Theology for an Inclusive World

Theology for an Inclusive World

Felix Wilfred

2019

Theology for an Inclusive World — published by the Rev. Dr. Ashish Amos of the Indian Society for Promoting Christian Knowledge (ISPCK), Post Box 1585, 1654, Madarsa Road, Kashmere Gate, Delhi-110006.

© Author, 2019

ISBN: 978-81-8465-685-5

Cover Credit: https://focuspocusnow.com/2014/11/23/indras-net/

Laser typeset by

ISPCK, Post Box 1585, 1654, Madarsa Road, Kashmere Gate, Delhi-110006
• *Tel:* 23866323/22

e-mail: ashish@ispck.org.in • ella@ispck.org.in
website: www.ispck.org.in

Contents

Part - II

Practice of Justice – Challenge to Theology

Part - III

Renewal of Faith and Reform of the Church Community

Part - IV
Ecumenism and "Wider Ecumenism"

Preface

With a number of commitments in hand, I was lingering over this book. What really made me accelerate the publication process was the encouragement I received especially from students and faculty of several theological institutions - Protestant, Pentecostal, Orthodox and Roman Catholic. It was a humbling experience for me when I heard them say that by reading what I wrote they were helped in their theological pursuits. The thought of helping to further the growth of students of theology and related disciplines, as well as those working in NGOs that are involved in taking up issues affecting diverse groups of people served as a powerful inspiration for me to work on the present volume. When a group of postgraduate students and faculty of the Missiology Department of St Peter's Pontifical Institute, Bangalore, visited me for a day of discussion on 18 December 2017, my wish became a firm resolve to complete this book as early as possible.

The shaping of this volume and the research, study, and reflection it involved will be worth this labour of love, if it is going to serve my readers. It is for this purpose that I have added after each chapter, a list of works that will help them delve deeper into the themes treated.

There is a growing realization about the limits of systems in general, and especially those that are in the sphere of knowledge. This is all the more true of authentic theology whose movement is from bottom up. Writing a systematic theological work could prove to be a distortion of reality as it would frame from above what is incommensurable. I have not attempted here anything like a systematic book. What is presented here are truly fragments, leaving the reader to develop a sense of the whole creatively. The various chapters are meant to be different windows that could illumine diverse aspects of our life and experiences as we struggle with them and try to make sense of them.

Often, I feel like a child looking at the chain of high mountains lost in the infinite cloud, admiring its marvel now from one angle, now from another, without end. Every view is unique and exciting. Each one of the chapters in this volume goes back to different contextual situations that called for a rethinking, a reflection or a clarification. For better understanding, I have given in the appendix the contexts that were at the origin of every chapter of this book. It is difficult to bring all of them into a coherent logic and sequence. And yet, the reader may find many threads binding these chapters together and the same spirit animating them. The thoughts, reflections, and suggestions spread through this volume may reinforce one another.

A thread running through this volume encodes the question how could theology serve for a more inclusive world that is more just and egalitarian. Many ideologies, projects, and institutions that once promised greater humanization have proved to be woefully disappointing. Theology is no panacea for the many ills of our world and society. However, it has the potential to trigger minds and hearts in the direction of a true humanistic and environmentally sustainable world.

I feel indebted to many people who have indirectly and directly helped me prepare and shape the book in this form. Foremost I think of the poor and my encounter with their suffering which has been all through my life an enduring inspiration to think of God, world, society, and nature in new ways. Their struggles and their hopes even when things fall apart remain a source of strength and redeeming knowledge. The primordial faith the poor manifest and the hope they nurture augurs well for the dawn of a new world where there will be no exclusion and negation; where every creature – from the blade of grass to human beings – will be respected and drawn in an inclusive and universal communion without end.

I think of students and scholars who listened to me and gave their feedbacks and raised critical questions on different occasions. Their comments and observations helped me sharpen my ideas and elaborate them further.

Since the time I met him as a young professor at Sacred Heart Seminary, Poonamallee, Chennai, Amirtharaj Arockiyam, impressed me as a perceptive thinker, gifted with fine artistic and aesthetic sense. He is also someone to whom I could sound my ideas and get very original feedbacks. I requested him to go through the manuscripts and give his comments chapter by chapter. I wish to record my debt of gratitude to him for his great support in preparing this volume for publication.

Dr Preeti Oza, St Andrew's College, Mumbai, went through most of the chapters and Dr Amitha Santiago, Bishop Cotton Women's Christian College, Bangalore, read through some of the chapters, suggested stylistic changes in language, and checked grammatical errors. To both of them I wish to express my sincere thanks. Dr Mary John, my former doctoral student, came to my aid by helping prepare the index for the book. I express my gratitude to him for doing it with great care and within a relatively short period of time. Another former student, Professor James Ponniah, University of Madras, gave me from time to time very pertinent suggestions, which I wish to acknowledge with appreciation and thanks.

My sincere thanks goes to Ashish, Ella, and Sandeep of ISPCK for their interest in my writings, their encouragement, and for having done a neat work of publishing this volume.

For the past several years, Ms Nirmal has been an unfailing support in my intellectual pursuit. Like in the preparation of other volumes, also for this one, she extended right from the beginning her assistance full of dedication. Her amazing concentration helped to check carefully many details of the references and bibliography. I wish to thank her very warmly.

Felix Wilfred

Introduction

Role of Theology Today

Struggle for an Equitable and Inclusive World

All of life is a journey; so too liberation. Equality and inclusion are the two eyes of liberation; they are also the means to gauge the distance we have travelled on the path to freedom - the more equality and inclusion, the greater liberation. The absence of equality and inclusion would spell a world of increasing violence and contradictions. Every grand narrative projects master-plans of liberation and is teleologically oriented with ideologically tinged strategies of revolution, evolution, and so on.

In the globalising world, neo-liberalism and advanced capitalism, as master narratives, pervade and control all areas of life both as a praxis and as an ideology. Humanity and nature need to be progressively liberated from their stranglehold. This may not be realized by projecting any alternative grand narrative of liberation, but through constant and widespread struggles for equality and inclusion, and by confronting the contradiction of this ideology with the actual lived reality on the ground. Further, in our human condition, a perfect state of justice, equality, and inclusion may elude us. All that can be done is to strive to move from conditions of less justice to more justice, to greater equality and inclusion. In this journey of struggle towards liberation, jointly undertaken with hope by women and men across nations, religions could play an important role, thanks to their abundant humanistic resources.

The role of theology is situated in the context of struggle for equality and inclusion inspired by compassion and solidarity. In the footsteps of Jesus, genuine theology will address the burning issues that affect humanity and nature, and weave into these concerns the question of God, since the human, the divine, and the universe are inextricably intertwined to form one single mystery that envelops us.

Forms of Inequality and Exclusion

In the past, slaves were discriminated against, but they were acquired as a wealth producing force. So too vassals in a feudal society and the lumpen proletariat in industrial society. What is alarming today is that the poor are viewed as *redundant*, excluded and made to feel unwanted. This is the worst attack on the dignity of a person. One has ceased to analyse the structural issues that generate and sustain poverty and the growth of inequality. Even worse, the poor as victims of structural crimes are blamed for their lot. The market economy has become the proverbial elephant in the China bazaar playing havoc and trampling even nature under its feet.

In no less dramatic a form, the market economy as a hegemonic force, has also become a source of modern forms of social, cultural and political exclusion and discrimination. It marginalises vulnerable groups such as indigenous peoples, tribals, migrants, refugees, stateless people, bonded labourers, *los mestizos, los camposinos, los indignados*, the minorities, the disabled, transgenders, homosexuals, lesbians, inter-sexuals, and so on.

The Costs of Inequality and Exclusion

Inequality and exclusion cost dearly as they are at the root of malnutrition, chronic hunger, homelessness, and the absence of minimum health-care. Inequality deprives victims of their *agency* and selfhood. It narrows and limits the range of choices and alternatives to shape their individual and collective life. Then, there is the whole aspect of *humiliation* that inequality heaps upon those discriminated against and excluded. As Pierre Bourdieu rightly points out, "there is no worse deprivation, no worse privation, perhaps, than that of losers in the symbolic struggle for recognition, for access to socially recognized social being, in a word, humanity".[1] Material poverty as the Gospels testify is the result of exclusion from communion and community.

Further, inequality destroys the social fabric, robs the community of trust, solidarity, and mutuality that cement human relationships. There is another cost to the community that results by excluding others. One deprives the community of the possibility of enriching itself through the talents and capabilities of the excluded. It is no less a loss to the community than to the excluded victims. Inequality gives rise to a host of social problems too – violence, drugs, alcoholism, mental illness, chronic unemployment, erosion of the rule of law, lower life-expectancy, and so on. Studies show that in the North too, those countries that have achieved greater equality, witness less social problems and enjoy a higher quality of life, while on the contrary, countries with greater inequality are also the ones with serious social problems.[2]

Denial of opportunities is yet another serious consequence of inequality and exclusion. It forms part of the reigning economic paradigm. The present economic system advocates free market and competition as the essential dynamics of development, unmindful of the initial conditions of disparity, asymmetry of power, and opportunities. In earlier times, oppression, inequality, and exclusion took on more direct forms. Today, they have become more and more subtle and get deeply embedded in economic, social, cultural, and political systems. The clever concealment of inequality and exclusion under the cloak of sophisticated ideology and arguments, mathematical data, and statistics, necessitates that we develop more subtle analyses and approaches to be able to unmask them.

Neo-Liberal Roots of Inequality and Exclusion

At the root of inequality is the fact that the forces of production such as capital, large tracts of land, ownership of various forms of natural resources, etc., are today concentrated in ever smaller groups of powerful elites. This inequality is the foundation on which modern market economy is built. And this inequality expresses itself in everyday life. The recent increase in the growth of inequality is to be traced also to *political attitudes and policies*. With the waning of the communist-threat, the political policies and measures to support the poor experienced a retreat. It further resulted in the privatization of public utilities, the drastic weakening of workers unions all over the world, and the absence or abolition of minimum wage legislations in different parts of the world.

The assertion of the political right and its extolling of a free market started a trend that culminated today in an unprecedented inequality in income and in the just sharing of resources. Liberal *laissez faire* economy today has assumed the character even of a religion with its own pontiffs like Friedrich von Hayek, Milton Friedmann, and Thomas Friedman who expect us to have blind faith in the market. They claim to provide infallible economic remedies. They have managed to recruit disciples like Michael Novak who can theologically justify the economic status quo and sanctify the market.

The Neoliberal Response to Inequality and Exclusion

We are battling against an insidious ideology that does not really evidence equality and inclusion. Rightly then, Pope Francis in *Evangelii Gaudium* has come out in the strongest terms against an economy that kills. In his words,

> Just as the commandment: 'Thou shalt not kill' sets a clear limit in order to safeguard the value of human life, today we also have to say 'Thou shalt not' to an economy of exclusion and inequality. Such an economy kills. [3]

The philosophy of neo-liberalism behind this economy, not only does not challenge inequality, but strangely views inequality as tolerable and even necessary for growth. The conception of society underlying a neo-liberal market economy is one based on the *theory of social contract*. The contractual theory empties the richness of human relationships. It is not capable of sustaining communities since it is based on self-interest. It has no heart for those who suffer, for the victims, for refugees, and the tortured. Solidarity and compassion are banished and replaced by competition inspired by the philosophy of the survival of the fittest. In a presumed situation of all round war – *bellum omnium contra omnes* (as Thomas Hobbes would say), those who do not enter into contract are the losers, and have no rights. They become the excluded. There is no consideration of the unequal conditions into which individuals and groups are born or thrown. If they are not able to keep the contractual obligations, they are left behind. This theory flies in the face of the truth that not all human relationships can be framed within contracts.

The neoliberal economy presents capitalism as a historical inevitability whose ultimate triumph is already proclaimed. It is a type of modern fatalism. Think of Francis Fukuyama and his "*End of History and the Last Man*".[4] In this system, inequality is explained as the collateral effect of the development process. To consider the suffering and privations of millions and millions of people as collateral damage cannot but be described as a bizarre and non-redemptive reasoning. To hide the damages, market capitalism cleverly dons the mantle of Good Samaritan and co-opts the discourse of liberation. To all this we must add the fact that in many societies, especially in the South, there are strong traces of feudal culture and modes of practice that thrive on the hierarchy of high and low – *secundum sub et supra*. We find in these societies an intermingling of these vestiges with the neoliberal market economy.

Economy Needs a Sabbath

Like in the times of Egyptian Pharaohs, what we have today is a system of production and consumption that keeps everyone anxious.[5] The production units which go on without stop throughout the day, week, month, and year are symbolic. So are the many businesses and economic activities. Like the devil, business never sleeps. This mad rush in the name of development requires a sane *interruption*.

Sabbath in the Biblical tradition is not only a day of rest to recuperate and continue further along the same lines; it is in a way *an interruption* that is necessary to relieve us of our anxiety. Sabbath is a metaphor of freedom from the enslavement of the greed that propels endless production and consumption in an effort to find happiness in this mad cycle. Sabbath is a liberating break to remind us of our authentic self, of others, and of values that matter.[6] It helps us perceive the neighbour with new eyes – not as threatening competitors or as objects of exploitation, but as true human beings with dignity. This being the case, there is a certain sacredness about the Sabbath. "Remember the Sabbath day, and keep it holy" (Ex. 20:8). The Sabbath also brings in the element of contemplation and a primordial aesthetics. God saw everything God made very good (Gen. 1:31) "God blessed the seventh day and hallowed it, because on it God rested from all his work which God had done in creation" (Gen. 2:3). The trouble with our economy and our politics is that they are mechanisms without Sabbath, without the mystical and the contemplative. Hence, they can become very violent and aggressive, brutal and destructive.

Buddhism speaks of "*tṛṣṇā*" the insatiable thirst or craving for accumulation. Accumulation is the source of division, inequality and exclusion. Sabbath is a liberation from commoditisation of everything, including self and others. Sabbath is a reminder of the fundamental equality of all human beings regardless of their profession or achievements. Equality springs from the common origin and destiny of all human beings, their sharing in a common human nature, and their experience of the same kinds of needs and aspirations. If the "earth is the Lord's" (Ps. 24:1), all God's children have the right to share its resources in an equitable manner. Church Fathers vigorously condemn the privatisation of common goods by some and deprivation of the legitimate rights of others.[7] Today, our faith spurs us on to resolutely challenge the commercialisation of the earth and its resources, which disrupts communion and the life of communities. This is a point that Pope Francis has brought home exceedingly well in his *Laudato si*.[8]

Theology Focused on the Essentials

Theology needs to become alert to the crises that humanity is facing, and needs to gain competency in order to cooperate with diverse forces at play. In a world of fragmentation – of knowledge, self, community, economy, politics, etc. – theology, I believe, could offer some glimmer of hope. For, theology that is inclusive is a disciplinary enterprise that has the potential for a holistic vision of reality and an integral approach to life. This is today's requirement in order to respond to inequality and exclusion, oppression and injustice.

When the house is on fire, we have time to save only the essentials. When humanity and nature are in deep crisis and immersed in inequality and exclusion, we need to come up with theologies – both in the North and the South – that address the crisis situation of both humanity and the creation. Theology is accountable and has a responsibility towards humanity and God's creation. It may be interesting to study about the virginity of Mary and make fine theological distinctions between virginity *ante partum, in partu, post-partum,* etc. It may be exciting to discuss the rapprochement between the Protestants and Catholics on the understanding of the doctrine of justification. Such doctrinal concerns that occupied and continues to occupy so much attention of theology have to recede to the background in the face of the magnitude of problems that humanity is facing: problems of inequality, exclusion, violation of human dignity and rights, violence, war, peace, the oppression of women and discrimination against them, and environmental issues. Unfortunately, much of theology today, including those claiming to derive inspiration from Vatican II, are often evasive about the question of poverty, inequality, and exclusion. They are lost in the exegetical minutiae in the hermeneutics of the Conciliar texts. Theology that limits itself to explaining the doctrinal aspects of Christianity and its symbolic system would be doing little good for humanity if it fails to turn its gaze on the world and the burning issues of our times.

There is a big gulf between the classicist theology and the empirical everyday experience of life and its struggles. God has identified God's self with humanity (*verbum caro factum est*). Rightly then, Nicholas of Cusa reminds us, God is an infinite circle whose center is everywhere and whose circumference is nowhere.[9] The exiling of God and the neighbor from the horizon of economy to pursue crass selfishness and individualism presents the greatest challenge to theology today. If Sabbath, as we have seen, represents an interruption, a break to think of the whole in view of creative transformation, then the role of theology would be to promote the practice of the Sabbath in every field of human and collective life. It would mean to help connect every fragment with the whole, and bind every day with the day that will have no end. In following humanity in its journey towards liberation, theology needs to effect a re-location of the sacred from traditionally venerated spaces and objects to the entire creation and learn to respect all forms of life. It is one of the fundamental intuitions of the Bible that the quality of a community is measured by the way it takes care of its weaker and vulnerable ones, for whom equality and justice are quintessential. This runs through the entire corpus of the Biblical tradition in which *idolatry and injustice* are interlinked. For, the abandoning of Yahweh caused injustice and inequality in society. Reversely social injustice led one away from Yahweh to the idols.

As for exclusion, it is diametrically opposed to the dynamics of *interdependence* the story of creation in Genesis tells us. In creation, God binds everything together in harmony; creation, however, confers also distinctness and identity to every creature. When exclusion is practiced as assimilation of the other, it denies the legitimate difference and plurality. What God exercised in creation should characterize also human communities. Here is an important task for theology. It is the task of contributing to create communities without exclusion; communities that will respect difference and plurality. This is a crucial task in these times when the reigning economic system has become a force of division and detrimental to the nurturing of communities.

Liberation and the pursuit of equality and inclusion will be inspired by a new sense of the sacred, and nourished by a faith as deep as that of Jesus. In a world that sacralised the hierarchy and power, cultivated inequality and practiced exclusion, Jesus stood for the dignity of every human being as the new temple of God. Exclusion of the poor from knowledge, freedom, dignity, and from participation and community was the real sacrilege. The Gospels tell us that Jesus was concerned about *human suffering* and privations rather than about *sin*. Unfortunately, Christian soteriology came to be constructed around sin and not on the most important aspects of Jesus' praxis for the wellbeing (*salus*) of human beings and of communities. His vision of liberation was anchored in the experience of the divine as a compassionate God in solidarity with the suffering humanity. The experience of human suffering, poverty, deprivation, and enslavement touched him deeply. Compassion and solidarity came gushing forth from his inner being. A theology in the footsteps of Jesus will incorporate his vision, passion, and praxis. Like Jesus, it will question what passes for the norm, and which is rationalized as being self-evident, and therefore beyond questioning.

Humanistic Role of Theology

Time was when discussions veered around the question of reason and faith. The way the two were related was also to distinguish Catholic and Protestant orientations, for example. I think the age for this kind of approach is gone. Today, theology is pursued not by counterposing it to the role of reason, but rather by following a rational and humanistic approach in varied spheres of life. The world today, with its technology and end-means pragmatism, has lost its reason. This is a challenge for theology, so that the world becomes less absurd and more rational and humanistic. The irrationalities that have creeped into the dominant system of economy, in the model of development, and in inter-human relationships are such that they have brought humanity and the world to the brink of disaster.

There is no claim that theology is going to be the redeemer. That would further an unwarranted triumphalism, which theology often exercised in the past. Rather, what theology could do is to help see the reality, the present history and its processes in a broader light, more rationally and humanistically. There is yet another important role theology could play. This refers to the situation of fragmentation in all the areas of life that we experience today. A sense of the whole and an effort towards integration will make our world more humanistic and environmentally sensitive. Theology could play this role of infusing into the various fields of life the aspiration to go beyond the fragment, and the momentary, and help see these in the light of a larger picture.

Another important humanistic role that theology is called upon to play is to facilitate the understanding and practice of plurality and diversity. Living with difference is a great challenge humanity faces today. While globalisation might give the impression that differences are being eliminated, in fact, what is happening is that the differences come face to face more than ever. Living with difference is an art that needs to be cultivated. Theology more than being a theory on difference could serve as a force of transformation that can help individuals and communities to develop the art of living with difference. As many conflicts in our world demonstrate, the world is struggling with the issue of coming to terms with the distinct other – geographically, culturally, ethnically, religiously, sexually, and ideologically. Short-sighted solutions are offered for more complex problems of diversity. Ultimately, it is important to hold high a vision that sees the other as part of oneself. Here is a universal humanism, beyond all kinds of barriers and divisions. While individuals, groups and societies are struggling to come to terms with the "other", theology could help this encounter by projecting a universal humanistic vision for the wellbeing of society and the future of the world.

The journey to liberation is strewn with many a wilderness, which needs to be crossed in hope. Movements of *resistance* all over the world against inequality, and refusal to take exclusion lying down offer hope for the future. These movements are the conscience of the world today, and they embody ethics in practice.

In this journey of struggle and liberation, jointly undertaken with hope by women and men across nations, a right kind of theology could play a significant role. You may ask "What do you mean by a right kind of theology?" Let me respond by recalling a 2500 year old parable of the Buddha: the parable of the poisoned arrow. A person was hit by an arrow as he was passing through a forest. When his friends and kin wanted to help him, he would not have the arrow removed until he was sure as to who the person was who had targeted him with the arrow. He wanted to know his name, age, village, his physical size, the length of the bow he used. He insisted on knowing whether the feathers of the arrow used were from a vulture, a stork, a hawk or a peacock! This parable was a trenchant critique of Buddha against the high caste Brahmin theology of his time and its abstruse metaphysical speculations, which seriously failed in praxis. The Buddha called everyone to respond without delay to human suffering and oppression with *karuna* or compassion. He upheld the equality of every man and woman without distinction in his teachings, based on the knowledge that everyone is equally capable of *enlightenment*. He broke the social stratification of caste that excluded people.

When he was asked about God, the Buddha kept his silence. The enigmatic silence of the Buddha is a great theme in itself. Five hundred years after Buddha, Jesus identified himself with the suffering humanity. What is striking is that Jesus broke the silence of the Buddha. He opened his mouth to speak of a God, indeed of a God Father and Mother who is deeply involved in the life of human beings and their suffering. This God is not an alienating God, but a God of compassion, mercy and solidarity who treats with equality all sons and daughters. Through this God, we have a great message of hope that inspires us to continue the struggle for equality and inclusion and to journey on the path of liberation in these times when human life and coexistence are threatened by the liberal market and its model of development. A theology sensitive to the issue of inequality and exclusion in our world today has the liberating task of de-sacralizing the "golden calf" of the free market. Theology will try constantly to weave the question of God into the burning issue of inequality and exclusions afflicting humanity. It will continue to provide a vision that will be based on the ultimate unity and communion of the mystery of the human, the divine, and of the universe.

Endnotes

[1] Pierre Bourdieu, *Pascalian Meditations* (Stanford: Stanford University Press, 2000), p. 241.

[2] Cf. Richard Wilkinson and Kate Pickett, *The Spirit level: Why Greater Equality Makes Societies Stronger* (New York: Bloomsbury Press, 2009); Thomas Piketty, *Capital in the Twenty-First Century* (Cambridge MA: The Belknap Press of Harvard University Press, 2017); Heather Boushey, et al., eds, *After Piketty. The Agenda for Economics and Inequality* (Cambridge MAA: Harvard University Press, 2017).

[3] Pope Francis, *Evangelii Gaudium* no. 53.

[4] Francis Fukuyama, *The End of History and The Last Man* (New York: Penguin Books, 1992).

[5] See Walter Brueggemann, *Disruptive Grace: Reflections on God, Scripture and the Church* (London: SCM Press), 55 ff.

[6] *Ibid.*

[7] Charles Avila, *Ownership: Early Christian Teaching* (Eugene: Wipf & Stock Publishers, 2004).

[8] Cf. Felix Wilfred, chapter 8 in this volume.

[9] This thought attributed to Nicholas of Cusa (*Docta ignorantia* II. 2), derives from neo-platonic traditions, and was expressed differently by Alain de Lille, Pascal and others.

PART - I
DIVERSITY, RECOGNITION, AND PLURALISM

CHAPTER 1

Christian Faith and
Multiple Rationalities

A couple of years ago, during a visit to Brassanone in the South Tyrol in Italy – a town where Nicholas of Cusa was once bishop – I entered a monastery adjacent to the cathedral. Here on the roof I saw a fifteenth century fresco of a strange animal figure – a big and powerful horse with two elephant tusks, a trunk and two large ears. It was intriguing. Having watched elephants move around from my childhood, I could only smile at the attempt of the artist to portray something he never experienced – an elephant. On the other hand, I was in admiration for the ingenuity of the painter - Leonhard of Brixen. When portraying the biggest animal, logically, he could only think of the biggest horse in his experience, and then add on to it what he might have heard from descriptions about elephants - two tusks and two large ears and one long trunk.[1] From the point of view of the artist, there is perfect logic and rationality in the reconstruction of the image; at the same time there is such a wide chasm between the representation and the real elephant!

Plurality of Rationalities

Theology is in need of approaching reason in new ways, profoundly conscious of its (reason) serious limitations, and at the same time aware of the plural forms of rationality stemming from history, culture, tradition, philosophy, visions of the world, and so on. A closer analysis would show that the mode of reasoning is a function and an expression of one's culture. Though the debate around the polysemous understanding of the rational has been on for the past several decades,[2] and some may even consider such a debate outdated, what is surprising is that the concept of a single and univocal rationality that denies alternative approaches and standards continues to be still dominant. It is the way how the colonial continues to be present and operative at a deeper and subtle level. In other words, certain conditions are to be fulfilled if any belief or action is to be considered rational, and norms to be adhered to in order to pass for rational.[3] Anthropologists have tried to present a plurality of ways of reasoning through their case studies. For example, the rationality of a *shaman* or diviner is contrasted with that of so-called scientific rationality. What the anthropologists have succeeded is to show the contrast between the rational behaviour of the locals and the dominant understanding of rationality with its standard procedures of logic and inference.

Our concern here goes beyond such debates of the past and the contributions of anthropologists. It begins with the actual fact of polymorphous or plural rationalities.[4] This plurality needs to be based on something deeper than what has been attempted. That is why we turn to the relationship between rationality and language which is the foremost expression of culture. In my view, the project of inculturation has hardly gone into the investigation of the cognitive modes and processes and the social and cultural constructs of different rationalities and their import in the formation of different theologies.[5]

Rationality and Structure of Language

There is a correlation between the structure of language and the structure of thought; between the genesis of language and the crystallization of ideas. One's language, its patterns and functioning make a clear impact on one's reasoning, analysis and interpretations. Ancient theoreticians of Indian medieval hermeneutics such as Anandavardhana (820 – 890),[6] and modern western structural linguists such as Ferdinand de Saussure have debunked the naïve view that language is simply a vehicle of thought.[7] Asian tradition and modern western linguistics have brought to our awareness that language is more a *source of thought* than its form or expression. We experience the world the way we do because of our language. In other words, depending on the language, our perception of reality and experience of the world become different. Certain schools of Buddhism would go to the point of total constructivism, namely that reality is created by our language. A chariot exists because there is a word called chariot. To bring in a citation from the western tradition, from second Heidegger, it is not so much that we speak a language but rather the language speaks us – "*die Sprache spricht*".[8] Precisely because the Chinese language, Arabic, Tamil, and the French operate with different linguistic modes, we have distinctly different reasonings, consequently different experiences of the world, approaches to reality, many ways of ordering and interpreting the world, and structuring society. In short, cognitive processes and construal of thought follow linguistic patterns.

Let us take the simple case of the English word "uncle". It could be applied to the brother of one's father or mother. The word does not indicate anything more. On the other hand, most Indian languages have one term to refer to the brother of the father and another term to the brother of one's mother. Often the kinship word would indicate also whether the brother is an elder brother or a younger one to one's father or mother. To cite an example from my mother-tongue Tamil, we refer to the elder brother of father as "*periappa*" and younger brother as "*chitappa*", and the brother of mother as "*mama*". Someone who thinks through these words of kinship is brought up in a linguistic and cultural community that has invested these words with meaning. Therein are inscribed certain rights and duties in the affairs of the family, particularly on important occasions like birth, marriage and death. The structuring of the family and society are inextricably intertwined with the language of kinship. Here is the fabric of human relationships woven with threads of a rationality of its own, which an outsider may not be able to grasp fully.

If we take seriously into account these inputs of linguistics, we will readily acknowledge not only a plurality of reasonings and culture-specific universals, but also challenge the absolutization of any one of them - be it Latin or Greek.

I am afraid that theology, in general, has not benefitted from the study of structural linguistics, which could open the doors to recognize plurality of rationalities and understand their implications. Further, the failure to deploy consistently the heritage of Asian and modern hermeneutical insights explains also the difficulty of traditional theology to understand Christian faith in relation to reasonings and approaches obtaining in differing socio-cultural contexts. On a practical note, the turn to plurality of cultural reasoning seems to be vital for the future of the world, for its peace and security. Theology will be accomplishing its mission to humanity by bringing into play a plurality of reasoning in the cognitive and interpretative processes of faith.

Looking back at Christian History

In Christian history, there has been a dichotomous and antagonistic approach in defining the relationship between faith and reason.[9] The manner and the measure in which reason was deployed made the difference in defining the nature of and approach to theology. On one extreme were the ones like Saint Bonaventure who thought that the pure wine of faith should not be diluted by pouring into it the water of reason. Others argued for a theology that harmoniously blended faith with reason. For the former, it is faith that leads to understanding (*crede ut intelligas*), whereas for the latter, faith should not be blind and obscurantist, or based solely on testimony but should seek reason (*fides quaerens intellectum*).[10] Around these two major axes, I think, the entire western history of theology up to our times could be re-written.

Theology becomes inauthentic and loses its anchor when it succumbs to a rationality that claims universal validity - *Allgemeingültigkeit*. Furthermore, legitimate theological pluralism is compromised when one particular understanding of reason – the Greco-Roman – is raised to be *the* reason consonant with faith, and indeed as part of it. This is what Pope Benedict XVI expounded in his unfortunate and controversial lecture in Regensburg in 2006. Referring to the Greco-Roman reason, he stated, "the fundamental decisions made about the relationship between faith and use of human reason are part of the faith itself; they are developments consonant with the nature of faith itself".[11]

What we have here is an idealization and even a romanticization of a particular brand of reason, namely, the Greco-Roman, which was attached to the Christian faith with the implicit claim that other religions have divorced reason and faith. In terms of methodology, this is a deductive approach; it is also and ill-informed as regards the history of religions and the developments of their doctrines and practices.

The dichotomy between *reason and faith* had serious consequences in the understanding of other religions. These were seen at best as the work of reason, whereas, God's revelation in Christian faith was viewed as a gift and the work of grace. Such a dichotomy contradicts the truth. Closely connected with this is the opposition between *nature and grace*. In both cases, one forgets that reason and nature are *concepts* and not realities. The reality is that human beings are right from their birth in a graced situation, and this is true of all human beings across religious traditions. It is a situation of the *"supernatural existential"*. Early and Medieval Christian thinkers – Nicholas of Cusa, Alain de Lille, for example – tell us that God's centre is everywhere; God's circumference is nowhere. If that is the case, then, all human beings are enveloped in the realm of divine mystery beyond any conflict between reason and faith. By our birth we are placed existentially in a supernatural situation, which makes the divide between reason and nature only as real as the imaginary equator that we use to mark the globe.

Rationality in the History of Mission

Missionaries believed earnestly that people could be led to the truth of Christian faith through the help of rational arguments. There are numerous stories in India, China, Japan and elsewhere, which narrate how missionaries entered into disputation with *pundits* and *mandarins* of Hinduism and Buddhism, and demonstrated through their arguments the falsehood of the beliefs of their opponents. The arguments of missionaries to prove the untruth of the beliefs of other religions and the truth of Christian faith could not win over scholars to the Christian faith as was expected.[12] They were at a loss to understand this. What they did not realize was that the instruments of rationality they deployed could not make any dent on the modes of thought and practical logic of the people. The cognitive processes the local people followed, their way of acquiring, accumulating, classifying and transmitting knowledge were different; so too the manner of reasoning. The missionaries failed to understand that the people have their own rationality of why they do what they do – a rationality deeply embedded in their millennial culture and tradition.

To speak in imagery, even while the missionaries were trying to build a tunnel of arguments in the hope of reaching the people, the people built their own tunnels with their distinctive rationalities. Both the tunnels never met. The underlying missionary argument that error has no rights succeeded to exclude peoples, religions, cultures, practices, and indeed the exercise of reason and freedom. It has served also as an ideology underpinning the horrendous and irrational practices of inquisition. [13]

Tailored Reason for the Justification of Christian Faith

A general theme running through the western history of theology is that Christian faith does not contradict reason; rather it enhances and fulfils reason. This argument was advanced by early Christian thinkers who wanted to justify faith as reasonable and reconcile it with the Greek intellectual world. There is no conflict between Jerusalem and Athens. That was the position held by Justin, Clement of Alexandria and others. In the modern period, Hegel justified Christianity theoretically saying that it fits perfectly into the world of reason (also differently named as "idea" "World Spirit" "logic", etc.) and into his philosophy of religion. Christianity makes explicit what reason and philosophy have to say about ultimate reality and its becoming self-conscious in humanity. As ultimate and universal truth, Jesus himself would be for Hegel, the historicization of reason. Karl Rahner, on his part, deploying his transcendental method tried to examine on the basis of an analysis of the structure of the human spirit, the *a priori* conditions for the possibility of Christianity and its various beliefs.[14] In recent times, Pope John Paul II in his *Fides et Ratio* holds that faith makes up for the deficiencies and weaknesses of reason and guides it. The point is clear: sincere rational enquiry cannot but lead to the fullness and absoluteness of truth, which Christian faith offers.[15] These are some of the ways by which faith has been justified, and so to speak, rationalized without however reducing it within the parameters of reason. This is what I call "tailored reason" that serves the philosophical justification of Christianity.

Lights from Asian Traditions

Markedly different from the above approaches, Asia bases itself on the trans-rational realm of *experience* (*anubhava*) as the foundation for the truth of Christianity, rather than try to argue how Christian revelation can be reconciled with the claims of reason. In so doing, Asia has let itself be inspired by the early Christian period when experience and witness were points of reference and litmus tests for the claims of Christianity. Further, the Asian theological reasoning is one that is in harmony with the experience of faith as recorded in the Sacred Scriptures, which is different from a reasoning harnessed to elaborate the tenets of faith. Experience of faith is, as the Scriptures testify, an experience of liberation. "The truth will set you free" (Jn 8:32). In Asian theologies, reason and rationality as subsidiary instruments of knowledge, are directed to the goal of liberation and salvation, which are trans-rational and experiential realities requiring for their expressions something more than the language of reason.

Asia and the Trans-rational Mystery

There is another important Asian approach that calls for a plurality of rationalities in theology. St Thomas Aquinas reminds us that the act of faith does not end in its expression but in reality itself - "*Actus autem credentis non terminatur ad enunciabile, sed ad rem*".[16] Now the object of this faith is a mystery, which precisely because of its incommensurablity defies any one single approach. It, however, calls for multiple human cognitive and affective means, which could cumulatively help explain its various inexhaustible dimensions.

"Truth is one, sages have called it many" (*ekam sat viprā bahudhā vandanti).*[17] This statement from the Rig Veda is the leitmotif that runs through the Asian approach to reality as a whole, and to the truth of religion in particular. The ways of approaching truth, experiencing it and expressing it go beyond discursive thought and conceptual elaborations. Truth in the Asian tradition is never something once and for all given to be possessed but something that is to be continuously sought after. The journey (*yātrā*) is a root metaphor in the Asian tradition, and it provides dynamism and movement in the quest for truth and its deeper experience and understanding. All this is well-expressed in the form of a prayer in the ancient Upanishads:

> From ignorance, lead me to truth; (*asato mā sadgamaya*)
>
> From darkness, lead me to light (*tamasomā jyotir gamaya*)
>
> From death, lead me to immortality (*mrityormā amritam gamaya*)
>
> Om peace, peace, peace (*Oṃ śhānti śhānti śhāntiḥ*) [18]

Having found the conceptual tools of traditional theology too static and as having failed to come to terms with the dynamic character of faith, Asian theologies have sought to overcome these shortcomings through rationalities that reflect the spirit of search and quest. Even though the truths of faith are known, yet they are also objects of our unending quest. To recall St Paul, "Now we see indistinctly, as in a mirror; then we shall see face to face. My knowledge is imperfect now; then I shall know even as I am known" (I Cor. 13:12). Any genuine theology, precisely because the divine mystery is inexhaustible, will become apophatic and mystical, and this is important since it relativizes reason and sets limits to its role and its claims. Something of this is reflected in contemporary philosophy that speaks in terms of *incommensurability* on the one hand and *human fallibility* on the other. When these are acknowledged, we confess the limits of reason and move into the sphere of mystery that could equally be treated by theology as by philosophy. In this way, reason is not that which dismisses mystery but points towards it. The absence of this sense of mystery in his system led Kant to think of "*Religion within the Limits of Reason*".

Absence of Emotions as the Absurd

Very often, emotion and reason are set one against the other. Emotion is viewed as an obstacle on the path to reason. A person is thought to be rational to the degree she does not display emotions. But how human is this? We are reminded of a character in the great novel by Albert Camus, "*Stranger*". Here the character Meursault is indifferent and does not display any emotion either at death of dear ones or on being condemned, and goes without any emotion into a relationship with his girlfriend.[19] Meursault could say dispassionately, "Mother died today; may be yesterday; I can't be sure."[20] For those who advocate an abstract reason, this should be the ideal person; and yet what we could say of such a character and his way of behaving is that it is inhuman and irrational, precisely because of the lack of emotion in his dealings with the reality around him.[21] When 97 million children are undernourished in India,[22] and with so many deaths happening due to want of basic nutrition, how reasonable is it to focus on the fastest bullet train from Mumbai to Ahmedabad with crores of rupees spent on this project? It is a policy and system that lacks any emotional content as regards the plight of the children deprived of their daily food. A cold, calculative reasoning, indifferent to the human, is at work in the reigning model of development and in the political sub-culture. The "rationality" here is nothing but another name for pathology. It does not matter if children are sexually abused, maimed, killed and dumped; it does not matter if women become increasingly targets of violent attack and sexual assaults; it does not matter if tribals are displaced and Dalits are discriminated and excluded. What counts is moving ahead technologically and catching up with other 'advanced' nations. At work here is also an ideology of nationalism that sacrifices people for the sake of an imagined development. If anything is irrational, this is.

In modern economy, rationality is understood as taking the most effective means to achieve predetermined ends. Rational choice theory is something familiar to economists. It is this kind of understanding of rationality that is at work in one of the greatest political philosophers of twentieth century: John Rawls understands justice as fairness. According to him,

> A rational person is thought to have a coherent set of preferences between the options open to him. He ranks these options according to how well they further his purposes; he follows the plan which will satisfy more of his desires rather than less, and which has the greater chance of being successfully executed.[23]

Rawls is concerned more about the formal aspect of rationality, its effectiveness and coherence in achieving ends made up of aspirations, desires, etc. This formal approach to rationality does not allow him to interrogate the morality of these desires and aspirations themselves. Once again, this cannot be achieved without sensitivity and compassion to the other, especially the suffering and weaker others. In fact, in the western tradition, Max Weber, one of the leading scholars who went into the study of rationality and the process of rationalization had a multivalent understanding of rationality. He distinguished no less than four types of rationalities – practical, theoretical, formal and substantive. What has happened is that the first three have dominated our understanding of modernity, globalisation, and planning for the future of the world. We have woefully left out the substantive rationality. A value-based and substantive kind of rationality will identify the areas of irrationality in capitalism and the dominant economic system today.

Though Jürgen Habermas has the merit of re-defining the western Enlightenment and reason in communicative terms, nevertheless, in my view, his approach to reason and his efforts to propose a universal ethics and normativity remain unaffected by contemporary burning issues such as identity-construction, cultural and cognitive pluralism across the world. Hence his formulations cannot but be taken as a partial, constricted and "truncated" view of reason.[24] It is interesting to note that the western Enlightenment understanding of reason Habermas seeks to defend has been object of sharp critiques, starting from Leftist Hegelians, Martin Heidegger, Theodor Adorno, Michael Foucault, Jacques Derrida, and an increasing number of scholars from every part of the world and in every field.[25] Further, any consideration of reason in the abstract without taking into account factors such as interest, desire and passion – all of which can cloud reason – cannot but be viewed as appallingly incomplete. There is the need to challenge the means-end rationality at work in every sphere of life. This calls for a broader orientation and outlook. That leads us to the next point.

Widening the Scope of Reason

That reason is not the sole instrument of knowledge is portrayed so well by the celebrated words of Blaise Pascal, "*Le coeur a ses raisons que la raison ne connait pas*" – the heart has its reasons which the reason does not know.[26] Besides, reason plays another role, namely, serve as an instrument of control. We recall here Plato's allegory of two winged horses driven by a charioteer. One of the horses is of noble breed and the other is the opposite. They therefore are pulling in different directions. Reason symbolized as the charioteer has to control the disparate pulls of the horses, the one representing the rational force and the other the irrational one, and they have to be guided towards the goal.[27]

Asian tradition is full of references to self-control, self-discipline and restraint, which sustain one on the ethical and spiritual path. Reason not only helps us in framing knowledge, processing experience, and expressing faith, but as *practical reason* it helps us to draw out the moral and spiritual implications of the same faith. Here practical reason takes on the form of efforts towards integration and wholeness of mind and body, which all facilitate appropriate ethical practices. Seen in this light, the many practices in the Asian tradition such as *yoga* and *zen* used to control the mind and body, could be considered as practical reason helping us to live out the implications of faith in an integral way and making it fruitful through self-transformation and the transformation of the world. Hence, it is difficult to understand the warning by the Congregation for the Doctrine of the Faith (1989)[28] against the use of such "eastern methods." Regrettably, as it associates faith with a particular brand of reason and betrays almost total ignorance of the nature of these practices of practical reason in the Asian context.

Care: A New Name for Reason

The neutrality of procedural rationality comes at the cost of the victims whose concerns do not have any role in determining what is rational and what is irrational. On the other hand, where there is care and solidarity rationality is at home. Hence today, we require a re-definition of rationality in conjunction with care and solidarity, and not divorced from them. Theology will betray its mission of care if it uses calculative reasoning (what Heidegger called *das rechnende Denken*) to gain the aura of 'scientific'.

Where there is care, there is emotion. Without emotion, philosophy and theology could become blind to reality. For, as Robert C. Solomon observes:

> What is essential in this analysis for our understanding of rationality is
> that the concepts and judgments that are constitutive of our emotions are
> in turn constitutive of the criteria for rationality as well. If an offense is
> worthy of anger it thus becomes rational (that is, warranted) to be angry
> about it.... The idea that emotions as such are not rational thus begins
> with a basic misunderstanding of both the nature of emotions and the
> nature of rationality, and the idea that emotions as such are irrational is a
> confusion of certain sorts of specialized procedures - appropriate perhaps
> to the seminar room and the negotiating table - with rationality as such.[29]

When Jesus stood before the tomb of Lazarus as the evangelists tell us, he was deeply moved Then we have from the Evangelist, one of the shortest and most pregnant sentences in the entire Bible: "Jesus wept". (Jn 11:35). If Jesus was angry with those doing commerce in the temple, his emotion was something reasonable since such an use of the temple was unethical and should not happen. Behind emotions of this kind there is a close perception of reality and truth, which a dispassionate reason is not capable of reaching. Jesus' responses to situations of human suffering were all charged with deep emotions. Emotions help theology to see the reality, see the truth as it is. How true it is that the greatest things in the world happen, thanks to emotions.[30] Emotions are sensitive to context, to circumstances, which rationality is most often not. It is a mark of genuine reason if we are moved by the suffering of the other and reach out to the other in solidarity and care. Care for the other is something that would redeem us from dispassionate and cold reason. Care-filled reason is the one we need to relate to faith. It closely reflects the way of Jesus. The prophets of the Old Testament too were moved by rage in the face of injustice and exploitation. This rage and sensitivity to the conditions they experienced around them made them sane, compassionate, and rational human beings.

It would make a lot of sense to relate thus understood reason with faith. But very often one tries to relate the two as if reason were human effort and faith were something to do with God's revelation and grace. On the assumption of an inherent conflict between reason and faith, one tries to reconcile the two. This was also the effort made during medieval times to connect philosophy and theology. Neo-scholasticism has followed this method. Pope John Paul II came out with an encyclical *Fides et Ratio* which reflects the spirit of neo-scholastic arguments. Scholasticism views reason as an attribute characterizing human beings and distinguishing them from other creatures.

Protests and Resistance: Expressions of Faith and Reason

Reason is not neutral. Theoretical operations like analysis, synthesis, classification, inference, dialectics, etc. are not immaculate conceptions. They reflect cultural inclinations, social conditions, and dispositions.[31] The way the poor perceive, judge, and analyze situations and put reason to use is different from the way it is used by the dominant classes, castes, and elite groups in society. The resistance to domination and injustice by the poor reveals incisive analysis of complex situations and sound reasoning.

In movements of resistance, protest, and revolution, generally, the element of passion is highlighted. What is forgotten is that these movements are also the fruits of cogent reasoning; they are ethics in action. It is the kind of reasoning that Jesus uses while confronting the Pharisees and Sadducees. "Let anyone of you without sin be the first to throw a stone at her" (Jn 8:7). Such substantive reasoning is the flowering of wisdom, and is required for any public philosophy or theology that wants to be prophetic or different from formal and procedural rationality. Prophetic reasoning indeed is the need of the hour. Protests and resistance are also expressions of faith. For, the poor, like the prophets, are not at home with the existing order of things. They have an unshakable faith in a different order of things, which they yearn for.

It is striking that reason is not among the seven gifts of the Spirit, although *wisdom* is. For, wisdom is perceived as something greater than rationality and reasoning. The prophetic wisdom of Jesus indicates that wisdom flows from faith and is set forth by the Spirit. "Whoever believes in me, as Scripture has said, rivers of living water will flow from within them." (Jn 7:38). Reasoning flowing from within comes from faith, from the Spirit. Like the Pharisees, those who are haughty, arrogant and self-satisfied are involved in a sophistry (*kutharka*) of reasoning, which far from illuminating reality twists it so that truth becomes the victim of distortion.

Contemporary politics in our country is the best illustration. Sound reason and wisdom belong to the poor and the childlike who combine faith and reason marvelously in their daily lives. Hence the prayer of Jesus:

> "O Father, Lord of heaven and earth, thank you for hiding these things from those who think themselves wise and clever, and for revealing them to the childlike." (Mathew 11:25).

Conclusion

By way of conclusion, let me make some concrete suggestions for the future of theologies in Asia and across the world.

To do critical philosophy and authentic theology we need to acknowledge the historicity of reason, attend to the social conditions of its exercise, and pursue liberation from the fallacy of universalizing any particular culturally-conditioned rationality and mode of thought. Given the plurality of rationalities, the various philosophies and theologies will distinguish themselves in their methods, on the basis of the difference in socio-cultural rationalities. This indicates the paramount importance of understanding any philosophy or theology in its context.

What follows is that the judgment about authenticity and orthodoxy of faith has to be sorted out in context. What is said theologically in one context and within a particular world of cultural rationality may appear as heterodox when viewed and interpreted through the prism of another world of rationality. It is then impossible to have one single and centralized way of judging the soundness of Christian faith and its expressions. The failure to recognize this has led, unfortunately, to much unfair treatment of many creative and innovative theological enterprises in context. Today, doctrinal difficulties with theologians need to be understood by the people and the pastors and theologians with reference to a particular context, and not with reference to some presumed neutral and universal doctrinal normativity. This will avoid the caricaturing of theological thought from another cultural world and shadow-boxing. Theologians need to be involved in understanding and interpreting what their colleagues are saying. Regional and national bishops' conferences while playing a decentralized doctrinal role will also be in a position to judge the statements of theologians regarding their orthodoxy in a definite pastoral situation, provided the bishops themselves are not alienated from their own intellectual and cultural worlds.

From what we have said follows a critical question regarding the epistemological soundness and theological legitimacy of an institution like the Congregation for the Doctrine of the Faith within the Roman Curia. There are many assumptions in the way it judges theological soundness of faith and doctrines, which are difficult to uphold today, as they belong to a bygone age. The Congregation would be undertaking an impossible task of having to master innumerable ways of socio-cultural reasonings to be able to function. This is better left to the local Churches, which are in a position to judge matters of orthodoxy and heterodoxy in context. This means that the Roman Catholic Church may not need such an institution as the Congregation of the Doctrine of the Faith. It needs to become soon a matter of history. Is not its disappearance long overdue?

Faith is, so to say, an alarm vis-à-vis reason. For, not seldom does reason go into slumber, and it needs to be awakened. When the National Socialism of Hitler annihilated six million Jews, the European Enlightenment with its reason was sleeping. In such contexts precisely because faith sees more than reason, it has the obligation to challenge the corruption of reason, which it often did not do. Faith and theology need to have today the courage to sound the alarm in all realms, including religion and religious establishments, where reason is corrupted. This would be the character of a theology for an inclusive world.

Reason is often employed to justify the status quo, the logic of power, the system of the Empire. On the other hand, faith moves ahead into the future, even if it is a distant dream, and keeps alive what is to come. Let me conclude with the words of a Palestinian theologian, Mitri Raheb, reflecting from the oppressive history of occupations, wars and conquest by many empires that have characterized the history of his land:

> For we lose the future the moment we lose our capability for imagination. Without faith, there is no imagination; and without imagination, there is no future. Faith embodies the view that we can imagine something that was not, until the present part of our history.[32]

Bibliography

Boeve, Lieven. *Theology at the Crossroads of University, Church and Society: Dialogue, Difference and Catholic Identity* (Edinburgh: T&T Clark, 2016).

Brown, Harold I. *Rationality. The Problems of Philosophy* (London: Routledge, 1990).

Crosby, Donald A. *Faith and Reason: Their Roles in Religious and Secular Life* (Albany, N.Y: State University of New York Press, 2011).

Culture and Rationality: Colloquium Revised Papers (University of Hawaii: Hawaii Press, 1992).

Epstein, Brian. "The Diviner and the Scientist: Revisiting the Question of Alternative Standards of Rationality." *Journal of the American Academy of Religion* 78 (4) (2010), 1048-086.

Evers, C.W., and Mason, Mark. "Culture, Cognitive Pluralism and Rationality." *Educational Philosophy and Theory* 39 (4) (2007), 364-82.

Eze, Emmanuel Chukwudi. *On Reason: Rationality in a World of Cultural Conflict and Racism* (Durham, N.C.: Duke University Press, 2008).

Gasché, Rodolphe. "Postmodernism and Rationality." *The Journal of Philosophy* 88 (10) (1988), 528-538.

Gibson, Nigel C. "The Specter of Fanon: The Student Movements and the Rationality of Revolt in South Africa." *Social Identities* 23 (2017), 579-99.

Habermas, Jürgen. *An Awareness of What Is Missing: Faith and Reason in a Post-Secular Age.* Translated by Ciaran Cronin (Cambridge: Polity, 2010).

Halbfass, Wilhelm. "Human Reason and Vedic Revelation in Advaita Vedanta." chapter 5 in ID., *Tradition and reflection. Explorations in Indian Thought* (New York: State University of New York Press, 1991).

Halbfass, Wilhelm. *India and Europe. An Essay in Philosophical Understanding* (Delhi: Motilal Banarsidass, 1990).

Heal, J. "'Back to the Rough Ground!' Wittgensteinian Reflections on Rationality and Reason." *Ratio* 20 (4) (2007): 403-21.

Hollis, Mark and Lukes, Steven., eds. *Rationality and Relativism* (Oxford: Basil Blackwell, 1982).

Krausz, Michael. *Relativism: A Contemporary Anthology* (New York: Columbia University Press, 2010).

Paffenroth, Kim. *In Praise of Wisdom: Literary and Theological Reflections on Faith and Reason* (New York: Continuum, 2004).

Peters, James R. *The Logic of the Heart: Augustine, Pascal, and the Rationality of Faith* (Grand Rapids, Mich.: Baker Academic, 2009).

Robbins, Philip., and Aydede, Murat., eds. *The Cambridge Handbook of Situated Cognition* (Cambridge: Cambridge University Press, 2009).

Smilde, David. *Reason to Believe: Cultural Agency in Latin American Evangelicalism.* (Berkeley, Calif.: University of California Press, 2007).

Solomon, Robert C. "Existentialism, Emotions, and the Cultural Limits of Rationality." *Philosophy East and West* 42 (4) (Oct., 1992), 597-621.

Solomon, Robert C. *Thinking about Feeling: Contemporary Philosophers on Emotions* (Oxford: Oxford University Press, 2004).

Weithman, Paul J. *Rawls, Political Liberalism, and Reasonable Faith* (Cambridge: Cambridge University Press, 2016).

Wilson, Bryan R. *"Rationality." Key Concepts in the Social Sciences* (Oxford: Basil Blackwell, 1987).

Endnotes

[1] In medieval royal courts of Europe, there were menageries with exotic animals. With little mobility in that period, very few people probably saw them. Though manuscript illuminators painted exotic animals, it is doubtful how many of them got to see an animal like elephant. In reproducing an animal like elephant, they depended a lot on their imagination, narratives in travelogues, and some descriptions in bestiaries of the time.

[2] Mark Hollis – Steven Lukes, eds, *Rationality and Relativism* (Oxford: Basil Blackwell, 1982).

[3] For a sharp critique of such views and assumptions see, Robert C. Solomon, "Existentialism, Emotions, and the Cultural Limits of Rationality", *Philosophy East and West*, 42:4 (Oct., 1992), pp. 597-621.

[4] Cf. Stefano Occhipinti – Micahel Siegel, "Cultural Evolution and Divergent Rationalities in Human Reasoning", *Ethos,* 24:3 (1996), pp. 510-526; see also Hajime Nakamura, *Ways of Thinking of Eastern Peoples* (Hawaii: University of Hawaii Press, 1964).

[5] Felix Wilfred, "Inculturation as a Hermeneutical Question. Reflections in the Asian Context", *Vidyajyoti Journal of Theological Reflection*, 52 (1988), pp. 422-436.

[6] Cf. Kunjuni Raja, *Indian Theories of Meaning* (Madras: The Adyar Library and Research Centre, 1963); P.C. Muraleemadhavan, ed., *Indian Theories of Hermeneutics* (Delhi: New Bharatiya Book Corporation, 2002).

[7] See Ferdinand de Saussure, *Course in General Linguistics* (London: Duckworth, 1983).

[8] Martin Heidegger, *Unterwegs zur Sprache*, 4th ed. (Pfullingen: Neske, 1971), p. 19.

[9] Cf. Yves M.-J. Congar, *A History of Theology* (Garden City-New York: Doubleday & Company, Inc.1968); ID., *La foi et la théologie* (Tournai: Desclée, 1962).

[10] The problematic of the relationship between reason and revelation has been dealt with also in the Indian tradition. However, the manner of relating and reconciling the two has been quite different. See, Wilhelm Halbfass, "Human Reason and Vedic Revelation in Advaita Vedanta", in his volume *Tradition and Reflection. Explorations in Indian Thought* (New York: State University of New York Press, 1991), pp. 131-204.

[11] *L'Osservatore Romano* (September 14, 2006).

[12] Missionaries entered into disputation with the local intellectuals – *pundits* in India and *mandarins* in China, for example. With the increase of the print media, they took to apologetic and defensive pamphleteering with arguments, which in their estimation was very convincing. See Jacques Gernet, *China and the Christian Impact. A Conflict of Cultures* (Cambridge: Cambridge University Press, 1985).

[13] The statement that error has no rights, found in the *Syllabus* of Pius X (1864) and in some subsequent pontifical documents, was a stumbling block to the acknowledgement of Religious Freedom by Vatican II in *Dignitatis Humanae.*

[14] Cf. Thomas Sheehan, "Rahner's Transcendental Project," in Declan Marmion - Mary E. Hines, eds, *Cambridge Companion to Karl Rahner* (Cambridge: Cambridge University Press, 2005), pp. 29-42.

[15] Pope John Paul II, *Fides et Ratio* (14 September, 1998).

[16] *S.Th.* II-II, q. 1, a. 2 ad 2.

[17] *Rig Veda* 1:164:46.

[18] *Brihadaranya Upanishad* 1.3.28

[19] Robert C. Solomon, "Existentialism, Emotions, and the Cultural Limits of rationality." *Philosophy East and West*, 42:4 (Oct., 1992), 597-621.

[20] Albert Camus, *The Stranger* (New York: Vintage Books), p. 4.

[21] Today philosophers, psychologists and sociologists present a different view of the interconnection between reason and emotion. See, Dylan Evans and Pierre Cruse, eds, *Emotion, Evolution and Rationality* (Oxford: Oxford University Press, 2004); Robert C Solomon, ed, *Thinking about Feeling: Contemporary Philosophers on Emotions* (Oxford: Oxford University Press, 2004).

[22] This figure is according to the latest World Hunger Index

[23] See John Rawls, *A Theory of Justice* (Cambridge MAA: Harvard University Press 1999), 124.

[24] See also Fred Dallmayar, "Habermas and Rationality", *Political Theory*, 16:4 (1988), 553-579.

[25] See Rodolphe Gasché, "Postmodernism and Rationality", in *The Journal of Philosophy*, 88:10 (1988), 528-538.

[26] Blaise Pascal, *Thoughts*, section IV. No. 277

[27] Plato, *Phaedrus* 246a – 254e.

[28] *Congregation for the Doctrine of the Faith: Letter to the Bishops of the Catholic Church on Some Aspects of Christian Meditation*, October 15, 1989.

[29] Robert C. Solomon , "Existentialism, Emotions and the Cultural Limits of Rationality", *art.cit.*, at 611.

[30] This thought is attributed to Hegel.

[31] Gemma Edwards, "Social Movements and Protest", *Key Topics in Sociology* (Cambridge: Cambridge University Press, 2014).

[32] Mitri Raheb, *Faith in the Face of Empire. The Bible through Palestinian Eyes* (New York: Orbis, 2014), p.127.

CHAPTER 2

Plurality, Recognition, and Coexistence:
Beyond Liberalism and Secularism

Way back in the 1970's in Italy, as a student, I saw a tourist view-card that had the leading politicians of the time, Charles de Gaulle, Aldo Moro, General Franco, Willie Brandt, Leonid Brezhnev and others, depicted as part of a football team wearing shorts and sportive T-shirts. Pope Paul VI was shown as the goal keeper, also dressed in shorts like others on the team. I know of no serious protest over the Pope being represented this way. Is this a sign of the victory of western secularism that one may like to contrast with what happened to *The Satanic Verses* of Salman Rushdie?[1] Some may take pride in this western secularism. This, however, is to miss the point.

Europe is not outraged by such a depiction of a sacred person, not because of its secularism, but probably because of its pre-modern tradition of the *carnival.* Carnival was a playful mockery of the sacred and reversal of the established order of things, and was meant to contribute to the equilibrium of the society. But if one were to project the European carnival tradition or European secular tradition as something universal and expect other religions not to react in such cases, it is a clear sign of a misunderstanding of what secularism is in the rest of the world. Because Islam will not allow such depictions, it does not become less secular. On the other hand, for Hinduism there is no difficulty to make even semi-nude representations of goddesses,[2] and depicting explicit human sexuality in temple arts as is the case of the Khajuraho group of temples in Madhya Pradesh. That, however, does not make Hinduism more secular.[3] All that we can say is that religions are different; so are cultures. They have contributed to shape the identities of nations, groups, and peoples. This is important in order to come to terms with the question of diversity and co-existence.

Diversity, tolerance, and co-existence are issues that are an integral part of human history. In every epoch, they pose new challenges and questions which need to be addressed afresh. These questions have been sharpened today with the problem of migration, the plight of refugees, and the displacement of large numbers of people in the name of development. Coming to terms with these groups of people calls for new frames of reference and theories. In this chapter, I intend to reflect on the limits of the theory of liberalism and its version of secularism and to indicate the need to look for alternative points of reference. This is done with reference to the experiments in Asia. I name them as "experiments" because it would be too presumptuous to project these undertakings as an ideal. May be these experiments could also at some level inspire Europe and the rest of the world.[4]

A Liberal Approach to Diversity and its Limitations

The difficulty with the liberal conception is that in theory it treats everybody equally with no consideration of the factual situation of existing inequalities that impede some people from enjoying the same kind of freedom and autonomy as the rest. In other words, the ideal proclamation of equal rights for everyone without distinction does not solve the factual situation of inequality. The liberal conception and its regime of individual rights in fact, help to undo claims of ranks, honours, and privileges characteristic of feudal or monarchical traditions. In its own way, it challenges the hierarchical ordering of the society, and views every one as citizens with equal rights. And this is important in a casteist society like India.

Unfortunately, the liberal conception is proving a poor instrument to face complex situations of identity-assertion, which is the claim of cultures for survival, especially in minority situations. It is not able to address the phenomenon of increasing migration in our global world with consequences for tolerance and co-existence.

The hard version of liberalism does not attend to the collective reality and its implications. But if this version of liberalism is consistent, then, it should also call for the cessation of all nation-states, which is also at the root of modern collective identities invoking culture, language, and history.[5] The right of individual person to belong to a particular identity – cultural, linguistic, religious, etc. – is readily accepted by liberalism. But the collective reality does not become a title for claims of rights. On the other hand, the exercise of individual rights and the choice one makes as an individual, are both very much dependent upon the group to which one belongs. Hence the claims for a group's survival are legitimate as in the case of the French language and culture in Quebec, Canada.

The question turns more problematic when identity – ethnic, cultural, geographic, etc.– becomes the source of discrimination. Ideally, the liberal neutral position of a non-differentiating and blind application of equal rights for all is intended to safeguard the autonomy and freedom of the individuals. However, when people are discriminated against and excluded because they belong to a particular group or identity, the autonomy and freedom of the individual is not guaranteed without addressing the issue of identity.

In a soft version of liberalism like the one proposed by Charles Taylor and Will Kymlicka, some space is accorded to the reality of identity. But then it is the individual rights that take precedence over any community identity and rights.[6] This soft liberalism would appear tailor-made (yes, Taylor-made!) to fit the situation of Canada. Today, one needs to expand the discourse of diversity and coexistence to the situations in our global world. Moreover, even if such spaces for recognition are allowed a liberal constitutional state would not want to guarantee the survival of the cultural identities of various groups.

The crucial matter of recognition and coexistence in pluralistic societies is not solved by ending the theoretical debates between those who hold the primacy and precedence of individual rights and those who advocate the rights of collectivities – especially among the marginalized and discriminated ones. The question comes into greater relief when faced with the issue of migration and xenophobia. Think, for example, of those different peoples with their cultures, traditions, religions, and ethnicities making Europe their new home. The domination of a liberal thought based on individual rights has not allowed, in many instances, any policy or practice that would do justice to the identity of these groups of migrants.[7] Here is another intriguing question.

The difficulty with acceptance of different cultures with their distinct identities is closely connected with a monocultural conception of nation. It is often assumed that one nation means one culture. Though migrants may enjoy citizenship, however, as for culture, they need to fall in line with the national culture. Thus, the French would want all the immigrants to follow the "French culture" and the Germans would want that the immigrants follow "German culture". But the point to note is that one culture and one [8]nation is an illusion which is neither acceptable nor empirically realizable. Unfortunately, this failed model of connecting nation with culture is followed in a warmed-up version by religious nationalists of our country. In Europe too, there are sediments of this dangerous conception as is shown in the attitude of right-wing movements towards migrants and refugees. The fact of citizenship does not call for giving up one's culture as expected by narrow national chauvinists. The future anyway is going to be one in which we are bound to have more and more multicultural nations. Here it is good to turn our attention to the Asian – especially South Asian – experiments with diversity, recognition and co-existence. We could discuss in this context, how Indian and Asian communitarian thinkers have critically responded to liberalism out of their local experiences. This would involve a lot of critical questions regarding infringements on individual rights, including those concerning the right to privacy, which is today a fundamental right.[9] These infringements are made possible in the name of a homogenously defined national and cultural community or in the name of some pre-modern forms of community.

What kind of community do we envisage to stand up to liberal individualism? Are they caste communities or religious communities? Who would guarantee against the abuses of such communities which often cause communalism and violence? Should we then opt for liberal individualism? Instead of entering into any Asian debate on liberalism versus communitarianism,[10] what I intend to do here is to indicate some of the Asian cultural resources that further a life of recognition, tolerance and peaceful co-existence today. Freedom and rights of individuals are to be set in a context of mutuality and healthy interdependence. This would give us some important impulses to overcome the inherent limitations of liberalism to create a world of mutuality and understanding.

Asian Diversity

There is probably no continent on the earth that is as diverse as Asia. For example, no one knows exactly the total number of languages spoken by the 1.2 billion people of India. According to Peoples' Linguistic Survey of India, the country has as many as 780 languages spoken, and 86 different scripts are used. Of these languages, 122 are spoken by no less than 10,000 people.[11] The Philippines is made up of over 7000 thousand islands (more or less depending on the tides!) with a wide variety of languages, ethnicities, and traditions. So too Indonesia, which contains a multiplicity of cultures and ethnicities spanning a stretch of over 5100 kilometres from one end to the other along the equator. When Asia is torn and pulled apart on every side with different identities and collectivities in the same nation,[12] one may imagine liberalism has the answer for the Asian situation. Yes, it does provide an answer, but it is too simplistic to be real in Asia. One should remember that centuries of colonialism did not succeed to obliterate this diversity, and that all projects in the past to steamroll differences proved to be colossal failures. I point to the most natural reaction of liberals and secularists who would recommend the levelling of these differences so as to create a society based on equal rights as a guarantee for peace and coexistence. But then, this levelling would not only mean an impoverishment but would also be utopian in terms of its intended effect.

What has helped Asia to sustain its diversity and multiplicity of identities is a certain vision of reality and ethos in its understanding of the "other". The "other" both as an individual and a collective, is more than an equal bearer of rights like oneself, and therefore deserving respect. The 'other', to use a postmodern vocabulary is *incommensurable*. The rights approach is too weak a foundation for most Asian peoples to relate with each other, as it represents, at most, the lines of a work of art and not the richness of its colours. Every culture, as a dynamic code that organizes a people's experience, knowledge, and practices is something that goes beyond the self of the individual. For most Asians, a definition of self or individual without reference to the group through which the self is nurtured and shaped would simply be an abstraction. The root for this attitude and practice is the various forms of community-life Asia has developed in its history, which are still active.

Recognition and Co-existence: Ethos in the Asian World View

One of the reasons why Asia could feel at home with diversity and multiplicity is the fact that its ethos allows fluid and porous borders. It shuns rigid walls of separation. In the relationships of the self to the "other", of God to the world, and of humans to nature, there exists an osmosis that makes it almost impossible to think and act in terms of borders and boundaries. This is true of the individual in relation to the community he or she belongs to as well as in the relationship of one community to other communities. The web of interdependence of the entire reality within which the individual is placed has been fostered by the great Asian religious traditions of Hinduism, Buddhism, Jainism and Daoism. Interdependence has become part of Asian civilizational experience. This experience, which includes the different 'other' as part of one's own self, does not take away one's freedom. In fact, an individual is free to choose the path (*mārga*) or as one calls it today, "the conception of a good life", which is most suited to her fulfilment. In Hinduism, for example, there is no single means prescribed for everyone. One can choose the path of devotion (*bhakti*), the way of enlightenment (*jñāna*) or the path of action (*karma*) as one's fundamental life-option.[13] This is a conception of freedom and autonomy of the individual that is quite different from the western Enlightenment tradition. For, here, the freedom of the individual to be oneself and to pursue the conception of a life one thinks fit does not isolate her from the rest, but rather, this pursuit is harmonized with the community's identity and aspirations. anekānta-vāda

Philosophical Underpinnings

Realizing interdependence to be the basis for recognition of the "other" and of plurality at the ideational level, Jainism, one of the ancient Asian religious traditions, has developed the doctrine of *anekānta-vāda*.[14] It is a philosophical perspective that holds the legitimacy of a plurality of viewpoints and refuses to identify the truth with any one of them. The "other" becomes part of one's own search for truth in its more integral form.

The classical Indian story of "five blind men and an elephant" illustrates this point. As history and experience show, one of the difficulties to accept the "other" in his or her otherness, and hence to accept plurality and difference, is the claim of absoluteness for what is only a limited experience and a partial viewpoint. Here again, Jainism proposes the doctrine of *syad-vāda*. Literally translated, it means the "may-be position". This philosophy advocates that every statement would require to be premised by a "may-be".[15] This is an antidote to all kinds of absolutism, the root of intolerance, aggression, and violence. Absolutism shirks the responsibility of listening to the "other" in all that makes her and her identity. The "may-be" philosophy sets people in a mood of quest for truth, and takes them on a journey full of surprises.

The "other", with her culture, identity, and tradition is not someone to be tolerated. This is what an autonomous individual would tend to think. On the contrary, here the "other" with her culture and tradition becomes a new source for the redefinition of one's own self. Even more, there is an ecstatic sense about the "other". The "other" becomes a source of pleasant surprises, new knowledge and experience. In the face of the "other", one does not think about how one could safeguard one's autonomy and freedom, but rather one is beholden to the other.

These are the things that one may not expect to learn from the liberal tradition of Enlightenment vintage. It has an individualistic, abstract, and legalistic understanding of the "other". I think one needs to turn to the Christian and other religious traditions for help to discover the face of the other. The reality is that the "other" and all that makes up the identity of the "other" are enveloped in a much larger realm of mystery. From this realization flows a sense of respect for the knowledge, beliefs and practices of others. For example, as far as religious diversity is concerned, there exists an embedded sense of mystery in the Asian ethos that recognizes the sacred in the religious tradition and rituals of others, even though these are quite different from one's own. Implicit herein is also the conviction that the sacral mystery may not be encapsulated in any one single frame or limited to one path. It is not by trying to create unity of creed that harmony and concord are brought about, but by moving together in a common quest carrying along all kinds of differences. Asian ethos does not strive to somehow reconcile the differences quickly to arrive at a point of unity. It is rather carried forward by the thought that differences meet at some point even though one is not able to see it. This sense of the unfathomable behind plurality is the binding force that holds all the immense diversity of Asia together. There is no intention here to idealize Asia and demonize the West as some may be led to think. The following paragraphs will show the difficulties and struggles Asia is going through to grapple with diversity and coexistence. At the same time, Asian encounters with the "other" point to definite challenges that call for an ethos and a means that go beyond liberalism and western secularism.

Asian Struggles with Diversity

While it is deeply rooted in its tradition of pluralism and diversity, Asia needs new means to be able to sustain itself in the contemporary global world. Traditions such as the caste-system that have been fostered on Asian soil have gone against outcast groups. Rampant today is discrimination on the basis of caste, class, gender, language, and ethnicity. This negative legacy of the past cannot be made good by the liberal approach of equality of rights. Justice is not done to the discriminated groups and minorities when the starting-point is different for the individuals because of their belonging to a particular group. Declaring that everyone is equal without paying attention to the initial condition of inequality, as liberalism does, would be to sacrifice justice on the altar of freedom and autonomy. Nay, even freedom is not ensured for all. For, it is only when justice is delivered to these groups that freedom for the individuals of these groups is also secured.

One of the experiments Asia has made is to make different kinds of provisions for the minority groups and other identities. The so-called system of "reservation" or affirmative action in India is a case in point. Within the democratic and secular framework of the Constitution, India, for example, provides for preferential treatment of the scheduled castes and the tribal communities in education, employment, etc., and these provisions are legally binding on the entire community of the nation.[16] Interestingly, the elites and upper castes tend to resent this policy and argue, like the liberals, that everybody should be given the same rights in a colour-blind manner. If one were to follow the liberal tradition espoused by the elites in India, justice will never dawn for the marginalized. Equality of rights will only perpetuate the many existing discriminations and forms of injustice. Here is again the limit of the liberal tradition in Asia. In other words, the provision, like "reservation" for the marginalized, takes Asia beyond liberal and secular traditions. This experiment is proving effective, and as a matter of fact, its application has brought a modicum of justice and freedom to the marginalized groups and identities.

One may be completely mistaken to think of these provisions as "ghettoization." Only with a deeper understanding of the history of discrimination suffered by the victims for millennia will one be able to appreciate the wisdom of employing affirmative action in their favour.

Multiple Layers of Identity

Identity-affirmation and identity-politics are viewed with scepticism by liberalism, not without reason. No doubt, identity has been a source of violence. What could prove dangerous is when people are viewed from a singular identity view-point, whereas, most people live in situations of many layers of identity. The danger of a singular identity is illustrated today by the Rohingyas who are viewed and judged on the basis of their

Muslim identity. Amartya Sen argues against viewing any single identity as destiny and views this as an illusion:

> In our normal lives, we see ourselves as members of a variety of groups – we belong to all of them. A person's citizenship, residence, geographic origin, gender, class, politics, profession, employment, food habits, sports interests, taste in music, social commitments, etc., make us members of a variety of groups. Each of these collectivities, to all of which this person simultaneously belongs, gives her a particular identity or singular membership category.[17]

It is precisely the awareness of multi-layered identity that has prompted the encounter of peoples, and has enabled the co-existence of, cultures, and traditions on the Asian continent.

We need to also sound a caveat against the imposition of any ossified community identity that would stand in the way of the freedom of the individual and her legitimate rights, which include the right to dissent from the community. It calls for a delicate balance. We acknowledge the contribution of liberal thought historically, in as much as it stood against all authoritarian structures that did not respect the freedom of the individuals. This was something positive. On the other hand, freedom of the individual may not be interpreted against the community. It is a freedom to be exercised in solidarity with the community. One should be attentive, however, that the solidarity with the community does not take away the right to dissent. As Sarah Joseph puts it,

> But to give importance to communities without at the same time confronting the need for greater democratization of communities and state and without expressing commitment to egalitarian ideals could send all the wrong messages about what is needed to strengthen inter-group tolerance in our society.[18]

This could be illustrated by ground realities of today. For example, cow vigilantism and love jihad in the name of religious and caste identity and the violence they unleash are diametrically opposed to democracy and the values of the individual freedom. Here is a case of some individuals in the name of the community they claim to represent imposing ideologies and practices (with which other members of the same community themselves may not be in agreement), and in the process going against the individual freedom of its own members and causing conflicts with other communities.

Another experiment Asia is following is to promote inter-religious understanding and dialogue in the new circumstances of today.[19] Religious identities are a permanent feature in the life of the peoples of the Asian continent. Cooperation and understanding among the religious groups have become indispensable to the pursuit of what is termed as "secular goals" – freedom, equality, justice. This experiment takes seriously the fact that religions play an important role in the life of the society. A few western thinkers like Jürgen Habermas who once upheld liberalism and secularism rigorously have now come to realize that religion not playing any public role is an exceptional European situation which cannot be universalized.[20] Encounter between religion and the life of the society has been a permanent feature of Asia, and this has been repeatedly voiced by Asian thinkers.[21] Therefore, when we hear the new realization by western thinkers, it sounds like "Columbus discovered America!". The promotion of inter-religious understanding for co-existence has become an imperative also in traditionally "secular" countries whose composition today is increasingly becoming multi-cultural and multi-religious. Curiously, it is now the case of Europe considering the experiments of Asia for coexistence in multicultural and multi religious societies, rather than Asia taking on European liberalism and secularism.

Multi-layered identity is not a matter of religion alone. Also, individuals and communities who declare themselves not bound to any religion, doctrines and practices, need to be acknowledged and their contribution to co-existence needs to be vindicated. In fact, we have in India strong atheist movements like the one represented by E.V. Ramasamy (Periyar) of Tamilnadu, which have practiced deep humanism, respecting the rights and freedom of the individuals. They have freed themselves from the stranglehold of single identity.

Inclusive Conception of the Secular

The prevailing western understanding of the secular is exclusive and partial. Indian and Asian experience and the elaboration of the secular has shown that it is not anti-religious but that all religions and religious groups are treated equally without anyone getting privileged. But we need to consolidate this Asian understanding by examining and correcting some of its inherent flaws and presuppositions. An inclusive and integral understanding of the secular calls for thorough revision of the dominant conception of the secular.[22] The secular is not opposed to the religious. Therefore, people who are believers can and should take active part in matters relating to public life.

It is important at this juncture to make a distinction between *religion* and *faith*. Faith is a much larger category than religion. People who do not have religion and declare themselves to be agnostics and atheists profess a faith, just as religious believers do. As it is, liberalism would consider as anti-secular, people acting in the public sphere influenced by their faith, whereas it would consider as secular, atheists and agnostics who nevertheless profess a faith like the religious ones. If an atheist or agnostic could give expression to her faith in public life, why is this denied to religious believers? In other words, only an inclusive and pluralist concept of the secular will be able to support the cause of diversity and tolerance that is expected of secularism. Excluding religion from the secular and opposing the one with the other neither responds to our experience in Asia, nor does it contribute to a much needed inclusive conception of the secular.

The need for such an inclusive conception of the secular is not only felt in Asia, but also in other parts of the world. The articles relating to religious freedom in South Africa and Canada, for example, have incorporated an inclusive conception of the secular.[23] Liberalism would be contradicting its own principle of freedom, if, in the name of the secular it admits only the freedom of non-religious persons to formulate public policies, whereas, such a freedom is denied to a believer who acts on the basis of religiously inspired consciousness in the public sphere to promote the wellbeing of all. Secularism needs to regain its credibility by being inclusive to a diversity of views – not by excluding the religious ones – in terms of life in public. Further, true democracy is at work where diversity of views and perceptions of reality are brought together in the spirit of coexistence without any one of them being excluded. Exclusion cannot be the basis of neither secularism nor democracy.

Conclusion

In the history of humanity, there have been many other ways and means than liberalism and secularism to live with differences in mutual understanding and respect. Michael Walzer peaks of "regimes of tolerance" and elaborates a few of them.[24] Asia, on its part, has developed its own approach to plurality and diversity. How far can liberalism come to terms with such diversity of Asian identities with which people have harmoniously lived through centuries and millennia in the spirit of mutual recognition and tolerance? The project of liberalism and secularism is not what Asia looks for if it means flattening and divesting of identities to make room for right-bearing individuals as the unique point of reference. This is something that would not find acceptance among Asians who have a different experience of plurality and diversity.

Today, Europe, like many other parts of the world, is facing the critical question of how to come to terms with the "other"; with the different. In a recent book, Edward Luce, a journalist, has shown how today western liberalism is getting weakened and he sees the cause of it in the arrogance about the invincibility of liberalism and capitalism after the fall of the Berlin Wall.[25]

The ruptures in liberalism have come out in the open in the face of the growing migration of peoples from the ends of the earth who are settling down in different countries of that continent. In resolving the problem, many European intellectuals, it seems to me, have recourse to the Enlightenment tradition of liberalism from which also flows, secularism and the conception of the autonomous individual based on a contractual theory of society as well as the theory and regime of rights. But all these intellectual ammunitions today seem to have been dampened with no firing power. The European discourse of the "other", it seems to me, is dead-locked at this point. Not being able to face the crisis of the "other" has provoked a serious crisis for the European world. New avenues to the "other" can be opened up only when Europe does not absolutize one of its heritages namely, the Enlightenment, but draws also from other sources of its civilization, such as the Greco-Roman culture, the Renaissance and especially Christianity. Centuries after centuries the Christian tradition has shaped Europe, and it is important that it draws from this resource new energies and perspectives to reach out to the "other" as one's very self in the spirit of solidarity and compassion.[26] It is true that modern European history is full of power-conflict with Christianity as an institution. The entire spiritual and mystical legacy of Christianity may not be written off on account of the past untoward experiences. Rather more than ever, the continent of Europe seems to be in need of new energies from Christian sources to come to terms with the "other".

Bibliography

Chakrabarty, Bidyut. "BR Ambedkar and the History of Constitutionalizing India." *Contemporary South Asia* 24 (2016), 133-48.

Delaney, C F. ed. *The Liberalism-communitarianism Debate: Liberty and Community Values* (London: Rowman & Littlefield, 1994).

Dobbernack, Jan, and Modood, Tariq., eds. *Tolerance, Intolerance and Respect: Hard to Accept?* Palgrave *Politics of Identity and Citizenship* Series (New York: Palgrave Macmillan, 2013).

Grande, Sandy. "Accumulation of the Primitive: The Limits of Liberalism and the Politics of Occupy Wall Street." *Settler Colonial Studies* 3 (2013), 369-380

Jessop, B., Mudge, S., Derbyshire, J., Davies, W. "The Limits of Neo-liberalism." *Renewal: A Journal of Social Democracy* 22 (3/4) (2014), 81-100.

Joseph, Sarah. "Politics of Contemporary Indian Communitarianism." *Economic and Political Weekly* 32 (40) (Oct. 4-10, 1997), 2517-2523.

Laden, Anthony Simon. *Reasonably Radical: Deliberative Liberalism and the Politics of Identity* (Ithaca: Cornell University Press, 2001).

Mahmood, Saba. *Politics of Piety: The Islamic Revival and the Feminist Subject* (Princeton, Oxford: Princeton University Press, 2005).

Momin, A. R. "India as a Model for Multiethnic Europe." *Asia Europe Journal* 4 (4) (2006), 523-37.

Morrice, David. "The Liberal-Communitarian Debate in Contemporary Political Philosophy and Its Significance for International Relations." *Review of International Studies* 26 (2) (2000), 233-51.

Parekh, Bhikhu C. *A New Politics of Identity: Political Principles for an Interdependent World* (Baskingstoke: Palgrave Macmillan, 2008).

Ray, Raka. "Saba Mahmood and the Challenge to Liberal Thought." *Economic and Political Weekly* (March 31, 2018),13-14.

Robb, Peter. *Liberalism, Modernity, and the Nation. Oxford Collected Essays* (Delhi: Oxford University Press, 2007).

Ryan, Alan. *The Making of Modern Liberalism* (Princeton: Princeton University Press, 2012).

Sanders, Michael. *Liberalism and the Limits of Justice* (Cambridge: Cambridge University Press, 1982). 2nd ed. 1998.

Smith, G. W. *Liberalism: Critical Concepts in Political Science* (London: Routledge, 2002).

Tan, Sor-hoon., ed. *Challenging Citizenship: Group Membership and Cultural Identity in a Global Age* (London: Routledge, 2017).

Taylor, Charles. "Cross-Purposes: The Liberal-Communitarian Debate." In *Liberalism and the Moral Life*, edited by Nancy L. Rosenblum (Cambridge MA: Harvard University Press, 1989).

Veer, Peter Van Der. *The Modern Spirit of Asia: The Spiritual and the Secular in China and India* (Princeton: Princeton University Press, 2014).

Vitikainen, Annamari. *The Limits of Liberal Multiculturalism: Towards an Individuated Approach to Cultural Diversity.* (Basingstoke: Palgrave Macmillan, 2015).

Walzer, Michael. "The Communitarian Critique of Liberalism." *Political Theory* 18 (1) (1990), 6-23.

Wetherell, Margaret and Mohanty, Chandra Talpade., eds. *The SAGE Handbook of Identities* (London: Sage Publications 2010).

Endnotes

[1] I would recall here the brutal killing of those associated with the Charlie Hebdo magazine on 7 January, 2015, for caricaturing Prophet Mohammad. While this terrorism is condemnable, on the other hand, one needs to ask also to what extent can one go to trivialize another religion in the name of secularity and freedom of expression. There was the least concern about the grade of religious sensitivity. If Islam does not allow images, one does not become secular by questioning this or by installing images in a Mosque. Islam is simply another type of religion than popular Christianity and has its own reasons for prohibition of images. Some commentators have seen in the Charlie Hebdo event, an uncalled provocation, and the killings as Charlie Hebdo's own making, which wanted to wear secularism on its sleeves. See, Brian Trench, "Charlie Hebdo", Islamophobia and Freedoms of the Press", *Studies: An Irish Quarterly Review*, 105:418 (2016), 183-91.

[2] In the context of religious nationalism in India today, this tradition is set aside, and one takes offence easily as illustrated by the case of the artist M.F. Hussain (1915-2011) for his paintings of nude Hindu goddesses.

[3] Like there are manifold forms of modernity which allow us to speak of "modernities" in the plural, so also are there wide varieties of secularism conditioned by a particular people's history and tradition. For example, when the French speak

of "*laïcité*" and object to veils in public, they are probably thinking unconsciously of the veils of nuns in their secular fight against the Catholic Church and its historical hold of power on society. See the interview of Sanjay Subramaniam (Collège de France, Paris) in The Hindu, November 30, 2013. The irruption of Buddha into Indian history with his negation of soul and God resulted in a radically secularizing moment over and against the exaggerated religious control of the priestly class of the Brahmins. Many of the concepts associated with Buddhism pulled from under the feet of the established religious agents their very *raison d'être*.

[4] Georg Evers is of the view that the experiences in inter-religious dialogue in Asia could be an inspiration for the integration of Islam into Europe. See Georg Evers, "Entwicklungen des Chritentums in Asien. Vorbild fuer eine Integration des Islam in Europe?", *Herder-Korrespondenz,* 70 (2016), 41-45. See also A.R. Momin, "India as a Model for Multiethnic Europe," *Asia Europe Journal* 4:4 (2006), 523-37.

[5] Cf. A. D. Smith, *The Ethnic Origins of Nations* (Malden, MA: Blackwell Publishers, 1986); R. Caplan, J. Feffer, eds, *Europe's New Nationalism: States and Minorities in Conflict* (New York: Oxford University Press, 1996).

[6] Cf. C. Taylor, *Multiculturalism: Examining the Politics of Religion* (Princeton: Princeton University Press, 1992); C. Taylor, *A Secular Age* (Cambridge, MA: The Belknap Press of Harvard University Press, 2001); W. Kymlicka, *Multicultural Citizenship: A Liberal Theory of Minority Rights* (Oxford: Clarendon Press, 1995); W. Kymlicka, *Contemporary Political Philosophy: An Introduction* (New York: Oxford University Press, 2002); W. Kymlicka and W. Norman, eds, *Citizenship in Diverse Societies* (New York: Oxford University Press, 2000). Charles Taylor speaks of two variants of liberalism, which Michael Walzer has characterized as Liberalism I and Liberalism II. I am characterizing them as hard liberalism and soft liberalism, respectively.

[7] While seeming to espouse liberal and democratic values, the change of immigration laws by some European states to defend the cultural identity of the nation, its ethnicity, blood and soil is nothing but hypocrisy. See David Cesarani, and Mary Fulbrook, eds., *Citizenship, Nationality and Migration in Europe* (London: Routledge, 1996); Ernst Spaan, Ton van Naerssen, Felicitas Hillmann, "Shifts in the European Discourses on Migration and Development", *Asian and Pacific Migration Journal,* 14:1/2 (2005), 35-70; Natalia Ribas Mateos, *Border Shifts: New Mobilities in Europe and Beyond* (New York: Palgrave Macmillan 2015); Vicki Squire, "Governing Migration through Death in Europe and the US: Identification, Burial and the Crisis of Modern Humanism", *European Journal of International Relations*, 23:3 (Sept 2017), 513-532.

[8] In Asia, most nations have multiple cultures. When Hindutva, wants to make its own the theory of one nation/one culture, it falls into the same trap as the

West which is unable to come to terms with a plurality of cultures. Hindutva, in this respect, is, ironically, the westernization of India, since its principle of one culture/one nation is not really Asian in its spirit and orientation.

[9] The supreme court of India made history on 24 August 2017 by an unambiguous and unanimous verdict that the right to privacy belongs to the fundamental right. This places checks on the intrusive state that wants to curtail the legitimate freedom of the individuals. It also sets limits to unwarranted intervention and pressures on the part of various communities and identities.

[10] Sarah Joseph, in a concise article introduces us to the views of Indian communitarians in relation to liberalism and secularism. See, Sarah Joseph, "Politics of Contemporary Indian Communitarianism", *Economic and Political Weekly*, 32:40 (Oct. 4-10, 1997), 2517-2523.

[11] See http://www.hinudstantimes.com/lifestyle/books/780 [accessed on 13 July, 2018].

[12] D. L. Sheth and G. Mahajan, eds, *Minority Identities and the Nation-State* (Delhi: Oxford University Press, 1999).

[13] For some of these concepts, See Knut A. Jacobsen et al., eds, *Brill's Encyclopedia of Hinduism*, vol. II (Leiden-Boston: Brill, 2010).

[14] Bimal Krishna Matilal, *The Central Philosophy of Jainism (Anekānta-Vāda)* (Ahmedabad: Institute of Indology, 1981); R. C. Dwivedi, ed, *Contribution of Jainism to Indian Culture* (Delhi: Motilal Banarsidass, 1975); Naagin J Shah, ed, *Jaina theory of Multiple Facets of Reality and Truth* (Delhi: Motilal Banarsidass 2000).

[15] Cf. S. Radhakrishnan, *Indian Philosophy*, Vol. 1 (Delhi: Oxford University Press, 1994), 302ff; (seventh impression).

[16] Cf. Felix Wilfred, *Dalit Empowerment* (Delhi: ISPCK, 2007); Felix Wilfred, *Asian Public Theology* (Delhi: ISPCK, 2010); R. Deliège, *The Untouchables of India* (Oxford: Berg, 1999), 192ff.

[17] Amartya Sen, *Identity and Violence: The Illusion of Destiny* (London: Allen Lane Penguin Books, 2006), 4-5.

[18] Sara Joseph, "Politics of Contemporary Indian Communitarianism", *Economic and Political Weekly*, 32:40 (Oct. 4-10, 1997), 2517-2523.

[19] Inter-religious dialogue is not new in Asia. For example, in medieval India, we have an example set by the Mughal Emperor Akbar (1542 – 1605). The need for tolerance and mutual trust among the religious communities, led him to regularly hold interreligious dialogue sessions in his court with the participation of Hindus, Christians, Jews, Parsis, Jains, and even atheists. Such was the trust Akbar placed in his Hindu collaborators that he did not hesitate to appoint them as generals in his army.

[20] Cf. M. Junker-Kenny, *Habermas and Theology* (New York: T & T Clark International, 2011), 132ff; cf. also G. Davie, *Europe-The Exceptional Case: Parameters of Faith in the Modern World, Sarum Theological Lectures* (New York: Orbis Books, 2002); N. Biggar and L. Hogan, eds, *Religious Voices in Public Places* (New York: Oxford University Press, 2009).

[21] Cf. R. Bhargava, ed, *Secularism and its Critics* (New Delhi: Oxford University Press, 1998).

[22] Peter Van Der Veer, *The Modern Spirit of Asia: The Spiritual and the Secular in China and India* (Princeton: Princeton University Press, 2014), pp. 253-70.

[23] Ian T. Benson. "Taking Pluralism and Liberalism Seriously: The Need to Re-understand Faith, Beliefs, Religion, and Diversity in the Public Sphere", *Journal for the Study of Religion,* 23:1/2 (2010), 17-41.

[24] The following are the five regimes that the author develops in his work: the millet system as practiced in the Ottoman Empire, International Society; consociations as seen in Belgium, Switzerland, Cyprus, Lebanon; nation-states; immigrant societies. cf. Michael Walzer, *On Toleration* (Noida: Frank Bros. & Co., 2004) - Indian reprint.

[25] Edward Luce, *The Retreat of Western Liberalism* (London: Little, Brown, 2017). According to him one may not attribute the cause of this weakening to a president like Donald Trump; rather according to him, Trump is a symptom of a weakened western liberalism.

[26] I am not able to understand it when some European intellectuals want to define Europe in terms of Greco-Roman culture, Renaissance and Enlightenment, dissimulating, it would appear, the Christian heritage of Europe. And this happened, for example, when attempting to draw up a common European Constitution (2000). See David Morrice, "The Liberal-Communitarian Debate in Contemporary Political Philosophy and Its Significance for International Relations", in *Review of International Studies,* 26:2 (2000), 233-51. Peter Van Der Veer, *The Modern Spirit of Asia: The Spiritual and the Secular in China and India* (Princeton: Princeton University Press, 2013).

Chapter 3

Fundamentalism and Kenosis: Multidisciplinary Analysis and Reflections

Term, Concept, and Genre

Fundamentalism is a very loosely used term that defies being fit into any coherent conceptual frame. Often caricatured, the use of this term is also ambiguous as its connotation depends on the perspective of the one who employs it.[1] Moreover, fundamentalism refers to such a wide variety of situations and contexts, that, as a concept, it can hardly be generalized.[2] The phenomenon of Protestant fundamentalism in the United States, the revolution of Iranian fundamentalist forces to overthrow repressive regime of Shah, and the Indian Hindutva nationalism could hardly be interpreted in the same terms. Fundamentalism is like the *rangoli* (*kōlam* in Tamil), which has no one definite meaning, but has so many nuances and shades of meaning, according to different geographic regions, cultures, and languages.

We need to be attentive also to the fact that the *discourses* on fundamentalism, namely how it is spoken about and discussed, differ from one context to the other, in spite of the family-resemblance among different varieties of fundamentalism. These discourses, in a way, construct different fundamentalisms and the term is invested with specific meanings in context. People who are aware of the ambivalence of terms like "fundamentalism" or "fundamentalists", choose to a different terminology like extremists, militants, fanatics and so on. There is also some hesitation to use the term "fundamentalism", since it originates from an American Protestant tradition. But the term is today extrapolated both in secular and religious spheres. There are other scholars like Iannaccone who think that fundamentalism cannot be the object of scholarly study at all, and any attempt to define it could lead only to a dead-end. Quite the contrary, today fundamentalism has been studied intensely from the perspective of different disciplines.[3]

The first thing to note is that there are different genres of fundamentalism, the most discussed and researched being religious fundamentalism.[4] Fundamentalist traits can be observed in least suspected spaces like secularism. There is room for "secular fundamentalism" when the boundaries are closed for any other views or opinions, and anti-religious tirades and attacks are defended with almost the same zeal as religious dogmas.

Some varieties of Marxism in eastern Europe before the fall of the Berlin wall could be, in this sense, characterized as secular or ideological fundamentalism. In a similar sense, there could be a 'scientific fundamentalism' when science does not allow any form of knowledge other than the empirical one, claiming to have within its purview the total truth about reality.[5] There could also be a "market fundamentalism', when present-day capitalism claims the market as the directive principle of life and forecloses all other options for an alternative mode of economy. Fanaticism and extremism characterize all these varieties of fundamentalism.[6]

Having taken note of how fundamentalism could have connotations in other fields, we need to acknowledge that it is the religious or theistic fundamentalism, which has become a global issue of serious concern. The complexity of religious fundamentalism is such that we could understand it more fully only when we take a multi-disciplinary approach.[7] Hence, any attempt to enlighten this concept from the biblical perspective needs to be situated, so that what is worked out biblically does not remain a mere abstraction. Each and every situation of religious fundamentalism is unique and the result of certain constellations of social, cultural, political, and ideological forces. At the same time, it is also the cause of social convulsion, intolerance, and violence.

What is most preoccupying is the increasing *political role* fundamentalism plays. It seems to determine the destiny of nations and erodes the democratic structures and processes, which we are experiencing presently in our country. The present situation in India has raised well-founded fears as to whether the country would go the way of Pakistan, Egypt, Morocco, Israel and Indonesia, to become in practice a Hindu theocratic state. The other serious concern about fundamentalism is the *unleashing of violence*, both physical and moral, in the name of God.

Since the question of religious fundamentalism is a larger one, it would be naïve to believe that we could solve it by counter-posing right religious beliefs. In that sense, *theistic fundamentalism* is not solved by expounding *theistic kenosis*. It does not imply any such presumption. There is, certainly a role for religious beliefs and ideologies in fomenting fundamentalism as well as in trying to overcome it. The Muslim *"ulamas"* (theologians) may complain about the degeneration that has happened in Islamic doctrines through adopting practices alien to it and hence the need of purifying Islam. This religious doctrinal motive could become a force for fundamentalism. Similarly, the Christian Right could oppose the theory of evolution or become fanatic like pro-life Christian groups who bomb abortion clinics, kidnap and kill doctors and other abortion providers.[8]

Doctrinally motivated manifestations of fundamentalism need to be situated within the larger frame of political, economic, social and cultural conditions. Thus we understand different forms of fundamentalism in West Asia (Middle East), South Asia, South-East Asia, in Africa, Latin America and North America. If we analyze the conditions in these geographical regions, we will also realize that fundamentalism may not be univocally applied to every situation. Protestant fundamentalism of the USA and Protestant fundamentalism in Latin America are markedly different, because of their different histories and socio-political contexts. Moreover, each religious group has its own form of fundamentalism. As a result, the fundamentalist character of Islam, Judaism, Christianity, Hinduism, Buddhism, and Sikhism, in many respects, differs in spite of many commonalities. The religious conflicts in the Balkan states in Europe such as the Bosnian and Kosovo war, are different from the ones we find in India, Bangladesh, Malaysia, or Indonesia.

In the first part of this chapter I intend to highlight how material forces are entangled in the emergence and growth of religious fundamentalism. In the second part, we shall look at fundamentalism as a theological category. The challenging counter-theology, theistic kenosis, is an approach to God through emptiness rather than through fullness. The emptiness, from the biblical point of view, illuminates the divine mystery. This is a valid theological approach. But the phenomenon of fundamentalism is more than theology. Hence, we need to widen the discourse on religious fundamentalism before coming back to the theological and scriptural response to fundamentalism. The second part of the chapter will then focus on some of the theological issues underlying fundamentalism. We shall conclude with some reflections on the place of theistic kenosis, which needs to be interpreted in more radical terms.

Part I: Analysing Fundamentalism and Its Dynamics

Global Resurgence of Religious Fundamentalism

The end of the Cold War, symbolized by the collapse of the Berlin Wall in 1989, and the dismantling of the Soviet Union, were celebrated as the triumph of liberal democracy. However, the ghastly events of 9/11 of 2001 brought on to the world stage the power of religious fundamentalism, revealing at the same time the inherent weaknesses of liberal democracy and its market fundamentalism. Today, the political discourse has shifted from the ideological divide of capitalism and socialism to liberal democracy versus religious fundamentalism. We have in India quite a different and strange model of development from what we witness in the rest of the world. Market fundamentalism and religious fundamentalism are in an unholy alliance, throwing democracy to the winds along with the spirit of the Indian Constitution. This is what critical observers sense happening in the country with the BJP government in power. Ominous signs are all around that challenge us to reflect deeply on religious fundamentalism and its consequences for our people, society, and the country at large.[9] It would be too narrow to see the rising of religious fundamentalism as a threat to the minority Christian communities alone. The danger is for all the people in this country and is a common and indeed pressing concern.

We find increasing influence of religious fundamentalism on the politics of several countries in the world. We have striking examples in the Egyptian Muslim Brotherhood and the Right Wing Jewish fundamentalism in Israel. Then there are religious fundamentalist movements causing civil wars in Sudan, Nigeria, Kenya, Mali, Somalia, and in other parts of the African continent. Moreover, there is a surge of politically active fundamentalist groups in many countries of South America. It would be wrong to imagine that this phenomenon is connected with the developing world alone. We could observe the influence of the Christian right in the elections in the US during the past two decades or so.[10]

Caveat: Reductionism

It is clear that social, political, economic, and cultural situations determine the emergence and growth of fundamentalism. Today, media too plays an important role in fomenting and disseminating fundamentalism. On the other hand, one may not argue that religious fundamentalism could be reduced to these material causes and factors. That would be a gross reductionism. Any such attempt would be as successful as to believe that a critique of religious beliefs will bring an end to religious fundamentalism. One school of analysis of the phenomenon of fundamentalism tends to see it as nothing but a certain configuration of socio-political conditions in which religion becomes an important instrument for the purpose of acquiring power. There is another school of analysis that views it exclusively in terms of religious beliefs, convictions, and theologies, with no reference to context. A more complete picture of fundamentalism emerges when both these sets of analysis enter into dialogue with each other.

Misconstrued Theories and New Awakenings

In the face of contemporary forms of religious fundamentalism, the western academia was quick in providing theoretical frames of interpretation.

Religious fundamentalism was viewed by several authors as resistance to modernity and to the process of secularization it set in motion.[11]

Closer analysis of the phenomenon of religious fundamentalism has led us to be attentive to its complexity and to critically question the view that religious fundamentalism is the result of a threat represented by modernity and secularization. Max Weber saw the role of religion shrinking in the world through a process of disenchantment or demystification.[12] From this perspective, the fundamentalists would be misguided fanatics wedded to pre-modern values. They want to lead us to the dark ages of the past. They are those who confound the social and political order by their obscurantist religious beliefs, intolerance, and patriarchal practices that are out of step with the modern world. Such people pose a serious danger to the stability of our societies and to the world. Hence, for those who view fundamentalism from this perspective, the pursuit of secularization would be the solution. It was projected that with the rise of the sun of secularization, the darkness of religious fundamentalism would vanish into thin air. Most analyses fail to go further than viewing fundamentalism as a violent reaction to modernity and secularism and this thesis gets repeated. Those who uphold this position fail to go deeper into the social, political, economic, cultural, and historical factors that lie beneath the emergence and growth of contemporary religious fundamentalism.

The resurgence of fundamentalist religious forces from the late 1970s led one to revise past theoretical frameworks of interpretation. A very significant event was the Iranian revolution of 1978, which became a wake-up call for those who had underestimated the power of religion, and had even written its obituary.[13] As Peter Berger has pointed out, the secularization thesis explaining religious fundamentalism failed to anticipate two interrelated developments. First, secularization carries within itself the seeds of a re-mystification of the world. Second, there would be resistance to demystification.[14] Those who were involved in the religious re-mystification and resisted demystification came to be labelled as fundamentalists. This religious process did not take place in a vacuum but in particular socio-cultural contexts and environments in which groups of people were involved in power-conflicts. The religious process exacerbated the socio-political conflicts.

There is something still missing in the new awakening. This is evident in most western analyses of fundamentalism. There is a failure to take into account the underlying forces that foment fundamentalism and fanatic violence. The experience of injustice – real or perceived, discrimination, exclusion, failure of recognition, and similar factors are some of the serious issues which need to be studied as forces that lead to terrorism and violence. When there are gross economic disparities among groups, or when economic opportunities are denied, religion becomes a force in the conflicts among communities. To cite an example from history, while the Hindu elite took on English education, the Muslim elite of the nineteenth century felt that the change to English adversely affected their opportunities, as they were employed by the Mughal courts in its administration, which was done in Urdu. Switching over to English meant the advancement of the Hindu elite; the Muslim elite felt left behind and were aggrieved that they were denied opportunities.[15] In more recent times, the privileging of the Tamils in Sri Lanka by the British in their administration and bureaucracy was resented by the Sinhalese majority, who turned their Buddhism into a fundamentalist and extremist force to suppress the Tamils and dislodge them from their privileged position in the post-independent period.

In our contemporary world, fundamentalism is associated also with *identity-assertion* of different kinds. Both the powerful and the powerless could resort to fundamentalism as a means for their identity assertion. We have cases of a powerful majority making use of fundamentalism to assert itself, as illustrated in the case of the Hindutva. But we have also instances where a situation of powerlessness and marginalization could drive a discriminated minority to take recourse to religious fundamentalism in support of its cause, as with the case of Indian Muslims. We need to immediately add that it is wrong to point to the whole group as gripped by fundamentalism. Rather, the situation experienced by an oppressed and discriminated minority could lead some members or some fringe section of it to resort to fundamentalism as a means to express their grievances and to claim their due share.

Further, simply to maintain that fundamentalism is a reaction to modernity and imply thereby that the fundamentalists are in a pre-modern and underdeveloped state, is to remain on the surface of a deeper problematic. Here is an area for deeper study and research in the future.

Another missing aspect in the present study of fundamentalism is the use of religion for anti-colonial struggles. History shows that, in different parts of the world, religious fundamentalism came to the fore as a force to resist colonial powers. Most western analysts of fundamentalism pass over this in silence or ignore it. In fact, those who fall into the trap of fundamentalism are not against modernity. Rather, many of them feel deprived of the benefits of modernity through structural injustices. The frustration and disappointment that accompany the lack of opportunities to reap at least some benefits of development drives them to despair, as for example in the situation where the youth are deprived of job opportunities with bleak prospects for their future. In such cases (which abound) rather than opposing modernity with the weapon of religion, they resist inequality and the process of marginalization. In many Islamic countries we notice how the absence of fairness and justice on the part of autocratic rulers fomented resistance through religious fundamentalism. Fundamentalist groups recruit people for their militancy among those disillusioned with the leaders of nations, and affected by their repression and mis-governance. This is what happened in Iran, Afghanistan, Egypt, Algeria, Saudi Arabia, and so on. Historically, in India, many subaltern movements were inspired by popular religious traditions. They provided a rallying point for resistance against oppression and marginalization, and they bear some traits of fundamentalism. The Subaltern Studies series initiated by Ranajit Guha has many case studies which would illustrate this point.[16]

Intra-Religious Fundamentalism

Fundamentalism is practiced not only vis-à-vis those outside one's religious fold but is played out also as intra-fundamentalism. In fact, in the case of the earliest use of the term by the Protestant conservative movement of the early twentieth century in the USA, fundamentalism was an attitude and practice directed against the modernizing and liberal stream among the Protestant groups.[17] In Islam, for example, Wahhabism represents a restrictive and fundamentalist trend, while the Sufi stream, is more open and flexible. Hence, there are conflicts within Islam between those attached to Wahhabism and those inspired by Sufi mysticism. This could be seen all over the Islamic world. In nineteenth century India, the Wahhabists, invoking the authority of thirteenth century Ibn Taymiyya of Damascus, turned their criticism against those who, in their view, were trying to accommodate Islam to the Hindu surroundings. In the Roman Catholic Church, there are movements that challenge the renewal of the Second Vatican Council and consider it a degeneration of Christian faith and dogma. They find orthodoxy in the Council of Trent and First Vatican Council. They do not even spare Pope Francis, whose orthodoxy of faith is brought under a cloud of suspicion! A most recent example would be the letter of four cardinals – Raymond Burke, Carlo Caffara, Walter Brandmüller and Joachim Meisner – who raised questions (*dubia*) about the open and pastorally-inspired views of Pope Francis on issues of family and marriage in his Apostolic Letter, *Amoris Laetitia*.[18]

Fundamentalism and Escalation of Global Violence

The impact of fundamentalism is most intensely felt in its capacity for brutal violence suicide bombs, attacks on peoples of other faiths, and demolition of their places of worship. Hardly a day passes without some form of religiously motivated violence on people, and the number of such events and victims keep growing. Mark Juergensmeyer, in his work *Terror in the Mind of God*, tried to study and analyse through personal interviews with those involved in terror-activities, their friends and relatives, what motivated them to do such things in the name of religion.[19] One of the things that has come out from these interviews is that there are not only religious motives to cause damage and destruction to the life and property of the other; there is also a *performative or symbolic* aspect to violence. It is meant to draw attention by creating a dramatic effect in the consciousness of the society and make the religious cause of the perpetrator of violence felt profoundly and shockingly.[20] These acts of violence are directed not only against the religiosity of the other but also against those within one's own religious fold, if they are found to hold a different view, or if they do not act in conventional ways. They are viewed as traitors deserving violent treatment.

Critical analysts point out the inextricable connection of religion with violence throughout human history.[21] From a theological point of view, this is substantiated by René Girard, who held that religions vicariously try to overcome the human tendency to violence by symbolically doing violence to the sacrificial animal – the "scapegoat" theory.[22] This reminds us of the thesis of Sigmund Freud, for whom the birth of civilization needs the repression of instincts through superego, without which there will be only chaos.[23] Religious fundamentalism gives rise to violence when religious rights are curtailed, or religious convictions are idealized or made absolute. For this reason as well, religion and violence remain theologically connected and the spiral of violence becomes uncontrollable.

Part II: Fundamentalism as a Theological Stance

In this second part, we shall focus our attention on fundamentalism from a theological perspective and examine briefly some of the underlying convictions and assumptions behind this phenomenon. Fundamentalism is characterized by its belief in the immutability and inerrancy of one's scriptures and faith-tradition; resistance to deployment of critical hermeneutics; dualistic world-view (good/bad; holy/profane etc.); closeness and exclusionary identity-construction with attendant attitudes and practices. We shall go into some of these theological questions as handled by the fundamentalists.

Immutability and Inerrancy

In the classical scheme of things, anything that is of value means it is unchangeable. Absence of change has been associated with the identity of God in the Scholastic philosophy; God is – *ipsum esse* – the very Being itself. Change is associated with limitation, finitude and lack of fullness or perfection. Fundamentalists would like to protect their faith by insulating it from the vagaries of change associated with temporality. I am reminded about the Episcopal motto of Cardinal Alfred Ottoviani, once the Prefect of the Congregation for the Doctrine of the Faith. It read *"semper idem"*- always the same! Given the preoccupation of fundamentalists to protect faith, they become resistant to anything that could compromise its inviolable sacredness and certainty. In a world full of uncertainties, faith for the fundamentalists offers a haven of certitude, anchor in the turbulent sea of views and opinions, a fortress against the onslaught of attacks, and a guarantee against attempts to dilute or compromise it. From the perspective of the fundamentalists, it is not their religious doctrines and faith which have to change, but rather, the world and society. And they should indeed change according to the immutable truth of faith. Inerrancy relates to the belief that one's sacred books and traditions give nothing but truth and are free from any error.[24] This position involving literalism is the cornerstone of many a theological fundamentalism.

Insulated from Critical Hermeneutics

Given the belief in the immutability and inerrancy of their faith, the fundamentalists adhere to the literal meaning and believe in the absolute and incontestable nature of sacred writings, for example, the Bible, Quran, Bhagavad Gita, Bhagavata Purana, Tripitaka, and the Adi Granth. They resist any historical and contextual interpretation of the sacred writings. The texts are placed on a de-historicized universal plane. These sacred writings, according to them, are the foundations, and they should not be shaken by applying any critical hermeneutics. The sacred books are not subjected to changing times and ephemeral opinions. This explains why the historical-critical method in biblical interpretation has been anathema to Christian fundamentalist groups. There is no room for allegoric, moral and anagogic interpretation of the Christian scriptures, or for *sensus plenior*. All that matters is the literal meaning of the texts. Nor are there any real distinctions between the author, the text, and the reader. Sacred writings are seen as the repository of revelation, and so to be safeguarded from any momentary whims and fancies.[25]

Closeness and Exclusive Identity

Among the fundamentalists, there is a sense of special election. They feel passionately a sense of divine destiny, as chosen instruments to fulfil the will of God. From here flows their commitment even to the point of giving up their lives for the cause of God as they perceive and interpret it. The theology of election leads them to believe in an exclusionary identity, and to create a "we" versus "they"; "they" denotes those outside of the fold of election. Fundamentalism seeks to demarcate clear religious boundaries. It lays down in unambiguous terms who is in and who is out, and establishes criteria for religious belonging. Whereas in reality, as a result of encounters and exchanges, fluidity has characterized the life of religions and their practices. Fundamentalist movements aim at purity of identity, which it believes is safeguarded by erecting borders. Such a view suffers from an essentialist conception of religion and an exclusionary theological conception. Moreover, defining religious identity in the fundamentalist movements has political implications, as for example, in the case of constructing Sikh identity, which has been a major issue since the nineteenth century.[26]

Dualism, Cosmic War and Apocalypticism

Fundamentalists describe the situation of the world in terms of a struggle between the forces of good and evil. It is the duty of the believers to throw out of power the political forces that support in any way immoral policies and practices. Some of the fundamentalist groups go even further and see a cosmic war at hand, and urge the need to be prepared to combat the evil one – the Satan – and overthrow its kingdom and power.[27] In the imagination of the fundamentalists, the satanic force is represented by communism, which should be combated to establish the kingdom of God.

The idea of a God of war is not something totally new. Some of the Christian fundamentalists refer to the Old Testament and see how God avenges God's enemies. The Islamic concept of *jihad* is well-known. At one extreme is the interpretation of it as a spiritual struggle that a person needs to undertake to become a true believer. On the other extreme is the use of it as justification for aggressive wars and brutal violence against the "infidels". In the Hindu extreme fundamentalism, Ramayana and Mahabharata are invoked as examples of war to be waged against enemies. Such use of Hindu epics leads to violence against minorities, and anyone who opposes the Hindutva ideology.

The motive of war gets heightened when it is couched in apocalyptical terms. Some of the fundamentalists see the ultimate struggle between God and God's enemies as a veritable Armageddon of cosmic proportions. The Japanese Aum Shinrikyo fundamentalist movement, which attained notoriety through the chemical gas killings in the Tokyo subway in 1995, was gripped by this impending doom. We could find different kinds of apocalypticism, depending on the fundamentalist movements and their respective religious affiliations. The apocalyptic grip on the consciousness of the fundamentalists and a sense of urgency allow little room for any accommodation, negotiation or compromise. The believers become the soldiers of God, and they have to take a definite stand with God in the battle against the evil forces. All this explains why there is some kind of "spiritualization of violence". Violence and terror become a means to attain the spiritual good in the apocalyptic imagination of the fundamentalists. The apocalyptic and messianic traits of fundamentalism[28] could go to the extent of collective suicide as was the case with the members of the Solar Temple in Switzerland, where the leaders convinced their followers that they should burn themselves to attain eternal bliss in the next world.

Intransigent Theological Views on Gender and Morals

The fundamentalists take a rigorous view of the moral situation of the society and of the world. They see sin and moral degradation taking hold of the lives of the people as seen in the increase of drugs, abortion, homosexuality, and so on. This is often related to flag-waving nationalism. An example of this type of fundamentalism would be the Christian Right in the United States who want to save their country from decline and from losing its privileged leadership position in the world. For, they believe that America is the chosen instrument of God to achieve God's purpose in the world. We see them quoting from the holy scriptures to judge the immoral situation of the present world, and fighting against all those who they think are the cause for it. Jerry Falwell of Moral Majority became a rallying point for the Christian Right as he justified his position on the basis of Christian scriptural passages. We are witnessing similar developments in India with the Hindutva right-wing activists who do moral policing in the name of cultural and religious purity, and this is intimately connected with their brand of nationalism. The strident moral stance also justifies their violence against those who in their view are perpetrators of immorality, or going against traditional Indian culture, as defined by them.

Most fundamentalist groups target women, and seek to control their bodies by intervening in issues of reproduction, and control their minds by imposing severe restrictions on their thinking and free expression.[29] These groups flaunt patriarchal values to subjugate women, and seek to stunt their free development as human persons. There is little difference in this among the Islamic, Christian or Hindu fundamentalist movements. The Hindutva fundamentalists, for example, would call for Hindu women to produce more children so as to counter the threat represented by the Muslims and their fast growth. We could observe similar kind of polemics between the Catholic Croatian fundamentalists and the Orthodox Serbian fundamentalists in the Balkans – both of them instigating their women to produce more children in their fight against the enemy. Women are at the receiving end in these schemas, with no voice and agency of their own.

> Despite some evidence of accommodation …a consistent finding - whether qualitative or quantitative approaches are used - is that fundamentalists are strong traditionalists on matters of family and gender relations. Patriarchal families, with distinct and separate roles for males and females, are core components of fundamentalist beliefs and practices across religions and continents.[30]

In India, during the anti-colonial struggle, the Hindu fundamentalists wanted to show that the colonizers could not erode India's culture. In this context, women were forced to take on the role of the guardians of tradition. Women in this role are employed to symbolize the purity and honour of one's tradition.[31] Their autonomy is viewed suspiciously by fundamentalists as it could, in their estimation, upset the social order.

Fundamentalism and Restoration

Another theological characteristic of fundamentalism is that it sees the golden age in the past, and hence there is an endeavour to restore what was there before. This restorative mindset is found in the fundamentalists in all religions. If we apply this yardstick, the Pentecostals may not be characterized as fundamentalists as they focus attention on the direct and unmediated present action of God as Spirit, and on the experience of salvation of body and soul here and now.

This feature also distinguishes revolutionaries from fundamentalists. Revolutionaries intend to change and transform the present order, whereas, fundamentalists seek to re-establish the past glory: *the status quo ante*. In the New Testament times, we have the Zealots and the Sicarii of the second temple Judaism, who, in spite of the impression of their being revolutionaries, were in fact groups intent on restoration of the past. The Jesus movement of the time makes a departure from such restorative movements, as it is focused on the (then) present and future of the coming of God's Kingdom. It was a forward-looking movement of hope.

Hindutva is a restorative movement of fundamentalism since, in its efforts to construct a world of past glory, it turns myths into history. It claims through pseudo-scientific evidence to establish that the modern developments in technology and science were already invented in ancient India, and that they are indeed the best! In the Roman Catholic Church, resistances to the spirit of innovation came from right wing groups of different hues. There was outright rejection of the Second Vatican Council and its renewal, in an effort to go back to the Council of Trent and to re-establish the Tridentine liturgy as it happened in The Society of Saint Pius X, founded by Archbishop Marcel Lefebvre in 1970. A milder version of the above restorative tendency is to be found in the various movement of Catholic Fundamentalism. Wahhabism would be another example of restoration of the past in Islam, and so also all those movements calling for the re-establishment of the Caliphate of the past.

Conclusion: Kenosis

Religious fundamentalist movements present the same kind of threat to humanity as political totalitarianism. Both are a serious menace to human dignity, rights, and freedom. Experience and observation tell us that in spite of the efforts of the past many years in the field of inter-religious dialogue, we are far from creating a world of peace and religious harmony. Inter-religious dialogue could sometimes give the impression of conversing with and preaching to the converted. Further, one of the weaknesses of the inter-religious dialogical practice is that it is not sufficiently based on social, political, and cultural analyses of religious identity and belonging. All this seems to be too heavy a matter for an inter-religious dialogue to deal with, and it is not able to really take on religious fundamentalism with its stubborn theological positions.

Fundamentalism is a complex phenomenon, the addressing of which calls for a multipronged approach: social, cultural, and political. Since there is a theological component to fundamentalism, in terms of religious doctrines and faith-convictions, it needs to be addressed at that level too. This should be done with the humble acknowledgement that a theological antidote is no panacea for fundamentalism. It can however, make a small but significant contribution. In this sense, the reality and concept of *kenosis* that is embedded in the Christian Scriptures could be very helpful. Against the conviction that one's faith has fullness, kenosis calls for acknowledgement of human vulnerability even when speaking of things divine. It is a call to climb down from the height of triumphalism and exclusion. It is an invitation to nothingness vis-a-vis claims of fullness. Religions will look different if they begin from emptiness or '*suniyata*' as the point of reference.[32]

While proposing theistic kenosis as a counter-theology to fundamentalism, we need to attend to two things: First, *kenosis* needs to be set in a concrete context. An abstract discourse on theistic kenosis may not have any socio-cultural impact. Second, we need to take kenosis to its radical conclusions. For, the Incarnation as the kenosis of God in the scriptures is not a dogma to be defended or held on to, but rather an opening of a new path (*odos*) to be followed with freedom towards its ultimate consequences. The Incarnation as kenosis should not be viewed as a closure of history, but as a disclosure for the future course of history. The way of kenosis is the path to truth and life. It is by walking on this path that we discover both truth and life. To think in these terms is to move in a completely different direction from fundamentalism.

Religions by their very nature are defenders of the universality of their truth; the truth they hold is not only theirs, but is universally valid for all. The theological programme of fullness of truth needs to be questioned by a kenotic theism. Kenotic theism is the espousal of non-violence because the sense of obligation to defend the truth of one's religion gives birth not only to moral violence, but leads almost inevitably to physical harm, torture, inquisition, death, and all round destruction. The Incarnation as the supreme kenotic act is a matter of giving up the claim of infinite and universal as positions of power. It is God's espousal of finitude, symbolized by flesh and by the tent pitched among us (*kai o logos sarx egeneto kai eskēnōsen en ēmin*), as we read in the Gospel of John (Jn 1:14). Incarnation means to become one with the vulnerability and relativity of the particular, and so we could say that Incarnation is indeed a kenotic act.

We will do well to follow theistic kenosis in Christianity. Expressed in simple terms, there will not be any trace of fundamentalism – theological or scriptural in Christianity because there are no truths to defend, but only a sublime divine vocation that helps us to move ahead in history and respond to its ever-new challenges. The sense of a call to something yet to come will override the pathology of the defence of truth which is at the bottom of every fundamentalism. Our interpretation of the scriptures will foster this call and contribute to the overcoming of theistic fundamentalism. I have cited the case of *kenosis* as an example. Other religious traditions have within their scriptures and traditions important conceptions and motifs, which could help address the problem of fundamentalism at the local and global levels.

Bibliography

Akkara, Anto. *Shining Faith in Kandhamal* (Bangalore: Asian Trading, 2009).

Ammerman, N.T. *Bible Believers: Fundamentalists in the Modern World* (New Brunswick, NJ: Rutgers Univ. Press, 1987).

Antoun, Richard T. *Understanding Fundamentalism: Christian, Islamic, and Jewish Movements* (Walnut Creek, CA: AltaMira, 2001).

Appleby, R. Scott., and Marty, Martin E., "Fundamentalism." *Foreign Policy* 128 (2002), 16-22.

Appleby, R. Scott., and Marty, Martin E., eds. *Fundamentalisms Comprehended* (Chicago; London: University of Chicago Press, 1995).

Barr, James. *Fundamentalism.* 2nd ed. (London: Xpress Reprints, 1995).

Bjorkman, James Warner., ed. *Fundamentalism, Revivalists and Violence in South Asia* (New Delhi: Manohar, 1988).

Byrd, Dustin J. *Islam in a Post-Secular Society: Religion, Secularity and the Antagonism of Recalcitrant Faith* (Leiden; Boston: Brill, 2017).

Durrany, K. S. *Impact of Islamic Fundamentalism* (Delhi: Published for the Christian Institute for the Study of Religion and Society, Bangalore, 1993).

Fernandes, Edna. *Holy Warriors: A Journey into the Heart of Indian Fundamentalism* (New Delhi; London: Viking, 2006).

Filiu, Jean-Pierre, and DeBevoise, M. B., eds. *Apocalypse in Islam* (Berkeley, Calif.; London: University of California Press, 2011).

Gregg, Heather Selma. "Three Theories of Religious Activism and Violence: Social Movements, Fundamentalists, and Apocalyptic Warriors." *Terrorism and Political Violence* 28 (2016), 338-60.

Hardy, Mike, Mughal, Fiyaz., eds. *Muslim Identity in a Turbulent Age: Islamic Extremism and Western Islamophobia* (London: Jessica Kingsley Publishers, 2017).

Kalliath, Antony and Raj Irudaya., eds. *Indian Secularism. A Theological Response.* Indian Theological Association 33rd Annual Conference cum Seminar (Bangalore: NBCLC, 2011).

Kenny, Dianna T. God. *Freud and Religion: The Origins of Faith, Fear and Fundamentalism* (London: Routledge, 2015).

Kurti, Peter, *Terror in the Name of God: Confronting Acts of Religious Violence in a Liberal Society* (Sydney: The Centre for Independent Studies, 2017).

Ling, Trevor., and Rylands, John. *Islam's Alternative to Fundamentalism* (Manchester: John Rylands University Library of Manchester, 1981).

Lobo, L. Heredia, R.C. "Religious Fundamentalism - A Challenge to Democracy in India." *Social Action*, 59:2 (2009), 143-58.

Madan, T. N. *Modern Myths, Locked Minds: Secularism and Fundamentalism in India*. 2nd ed. Oxford India Paperbacks (New Delhi; Oxford: Oxford University Press, 2009).

Marty, Martin E., and Appleby, R. Scott. *The Glory and the Power: The Fundamentalist Challenge to the Modern World* (Boston: Beacon Press, 1992).

Milton-Edwards, Beverley. *Islam and Violence in the Modern Era* (Basingstoke: Palgrave Macmillan, 2006).

Newport, Kenneth G. C., and Gribben, Crawford, eds. *Expecting the End: Millennialism in Social and Historical Context* (Waco, Tex.: Baylor University Press, 2006).

Pable, Martin W. *Catholics and Fundamentalists: Understanding the Difference*. 2nd ed. (Milwaukee, WI: HI-TIME; Chicago, IL: ACTA Publications, 1997).

Pedersen, Lars. *1951- Newer Islamic Movements in Western Europe* (Aldershot: Ashgate, 1999).

Puniyani, Ram. *Religion, Power and Violence: Expression of Politics in Contemporary Times* (New Delhi; London: Sage, 2005).

Riesebrodt, M. "Fundamentalism and the Resurgence of Religion." *Numen* 47 (2000), 266-87.

Riesebrodt, M. *Pious Passion: The Emergence of Modern Fundamentalism in the United States and Iran* (Berkeley: Univ. Calif. Press, 1993) [1990].

Schlee, Günther. *How Enemies Are Made: Towards a Theory of Ethnic and Religious Conflicts* (New York; Oxford: Berghahn Books, 2010).

Strozier, Charles B., Terman, David M., Jones, James William., and Boyd, Katharine. *The Fundamentalist Mindset: Psychological Perspectives on Religion, Violence, and History* (New York; Oxford: Oxford University Press, 2010).

Thomas, Pradip. *Strong Religion, Zealous Media: Christian Fundamentalism and Communication in India* (Delhi, London: SAGE, 2008).

Walzer, Michael. *The Paradox of Liberation: Secular Revolutions and Religious Counterrevolutions* (New Haven: Yale University 2015).

Endnotes

[1] The use of this term goes back to the Protestant conservative movement in the USA at the end of the nineteenth and beginning of the twentieth century. More directly, the term 'fundamentalism' is connected to a series of pamphlets brought out during 1910–1915 by this movement under the title *The Fundamentals: A Testimony of the Truth*. The scope of this series was to lay down in clear terms non-negotiable Christian truths as perceived by the followers of this conservative movement. For the results of a significant contemporary research project on fundamentalism, see Martin E. Marty and R. Scott Appleby, eds, *Fundamentalism Observed* (Chicago: University of Chicago Press, 1991). This volume was followed

by a series of publications on the various aspects of fundamentalism bringing together the fruits of a worldwide research.

[2] This has prompted some scholars to propose that instead of speaking of fundamentalism, that is vague and disparate, we should concentrate on the study of *sects*. Sects represent a strict form of religion, religious identity, and belonging. Its nature and features can be understood and defined more precisely than fundamentalism. The phenomenon of a sect is not new, it has existed for millennia in the history of religions. If we interpret what is said of fundamentalism today in terms of a sect, then we need not go into explaining the why of its appearance in the contemporary world since the 1970s. Cf. Michael O. Emerson and David Hartman, "The Rise of Religious Fundamentalism", *Annual Review of Sociology* 32 (2006), 127-144.

[3] L.R. Iannaccone, "Toward an Economic Theory of 'Fundamentalism'", *Journal of Institutional and Theoretical Economics*, 153 (1997), 100-16. His proposal is that we study sectarianism rather than fundamentalism. Sectarianism in religion has been a phenomenon we observe throughout history.

[4] R. Scott Appleby, and Martin E. Marty, eds, "*Fundamentalisms Comprehended*", (Chicago, London: University of Chicago Press, 1995); Martin E Marty, and R. Scott Appleby, *The Glory and the Power: The Fundamentalist Challenge to the Modern World* (Boston: Beacon Press, 1992).

[5] R. Scott Appleby, and Martin E. Marty, "Fundamentalism", *Foreign Policy*, 128 (2002), 16-22. at p. 16.

[6] For an anthropological approach identifying some common characteristics of all these varieties of fundamentalisms, see Judith Nagata, "Beyond Theology: Toward an Anthropology of 'Fundamentalism'", *American Anthropologist*, 103:2 (2001), 481-98.

[7] In earlier times, there was a stereotypical understanding of fundamentalism. However, increasingly, fundamentalism as a phenomenon became the object of serious study and investigation from the last part of the twentieth century. It has been subjected to analysis from different disciplinary perspectives.

[8] There have been numerous such cases over the past forty years in the United States and Canada. See Chris Hedges, *American Fascists: The Christian Right and the War on America* (New York, London: Free Press, 2007); D. Pratt, "Religion and Terrorism: Christian Fundamentalism and Extremism", *Terrorism and Political Violence*, 22:3 (2010), 439-57.

[9] Cf. T.N. Madan, *Modern Myths, Locked Minds. Secularism and Fundamentalism in India*, 2nd ed. (New Delhi: Oxford University Press, 2009).

[10] It is being pointed out that, unlike the developing countries and the US, religious fundamentalism could not strike roots in Europe, barring some exceptions

like the Balkans. The reasons for this could be analyzed. See Michael O. Emerson and David Hartman, "The Rise of Religious Fundamentalism", *Annual Review of Sociology*, 32 (2006), 127-144.

[11] For example, Bruce Lawrence, *Defenders of God: The Fundamentalist Revolt against the Modern* (New York: Oxford University Press, 1982); N. T. Ammerman, *Bible Believers: Fundamentalists in the Modern World* (New Brunswick, NJ: Rutgers Univ. Press, 1987); Richard T. Antoun, *Understanding Fundamentalism: Christian, Islamic, and Jewish Movements* (Walnut Creek, CA: AltaMira Press, 2001).

[12] Cf. Max Weber, *The Sociology of Religion* (Boston MA: Beacon Press, 1993).

[13] See Peter Beyer, *Religion and Globalization* (London, New Delhi: Sage, 2000), p.160ff.

[14] Cf. Peter Berger, *A Far Glory: The Quest for Faith in the Age of Credulity* (New York: Free Press, 1992); see also Peter L. Berger, ed, *Desacralization of the World: Resurgent Religion and World Politics* (Grand Rapids: W.B. Eerdmans Publishing Company, 1999).

[15] See Asghar Ali Engineer, "Remaking Indian Muslim Identity", *Economic and Political Weekly* (20 April 1991), 1036-1038.

[16] Ranajit Guha, ed., *Subaltern Studies I: Writings on South Asian History and Society* (Oxford University Press: Delhi, 1982).

[17] This group, sidelined and even ridiculed by liberal stream of Protestantism, eventually isolated itself from the rest and built parallel structures and strategies of action. The global resurgence of religion in 1970s offered the occasion for the Christian fundamentalist group to re-emerge with great vigour to influence public life and become politically active. See Julie Scott Jones, *Being the Chosen: Exploring a Christian Fundamentalist Worldview* (Farnham: Ashgate, 2010).

[18] For the full text of this letter, see www.catholicnewsagency.com/news, full-text-of-dubia-cardinals-leter-asking-pope-for-an-audience 15105. [Accessed on 10 February, 2018].

[19] Mark Juergensmeyer, *Terror in the Mind of God: The Global Rise of Religious Violence* (Berkeley: University of California Press, 2000); see also Peter Kurti, *Terror in the Name of God: Confronting Acts of Religious Violence in a Liberal Society* (Sydney: The Centre for Independent Studies, 2017).

[20] Mark Juergensmeyer, *Terror in the Mind of God*, p. 14 & p. 221.

[21] Ellens, J. Harold, ed, *The Destructive Power of Religion: Violence in Judaism, Christianity, and Islam with an Ad Testimonium by Desmond Tutu* (Westport, Conn.: Oxford: Praeger; Harcourt Education [distributor], 2007); Juergensmeyer, Mark, Kitts, Margo, and Jerryson, Michael K. eds., *The Oxford Handbook of Religion and*

Violence (New York: Oxford University Press, 2013); Andrew Lee Gluck, ed, *Religion, Fundamentalism, and Violence: An Interdisciplinary Dialogue* (Scranton: University of Scranton Press, 2010); Ram Puniyani, ed, *Religion, Power & Violence: Expression of Politics in Contemporary times* (New Delhi; London: Sage, 2005).

[22] René Girard, *Violence and the Sacred* (London: Continuum, 2005).

[23] Cf. Sigmund Freud, *Civilization and Its Discontents* (New York: W.W. Norton & Company, 2010).

[24] See for example Ted G. Jelen, Clyde Wilcox, and Corwin E. Smidt. "Biblical Literalism and Inerrancy: A Methodological Investigation", *Sociological Analysis,* 51:3 (1990), 307-13.

[25] M. Abousenna, "Hermeneutics as the Antidote to Religious Fundamentalism." *Violence and Human Coexistence,* 1 (1992), 284-91.

[26] See Pashaura Singh and Louis E. Fenech, eds, *The Oxford Handbook of Sikh Studies* (New Delhi: Oxford University Press, 2014).

[27] See Reza Aslan, *How to Win a Cosmic War: Confronting Radical Religions* (London: Arrow, 2010); John Gray, *Black Mass: Apocalyptic Religion and the Death of Utopia* (London: Penguin, 2008); Dilip Hiro, *Apocalyptic Realm: Jihadists in South Asia* (New Haven, Conn.: Yale University Press, 2012); Jean-Pierre Filiu, and M.B. DeBevoise, *Apocalypse in Islam* (Berkeley, Calif.; London: University of California Press, 2011).

[28] L. Sargisson, "Religious Fundamentalism and Utopianism in the 21st Century", *Journal of Political Ideologies,* 12:3 (2007), 269-87; see also Dereck Daschke, "Millennial Studies for the New Millennium." *Nova Religio: The Journal of Alternative and Emergent Religions,* 12:4 (2009), 105-16.; Daniel Wojcik, "Embracing Doomsday: Faith, Fatalism, and Apocalyptic Beliefs in the Nuclear Age." *Western Folklore,* 55:4 (1996), 297-330.

[29] V. M. Moghadam, "Violence, Terrorism and Fundamentalism: Some Feminist Observations", *Global Dialogue,* 4:2 (2002), 66-76; Rayah Feldman, and Kate Clark. "Women, Religious Fundamentalism and Reproductive Rights", *Reproductive Health Matters,* 4:8 (1996), 12-20.

[30] Michael O. Emerson and David Hartman, "The Rise of Religious Fundamentalism", *Annual Review of Sociology,* 32 (2006),127-144, at 135.

[31] Cf. Partha Chatterji, *The Nation and Its Fragments: Colonial and Postcolonial Histories* (Princeton: Princeton University Press, 1993).

[32] See Felix Wilfred, "The Beginnings of New Identities", Editorial in *Concilium* 1999 Frontier Violations (New York: Orbis Books 1999).

CHAPTER 4

Religious Freedom in Asia:
Diversity, Contentions, and Complexity

In the western world today, religious freedom is a matter of an individual's conscience and an integral part of human rights regime. It is a touchstone of modernity and a benchmark of good democratic governance. As true as all these may be, if one were to use these yardsticks to interpret the Asian context, one is likely to misconstrue and misjudge what is a matter of greater complexity.[1] The Asian situation breaks conventional frameworks and assumptions on religious freedom. Multiethnic and multicultural as Asian societies are, freedom of religion has to do with a host of issues pertaining to the recognition and identity of different religious communities. Some of the issues include power relationships between majority and minority groups,[2] the relationship between the state and religion, the creation of a harmonious environment to achieve national objectives and goals guided by political expediency and stratagem.

Further, religious freedom concerns not only the legitimacy of a plurality of belief systems, but also an openness to a cluster of practices, behavior patterns, symbols, insignia, rituals, institutions, etc., that are different from one's own. Religious freedom has to do with the *freedom of a community* whose way of life and meaning-making schema an individual shares. These are important tools and perspectives necessary to analyse and understand the Asian approach to religious freedom. Moreover, freedom of religion in the West immediately evokes the notion of *conscience*, while in Asia it evokes the reality of *community*. To this we need to add a difference in the understanding of what religion is.

Different Understandings of "Religion"

In Asia, as we have seen above, if religious freedom has a host of issues to deal with, it is due to a different understanding of what religion means.[3] This is a fundamental question which we need to be aware of. The term "religion" and the concept of "religion" are western in origin and development. There is no corresponding word for it in any Indian or Asian language. We use several terms in India, which cannot be employed as a translation of the word, much less as an equivalent of the western concept of religion. For example, we speak of *mārga*, namely, religion as a path that gives a sense of movement and dynamism. *Dharma* is used to refer to the order of the universe and to righteous society; it refers to individuals as well as their ethical conduct. '*Sampradāya*' would refer to the various practices and rituals we engage in, and the traditions we follow. These concepts also provide a vision about the self, the universe, society, and the ultimate reality. We need to be aware of these different vocabularies and the complex of concepts they evoke. Within this complex context religions appear in a different light.

On the other hand, in the present day international order built around the institution of nation state, the western concept of religion has been dominant, and this has become part of our Indian constitution too. It is highly influenced by the western concept of religion. Hence, when one talks about the rights of the citizens in a state, an integral part of this discourse would be the pursuit of the religion of one's choice. Given this situation of two distinct frameworks: the traditional and the western, the question of freedom of religion becomes more intriguing and confusing.

Three Asian Situations of Religious Freedom

1. *The Overlap of Ethnic and Religious Identities*

Even at the risk of oversimplification, let me highlight three different situations in Asia with corresponding approaches to religious freedom. The first one is a situation in which religious identity overlaps with racial and ethnic identity. For example, in Sri Lanka, Thailand, and Myanmar, the majority are Buddhists, while Pakistan, Indonesia, Bangladesh, and Malaysia have an overwhelmingly large Muslim population. In these cases, national identity is viewed as religious identity.[4] To be a true Malay means to be a Muslim, and to be a true Thai is to be Buddhist.

Reinforcing this overlap, several of these countries have at the political level, the religion of the majority either as official state religion or religion enjoying sponsorship and special status guaranteed in the Constitution.[5] As for other religions, they are allowed to exist with different degrees of autonomy and freedom. At one end of the spectrum, minority religious groups are permitted to have their own places of worship, ownership of lands, religious education, and even freedom to run educational and charitable institutions, without however, infringing on the rights and privileges of the majority religious community. At the other end of the spectrum is a situation wherein the minority religious groups are deprived of many basic rights, oppressed, harassed, and discriminated against. They are to function in the private sphere with practically no space allowed for any public participation. This oppression is to be explained also from the fact that in many instances, the minority religious groups are ethnically and linguistically different from the group espousing the majority religion. Thus, in Myanmar where religion and majority ethnic identity of Burmese overlap, the Christian tribal groups of Karen, Chin, Kachin, and Liu, are oppressed. Further, the Rohingyas, who are racially different from the Burmese and practice Islam, suffer many forms of discrimination and oppression. The restriction of religious freedom relates not only to other religions but applies to intrareligious minorities or sects as well. These are viewed as unorthodox and so discriminated against and disowned. Such is the case, for instance with the Ahamadiyyas, an Islamic sect, in Pakistan and in Indonesia. Ahamadiyyas are not recognized as Muslims.

Moreover, the minority religious communities in most cases, do not have the right to convert, especially from the majority community. Any attempt to do so becomes a seriously punishable offence. There are numerous laws and injunctions that are restrictive of the freedom of ethnic religious minorities and internal minorities.

2. *Religious Freedom in Centralized States*

A second situation is one of control of all religions by the centralized state. The most obvious example is China, where, from imperial times through the Republican period up to present-day communist regime, there has been a continuous tradition of religion subjected to political power. It is striking that unlike the Indo-European tradition (wherein there have been two power centers – the altar and the throne in Europe and the priest [*Brahmin*] and the ruler [*Kshatriya*] in India, in China, the emperor or the political power also mediates heaven and earth, abolishing thus any intermediaries in the religious realm. This means absolute power is vested in the political authority which controls also the religious sphere. History attests to the fact that the political power-centre, whether it is the emperor or the communist party, does not tolerate any challenge or threat to it.[6] This is true of China as much as of Vietnam.

In the modern period, at the beginning of the communist take-over of China by Mao Zedong, religions were despised as unproductive and superstitious forces, and were allowed to function under very restrictive conditions. Things changed for the worse with the Cultural Revolution (1966-1976) when religious leaders and followers were persecuted, imprisoned, and tortured; properties owned by religious institutions were confiscated, and places of worship were either destroyed or turned into barracks, theatres, etc. The period beginning from 1978 which coincided with China's economic opening to globalization and market, marked also a change in its religious policies. Religious groups felt a greater sense of freedom, and there was an attempt to make good the past destruction of places of worship by rebuilding them, and restoring confiscated religious properties. The 1982 Constitution of China introduced a new statement on the freedom of religion. Though in theory religious freedom is admitted, in practice, religious freedom is stifled through highly restrictive measures. Since religion could turn into a destabilizing force, a fear heightened since the collapse of state socialism in eastern Europe, the Communist Party of China has been following a policy of *penetration, regulation,* and *control.* Far from allowing autonomy to religious communities, the state has tried to penetrate them, divide them through various strategies, and set one group against the other. This has happened for example, by creating a group of Catholics loyal to the state and its nationalist policies and programs, in opposition to a group of Catholics who tried to take on the state in their loyalty to the pope. This latter group could not act in public but only clandestinely, and so came to be called "the underground Church". To ensure loyalty to the state, a Catholic Patriotic Association was put in place, which wields today actual power over the Church and controls its affairs.

As a measure to regulate religions and their activities, China recognises only five of religious groups: Buddhism, Catholicism, Protestantism, Islam, and Daoism.[7] Only these have official sanction for pursuing religious activities. This restriction is meant to exclude many "sects", "superstitions" and popular cults. Throughout Chinese history, it is these marginal religious groups and cults, with their base in rural areas and hinterlands, that resisted the imperial power, and now the Chinese Communist Party. To form an idea of the deep insecurity of the communist rulers vis-à-vis marginal religious groups, we may recall here the case of *Falun Gong*, which stands up to the state, but is being continuously persecuted. Another example would be Tibetan-Buddhism, which has its own distinct traits, and is practised by a different ethnic community. But its people have been ruthlessly suppressed and its religious leader the Dalai Lama exiled. The Uyghur people, a Muslim minority in the province of Xinjiang, is yet another case of denial of religious freedom in China.

The officially recognized religions in China are controlled by a state apparatus called *Religious Affairs Bureau* whose permission is required for all sorts of activities. The Constitution says that the citizens have religious freedom for "normal religious activities". "Normal" is an ambiguous term. It is an euphemism to say that any activity that goes against the interests of the ruling power will be viewed as "abnormal" and "superstitious", and could invite punishment. When authoritarian and centralized states like China and Vietnam proclaim religious freedom in their constitutions but in practice deny it through excessive controls, the seriousness of this proclamation is to be gauged on the basis of whether there are public measures and institutional mechanisms to protect this freedom. One such measure would be an independent judiciary. Unfortunately, the judiciary at the local and national level, handpicked by the state, falls in line with its policies and cannot stand in defense of religious communities. The state is very vigilant with foreign religions, especially so with Islam and Christianity. The colonial inheritance makes the Chinese state suspicious that foreign powers may use Christian Churches to destabilize state power and cause social unrest. All religions are to follow the Three Self-Movements, namely, they should be self-governing, self-supporting and self-propagating. This explains why any foreign interventions are stoutly resisted as illustrated by the Vatican-China stand-off in the appointment of bishops. In effect, to say of China and Vietnam that the state controls religious freedom is to say too little. What is happening, in fact, is that the state is trying to redefine and reshape religions according to its own goals and policies.

3. *Religious Freedom and Democratic Nations*

A third situation of religious freedom is represented by countries with clear secular and democratic foundations. While democracy may appear a distant dream for many Asian countries where religious minorities continue to suffer, at least two countries – India and the Philippines - recognise the right to religious freedom in their Constitutions, based on secular and democratic principles. However, there is a difference in understanding both these principles. Procedural aspects of democracy are central to liberal thought. In Asia, what matters most is substantive democracy in a situation of great diversity and plurality. Any attempt at democratization of society and governance in Asia has to come to terms with identities: religious, regional, sub-national, linguistic, etc. whose concerns need to be represented justly and fairly. Hence, the concept and practice of democracy needs to be so reworked as to suit to the question of identity and diversity.

Contrary to most of its South Asian neighbors, India does not have a state religion or state-sponsored religion, even though the Hindus constitute the majority of the population. India defines itself as a secular state in its Constitution. However, the secular here, is not understood as a wall of separation between state and religion as we see in the US Constitution, nor is it seen as indifference to or animosity against it, as in the French *laicité*. Rather one engages with religions without privileging any one of them. It stands to signify the equidistance of the state from all religions, meaning that all of them are considered equal.

The Constitution grants the right and freedom "to profess, practice, and propagate religion" (art. 25). Restriction could be placed on religion only when it goes against public order, morality or hygiene. In the case of the Philippines, though the overwhelming majority are Christians, the country does not define itself according to the faith of its majority population. There is a considerable population of Muslims in the country who live mostly in Mindanao and in other territories in the South of the country.

For India and the Philippines there are number of practical difficulties in carrying out what is acknowledged in their Constitutions. In the case of India, there is a small though quite powerful and vociferous rightwing Hindu group which claims that India should be religiously defined as a Hindu nation; it challenges the freedom the minority religious groups enjoy. It is the extremist groups of Sangh Parivar who with impunity attack Christian places of worship, institutions, and seek to destroy Christian symbols. They also provoke the Muslims and try to polarize the society. It is important to note that the Sangh Parivar has *a different understanding of freedom*. It is focused on the freedom of the Hindu community which is viewed as being oppressed and marginalized, and having gone through progressive degeneration. Freedom is freedom of the Hindus which is being suppressed by others – Muslims, Christians, secularists and Marxists. In the Hindutva ideology there is no room for individuals and their liberties.

In all its forms, whether shrill or moderate, the Sangh Parivar does not have much to offer with regard to ideas about human emancipation. Not only does it subsume individual emancipation to collective will, it also goes against the universal recognition of group rights. There is a conspicuous absence of a conception of social freedoms against hierarchal oppressions. What are recognized as legitimate and central are the rights of Hindus as a majority community having a socio-political sanctity. The idea of individual liberties and freedoms is clearly absent. Also, the cultural rights of minorities are unacknowledged and unrecognized. In fact, they are subsumed within Hindu majoritarianism to an extent that they become meaningless. Its conception of freedom stands far removed from 'freedom' as is classically understood in any of the traditions of political theory. For the Sangh Parivar, it is the attainment of Hindu national regeneration, which spells freedom of the collective Hindu people.[8]

Fortunately, within the democratic set-up of our country there is an independent judiciary to whom the minority religious communities are able to appeal and get redress on the basis of the rights guaranteed to them in the Constitution. Further, the engagement of active civil society groups has also contributed to defend the religious freedom of the minorities against the excesses of radical right-wing Hindu groups.

In the case of the Philippines, though, as we noted, Christianity is not privileged officially, still the minority Muslim population feels neglected and discriminated against. Added to this is the fact that the migration of Christians in the traditional Muslim territories raises Muslim sense of insecurity as a minority religious group. There has been armed resistance by the Moro National Liberation Front (MNLF) against discrimination and inequality of development in Muslim areas.

Grey Zones and Borderline Issues

Having analysed the three different situations of religious freedom, we now turn to consider some of the areas that are ambiguous and present a lot of difficulties in practice. Does religious freedom extend, besides beliefs, also to the freedom to convert others to one's faith? To what extent could people exhibit the symbols, insignia, signs, apparels, etc. that belong to their life as believers of a particular religion? Does religious freedom imply also the freedom to be governed by the personal laws specific to one's religious community? Could a minority religious community legitimately play a public role and participate in what concerns the common good of the society, or is it reserved only to the majority community? Does the state violate freedom of religion if it intervenes in the name of equality to protect minorities and weaker sections? What happens when the Dalits are prohibited from entering the *sanctum sanctorum* of Hindu temples, or when women are discriminated and banned from ordination justified by religious beliefs? Is religious freedom violated if the state were to intervene in these situations? Asia is grappling with such issues of great social and political consequences. By way of example, let me elaborate just two issues here: conversion and personal or customary laws.

There are serious difficulties regarding the right to conversion[9] in different regions of Asia. Even though secular and democratic countries like India and the Philippines accept the right to conversion, the issue has presented itself politically as being highly sensitive. There are historical, practical, and theoretical reasons for challenging conversion as part of religious freedom. For a liberal person, the freedom to convert may seem like something natural and taken for granted; but not so for Asians with their much-resented colonial legacy in this regard. Many Asians feel that the Christian proselytizing mission, bolstered by the support of the ruling powers made aggressive inroads into their religions by luring them with material benefits and converting them. For some, conversion may appear as a right and as an expression of religious freedom. Those who challenge this view, maintain that they have the *right to protect their religious identity from intruding proselytizers.*

In colonial times, the converts were viewed as renegades entering into the camps of the ruling foreign powers – Portuguese, Dutch, French, and British. This unfortunate colonial experience has led most Asian nations to come out with stringent laws at the local and national levels against conversion, ironically, as an expression of freedom. Further, given the close familial, caste, and clan bonds, for an individual to convert to another religion has enormous social consequences as he or she would be cut off from these primordial ties with implications in terms of property, inheritance, marriage, etc.

From a theoretical perspective, the difficulty with conversion stems from the fact that religious belonging is not seen as a matter pertaining to the realm of human agency and choice. One may not shop around, so to say, and choose the religion one likes. Rather, like geography and parentage, religious belonging pertains to the realm of the given. It is a primordial vocation. Changing one's religion would be tantamount to betrayal. To rephrase it in Christian terms, it would be going against one's vocation and the will of God. There is also a further argument against the right to conversion. It is the claim that for many people, religion is an integral part of culture. Protection of one's religion from zealous proselytizers is to affirm one's cultural rights. With all his openness, spirit of tolerance, and promotion of interreligious understanding, Gandhi was one who dealt a very mighty blow on religious conversion.

There are several historical and sociological arguments against the claims of conversion as being a part of religious freedom. The theoretical arguments against it could be countered. On the other hand, interestingly, Asian history and experience themselves provide arguments favouring conversion. For, Buddhism, was the first religion that from the 5th century BCE onwards, committed itself to mission and conversion. Through the mission of its preachers about the path of righteousness (*dhamma*) and through enterprising monks, it spread in every region, among peoples, civilizations and cultures of Asia. It is said that Francis Xavier when he arrived in Kagoshima in Japan in 1549, was taken for a Buddhist missionary preacher! May be drawing on the country's Buddhist heritage, the Indian Constitution affirms not only the freedom to profess religion but also to propagate it. Further, Asian people have claimed the freedom to change their religious affiliation, when they felt that they were discriminated against and oppressed within a particular religious system. That explains, for example, the conversion to Christianity or Islam or to Buddhism by the oppressed and discriminated Dalits of India, and several movements of mass conversion of the marginalized castes in a society where caste hierarchy is sanctioned by religious ideology. All over Asia, we also have cases of many tribal, indigenous, ethno-linguistic and kinship groups traditionally immersed in their primaeval religious practices, converting to Christianity, which helps them to carve out a new social identity for themselves.

The connection between religion and law is all too evident, the former serving as the basis for the development of many legal systems and practice of jurisprudence. In Asia, the different religious communities were governed by their personal or customary laws. Thus, we have Islamic laws binding Muslims, a Hindu legal system for Hindus, and the Canon law system for the Roman Catholics. Many of these traditional laws have to do with issues of marriage, inheritance, the position of women, etc. A very knotty question is whether one would be infringing on the right to religious freedom if these were to be abolished and people are asked to follow a common civil code on civil issues, independent of their religious belonging. We are at an intriguing intersection of legal pluralism and legal universalism. It involves, on the one hand, the legitimate autonomy of religious communities, and on the other, it carries with it also the danger of violation of some universal human rights, including laws relating to women and minorities. How does one approach the problem when a religious community claims its legal system as essential to its religion? How can it be reconciled with claims of universal rights?[10] During the colonial period, the British allowed these personal and customary laws which are still at work and have been provided a space in the Indian Constitution.[11] However, the contradiction continues to persist.

Asia's Civilizational Challenge to Widen Western Conception of Religious Freedom

The Asian perspective on plurality of religions has been quite different. It admits that "truth is one, the sages speak of it variously"[12]. The admission that truth has many channels and none of them may be reduced to the other has fostered an atmosphere where religious plurality is not only a matter of tolerance, but also a part of spiritual and mystical experience, and quest. It has fostered an attitude of deep reverence and respect to the religiously other, which served also as the civilizational bedrock of a substantive religious freedom. Besides this, in Asia, religious boundaries have been viewed as fluid and porous, and hence mutual exchange and fecundation have been spontaneously taking place. This can be observed even today in everyday practices of Asian peoples, in spite of religious conflicts fomented by economic and political forces as well as by identity politics. The substantive religious freedom, which allows other beliefs (conceptions of what constitutes a good life, practices, symbols, etc.) to coexist with one's own in a spirit of harmony,[13] can be considered as Asia's contribution to the entire human family in these times of global crisis.

For those familiar with the idea of religious freedom, understood as being part of universal human rights, it may sound strange to speak of negation of religious freedom in the West. On the other hand, one would do well to remember that the liberal approach to religious freedom is a matter of recent history in the West itself. What should not be forgotten is the fact that down the centuries, Christianity had serious difficulties with religious freedom; it even maintained such a claim as heretic and unorthodox.[14] Many traditional objections were voiced as *Dignitatis Humanae* of Vatican II was struggling to be born. The argument was simple: to allow religious freedom is to claim that error has the right to exist, while truth can be only one, with only one way to salvation, with no choice. Christian faith is the only true and final revelation of God and the Church is the only way to salvation, ruling out any choice in the matter. This claim of superiority and uniqueness of truth for one's own religion has been, perhaps, the greatest aggression on religious freedom, calling forth a veritable "religious disarmament". Even today, this belief that one religion is in possession of absolute truth gets expressed in different ways, and can be observed in the struggle Europe is going through to come to terms with immigrants from other religions. Much of the western grandiloquent discourse on the secular appears to be only skin-deep.[15]

It is unfortunate that the European Court of Human Rights has ruled against the use of veils by Muslim immigrants and has shown little understanding of Muslim personal laws. One wonders whether here "human rights" does not become a smokescreen to discriminate the immigrant Muslim minority and to deny the right of Muslims to a dress inspired by their religious convictions. In the court's insensitive approach, we could note a "holier than thou" attitude unmindful of the social, cultural, economic, and political marginalisation of the immigrant communities.[16]

The right to identity in a multicultural society, although highly controversial, nevertheless, remains one of the fundamental rights of minorities. There are several forms of Muslim identity, and the level of recognition accorded to them in the British society forms a contentious element in the debate on multiculturalism. Muslim communities increasingly maintain a specific dress code, have particular dietary requirements, and engage in distinct religious ceremonies and celebrations. An open and public exhibition of these identities represents the core of the right to identity and religious freedom insofar as British Muslims are concerned.[17]

Further, in the European Court's verdict cited above, what seems to weigh is the nation state and European culture, and whatever is felt as threat is warded off by interpreting it as being against human rights. If the European court and other agencies are serious enough about human rights, should they not take the European nations to task by letting thousands of refugees drowning in the Mediterranean Sea? What about their human rights? Is it a case of abuse of the language of human rights as a shield to protect white lives, white nations and cultures against others storming at the fortress Europe?

Conclusion

Religion is an identity marker, which is so very evident in Asian societies. Hence religious freedom has to do with the recognition of religious identities and the establishing of the necessary socio-political conditions for a peaceful and harmonious coexistence. As such, the promotion of religious freedom is a common task for all the communities involved. It has to do also with the balance of power in socio-political fields, especially with regard to the protection of minorities wherever religious and minority ethnic identities overlap. If religious freedom is, on the one hand, *immunity* of a religious community from unwarranted intervention by the state or other social and political actors or by the majority religious community,[18] it is also, on the other hand, an issue of the *protection* of the identity of minority groups. This is quite a different approach from religious freedom, as the right of the "unencumbered" individual or as a matter of conscience. In fact, neither liberal thought nor Marxism has any plausible theory about minorities, much less about religious minorities and their freedom. For liberal individualism, the two poles of relationship are the individual and the state. The intermediary group unity or identity is not given due place, but rather is absorbed within the horizon of the individual.[19] Marxism supports the formation of great nations, but neglects and is even hostile to sub-nationalities.

In Asia, religious freedom is first and foremost a community issue, and often a matter of sub-nationalities, given the overlap of religion and ethnicity.[20] In this continent, the recognition[21] and acceptance of a religious community and its freedom create the precondition for the discourse on the religious freedom of the individual.[22]

There is, however, also an intra-religious dimension to religious freedom in the sense that the individual may not be constrained by the dictates of his or her community in matters of doctrine or ethical issues (abortion for example) or gender issues, but has the right to dissent and hold other views without being penalised for non-conformity. Thus, religious freedom remains a project that needs to be constantly negotiated in inter-religious and intra-religious spheres. A formal invocation of religious freedom as a universal right in the abstract may not be very helpful unless it is read and interpreted through issues of conversion, personal laws pertaining to religious communities, public manifestation of religious symbols, etc. These are integral parts in a wholistic understanding of religious freedom in Asia.

New contexts have amplified the scope of religious freedom even in the West. For example, the right to intervene in public life by religions or religious agents, something which the secularists would challenge, gets a fillip in post-secular society where there is not only the recognition of the legitimacy of religion in public life; even more, the need for its involvement is also increasingly being voiced. Thinkers like Jürgen Habermas have acknowledged a new and redefined role of religion. Further empirical studies show how religions can transform public life, politics, and governance. New thoughts, orientations, and practices in the context of immigrants have raised new questions leading to a rethinking of the traditional understanding of religious freedom in the West. There seems to be a convergence of the post-secular thought in the West on the public role of religion and the relationship of religion and society as practiced throughout Asian history. This is markedly different from the liberal tradition of relegating religion to a private affair. The maintenance of public order is the duty of the state, and it cannot be equated with the common good, which goes beyond its role. This distinction creates the space for religion to play a public role and contribute to the common good.[23] Asia's millennial experience of respect and tolerance for the religiosity of the other is an invaluable heritage that can stand in good stead even as the continent struggles to grapple with religious freedom in contemporary times.

Bibliography

Adcock, C. S. *The Limits of Tolerance: Indian Secularism and the Politics of Religious Freedom* (New York: Oxford University Press, 2014).

Ahmed, Farrah. *Religious Freedom under the Personal Law System* (Delhi: Oxford University Press, 2016).

De Souza, Peter Ronald. "Politics of the Uniform Civil Code in India." *Economic and Political Weekly* 50 (2015),50-57.

Dhavan, Rajeev. "Religious Freedom in India." *The American Journal of Comparative Law* 35 (1) (1987), 209-54.

DuBois, Thomas David. "Religious Freedom in East Asia: Historical Norms and the Limits of Advocacy." *Journal of Religious and Political Practice* 4 (2018), 46-60.

Grim, Brian J, and Finke, Roger. *The Price of Freedom Denied: Religious Persecution and Conflict in the 21st Century* (Cambridge: Cambridge University Press, 2011).

Hamayotsu, K. "The Limits of Civil Society in Democratic Indonesia: Media Freedom and Religious Intolerance." *Journal of Contemporary Asia* 43 (4) (2013), 658-77.

Hertzberg, Michael. "The Rhetorical Shadows of the Anti-Conversion Bill: Religious Freedom and Political Alliances in Sri Lanka." *Nordic Journal of Human Rights*. 34 (2016), 189-202.

Jenkins, L.D. "Diversity and the Constitution in India: What Is Religious Freedom?" *Drake Law Review* 57 (4) (2009), 913-48.

Jereza, Veronica Louise B. "Many Identities, Many Communities: Religious Freedom amidst Religious Diversity in Southeast Asia." *The Review of Faith & International Affairs* 14 (2016), 89-97.

Katju, Manjari. "The Understanding of Freedom in Hindutva." *Social Scientist* 39 (3/4) (2011), 3-22.

Kim, Hyung-Jun. "The Changing Interpretation of Religious Freedom in Indonesia." *Journal of Southeast Asian Studies* 29 (2) (1998), 357-73.

Leung, Beatrice. "China's Religious Freedom Policy: The Art of Managing Religious Activity." *The China Quarterly* 184 (2005), 894-913.

Lindsey, Timothy., and Pausacker, Helen., eds. *Religion, Law and Intolerance in Indonesia* (Oxford; New York: Routledge, 2016).

Lipton, Edward P., ed. *Religious Freedom in Asia* (New York: Nova Science, 2002).

Madan, T. N. "Freedom of Religion." *Economic and Political Weekly* 38 (11) (2003), 1034-041.

Massey, James. *Minorities and Religious Freedom in a Democracy* (New Delhi: Manohar Publishers & Distributors in Association with Centre for Dalit/Subaltern Studies, 2003).

Mufford, Tina L. *A Right for All: Freedom of Religion or Belief in ASEAN* (Washington D.C.: United States Commission on International Religious Freedom, 2017).

Nayak, Premanand. *In Kandhamal...: There Are No More Cheeks to Turn* (Delhi: Media House, 2015).

Osuri, Goldie, *Religious Freedom in India: Sovereignty and (anti) Conversion* (London: Routledge, 2012).

Potter, Pitman B. "Belief in Control: Regulation of Religion in China." *The China Quarterly* 174 (2003), 317-37.

Puniyani, Ram. *Communal Politics: Facts versus Myths* (New Delhi; London: SAGE Publications, 2003).

Rehman, Javaid. "'The Sharia' Freedom of Religion and European Human-Rights Law." *Irish Studies in International Affairs.* 22 (2011), 37-51.

South Asia Human Rights Documentation Centre "Anti-Conversion Laws: Challenges to Secularism and Fundamental Rights." *Economic and Political Weekly* 43 (2) (2008), 63-73.

Srivastava, D. K. "Personal Laws and Religious Freedom." *Journal of the Indian Law Institute* 18 (4) (1976), 551-86.

Walzer, Michael. *The Paradox of Liberation: Secular Revolutions and Religious Counterrevolutions* (New Haven: Yale University Press, 2015).

Wellens, Koen. "Negotiable Rights? China's Ethnic Minorities and the Right to Freedom of Religion." *International Journal on Minority and Group Rights* 16 (3) (2009), 433-54.

Endnotes

[1] Given the special and intricate situation of the Middle East, which calls for a study all by itself, the present chapter does not cover that part of Asia.

[2] The term "minority" is often used in a fluid way. It needs to be defined more precisely. The following definition of Neera Chandhoke would also apply to religious minorities: "A minority is a group that is numerically smaller in relation to the rest of the population. It is non-dominant or not represented in the public sphere or in the constitution of social norms. It has characteristics which differ from the majority group and more importantly it wishes to preserve these characteristics". Neera Chandhoke, *Beyond Secularism: The Rights of Religious Minorities* (Delhi: Oxford University Press, 1999), p. 26

³ Wilfred Cantwell Smith in his classical work treats the development of this concept of 'religion.' He even predicted that the word would disappear. See Wilfred Cantwell Smith, *The Meaning and End of Religion* (New York: New American Library, 1964).

⁴ This model would correspond to the establishment model in the western tradition. For example, in England, the Anglican Church is the established Church with the Queen as its head. In Italy, Spain, Portugal, Austria, and Belgium, Catholicism enjoyed, and to some extent continues to enjoy, a privileged position.

⁵ For the Japanese too, Shinto religious practices are a matter of national identity.

⁶ Cf. Kim-Kwong Chan and Eric R. Carlson, *Religious Freedom in China: Policy, Administration, and Regulation* (Santa Barbara: Institute for the Study of American Religion, 2005); Eric O. Hanson, *Catholic Politics in China and Korea* (Maryknoll, New York: Orbis Books, 1980); Donald E. MacInnis, *Religion in China Today: Policy and Practice* (Maryknoll, New York: Orbis Books, 1989); Daniel H. Bays, *Christianity in China: From the Eighteenth Century to the Present* (Stanford: Stanford University Press, 1996); Philip L. Wickeri, *Seeking The Common Ground: Protestant Christianity, and Three-Self Movement and China's United Front* (Maryknoll, New York: Orbis Books, 1988). David A. Palmer et al., *Chinese Religious Life* (New York: Oxford University Press, 2011).

⁷ Similarly, in Indonesia, only the following religions are officially recognized: Islam, Protestantism, Catholicism, Hinduism, Buddhism, and Confucianism. For any group to enjoy civil rights it must be registered with the state.

⁸ Manjari Katju, "The Understanding of Freedom in Hindutva", *Social Scientist*, 39:3/4 (March-April 2011), 3-22, at 18.

⁹ Cf. Rudolf C. Heredia, "Religious Disarmament: Rethinking Religious Conversion in Asia", in Felix Wilfred, ed, *The Oxford Handbook of Christianity in Asia* (New York: Oxford University Press, 2014), pp. 257-272; Richard Fox Young, "Christianity and Conversion: Conceptualization and Critique, Past and Present, with Special Reference to South Asia", in Felix Wilfred, op. cit. 444-457; Sebastian C. H. Kim, *In Search of Identity: Debates on Religious Conversion in India* (Delhi: Oxford University Press, 2003).

¹⁰ This has become a crucial issue in Europe. See Rehman, Javaid, "'The Sharia' Freedom of Religion and European Human-Rights Law", *Irish Studies in International Affairs* 22 (2011), 37-51.

¹¹ Cf. Gerald James Larson, ed., *Religion and Personal Law in Secular India: A Call to Judgment* (Bloomington: Indiana University Press, 2001); Marc Galanter, *Law and Society in Modern India* (Oxford: Oxford University Press, 1989).

¹² *Rig Veda Book* I, Hymn 164, Verse 46.

[13] In Hinduism for example, there is no concept of *heterodoxy* as generally understood. For, it allows immense scope for plurality of beliefs and practices. At the one end is the high advaitic mysticism of non-dual unity with the Absolute, and on the other end of the spectrum sexuality as a means of spiritual elevation, practiced in the tradition of tantra.

[14] In the western tradition, the political philosophy of *cuius regio eius religio* stifled religious freedom. It was meant to be a means to settle religious wars in Europe. Ironically, it only contributed to suppress freedom of religion. See Javaid Rehman, "'The Sharia' Freedom of Religion and European Human-Rights Law", *Irish Studies in International Affairs* 22 (2011), 37-51. According to him, "The application of the Millet system and the induction of capitulations also provide striking examples of innovation in religious tolerance at a time when the rest of Europe, and indeed, the entire world, was wrestling with such horrific acts as the slave-trade and colonialism" at 43.

[15] Human rights has got so much politicized today that it has become increasingly difficult to distinguish between genuine engagement and political expediency. It has been a common observation by the developing countries that the accusation of violation of human rights by western nations against developing countries has been often motivated by political and economic factors. Today, the way European nations and the USA under Donald Trump are treating the immigrants has become scandalous for the observers in the developing countries. See T. Ramishvili, "Human Rights Violation in the Center of Europe," *International Affairs.* 4 (1998), 116-127; M. Fasti, "The restrictive approach taken by the European Court of Human Rights: Deportation of long-term immigrants and right to family life. Part 2: "Consensus enquiry and security of residence of long-term immigrants in Europe" *Tolley's Journal of Immigration, Asylum and Nationality Law* 16:4 (2002), 224-236; S.E. Berry, "Bringing Muslim Minorities within the International Convention on the Elimination of All Forms of Racial Discrimination-Square Peg in a Round Hole?", *Human Rights Law Review,* 11:3 (2011), 423-450; Oliver De Schutter, and Julie Ringelheim, "Ethnic Profiling: A Rising Challenge for European Human Rights Law," *The Modern Law Review,* 71:3 (2008), 358–384.

[16] Javaid Rehman has brought out this point concretely with reference to the situation of the Muslims in UK. See Rehman, Javaid. *art. cit.*

[17] Javaid Rehman, *art.cit.* 47-48.

[18] In Malaysia, Christians are forbidden to use "Allah" to refer to God in their worship or in Bible translations. It is claimed exclusively by the majority Muslim community.

[19] Will Kymlicka in his theorizing has tried to create a space for community rights, by negotiating between liberalism and communitarianism. See Will Kymlicka,

ed, *The Rights of Minority Cultures* (Oxford: Oxford University Press, 1995); ID., Contemporary Political Philosophy: An Introduction II edition (Oxford: Oxford University Press, 2002).

[20] Satish Saberwal and Mushirul Hasan, eds, *Assertive Religious Identities: India and Europe* (New Delhi: Manohar Publishers & Distributors, 2006).

[21] Cf. Axel Honneth, *The Struggle for Recognition: The Moral Grammar of Social Conflicts* (Cambridge: Polity Press, 1995).

[22] This is parallel to the political realm in Asia where democratic participation often involves the polity as a conglomeration of a plurality of communities and not the sum total of individuals.

[23] See Craig Calhoun, Eduardo Mendieta, and Jonathan Van Antwerpen, eds, *Habermas and Religion* (Cambridge: Polity Press, 2013); Maureen Junker-Kenny, *Habermas and Theology* (London: T&T Clark, 2011); Jacques Derrida and Gianni Vattimo, eds, *Religion: Cultural Memory in the Present* (Stanford: Stanford University Press, 1996).

PART - II

PRACTICE OF JUSTICE –
CHALLENGE TO THEOLOGY

CHAPTER **5**

Global Inequalities:
Through an Asian Window

The Human Development Report of 2013 by the United Nations is titled *The Rise of the South*.[1] It states that about forty countries of the South, whose development index was low in 1990, had shown remarkable improvement in human development in 2012; highlighted in particular were India, China and Brazil. However, this story of the "Rise of the South" could be misleading if we do not attend to ground realities which exhibit a range of inequalities, raising many questions about those countries that have achieved a level of development, defying predictions. Inequality is the most crucial issue to be confronted as it jeopardizes any development they may have achieved. The undeniable fact is that about one billion people in the South live in extreme poverty, struggling to meet the bare necessities of life: food, clean water, shelter, basic health care, and basic education. This state of affairs is due to persisting expressions of inequality, all of them intertwined, of which income inequality is only one.

In this chapter, I shall try to analyse the connection between neoliberal economy and the phenomenal growth of inequalities in our world, with reference to the South, and chiefly to Asia. In the second part, we shall study some of the ways and strategies that need to be put in place, so that the inequalities are contained, and we are able to move towards a global situation of greater equality, justice, and harmony. In the final part, which is relatively short, we shall discuss how religions could provide resources today for the project of a more equitable world.

Part I: A World of Inequalities

The Case of Asia

Inequalities are of different kinds and each one has its own specific contour in each society, depending on its culture, tradition, history, etc. But what appears to be universal today is that in every society, money, market, and competition are reinforcing the traditional inequalities of gender, caste, ethnicity, education, etc. Economic inequality has led to new forms of social inequalities and an asymmetry in political power.

Since the fast-economic development of Asia has become the talk of the world, let us begin by examining the case of this continent which is going through liberal economic transformations, with consequences in social, political, and cultural fields.

In Asia, although there is economic growth, there is no reduction in poverty. There does not seem to be any correlation between these two realities, resulting in a contradictory situation. China's colossal economy stands on political feet of clay. Taken up by the glamour of liberal economy and the goodies in the market, democracy seems to be the last thing the Chinese youth could be attracted to. Moreover, the pursuit of a crass liberal economy has led to serious violations of human rights, land-alienation, suppression of minorities, and gross disparity among the various Chinese regions and populations.

India, on the other hand, has not used the opportunities offered by its democratic political system (world's largest democracy) to overcome inequality and pursue the wellbeing of all its citizens. The democratic system is corrupted by liberal and capitalist forces. India, which has pursued a liberal economy since the 1990s, and has attained significant economic growth, deprives the poor of their basic needs and rights. Against the many parameters of development, India trails far behind Bangladesh, where there is greater equity in growth and development.

This discrepancy between growth and poverty in Asia and the world at large could be illustrated by drawing on the concept of the Human Poverty Index (HPI) which was introduced by UNDP in 1997. A country also has the Human Development Index (HDI) besides the HPI.

> What is the difference between the HDI and the HPI? The HDI measures progress in a community or country as a whole. The HPI measures the extent of deprivation, the proportion of people in the community who are left out of progress…HPI draws attention to deprivations in three essential elements of human life…- longevity, knowledge and a decent living standard.[2]

Often there is no correspondence between the two. A country which shows a high percentage in HDI may have a low HPI due to persistent structures of inequality. Only a comparison between the two indices will show how well or inequitably the benefits of development are distributed.

Inequalities are also divided along an urban-rural axis. Asian societies have been rural-based, so much so Gandhi said that the heart of India beats in its villages. Today, in Asian countries as well as in many developing societies, the rural gets marginalized whereas the lion's share of the benefit of economic growth goes to the relatively well-off sections in urban areas. What the rural population gets from the present-day form of development are but some crumbs. We need to pay attention to the rampant social inequalities in Asian societies on the basis of ethnicity, region, caste, religion, etc. The marginalized groups suffer many disabilities, because they have not been provided the *capabilities* in terms of health, knowledge, life-span, etc.[3]

The Price of Greed and the Struggle for Basic Needs

"The Price of Greed" is how *Time* magazine characterized the financial crisis that the world has been experiencing since 2008.[4] Greed begets more greed and finally the price has to be paid. Unfortunately, it is the poor of the world who pay a hefty price for the avarice of the rich money-spinners, speculators, and business interests. This is shown by the bail-out measures of the various states. The irony is that the tax money of the poor is spent to save the greedy rich. It is greed, again, that lays off workers in times of crisis to save costs and maintain profits. What we fail to realize generally is that it is the same greed that is at work in the mainstream economic system.

There are 2,170 billionaires around the world whose combined wealth has doubled in the past five years—up from 1.85 trillion pounds to 3.88 trillion pounds.[5] The number of billionaires in India has doubled in the past fifteen years indicating the phenomenal concentration of wealth in a country with 400 million people living below the poverty line. This fact has led Christine Lagarde, director of the IMF, to state that the net worth of the Indian billionaires is large enough to eliminate the country's absolute poverty twice over.[6] Something similar was stated by UNDP way back in 1997 in its annual report.

> The world has more than enough resources to accelerate the progress in human development for all and to eradicate the worst forms of poverty from the planet. Advancing human development is not an exorbitant undertaking. For example, it has been estimated that the total additional yearly investment required to achieve universal access to basic social services would be roughly $40 billion, 0.1% of world income, barely more than a rounding error. That covers the bill for basic education, health, nutrition, reproductive health, family planning and safe water and sanitation for all. [7]

Greed not only turns priorities upside down, it also expresses itself in atrocious and repulsive consumption patterns. Consumerism is increasingly reaching out to the rural hinterlands too. The greed ingrained in the system of capitalist economy followed by Asian states has risked such crucial areas of the wellbeing of the poor as nutrition, health-care, basic education, development of women, and the security of marginalized communities.

We could think of overcoming inequalities only when there is restraint on human greed, and greater focus on the common good. Restraint on greed is indispensable today to enable the freedom of all – especially the weaker ones – and provide them opportunity for the flowering of their freedom and capabilities which is true development.[8] There is a further reason for a curb on the endless pursuit of economic growth. Experience and study have increasingly led to the realization that economic growth and prosperity, if pursued beyond a certain limit, can become a threat to all stakeholders and their happiness.[9] Further, from a psychological point of view, the more greatly unequal a society, the higher its level of distress.[10]

Social Consequences of Inequality

Greed is accompanied by violence, because in order to wrest control of possessions, one needs to employ violent means. The imbalance and asymmetry of power to which greed leads is a situation of injustice. It exploits and marginalizes the poor. The greed that is deeply embedded in the capitalist system of economy continues to generate violence at all levels and in every part of the world. This is something obvious. A Buddhist text brings out very lucidly where the path of violence, greed, and exclusive possession lead to:

> Thus, from the not giving of property to the needy, poverty became widespread; from the growth of poverty, the taking of what was not given increased; from the increase of theft, the use of weapons increased; from the increased use of weapons, the taking of life increased.[11]

Greed brings forth unequal societies, and inequality is a permanent source of violence. The other becomes an enemy to be destroyed or a competitor to overcome. Increasing number of analyses show that countries and societies with greater inequality are also the ones prone to crime and violence. In societies where there is less inequality, the quality of life turns out to be higher.

Another social consequence of inequality is the destruction of *social coherence and quality of life*. This is something observed not only in Asia and other developing countries, but also in the western countries, something so well brought out in the work of Richard Wilkinson and Kate Pickett.[12] Inequality kills opportunity even though people abound in talents, as they can flourish only in a society of equal opportunities. Inequality harms the community in as much as it prevents the talents of the marginalized individuals, groups, and communities from playing an active part in the life of the society and contributing to its growth.

Further, the social condition of the working class has suffered enormously under the present-day global economic dispensation and its tendency to create inequalities. The gains of the workers' movement, acquired through a century and a half of struggles, are thrown to the wind today. We are back to the initial years of the industrial revolution in terms of exploitation of the working class. Maximization of profit that took a great toll is once again at work with the globalisation of liberal economy. The workers' welfare and quality of life have gone down drastically, and their condition is characterized by a sense of deep insecurity.

The Case of Privatization

Inequality increases when, without attending to the basic needs, a country goes on with privatization. In a country which has problems with malnutrition, basic healthcare and low literacy, privatization has disastrous consequences. With privatization, inequality grows beyond limits. Let me illustrate the point with an example from the field of healthcare.

The practice of privatization is not something abstract, but something to be viewed in context, and against the social history of people. China, for example, spends 2.7% of its GDP on public healthcare, whereas India spends just 1.2% of its GDP. The market economy has put pressure on the healthcare of the people in India, encouraging private healthcare which most poor people cannot afford. Unlike most developed countries as Britain, Japan, Korea, and developing countries like Brazil and China, India has not built up any solid base for public healthcare. Jumping into private healthcare, as India seems to be doing now, has enormous consequences for the life and wellbeing of the poor.[13]

During the British colonial times, there were recurrent famines in India in which millions perished. Following independence, India has, within a few decades, not only gained self-sufficiency, it also has become an exporter of food. With better nutrition, there has come about a drastic reduction of child-mortality, and the average life-expectancy in India has risen from just 31 years, when the British left, to 67 years now. The gains India has made in these respects, thanks to a strong public sector, are, however, being compromised by increasing privatization. India needs to build up a strong public healthcare system before launching into privatization of health, as the private healthcare, which is based on the capitalistic principles of competition and profit, is unaffordable to them, and is bound to leave them in the lurch.

Crony Capitalism and the Political Fallout of Democracy

Inequality results when there is a disproportionate sharing of political power and the concentration of it in a small group of elites. What follows is the absence of effective public policies aimed at the reduction of poverty.

In India, natural resources are heavily exploited by the business lobby with the blessings of corrupt politicians. The illegal mining and shipping of iron ore to China by Uday Vir Singh, who made a profit of $2 billion within a short period, is only the tip of an iceberg. The point is that this sell-out of national resources was possible only because of his proximity to the state apparatus and to politicians whose palms were substantially greased.[14] Democracy per se does not guarantee the overcoming of inequalities; rather, it creates conditions conducive to their overcoming. Where democracy remains a political ideal without impacting the economic agenda, it can become a convenient cover-up for corrupt practices, something amply demonstrated by the sham "democracies" (Banana republics!) across the globe.

We not only have the philosophy and anthropology of competition to challenge, but crony capitalism as well. Here, riches and money are made not so much through competition, as by connections involving the state, its power and bureaucracy. In short, corruption and bribery have become new sources for wealth and the creation of billionaires in poor countries. In developed countries, the wealth made by crony capitalism is much less, whereas, in developing countries it has gone up very high and very fast – something which explains the phenomenal growth of billionaires in India, China, Hong Kong, Singapore, Malaysia, Indonesia and so on.[15]

Part II: Towards Overcoming Inequalities

From Competition to Cooperation and Solidarity

It is well-known that the neo-liberal ideology, animating the mainstream economic system, is based on competition as a general law or principle. What happens in the economic realm is argued to be nothing but concretization of a general law of nature. Competition is associated with growth, greater effectiveness, and productivity.

It is important to closely examine the arguments fielded in favour of competition to be able to unmask the myths behind it. It is said that competition is something that is inherent in human nature, and therefore inevitable. Human nature is prone to be lazy, greedy and aggressive. In this connection, competition is seen, with reference to Darwinian socio-biology, as something that underlies the survival of the fittest because it injects a force of dynamism to overcome what is at the level of nature. Numerous studies have shown, however, that the so-called natural tendency to compete, win, and set oneself apart is nothing but a socially learned behaviour pattern.

Are we to assume that the competitive spirit is natural? On the basis of no less strong evidence, we could also assume that the spirit of cooperation too is natural. Apart from scientific studies to this effect, even ordinary observation makes it evident that cooperation is ubiquitous, and something without which the human species cannot survive. In fact, so many peoples and cultures of the world manifest such a spirit of cooperation in their ways of life and traditions, that we are forced to question whether the tendency of competing was not peculiar to a few cultures, and whether this limited experience was being extrapolated as a general principle. Christian vision, for example, sees human beings not as competitors but as members of a family, sharing the same origin, and journeying together towards a common destiny. Hindu tradition sees the entire humanity as one family – *vasudhaiva kuṭumbakam*. Such universal spirit of harmony and coexistence is found in Buddhism, Islam, Daoism, and so on. The same is true also of primaeval religious traditions which are shot through with the spirit of harmony, communion, and solidarity, far from the spirit of competition.

Another important argument that seems to lend plausibility for competition is the situation of scarcity. At first sight it may appear that precisely because there is want and the means are scarce, competition could be justified. On the other hand, actual lack of material resources could be viewed as an environment in which human agency, inspired by the spirit of solidarity and participation, could come into play.[16] Far from the Malthusian prognostics of doom for humanity because of the geometrical growth of population and arithmetic production of food, we realize in the light of Christian faith, that scarcity could trigger the spirit of generosity and sharing, especially as can be observed among the poorest of the poor. Moreover, it engages the human economic agency as an extension of God's ongoing work of creation. Further, the situation of scarcity can lead to maximizing the use of available resources, through a process of participation and sharing. It will sustain life for all. Christian Scriptures highlight the centrality of justice and love to get the better of poverty and destitution. Christian faith, which is anchored in the tradition of covenant, election, and in the vision of the Kingdom of God, calls for self-sacrifice in economic relations. There would be no poor (Deut. 15:4) if only people took seriously their obligations to reach out to the other. Chronic Malthusian scarcity is a prima facie evidence of moral failure whether by sins of omission or commission.

These considerations on competition lead us to conclude that the present economic system is not something that is inevitable. The serious consequences seen in the suffering of the innocent should trigger another system of economy that is based on the spirit of cooperation, solidarity, and sharing. Due to the limited availability of resources, human beings, forming one family, should share what is available equitably; competition is not at all called for. On the contrary, it is counter-productive. The vision of a society that the Kingdom of God evokes is one of communion, mutuality, and reciprocal support. Nowhere does the Bible tell us to follow the law of competition, which is diametrically opposed to the Kingdom of God. What transpires through the Scriptures and Christian tradition is a call to cooperation in love and in the spirit of interdependence.

Capitalism is premised on an anthropology that views the other as a competitor. Solidarity, instead, is based on an anthropology of human interdependence and cooperation for the common good, and an ethics oriented towards the other. In fact, the Chinese sage Mencius gives us a telling example of a child at the brink of falling into an open well. We reach out our hands to rescue it, not for any external motive of gaining favour with the parents of the child and neighbours, nor for the fear of being blamed for not helping. An inner voice simply tells us that this child should not perish; it should be saved.[17]

Welfare Measures and Resistance

Even when the state tends to act independently, as in the case of providing welfare measures to the benefit of the poor (food subsidies, healthcare, old age pensions, etc.), it is stoutly resisted by the corporates as well as religious conservatives on the plea that it is bad economics. Good economics, according to them, is one which can produce the best results which is possible only through free competition. In short, the argument is that the best way to create a developed and prosperous society is to teach the poor to compete! Such an argument is blind to the initial unequal conditions of competition. Speaking of the argument of competition and meritocracy, the Mandal Commission critiqued it with a picturesque image of a race where the able-bodied and the physically challenged are made to compete and the winners are rewarded.[18] This, obviously, is senseless, since it ignores the disparities in the initial conditions of competition. Market economy and *laissez faire* capitalism do the same.

It is argued that allowing the market to follow its own laws would automatically bring about equilibrium, and any intervention in the logic of market is bad economics. Catholic and Protestant fundamentalist movements endorse such views. They are found supporting the worldview of capitalism more than that of the Gospel. This philosophy of free market, represented by the Chicago school of economics and by Milton Friedman and the like, fails to understand the vastly differing initial condition, among other things. Believing that the functioning of market will bring with it equality is simply utopian, and is contradicted by the conditions of the poor masses in Asia and other continents. An unrestrained market is not an instrument of equality as claimed by pundits of *laissez-faire* economy, but its cause.

Participative Economic Life

In the mainstream global economy and market, some people, groups, and even some continents (Africa, for example) do not count. The reason for this is the presumption that they have nothing to contribute to the accumulation of wealth, the linchpin of modern economy. They are the excluded. A healthy economy, on the contrary, is one in which there is a dynamic flow of wellbeing throughout the social body. This can only take place when all parts of the body are involved.

Social inequality and other evils derive from the fact that people are excluded from participating as active agents in the economic life of the country. Either the economy is viewed as something that is to be directed by the experts in the field, or by a group of elites whose economic activities overlap the fulfillment of their own interests without benefiting the people. A primary form of participation takes place when people become active contributors through employment. Unemployment restricts opportunities for people to be participants in the economic life of their society which is important for their dignity and self-esteem as well as for the realization of their needs. Hence, any policy that deprives people of employment in the name of increasing profit or accumulation of capital is a process of exclusion, and must be challenged. Displacement of millions of people from their traditional means of livelihood in the developing societies of the South, and the lack of opportunities for growing numbers of young people are symptoms of a deep malaise afflicting the current political economy. It calls for immediate attention.

Economy and Democracy

A democratically inspired economic life contributes to overcoming inequalities. India could be considered a world experiment in the complex relationship between democracy and poverty reduction. The experiences here show that a formal democratic system can coexist with capital accumulation and mass poverty. This is an anomaly. Participative economy, on the other hand, is of vital importance for sustaining a substantive democracy.[19] An important study on Democracy in South Asia brings out this point lucidly.[20]

> Continued co-existence of mass democracy and mass poverty is both a challenge and paradox of democracy in South Asia. While the working of democracy has not led to freedom from want, it may have given more space for struggles for securing better economic conditions. A manifold mismatch informs the relationship between democracy and freedom from

want: between the objective economic condition of the citizen and their sense of satisfaction, between objective and subjective placement in the economic hierarchy, and between popular preferences on economic policies and the policies pursued by the state. While this mismatch between the 'objective' and 'subjective' economic conditions of the people creates a space of democratic contestation, it also allows for state inaction on poverty and destitution.[21]

In the immediate post-independence period, a state or a political party was judged in terms of its ability to alleviate the poverty and misery of the people. In the last few decades, on the contrary, this ideal has been simply ignored and not acted upon, weakened by the spell of neoliberalism. Fortunately, there is a growing realization that democracy should go hand in hand with abolition of want and destitution. It is important to sustain this democratic spirit. The masses of people who are becoming more and more concerned, due to their increasing pauperization, about the adverse economic policies are putting continuous pressure on the elected representatives and the state to pursue policies that will respond to their situation and needs. Holding the state accountable for its economic decision-making will be an important exercise in democracy.[22]

As it is, the present economic system does not incorporate and value the economic contribution of certain segments of people. The most glaring exclusion is the household work of women in the maintenance of the family and society. Women's economic contribution to the family, in terms of household works like cooking, cleaning and caring, remain hidden and invisible. If one were to take into account the economically measurable income that would be generated if women were to do the same work outside the domestic walls, the very understanding of economy would change.

In sum, we may not leave the economy as a matter to be decided by experts; rather the form of economy that works is to be indicated by the victims. Hence, the representation of all, especially the weaker sections and groups, is important to the framing of economic policies in democratic spirit. Listening to the voices of the subaltern is an indispensable means of overcoming the economic inequality of our days. If there is an absence of participation from people in shaping the economic life, it is often due to social exclusion. Social inclusion and economic participation mutually reinforce each other.

Strengthening the Commons

Way back in 1968, Garrett Hardin wrote a celebrated article in the journal *Science*, entitled "The Tragedy of the Commons".[23] He said that common resources like pasture land, forests, air, water, fisheries etc. which had served the community for millennia have entered into a situation of crisis, because some members have started overexploiting them out of greed. This results in destruction, which is ultimately to nobody's advantage. For him, what caused this tragedy was the absence of well-defined property rights. Decades later, Elinor Ostrom, who was awarded the Nobel Prize for Economics in 2009, came back on this question. She showed that the real tragedy is in the destruction of the community-based systems of conserving the commons.[24] These systems had the advantage of turning the people into active participants using common resources responsibly. It allowed the violators to be easily identified and dealt with – something that created greater accountability for, and control over the commons.

Situating the community as the important player and most effective manager of the common resources challenges the primacy given to individual actors in the neoliberal economy. Community management of what is common itself is an expression of culture, and it helps overcome the violence that competition and conflicts between individuals could cause. In former times, before neo-liberal economics, the state and the market were viewed as protectors of natural resources from overuse and destruction. The community management of commons comes as an alternative to these two traditional actors, whose credibility has come into question, especially in such times when nature's regenerative capacity is stunted by exploitative human interventions.[25]

From Profligacy to a Sustainable Way of Life

When the Club of Rome warned, in the 1960s, of severe limits to growth, it came as a shocking realization. Unfortunately, it has not led to any significant change in the economic realm; much less to any radical rethinking of the reigning neoliberal paradigm. For the mainstream economy, it is business as usual. If India, China, Brazil, etc. were to follow the logic of mainstream economy and chart for themselves a course of progress as in the developed nations, it is plain that the resources available are far from adequate, and probably two or more earths in addition to the present one would be required to sustain such a model of development. If every Chinese and every Indian were to own a car, will not our earth literally turn into a gas chamber choking people to death? What we need is not sustainable development, but the practice of *a sustainable way of life*.

Let me illustrate the point with reference to India whose neoliberal economy has created an environment for the flourishing of consumerism and opulence in a sea of misery. This is practiced by the well-to-do classes and castes at the expense of the poor and of the earth. It is changing the face of India and its traditional ethos. Pavan Verma tells us how the Indian middle-class of the immediate post-independence period lived with the ideals of Gandhi and Nehru, and how restraint and moderation characterized their lives. This has undergone such a tremendous change today that the middle-class has become a class of competitors, with Bill Gates, Ambanis and Mittals as their new icons of success. Instead of restraint and moderation, they give in to instant gratification, and increasingly to revolting exhibitionism and ostentation.

> Indians love the spiritual halo ascribed to them by foreigners, but they are, in truth, among the world's most ingenious and resilient entrepreneurs, with their feet on the ground and their eyes on the balance sheet. Indeed, in the world view of Hinduism, Artha, the acquisition of wealth, is among the four highest purusharthas or goals of life. There is no biblical injunction in Hinduism to the effect that it is more difficult for a rich man to reach heaven than it is for a camel to go through the eye of a needle. On the contrary, Lakshmi, the goddess of wealth and prosperity, is ubiquitous in homes across the country.[26]

What is most disturbing in today's world is its forgetfulness of the poor, a callous indifference and the absence of any sense of community and solidarity. Zygmunt Bauman tells us about the shift from the Other to self-fulfillment, of which consumerism is an expression.

> The concept of responsibility and responsible choice, which resided before in the semantic field of ethical duty and moral concern for the Other, have

> shifted or have been moved to the realm of self-fulfillment and calculation of risks. In the process, the Other, as the trigger, the target and the yardstick of responsibility recognized, assumed and fulfilled has all but disappeared from view, elbowed out or overshadowed by the actor's own self. "Responsibility" now means, first and last, responsibility to oneself...while "responsible choices" are first and last, those moves serving the interests and satisfying the desires of the [self].[27]

If such is the case, the poor have nothing to gain from this economy of consumerism. The kind of economy the poor envision is one in which the fulfillment of basic needs will be the priority, and not the gratification of consumerist instincts.

Forward to Labour and Employment

The greed that capitalism embodies has brought the world to a situation in which accumulation of wealth has taken absolute priority over labour and employment. With liberalization, the South has also fallen into a trap of sacrificing the livelihood and employment of millions for the profit of a small percentage of its rich. In the process, it has thrown to the wind the wellbeing of the workers, as exemplified in the case of Special Economic Zones.[28]

There has also been a drastic increase in worldwide unemployment in these years. Moreover, during the past years, productivity growth has exceeded wage growth, affecting the lives of the labourers, and this is particularly so in the case of women. This trend is glaring in India and Brazil. The world trend, as per the report of the International Labour Organization, shows that the proportionate share of women's wages has drastically declined: "Income gap between the top and the bottom ten percent of wage earners increased in 70 percent of the countries for which data are available."[29] Furthermore, the health of employees is not a priority with the government, nor with employers. As a result, employees with low wages are sometimes forced to spend as much as 80% of their wages on health care, leaving little for food and other basic necessities.[30]

Charting a new economic course means bringing the question of labour and employment to centre-stage. The private sector cannot throw overboard the labour movement's legacy of over one hundred and fifty years, which has ensured just wages, security, and healthcare for workers and employees. In a situation of crisis, private corporations and enterprises tend to cut wages and other benefits frantically, increase working hours, and even lay off workers. This trend needs to be arrested, and economic participation on the part of the people will help to check such anti-labour practices in the future. Besides, state intervention is important and it should hold the private sector responsible for the violation of the basic norms of social justice. The widely discussed notion of corporate responsibility is often a matter of make-believe in many countries of the South. It does not really address the question of social justice in the field of labour and the common good.

An Economy of Care and Mutuality

The present economic system is totalitarian in character. It makes everything and everybody into commodities and drags the whole world into its net.[31] A future course for an economy sensitive to the needs of the poor calls for rethinking priorities and consequent reallocation of resources. In a country like India where large masses of people are still illiterate and where poverty prevents children from attending school, education should be accorded high priority with allocation of adequate funds. Similarly, taxation and fiscal policies should be continuously re-evaluated so as to benefit the poor, rather than increasing the advantage of those who are already rich and well-to-do.

The worst thing the present neoliberal economy does is to distort the relationship between producers and consumers through the mechanism of market. There takes place impoverization of human relationality and a very dangerous reductionism that wipes out important dimensions of human life. Feminist critique challenges this reductionism for its commercialization of things that matter in life. The present crisis is basically a consequence of a mechanistic economy that needs to be redeemed today by prioritizing mutuality and genuine care, which were earlier devalued as feminine qualities. A feminist redemption of this situation, in terms of the wellbeing of humanity and the earth, would be to bring the soul back into the economy by foregrounding mutuality and solidarity. This *ethics of care*, will be the new software by which a new economy will operate. Part of this software must be the evolution of a new relationship with the earth and all that it implies, because the economy of care also extends to the whole of nature.

Challenge to the Discipline of Political Economy

Our foregoing reflections also lead us to ask about the state of the mainstream economics of the present times and of the social sciences in general. Christian theology could make a contribution by provoking the present economy to shift from its claimed neutrality. There is a scandalous superficiality in the present state of economy-related sciences, given their failure to address the conditions suffered by the weak and the marginalized. Today's economics has become a matter of theories, numbers, equations, and models.

Fortunately, the self-assurance of the present economy is shaken. There seems to be a sudden blackout, and the financial music has come to a halt. With all the sophistication vaunted by economics, and its claims of prescience and predictive capabilities, it is dumbfounded in its task of explaining the appearance of this financial disaster which now affects the economies of the entire world including, alas, those of the poor and developing nations. Even more, it is clueless today as to how to get out of the deep mire into which it has sunk the world. The present discipline of economics, and especially its neoliberal ideology, is far from capable of pulling the world out of this situation. There is a need for a radical transformation of the science of economics along with other social sciences. The reason is spelt out clearly by the Gulbenkian Commission on the Restructuring of the Social Sciences:

> For, unlike the natural world as defined by the natural sciences, the domain of the social sciences not only is one in which the object of study encompasses the researchers themselves but also one in which the persons they study can enter into dialogue or contests of various kinds with these researchers. Matters of debate in the natural sciences are normally solved without recourse to the opinions of the object of study. In contrast the peoples… studied by social scientists have entered increasingly into the discussion, whether or not their opinion was sought by scholars, who, indeed, frequently considered this intrusion unwelcome.[32]

Economics requires constant dialogue with the entire society and its various strata. We need voices from the ground and alternative perspectives that will awaken these sciences from their slumber in the abstruse world of self-isolation.

Part III: Religion and Overcoming of Global Inequalities

Religions have, unfortunately, often contributed to legitimizing the accumulation of wealth, and have supported practices of greed. Wealth is said to be a sign of God's blessing, and poverty and deprivation a result of sin. A classic example is the ambiguous position of Christianity vis-à-vis colonialism in its greed, robbery, and genocide during the appropriation of the wealth of the nations. The prosperity Gospel is perhaps an echo of the traditional legitimization of riches. In the past it was fate and sin which were seen as causes of poverty and inequality. Today, under the aegis of liberal economy, the victims are blamed. Because the poor are lazy, incompetent, inefficient, and lacking in entrepreneurship, they remain poor. Some trends in Christian theology reflect this kind of explanation.

On the other hand, we also find that all religions concur in the deep wisdom that attachment to riches is harmful to human beings and society. Greed (*lobha)* and acquisitiveness (*aparigraha*) have been viewed in some streams of Indian religious tradition as contradicting the call of a *dharmic* life. They are to be countered by the generosity of sharing (*dāna*) and wisdom (*prajñā*) that redeem us from delusion. Buddhism speaks of the insatiable thirst (*tṛṣṇā*) for riches that deviates us and leads us to suffering (*duḥkha*), instead of happiness. *Dāna* is to be understood not simply as almsgiving; it has a depth of signification; it combines in itself the Christian understanding of social justice and compassion.

Jesus tells his disciples, "Watch out! Be on your guard against all kinds of greed; a man's life does not consist in the abundance of his possessions" (Lk 12:15). Capitalism is nothing but organized greed with all the evil it produces. We are reminded of the words in the Letter to Timothy which help us to understand what is deeply at work in capitalism: "Love of money is the root of all kinds of evil" (1 Tim 6:10). No wonder Jesus said that it is easier for the camel to go through the eye of a needle than the rich to enter into the Kingdom of God (Mt. 19:24; Mk 10:25; Lk 18:25). The ugly nature of avarice gets exposed in times of crisis such as the one we are currently living through. How could the well-being of humanity be based on an economic system whose structuring principle is greed?

Freedom from greed and attachment is the cornerstone of Jesus' social teachings. He does not command this only to his close disciples; it is meant for all those who want to follow him. There is even more to his teaching. By enjoining renunciation and detachment, Jesus responds to a basic human and societal issue which rests on a deeper vision of human beings and society. Jesus commands his disciples to free themselves from greed and attachment, because this freedom will make them authentic human beings. The servitude which greed and attachment represent, diminish and corrode individual and societal life on earth.[33] Therefore, the exhortation against avarice and attachment are not to be interpreted as something esoteric or fostering otherworldliness. Further, his teachings on the dangers of riches and the need for detachment and renunciation are not meant simply as spiritual principles for individuals. They are principles for the life of the community as well. Absorbing the teachings of Jesus, the early Christians tried to create an ideal community free from greed and accumulation.

It appears to me that today every religion, and Christianity in particular, could bring in four kinds of resources to stem the tide of global inequalities:

1) Prophetically challenge the dominant economic order in all its consequences;

2) Draw from its Holy Scriptures and traditions a sense of hope for a world which is heavy-laden with inequalities. It can bring the message of hope that change is possible and necessary;

3) Collaborate with new social movements and civil society initiatives – especially where Christianity is in a minority situation. It is also important in the traditionally Christian regions of the West, so that they may regain their lost credibility. Programs of advocacy appear to be important as an integral part of the Christian mission to bring about greater global equality;

4) Bring in spiritual resources to restrain the economy from the path of accumulation and opulence; orient it towards the transformation of social order and inter-human relationships through spiritual forces and inculcation of values.

Theology, too, has an important role to play in transforming a world marked by gross inequalities. An engaged theological critique of the dominant political economy as well as the theoretical conceptions it has attempted to develop can be supported by a feminist critique. In this regard, one important thing theology needs to be aware of is that economy is not gender neutral. In its critical study and analysis of both macro and micro-economy (which would include the process of production, distribution, consumption, trade, etc.), theology needs to be aware of gender inequality as operative in the very economic structures. The unequal power relationships that patriarchy creates is operative in all economic processes. The dominant economic system simply reproduces and reinforces existing unequal gender-relationships of power.

Theology and economics need to come together today and reinforce each other. We are reminded of what Gandhi had to say about the relationship between religion and economics: "Whereas religion to be worth anything, must be capable of being reduced to terms of economics, economics to be worth anything must also be capable of being reduced to terms of religion and spirituality".[34]

Faith and theology, which help the flourishing of life, cannot subscribe to a death-dealing totalitarian economy. Just as political totalitarianism needs to be opposed in the name of faith (think of the National Socialism in Hitler's Germany), so too in the name of the same faith, an economic system that spells suffering and death to the innocent should be resisted. Along with a resistance, which can take different forms, there also needs to be efforts made to devise alternatives.[35] A sign of hope is that in different parts of the world, significant movements and micro-initiatives are emerging which challenge the claim of the inevitability of the present economic order. For me, an approach of Money and Mission would make sense from this perspective. Money is a symbol of the economy, and Christian mission is called today to make its contribution to transform it in the direction of the life and progress of humankind and nature. This is a global mission – in every part of the world – as much in the South as in the North.

Conclusion

When the Berlin wall was pulled down, it brought an era to the end. But Europe is encircling itself today with new walls of defense against immigration from the South. As long as the North was not touched, there was little concern about the issue of global inequality. Today, the issue of immigration from the South is putting pressure on the North, unsettling its people in their self-enclosed islands of affluence. With the mobility that characterizes the modern world, the wave of migrations will intensify and storm the fortresses of the North – something that is causing serious preoccupation for Europeans and those in the Northern hemisphere. The fundamental issue of migration is, ultimately, the portrayal of a world of abysmal inequalities. Lampedusa remains a constant reminder of tragedies that inequality can bring about. The North is feeling the heat, so to say, of what could become a conflagration unless the issue of inequality is addressed at its roots, and in its structures.

More than in the past it is becoming evident today that greater equality is good, even essential, as much as for the South as for the North. Therefore, the battle against inequality is on a global scale, which requires numerous forces of solidarity, support, and intervention. With all their ambiguities in the past, religions do possess many resources that could be channeled to shape a world with a sharper sense of equality and justice. Religions and theology could help promote a sustainable way of life that is attentive both to the groans of nature and to the needs of the poor of the earth.

Bibliography

Bardhan, Pranab. *Scarcity, Conflicts and Cooperation: Essays in the Political and Institutional Economics of Development* (Delhi: Oxford University Press, 2005).

Barrera, Albino. *God and the Evil of Scarcity: Moral Foundations of Economic Agency* (Notre Dame: University of Notre Dame Press, 2005).

Bauman, Zygmunt. *Consuming Life* (Cambridge: Polity Press, 2007).

Bauman, Zygmunt. *Does Ethics Have a Chance in a World of Consumers?* (Cambridge MA: Harvard University Press, 2008).

Blomberg, Craig L. *Neither Poverty Nor Riches: A Biblical Theory of Possessions* (Leicester, England: InterVarsity Press, 1999).

Boushey, Heather. et al., eds. *After Piketty. The Agenda for Economics and Inequality* (Cambridge MA: Harvard University Press, 2017).

DeMartino, George. *Global Economy, Global Justice: Theoretical Objections and Policy Alternatives to Neoliberalism* (New York: Routledge, 2000).

Drèze, Jean, and Sen, Amartya. *An Uncertain Glory: India and Its Contradictions* (Princeton: Princeton University Press, 2013).

Duggan, Lisa. *The Twilight of Equality: Neoliberalism, Cultural Politics, and the Attack on Democracy* (Boston MA: Beacon Press, 2004).

Graaf, John de – Wann, David., and Naylor, Thomas H. *Affluenza: How Our Consumption is Killing Us and How We Can Fight Back. 3rd ed.* (San Francisco: Berrett-Koehler Publishers, 2014).

Haan, Roelf. *The Economics of Honor: Biblical Reflections on Money and Property* (Grand Rapids: William B. Eerdmans Publishing Company, 2009).

Hardin, Garrett. "The Tragedy of the Commons." *Science* 162 (1968), 1243-1248.

Jackson, Tim. *Prosperity without Growth: Economics for a Finite Planet* (London & Washington: Earthscan, 2009).

Kiely, Ray. *Empire in the Age of Globalization: US Hegemony and Neoliberal Disorder* (Hyderabad: Orient Longman Pvt. Ltd., 2007).

Klein, Naomi. *The Shock Doctrine* (New York: Penguin Books, 2007).

Klein, Naomi. *No Logo* (Great Britain: Flamingo, 2000).

Knitter, Paul F., and Muzaffar, Chandra., eds. *Subverting Greed: Religious Perspectives on the Global Economy* (New York: Orbis Books, 2002).

Navarro, Vincent., ed. *Neoliberalism, Globalization and Inequalities: Consequences for Health and Quality of Life* (New York: Baywood Publishing Company, 2007).

Ostrom, Elinor. *Governing the Commons. The Evolution of Institutions for Collective Action* (Cambridge: Cambridge University Press, 1990).

Piketty, Thomas. *Capital in Twentieth Century* (Cambridge MA: The Belknap Press of Harvard University Press, 2014).

Reservations for Backward Classes: Mandal Commission Report of the Backward Classes Commission, 1980 (Delhi: Akalank Publications, 1991).

Rieger, Joerg. *No Rising Tide: Theology, Economics, and the Future* (Minneapolis: Fortress Press, 2009).

Sampat, Preeti. "Special Economic Zones in India." *Economic and Political Weekly* 43 (28), July 12 (2008), 25-30.

Sassen, Saskia. *Globalization and its Discontents: Essays on the New Mobility of People and Money* (New York: The New Press, 1998).

Sen, Amartya. *Development as Freedom* (New York: Anchor Books, 2000).

Sen, Amartya. *The Idea of Justice* (New York: Allen Lane, Penguin Books, 2009).

Sen, Sunanda, and Anjan Chakrabarti., eds. *Development on Trial: Shrinking Space for the Periphery* (New Delhi: Orient Blackswan, 2013).

Simmel, Georg. *The Philosophy of Money* (New York: Routledge, 2004).

State of Democracy in South Asia: A Report (Delhi: Oxford University Press, 2008).

Stiglitz, Joseph E. *The Roaring Nineties: Why We're Paying the Price for the Greediest Decade in History* (New York: W. W. Norton & Company, Inc. Penguin Books, 2003).

Stiglitz, Joseph E. *The Price of Inequality* (New York: W. W. Norton & Company, Inc. Penguin Books, 2012).

Stiglitz, Joseph E. *Globalization and its Discontents* (New York: Penguin Books, 2002).

UNDP. *Human Development Report 2014, Sustaining Human Progress: Reducing Vulnerabilities and Building Resilience* (New York: Oxford University Press, 2014).

UNDP. *Human Development Report 2013, The Rise of the South: Human Progress in a Diverse World* (New Delhi: Academic Foundation, 2013).

UNDP. *Human Development Report 1998* (New York- Oxford: Oxford University Press, 1998).

UNDP. *Human Development Report of 1997* (New York: Oxford University Press, 1997).

Varma, Pavan K. *The Great Indian Middle Class* (Delhi: Penguin Book, 2007).

Wallerstein, Immanuel., et al. *Open the Social Sciences: Report of the Gulbenkian Commission on the Restructuring of the Social Sciences* (Delhi: Vistaar Publications, 1997).

Wilkinson, Richard, and Kate Pickett. *The Spirit Level: Why Greater Equality Makes Societies Stronger* (New York: Bloomsbury Press, 2010).

Youngs, Gillian. *Global Political Economy in the Information Age: Power and Inequality.* (New York: Routledge, 2006).

Endnotes

[1] UNDP, *Human Development Report 2013, The Rise of the South: Human Progress in a Diverse World* (New Delhi: Academic Foundation, 2013).

[2] UNDP, *Human Development Report 1998* (New York- Oxford: Oxford University Press, 1998), p. 25.

[3] Cf. Amartya Sen, *The Idea of Justice* (New York: Allen Lane, Penguin Books, 2009).

[4] 'The Price of Greed' *Time,* (September 29, 2008); see also Joseph E. Stiglitz, *The Roaring Nineties: Why We are Paying the Price for the Greediest Decade in History* (New York: W. W. Norton & Company, Inc. Penguin Books, 2003).

[5] *The Times of India* (April 1, 2014), 10.

[6] Christine Lagarde, http://businesstoday.intoday.in/story/indian-billionaires-wealth-can-end-countrys-poverty-twice-imf/> [accessed on 14 July, 2018].

[7] UNDP, *Human Development Report of 1998* (New York: Oxford University Press, 1998), p. 37; see also the incisive analysis of the shocking and scandalous situation resulting from the current economic policies, Naomi Klein, *The Shock Doctrine* (New York: Penguin Books, 2007).

[8] Cf. Amartya Sen, *Development as Freedom* (New York: Anchor Books, 2000).

[9] Cf. Tim Jackson, *Prosperity without Growth: Economics for a Finite Planet* (London-New York: Earthscan, 2009).

[10] Cf. John de Graaf – David Wann – Thomas H. Naylor, *Affluenza: How our Consumption is Killing us and How We Can Fight Back,* (San Francisco: Berrett-Koehler Publishers, 2014).

[11] Quoted in Paul F. Knitter and Chandra Muzaffar, eds, *Subverting Greed: Religious Perspectives on the Global Economy* (New York: Orbis Books, 2002), p. 63.

[12] Cf. Richard Wilkinson and Kate Pickett, *The Spirit Level: Why Greater Equality Makes Societies Stronger* (New York: Bloomsbury Press, 2010); Joseph E. Stiglitz, *The Price of Inequality* (New York: W. W. Norton & Company, Inc. Penguin Books, 2012).

[13] See Jean Drèze and Amartya Sen, *An Uncertain Glory: India and Its Contradictions* (Princeton: Princeton University Press, 2013), p. 37.

[14] See *The Economist* (March 15, 2014), 21.

[15] Ibid., *The Economist*

[16] Albino Barrera, *God and the Evil of Scarcity: Moral Foundations of Economic Agency* (Notre Dame, Indiana: University of Notre Dame Press, 2005).

[17] Mencius, *The Works of Mencius,* Book.2, Part I, Chapter 6.3. Translated by James Legge, 1815-1897, with Critical and Exegetical notes (New York: Dover Publication, Inc., 1970).

[18] *Reservations for Backward Classes: Mandal Commission Report of the Backward Classes Commission, 1980* (Delhi: Akalank Publications, 1991).

[19] Cf. Pranab Bardhan, *Scarcity, Conflicts and Cooperation: Essays in the Political and Institutional Economics of Development* (Delhi: Oxford University Press, 2005). This book goes into the external environment of politics and governance required for economics, and appears to be of neoliberal inspiration.

[20] *State of Democracy in South Asia: A Report* (Delhi: Oxford University Press, 2008).

[21] Ibid., *State of Democracy in South Asia*

[22] Inequality and discrimination remain the greatest challenges for development and growth of peoples and nations. Cf. UNDP, *Human Development Report 2014, Sustaining Human Progress: Reducing Vulnerabilities and Building Resilience* (New York: Oxford University Press, 2014). The report's findings point to the reasons why governments must enact and enforce laws.

[23] Garrett Hardin, "The Tragedy of the Commons", *Science* 162 (1968), 1243-1248.

[24] Cf. Elinor Ostrom, *Governing the Commons: The Evolution of Institutions for Collective Action* (Cambridge: Cambridge University Press, 1990).

[25] See Tim Jackson, *Prosperity without Growth: Economics for a Finite Planet* (London & Washington: Earthscan, 2009).

[26] Pavan K.Varma, *The Great Indian Middle Class* (Delhi: Penguin Book, 2007), xxi.

[27] Zygmunt Bauman, *Consuming Life* (Cambridge: Polity Press, 2007), p. 92; See also *ID., Does Ethics Have a Chance in a World of Consumers?* (Cambridge MA: Harvard University Press, 2008).

[28] Preeti Sampat, "Special Economic Zones in India", *Economic and Political Weekly,* 43:28 (July 12, 2008), 25-30.

[29] Quoted in T.K. Rajalakshmi, "Wake-up Call", *Frontline* (March 13, 2009), 86-87. For instance, in the United States already in 2007, the chief executive officers (CEOs) of the largest fifteen companies earned over 500 times more than the average worker, ibid. 87. The disparity has increased further in recent years.

[30] Cf. T.K. Rajalakshmi, "The Other Half", *Frontline* (April 24, 2009), 90-92.

[31] Ray Kiely, *Empire in the Age of Globalization: US Hegemony and Neo-Liberal Disorder* (Hyderabad: Orient Longman Pvt. Ltd., 2007).

[32] Immanuel Wallerstein, et al., *Open the Social Sciences: Report of the Gulbenkian Commission on the Restructuring of the Social Sciences* (Delhi: Vistaar Publications, 1997).

[33] Roelf Haan, *The Economics of Honor: Biblical reflections on Money and Property* (Grand Rapids: William B. Eerdmans Publishing Company, 2009); Craig L. Blomberg, *Neither Poverty Nor Riches: A Biblical Theory of Possessions* (Leicester, England: InterVarsity Press, 1999).

[34] *Young India,* September 15, 1927. As quoted in Christopher Key Chapple – Mary Evelyn Tucker, *Hinduism and Ecology* (Cambridge MA: Harvard University Press, 2000), p. 227.

[35] Joerg Rieger, *No Rising Tide: Theology, Economics, and the Future* (Minneapolis: Fortress Press, 2009); see also Saskia Sassen, *Globalization and its Discontents* (New York: The New Press, 1998). The author questions the axiom "Rising tide raises all boats" (attributed to J.F.K. Kennedy) and shows its fallacy in the prevailing economic system.

CHAPTER 6

Postcolonial Theories and Asian Theologies

Over fifty years ago, as a teenage student in Italy, on a visit to London, I witnessed a demonstration of South Asian immigrants against the discrimination they suffered. Their detractors wanted them to go back to their countries. I saw a young Indian woman holding a placard that read: "*We are here, because you were there!*". Yes, as the theory of *karma* would have it, all actions create waves or ripples and they endure. The intensifying reverse migration today from the colonized South to the North is probably the karmic effect of colonialism. Colonialism is indeed a two-way traffic affecting both the colonizers and the colonized. The placard kindled a spark in me. It took me many more years to understand the deeper postcolonial implications of it.

Two Caveats

1. *Hurried Burial of Colonialism*

It is a fact that at the time of the First World War in 1914, about 85% of the surface of the earth was under the dominion of European powers as colonies, and it involved millions of people. Such a colossal fact of history that conditioned the life of humankind with its huge consequences may not be buried and forgotten so easily. I say this because there is a tendency to dwell on Christianity in the present, underplaying the past history of colonialism and its connection with the missions. Why awaken the ghost of a bygone colonial past, and why not reinvent theology and mission in our times, one may argue. Said viewpoint fails to acknowledge how deeply colonialism has affected the life of the people as well as the understanding and practice of Christianity. Postcolonialism and its theorizing is an important reminder that the legacy of the past domination is still very active in the present life and history of the people of Asia, as elsewhere in Africa, Oceania, and Latin America. One cannot wish it away; we need to analyze the ways in which colonialism continues to affect the frame of thought, epistemology, and hermeneutics. Colonial experiences and the missionary past have left such indelible imprints that a construction of Asian theology is not possible without coming to terms with them. Theology was part of the imperial force and its legitimization. This is why we turn to postcolonialism to decolonize theology and explore how and to what extent it (postcolonialism) could help a critical Asian theological and pastoral agenda of the Church.

A dialogue with postcolonialism could be a force for creativity for the varied forms of Asian theologies. Unfortunately, very little has been done to deconstruct missionary discourses, practices, and structures of power. This is an important premise for Asian theologies. Edward W. Said, in his path-breaking work *Orientalism,* brought out lucidly and with numerous illustrations how the colonial discourses and approaches continue to be at work conditioning the ways of thinking and acting.[1] In short, one does not get away with colonialism so easily; the colonial grand narratives are still around. Colonialism was violence, aggression, and a rupture in the life and culture of the people. This is true also at the level of discourse and ideology. There is a violent imposition of the narratives and perspectives that are advantageous to the colonizers. These can be deceitful when they are masqueraded and camouflaged but even worse, when they are internalized by the colonized themselves in such a way that they become normal and set beyond questioning. All this should prompt us to consider colonialism not as an issue of the past, but be alert of its continued presence in theology, since it could subtly carry the vision, goals, and perspectives of the colonizers.

2. *Postcolonial Theories in Their Place*

There are intense debates as to how postcolonialism is to be understood. There are scholars who think that the "post" in *post*colonialism could be misleading in as much as one could think of colonialism as a matter of the past, while it is something enduring, built into the present structures of power. For others, it is a question of reflecting critically on the colonial past and its conditioning of modes of thinking and discoursing with the aim of deconstructing the frames of colonial knowledge systems in different fields. [2]

> Postcolonial theory is an umbrella term that covers different critical approaches which deconstruct European thought in areas as wide-ranging as philosophy, history, literary studies, anthropology, sociology and political science. In this perspective, the term 'postcolonial' refers not to a simple periodization but rather to a methodological revisionism which enables a wholesale critique of Western structures of knowledge and power, particularly those of the post-Enlightenment period.[3]

The critical method of postcolonialism needs to be applied to theology as well. While acknowledging the importance of postcolonial critique of theology, we need to also realize its limits. For, today, there is an institutionalization of postcolonial studies in centres of higher education. In some streams of postcolonialism we note a metamorphosis of pretentious rhetoric into what are called postcolonial theories. The importance of emphasizing the materialist dimension of postcolonial studies is an urgent need today. A de-politicized postcolonial theory as much as a de-historicized theology will be caught in the prison of language. Furthermore, one may not stop with the textual and discursive realm, and define postcolonialism simply as a new intellectual tool of analysis. It is important for postcolonialism to be credible as a force of transformation that it becomes ethically and ideologically interventionist with a socio-political agenda. If postcolonialism throws to the winds its materialist dimension - as more and more vacuous theorizing of some strands of postcolonialism show - it would lose its distinctive character, and all its discourses could be well absorbed within poststructuralism and postmodernism.

This needs to be said, since decolonization has not brought to a complete close colonialism. It has taken a new avatar and a new face with globalisation, promoting neo-liberal economy in an empire that is as powerful as it is invisible. Peoples of the colonized world are today faced with the phenomenon of *neo-colonialism*. Hence, the postcolonialism we mean here is not a hyphenated *post-colonialism*, as if we are chronologically after a historical period of colonialism; rather it is *postcolonialism* that takes into account colonialism as a continuing reality of our experience. We are confronted in a different context and historical situation with the same old problems of domination, power, subordination, and exclusion. The power is not exercised today over the periphery from a single political center. Centers and peripheries are dispersed. Unlike in the past, nations today do not get accentuated as much as the power of economy. Those who control the economy control the nations, and new forms of exclusion and marginalisation are on the increase. It is this new context that led to the book "*Culture and Imperialism*" by Edward Said.[4] Subalterns are caught in the power vortex of the empire where their identities are stripped and their cultures get co-opted in a "global culture" created by the empire. New forms of racial discrimination and profiling are on the increase in the crisis situation of immigrants and refugees. These are questions which postcolonialism needs to grapple with if it wants to remain anchored in the world of subalterns and committed to their cause.

Feminist theorizing and environmental theorizing had their origin in feminist and ecological *movements* of liberation. What distinguishes postcolonialism is perhaps the absence of a movement as basis for theorizing. And theorizing developed in the extreme can easily turn verbose and flamboyant. Notwithstanding, postcolonialism has found its application in a number of disciplinary fields.

Postcolonial theories could serve as important analytical tools for theology in Asia and other erstwhile colonized worlds, provided they retain the passion and engagement that characterized its beginnings with anti-colonial struggles (Franz Fanon, Aime Cesaire and others). It needs to also come to grips with the experience and expressions of neocolonialism. Postcolonialism needs to become, true to its origin, a site for the resistance of the powerless, the neo-colonized, the marginalized, and the subalterns, and not an abstruse and pedantic discourse among a small elitist club of academics. Postcolonialism needs to come down from the heights of theory to address more concretely the continuation of the colonial exploitation in the chronologically *post*-colonial period. This will depend on whether postcolonialism could become a movement that mediates praxis-theory.

Connection between Mission and Colonialism- Through the Lens of Postcolonial Theories

It is undeniable that missionaries benefitted from the support of the economic and political structures of the colonial rule – at least partly. Missionaries were at times critical of the excesses of colonial powers. They wished for colonial administrators with moral credibility. The criticism of missionaries was directed at individual officials for their moral failings. However, with laudable exceptions, they did not question the *system* of colonizing peoples. On the contrary, they felt that the system was providential for the expansion of Christianity, not unlike Eusebius who thought that the Roman Empire was part of the divine providence facilitating the propagation of the Gospel. The missionaries in a way played the role of bridge between the colonizers and the local people.[5]

We should also highlight the theological support colonialism received from the doctrine of manifest destiny of the colonizing nations. These nations, it was argued, are destined and chosen to rule and civilize other peoples and nations. Hence, resistance to colonial powers was viewed by colonial theology as resisting the legitimate authority set by God. No wonder then that the non-violent movement of civil disobedience by Gandhi was critiqued by colonial mission theology for going against legitimately constituted authority. Further, there was something like what Robert Warrior calls "Canaanite" ideology which is an ideology of conquest and occupation connected with the exodus event in the Bible.[6] It served as inspiration for the western colonial conquests of a later period. A normative reading of the great mission command in the Gospels of preaching, baptizing, and converting was so overwhelming, that mission theology did not care about the oppression people were going through under the colonial regimes.

The discursive practices of the colonizers and missionaries were on the same page, and there was mutual reinforcement of both these discourses. Like the colonial powers that created their own cartography by exploring and dividing the surface of the earth among themselves, there was also a missionary cartography, namely, mapping of mission territories according to the country, the various Christian denominations, and religious orders. The "natives" were mute spectators, and they suffered disintegration of their spaces. It is sad that today a whole Roman curial congregation – the Congregation for the Evangelization of Peoples – seems not to be wholly free from the cartographic approach to mission. As part of the Curial Reform,[7] which Pope Francis wants to vigorously carry on, I would suggest that a good dose of postcolonial theory would help the officials of this Congregation to adopt a "new mindset'" (*novus habitus mentis*)[8]. Such institutions seem to still follow the Orientalist approach, and the mission territories become object of study. The so-called mission territory - of which this Roman Congregation is in charge - seems to refer to the colonial space and geography created jointly by the colonizers and missionaries. Postcolonialism can help such institutions to deconstruct such colonial space construction in regard to Christian faith, its practice, and mission.[9] Even more, we are led to question whether in these postcolonial times there is a need of such a Roman Congregation at all.

Postcolonial Critique of Inculturation

Inculturation, in my view, is a belated attempt to make good the negation of culture in the colonial and missionary past, without however challenging the cultural hegemony of the past, and without letting the subjectivity of the people to have its own creative course. What Asia needs is the cultural power to name its own form of Christianity, shape and mould it deploying collective subjectivity. Postcolonial theories could help review critically the project of inculturation.

Inculturation basically does not change the method and concepts of received theology but finds ways to accommodate it and make it locally acceptable. On the other hand, experience of faith in context creates a theology with the local *episteme*, and not in the likeness of colonial knowledge system. The language of this theology also will be necessarily different. The theological language will not be one that tries to express to the locals what is presented through colonial theology as the universal. What people of Asia and those in the South do are *indigenous theologies*. This is a completely different project from a centralized programme of inculturation of theology. The difference between colonial theology and indigenous theology could be illustrated by the distinction between commonwealth literature and postcolonial literature. Both postcolonial theology and postcolonial literature seek to find their own language and episteme to express the indigenous and contextual experiences, challenging the assumed cultural and philosophical presuppositions. The colonial theology tries to frame the questions with its own points of reference, and what is expected of colonized people in Africa, Asia, Oceania, is to respond to the questions already framed in the West. Postcolonial theology is one which would challenge the usurping of the privilege of framing theological questions for all and then invite responses. Contextual, postcolonial, and indigenous theologies will frame the question themselves, and deal with them in context.

Though the Japanese bishops may not know anything of postcolonial theology, they seemed to have acted in the spirit of this theology when they took a stand vis-a-vis the *lineamenta* of Vatican on the Asian Synod in 1998. The local Churches of Asia were asked to respond to the position taken by the Roman Church about Asia in its pre-synodal *lineamenta* and answer the questions they had framed. The Japanese bishops found that the text and especially the questions, not speaking to what they experienced in Japan. So, they formulated their own questions and answered them and sent their report to Rome – a true exercise in postcolonial theology! Furthermore, to the Roman preoccupation that the uniqueness of Jesus Christ as the Truth and as the universal savior could be compromised in Asia, Japanese bishops responded in postcolonial spirit when they said: "Jesus Christ is the Way, the Truth and the Life, but in Asia before stressing that Jesus Christ is the truth, we must search, in depth, into how he is the Way and the Life".[10]

Inculturation could be viewed as a religious parallel to the secular concept of *development*. Development is a model which does not address the question of power. Discourse and practice of inculturation could be socially decontextualized if it is not set in the context of power-analysis in the Church, much like the discourse and practice of development. There is yet another element in the postcolonial theory which could help review critically the project of inculturation. Postcolonialism shares, with poststructuralism and postmodernism, the critique of essentialism. Applied to the realm of culture it means that cultures may not be viewed as water-tight compartments or insulated monadic entities. They are fluid and porous with a lot of criss-crossing among them in such a way that there is hardly any culture that is not hybrid and in a constant process of change affected by social, political and economic factors. Seen in this perspective, we need to interrogate the essentialist understanding of culture behind the project of inculturation. Through its cultural analysis, postcolonialism could help understand the dynamic process in which expressions of faith, its language, and its symbols get constantly re-appropriated, reshaped, and renewed by the collective subjectivity of the community of the faithful whose subjectivity itself is also in a constant flow, and its culture in constant evolution.

Moreover, inculturation seems to presuppose a unified understanding of culture. This may respond to the need of cultural anthropologists to create a general framework of interpretation and in the interests of colonial administration in search of a totalized vision of the colonized people – a "grand narrative". However, the native people live their culture every day in its disparate forms and expressions. The natives are not in need of any unified understanding of culture. They simply live their culture. To understand really the culture of a people one has to follow the movement and rhythm of their lives and respect the dynamic creation of new cultural forms and tropes in the community. Postcolonialism could support theology to overcome a naïve understanding of culture and help a dynamic reconceptualization of it in relation to faith.

The project of inculturation could learn something from a new stream of renewed anthropology. This anthropology is not focused, like the traditional one, on representing the subjected and colonized people, often ending up in misrepresentation with enormous consequences. On the other hand, this anthropology gives voice to the people and serves as a bridge or conduit for their knowledge and perceptions.[11] If we take this example, what is most important is not how the people who have been missioned by the West adopt Christian beliefs and practices into their culture, but rather *the dialogue of the people with Christianity.* [12]This would prove a much richer area of experience and study, and help the people decolonize their theology, liturgy, practices, and so on. Like in the case of "anthropology of resistance", this dialogue would also include how the people have resisted in their own ways – covertly and overtly – theological and liturgical impositions during the Christian history.[13] This is an unexplored area of study and research.

Postcolonialism, Theological Epistemology and Hermeneutics

There are discussions about the connection between colonial powers and the missionaries. Against the conflation of both, it is argued and rightly so, that missionaries have been critical of colonial powers, regarding its excesses, and have also opposed them and their policies in defence of the indigenous people. That said, what brought colonizers and missionaries together was a shared epistemology and hermeneutics about the culture and religions of the people with whom they were actively engaged. The manner of their acquiring knowledge on the local people or the local converts had the European stamp of the times.[14] Both of them understood themselves as superior to the natives – the colonizer as representative of a superior civilization of knowledge over ignorant savage locals; and the missionaries as representatives of ultimate salvation. The cultural dominance and theological hegemony exercised by two distinct but interrelated actors – colonial establishment and Christian missionaries – concurred in the negation of the epistemological role of cultures and religions of the natives. On the other hand, the natives, precisely through these lenses perceived the world, interpreted it, interacted in the society, and progressed towards their salvation. In other words, there was a failure to acknowledge the mediatory role of culture and religion in the acquisition, transmission, and dissemination of knowledge – mundane and trans-mundane.

Postcolonial analysis goes deep into the issue of *representation* which is not a simple matter of epistemology but one loaded with the question of power. There is a certain parallel to the gender question here. As women are fitted into the normative and patriarchal frame of the male, so were the colonized people fitted into and judged as per the pre-designed norms of the western culture, religion, history and tradition.[15] As a result, colonial legacy was one of misrepresentations, biased knowledge and stereotyping of the indigenous in service of power and domination. This misrepresentation and distortion of the colonized subject are characterized as "*epistemic violence*". In the end, the colonized people were objects to be examined and explored, and not subjects creating their own selves, society, religion, culture, and so on. This is indeed the worst form of violence. Whereas culture, literature, and history have been analyzed from postcolonial perspective, religious studies and theology, have not been studied in depth, though there have been some good attempts to study the Bible from postcolonial perspective.

Colonial theology suffers from misrepresentation which needs to be exposed. The colonially tainted western theology, for example, claims that the Greco-Roman heritage is part and parcel of Christian faith, and wherever Christian faith is proclaimed, this heritage should follow. Moreover, the very measure of rationality is to be the Greco-Roman in comparison to which other peoples and nations are deficient or simply irrational. We could hear the echoes of such thinking in the controversial lecture of Pope Benedict XVI in Regensburg in 2006. This lecture and its assumptions could be deconstructed in the light of postcolonialism. Given the universality of salvation and the plurality of cultures and languages through which people approach God, as we noted in the first chapter, no single culture (the Greco-Roman) and its rationality could be elevated to the normative level.

Deconstructing Narratives and Interpretations

Postcolonialism is a deconstruction of colonial narratives, its rationality and practices. This applies also to theology, the interpretation of tradition and scriptures, and to narration of history. Postcolonialism presents counter-narratives from the perspective and experiences of the colonized. One of the most fertile areas of dialogue between postcolonial theories and theology has been the field of Biblical interpretation. Postcolonialism brings in a new dimension to historical-critical method which has served as an important methodological tool to expose fundamentalist biblical interpretations.

The point could be illustrated through the difference in the way the Great Commission (Mt 28: 16-20) is interpreted. In the colonial interpretation of this text, there was an overlap between the conquest of lands and the preaching of the Gospel. Today, besides deconstructing the colonial interpretation of the Great Commission, we could approach it creatively through an inter-textual reading. An attempt was made, for example, by the great Indian biblical scholar George-Soares Prabhu who did a very insightful intertextual reading of the New Testament text with a similar command of the Buddha to his disciples.[16] On his part, Yonghan Chung of Korea has tried to read the text through a Korean myth.[17]

To refer to another example, from the field of Christian history, the writings of missionaries in terms of letters and reports to their native lands were, with rarest exceptions, in the Orientalist frame, and these catered to the Euro-centric expectations in their native countries whose support and material means, the missionaries required for their work. The numerous "native" Bible women, whose contribution has not been sufficiently recognized, appear differently in the missionary reports of the time. In her critical study of missionary reporting on Bible women, Mrinalini Sebastian highlights how the women to whom the "Bible women" were sent to be instructed in Christian faith, respond from a very different perspective with their own beliefs, myths, convictions and so on.[18] It brings out in new ways the agency of the Hindu and Muslim hearers of the Gospel message.

Postcolonial Theology and the Subalterns

As I noted earlier, the postcolonial is inextricably related to the anti-colonial struggles of the colonized, especially its subaltern groups. The subaltern condition interpreted through postcolonial theory converges with the Biblical understanding of the poor and its perspectives on them. Marxist analysis on the working of the economic forces in society provided the tools to understand the biblical message of liberation in relation to our present experiences. Postcolonial theory is a new tool in the pursuit of liberation. It analyses the *cultural oppression and distortions*, and releases the oppressed subjects from the bondage stifling their subjectivity and agency. Poststructuralism and deconstruction which have close affinity to postcolonial thought are of great importance to free faith and theology from essentialist presuppositions and from the danger of it becoming an ideology. In the analysis of the society from the perspective of the subalterns, there is not only a class analysis but also analysis on the basis of caste, gender, geography, etc.

Having said that, we need to direct our attention to the fact that the Bible itself presents situations and practices in the context of colonialism of its time – Egyptian, Assyrian, Persian, Greek and so on. The New Testament has the backdrop of the imperial Roman rule and domination, as the people of Palestine in Jesus' time were under the Roman colonial rule. Such being the case, the Bible itself presents many ambiguous and complex positions, sometimes tending to favour the colonial rule and other narrations representing resistance and revolt against it. The Bible, in that sense, is an admixture of both colonial ideology and postcolonial theory, which fact necessitates that it should be subjected to critical scrutiny, and may not be used as an unambiguous text to speak of God, the world, and human beings. It requires as much the application of historical-critical method and literary criticism, as a good dose of postcolonial criticism.[19]

As many studies and researches have shown, the Bible was used as a tool to support colonial ideology, value system, practices, etc. The imported western theology occupied a dominating and controlling position, and was conditioned by the feudal world, its values and the concepts it had inherited, which all are prejudicial to the cause of the subaltern peoples. Further, new theories regarding race developed in Europe. These theories had their own impact on the colonial theology.[20] Postcolonial theology is critical as it deconstructs the transmitted theology during the missionary epoch from the perspective of the subalterns.

Postcolonial Theory – a Support to the Prophetic Role of Theology

History attests to the fact that religions more often than not have aligned themselves with the powers to reap advantages in the pursuit of their goals and in defense of their institutions. Like so, they have provided support and theological legitimation to systems of power (for example, divine right of kings). Postcolonialism especially in its critique of powers, domination, and imperialism is close to the Biblical vision which speaks of the mighty being pulled down from their thrones (Lk 1:46-555). There is a convergence between the prophetic critic of powers both in the Old and New Testaments and the postcolonial critique of colonialism and the logic of power woven into it.

Postcolonialism as an analysis and critique of the way power functions, could help theology and the Church to be critical and prophetic vis-a-vis the empire and all systems of domination. It can help purify any imperial or colonial traces in the structures and practices of the Church as well as in the thought-patterns of theology. Further, it can help critically resist being co-opted into these systems. Creation of counter-discourse is an important strategy of postcolonial thinking. The postcolonial strategy of counter-discourse could chime in with the prophetic, in that the prophets not only critique the establishment, but also create a counter-discourse, and project an alternative vision.

Postcolonial Theology and the Crisis of Western Classical Theology

Even while the universal pretensions of western theology were taken seriously, it came to be challenged by the then emerging Third World Theologies, starting from the late 1970s. Today, the western classical theology has got so weakened that, to challenge it today could become a futile exercise. The crisis is not only due to the progressive realization of the provincial and limited nature of this theology, and due to the process of secularization; it is also due to its failure to make any impact on its own western territory. This theology gives the impression of moving on the clouds while on the ground Christians are exiting en mass from the Churches. There is a big chasm between the theology pursued in western academic institutions and the pastoral ground situation. Postcolonialism has provided methodological insights and analytical tools to review critically the claims of western theology. Postcolonialism, so to say, could help us perform the post-mortem of western classical theology and nail its coffin shut. Though dead, the specter of this theology is around and its traces are there. Postcolonialism and its theorizing could serve to exorcise any lingering colonial traits of this theology in Asia. It serves as a caveat to Asian and other local theologies, so that at every step theology becomes self-critical and is grounded in experience.

Challenging Colonial Christian Historiography of Asia

One important positive contribution postcolonialism could make is to help theology rewrite history through the lens of postcolonial theory. It is true that the movement of liberation theology implied also writing of history from the periphery. In this connection, one could think of the project of Enrique Dussel in Latin America.[21] In socio-political history, the Indian subaltern studies has contributed to re-read and interpret history from the stand-point of the subalterns.[22] Postcolonialism not only provides a perspective, but also conceptual tools and strategies to *de-construct* this history. Colonial establishment and the missionaries were again at one with denying any history to the peoples of the colonies. I wish to refer here, as an example, to James Mill who wrote a "History of British India"[23] which was the standard reference work for civil servants and other employees of the colonial government. In James Mill's work, history of India begins with the arrival of the British. In general perception, mission begins with the sixteenth century expansion. One conveniently forgets that Christianity was present in several parts of Asia, even before most parts of Europe were not converted to Christian faith. In fact, one of the oldest Christian communities in the world is represented by the Thomas Christians of India. The stele erected under Tang dynasty in 781 in Xian (formerly Chang'an) in the Chinese imperial capital of the time, attests to the presence of active Christian communities for a long period.[24] There is a general trend today to speak and write about how Christianity is shifting to the South.[25] If that means ignoring the early Christian history of Asia, the "Church of the East", such discourses need to be reviewed and amended.

Overcoming Binaries – a Crucial Theological Task

One of the theological heritages of colonial times is the use of binaries. Much of classical theology has thrived on binary conceptions which gets interpreted in contrasting terms – nature and grace; human and divine; true and false; good and evil; this world the other world; salvation and damnation. Postcolonialism critically analyses the construction of the binaries and their working. The critique of binaries by postcolonialism is at the same time affirmation of an integral and wholistic approach, very characteristic of Asian world-view. Asian theologies which critique theologies that have dichotomies built into them will find support in the postcolonial critique of binary mode of thinking.

There is another dimension to the critique of binary polarization. Binary ignores the spaces in-between and the interactional constitution of social, cultural, ethnic, racial, and gender identities. Developing Asian theologies, therefore, is to grapple with "ambivalence" "hybridity" and "liminality", and to weave these into their methodology.[26]

The binary of center vs periphery is used in liberation theology and in the world system analysis of Emmanuel Wallerstein which had great influence on Latin American liberation theology. Postcolonial theology will question the essentializing of center and periphery which would give the impression that the liberative task is to integrate the periphery into the whole or to empower the periphery. In postcolonial approach, the periphery is not simply a place at the edge, but it is a matter of multitudes that raise their voice. It helps us discover the misplacement or dislocation of the center. It is this that needs to be challenged more than attempting to integrate the periphery with the center, or the so-called mainstream.

Beyond the Universal and the Particular to the Singular

This is an important epistemological question treated at times openly, and most of the times covertly, distinguishing different theological approaches. We note a tension in the way the universal and the particular is related – be it in the conception of the Church or in the understanding of theology or morality. For some, particular or local Church is only a concrete realization in a place of the Church universal. For others, contextual theology is but accommodation or inculturation in a particular cultural setting of a presumed superior universal theology. As a result, particular Church and contextual theology become a diluted version of the normative and the universal. Asian theology has been, so to say at gut level, resisting this kind of thinking, but never tried to articulate it in theoretical form. I think here postcolonial theory could come to its aid with its conception of "*singularity*" which challenges the way universal and the particular are related. Singularity, unlike the particular, is not an application of a normative universal, but something which is repeatable and each one of the repetition has a difference. In this sense, Asian Church is singular, and not a copy of a universal Church. The singularity of the Asian Church and Asian Christianity makes them endure as reality in their own right, and not as a derivative reality, or a realm of application. The correlate of singularity is not universality but *pluriversality*. The relationships among the Churches in the early centuries, each one very singular in its origin and development, were characterized by a spirit of pluriversality, of communion and exchange.

Postcolonial Critique of the History of Christian Doctrines

The connection between monotheism and imperialism has been, for long, a subject of study and research. Postcolonialism adds strength and concreteness to the critique of monotheism for its role of not allowing a plurality of approaches to the divine by introducing the concept of *idolatry* - a trivialization of the faith of others. In the pursuit of uniformity of belief and practices, other views, perspectives, and approaches have been sidelined or stifled. As the Sri Lankan Biblical scholar Sugirtharajah points out, right from the early centuries, the Hellenistic form of Christianity got privileged and the multiple and plural voices from the Jewish and Oriental traditions were sidelined and silenced for being heretical. This was already at work, according to Sugirtharajah, at the time of the building of New Testament canon, when writings representing different viewpoints got excluded from the canon.[27] The analysis of how in the Christian history diversity in belief got eclipsed helps Asian theologies in their pursuit of genuine pluralism in faith, theology, and worship.

Conclusion

Like culture, religion may not be essentialized and transported. There is a creative and formative moment of identity. "Being Christian"[28] – to recall the well-known work of Hans Küng - would be called into question by postcolonial theories for its essentialism and all the presupposition that go with it.[29] *Becoming Christian* is a dynamic conception and approach, and it opens up to an interactional identity than the self-insulated essentialism of Being Christian. What we have in Asia are Christianities in the process of becoming, and the constitution of Christian identity is a process of dialogue than a normative given. This has implications for global Christianity.

The most important task of Asian theology is not inculturation, but assistance in the process of becoming Christian ever more. This process brings the Christian communities in encounter with the world, and with other religious traditions. The received theology from the missionary period is far from helping in this process, since they are framed within a dichotomous worldview and formulated in the colonial setting. There is the need for a decolonized mindset to pursue theology in Asia. Asian theologies will be critical by deconstructing the colonial theology as the first step and build on a new relationship with the world and with other religious traditions. Vatican II is an important source for the construction of Asian theologies. However, Asian theologies will go beyond theoretical debates on the interpretation of the Council trying to find out the meaning of the texts intended by the Council Fathers. The question of Asian theologies is not whether Vatican II is to be interpreted in *continuity* with tradition or whether it represents a *rupture* – the grist to the mill of many western theologians today. There is a place for this kind of discussion up to a point. But this is not everything about the Council. Postcolonial theories can help Asian theologies to go beyond this kind of debate and see Vatican II as an open-ended text which needs to be interpreted with the questions and issues the Christian communities and the Asian people at large are facing. In short, Asian theologies could find a much-needed critical and methodological tool in postcolonial theories. This is all the more when we note that many significant theorists of postcolonialism today hail from Asia and draw a lot of inspiration from Asian history, tradition, and resources

Bibliography

Abraham, Susan. "What does Mumbai has to do with Rome?" Postcolonial Perspective on Globalization and Theology." *Theological Studies* 69 (2) (2008), 376-393.

Achebe, Chinua. *Things Fall Apart* (New York: Anchor Books, 1994); (1958).

Ahmed, Siraj. "The Colonial Intellectual: Prototypes and Paradigms." *Postcolonial Studies: Culture, Politics, Economy* 20 (2017), 237-43.

An, Choi Hee. *A Postcolonial Self: Korean Immigrant Theology and Church* (Albany, NY: Suny Press, 2015).

Andrade, Luis Martinez. "Liberation Theology: A Critique of Modernity." *Interventions: The International Journal of Postcolonial Studies* 19 (2017), 620-30.

Asad, Talal. *Genealogies of Religion: Discipline and Reasons of Power in Christianity and Islam* (Baltimore: Johns Hopkins University Press, 1993).

Ashcroft, Bill., Griffiths, Gareth., and Tiffin, Helen. *Key Concepts in Post-Colonial Studies* (New York, London: Routledge, 2004).

Ashcroft, Bill., Griffiths, Gareth., and Tiffin, Helen. *The Postcolonial Studies Reader* (London: Routledge, 1995).

Barker, Francis., Hulme, Peter., and Iversen, Margaret., eds. *Colonial Discourse/ Postcolonial Theory* (New Delhi: Viva Books Private Limited, 2012).

Betts, Raymond F. *Europe Overseas: Phases of Imperialism* (New York: Basic Books, 1968).

Bhabha, Homi K. *The Location of Culture* (London: Routledge, 1994).

Bhattacharya, Sourit. "What Postcolonial Theory Doesn't Say." *Interventions: The International Journal of Postcolonial Studies* 19 (2017), 144-46.

Bilimoria, Purushottama and Al-Kassim, Dina, eds. *Postcolonial Reason and Its Critique: Deliberations on Gayatri Chakravorty Spivak's Thoughts* (New Delhi: Oxford University Press, 2014).

Boer, Roland., ed. *Postcolonialism and the Hebrew Bible: The Next Step* (Atlanta: Society of Biblical Literature, 2013).

Brett, Mark G. Havea, J., ed. *Colonial Contexts and Postcolonial Theologies: Story Weaving in the Asia-Pacific* (New York: Palgrave Macmillan, 2014).

Brett, Mark G. *Decolonizing God: The Bible in the Tides of Empire* (Sheffield: Sheffield Phoenix Press Ltd., 2008)

Cesaire, Aime. *Discourse on Colonialism*. Intro. Robin D. G. Kelley, trans. Joan Pinkham (New York: Monthly Review Press, 2000); (1950).

Chambers, Iain., and Curti, Lidia., eds. *The Post-Colonial Question: Common Skies, Divided Horizons* (London: Routledge, 1996).

Choudhury, Bibhash. *Reading Postcolonial Theory: Key Texts in Context* (New Delhi: Routledge India, 2001).

Daggers, Jenny. *Postcolonial Theology of Religions: Particularity and Pluralism in World Christianity* (New York: Routledge, 2013).

Dirlik, A. "The Postcolonial Aura: Third World Criticism in the Age of Global Capitalism." In *Postcolonialism. A Guide for the Perplexed.* Edited by Pramod K. Nayar (New York: Continuum International Publishing Group, 2010).

Donaldson, Laura E., and Pui-lan, Kwok., eds. *Postcolonialism, Feminism, and Religious Discourse* (New York: Routledge, 2002).

Dube, Musa W. *Postcolonial Feminist Interpretation of the Bible* (St Louis: Chalice Press, 2000).

During, Simon. "Postmodernism or Post-colonialism Today." *Landfall* 39 (1985), 366-81.

Fanon, Franz. *Wretched of the Earth.* Pref. by Jean-Paul Sartre. Translated from the French by Constance Farrington (New York: Grove Press, 1965).

Fitzgerald, Timothy. *The Ideology of Religious Studies* (New York: Oxford University Press, 2000).

Gandhi, Leela. *Postcolonial Theory: A Critical Introduction* (New Delhi: Oxford University Press, 1999).

Gulati, Varun, and Dalal, Garima., eds. *Multicultural and Marginalized Voices of Postcolonial Literature* (London: Lexington Books, 2017).

Hill, John Bernand. *Prophetic Rage: A Postcolonial Theology of Liberation* (Grand Rapids: W. Eerdmans, 2013).

Huggan, Graham., and Law, Ian., eds. *Racism Postcolonialism Europe* (Liverpool: Liverpool University Press, 2009).

Irvine, Anderw B. "Liberation Theology as a Postcolonial Critique of Theological Reasons: An Examination of Early Writings of Gustavo Gutierrez." *Journal of the Academic Study of Religion* 25 (2) (2012), 139-162.

Iskandar, Adel., and Rustom, Hakem. *Edward Said: A Legacy of Emancipation and Representation* (Berkeley, Los Angeles, London: University of California Press, 2010).

Jagessar, Michael N., and Anthony Reddie., eds. *Postcolonial Black British Theology: New Textures and Themes* (Peterborough: Epworth, 2007).

Jefferess, David. *Postcolonial Resistance: Culture, Liberation, and Transformation* (Toronto; Buffalo; London: University of Toronto Press, 2008).

Keller, Catherine. *Postcolonial Theologies: Divinity and Empire* (St Louis: Charlie Press, 2004).

King, Richard. *Orientalism and Religion: Postcolonial Theory, India and 'The Mystic East'* (London: Routledge, 1999).

Kumar Das, Bijay. *Critical Essays on Post-Colonial Literature*. 3rd ed. (New Delhi: Atlantic Publishers, 2012).

Kwan Shui-Man, Simon. *Postcolonial Resistance and Asian Theology* (London- New York: Routledge, 2014).

Lartey, Emmanuel Yartekwei. *Postcolonializing God: New Perspectives on Pastoral and Practical Theology* (London: SCM Press, 2013).

Liew, Tat-siong Benny., ed. *Postcolonial Interventions: Essays in Honour of R.S. Sugirtharajah* (Sheffield: Sheffield Phoenix Press, 2009).

Loomba, Ania. *Colonialism/Postcolonialism* (London and New York: Routledge, 2015).

Mariko, Aguilar. "Postcolonial African theology in Kabasele Lumbala." *Theological Studies* 63 (2) (2002), 302-323.

Masuzawa, Tomoko. *The Invention of World Religions, Or, How European Universalism Was Preserved in the Language of Pluralism* (Chicago: University of Chicago Press, 2005).

McLeod, John. *Beginning Postcolonialism* (New Delhi: Viva Books Private Limited, 2012).

McLeod, John. ed. *The Routledge Companion to Postcolonial Studies* (New York and London: Routledge, 2007).

Mendieta, Eduardo. "Re-Mapping Latin American Studies: Postcolonialism, Subaltern Studies, Postoccidentalism and Globalization Theory." *Dispositio vol.* 25, no. 52 (2005), 179-202.

Mongia, Padmini., ed. *Contemporary Postcolonial Theory: A Reader* (New Delhi: Oxford University Press, 1996).

Nayar, Pramod K. ed., *Postcolonial Studies. An Anthology* (Oxford, UK. Wiley Blackwell, 2016).

Parry, Benita. *Postcolonial Studies. A Materialist Critique* (London & New York: Routledge, 2005).

Pui-lan, Kwok. *Postcolonial Imagination and Feminist Theology* (Louisville: Westminster John Knowx Press, 2005).

Punt, Jeremy. "Postcolonial Biblical Criticism in South Africa: Some Mind and Road Mapping." *Neotestamentica* 37 (1) (2003), 59-85.

Punt, Jeremy. "The New Testament Theology and Imperialism: Some Postcolonial Remarks on Beyond New Testament Theology." *Neotestamentica* 35 (2001), 129-145.

Ramone, Jenni. *The Bloomsbury Introduction to Postcolonial Writing: New Contexts, New Narratives, New Debates* (Bloomsbury: Bloomsbury Academic, 2017).

Rivera, Mayra. *The Touch of Transcendence: A Postcolonial Theology of God* (Louisville: Westminster John Knox Press, 2007).

Said, Edward W. *Culture and Imperialism* (New York: Vintage, 1994).

Said, Edward W. *Orientalism* (New York: Vintage, 1978).

Styers, Randall. "Postcolonial Theory and the Study of Christian History." *Church History* 78 (4) (2009), 849-54.

Sugirtharajah, R. S. *Postcolonial Criticism and Biblical Interpretation* (Oxford: Oxford University Press, 2002).

Sugirtharajah, R. S. *The Bible and the Third World: Precolonial, Colonial, and Postcolonial Encounters* (Cambridge: Cambridge University Press, 2001).

Sugirtharajah, R. S. *Asian Biblical Hermeneutics and Postcolonialism: Contesting the Interpretations* (Maryknoll, N.Y.: Orbis Books, 1998).

Thang, Moe David. "Postcolonial and Liberation Theologies as Partners in Praxis against Sin and Suffering: A Hermeneutical Approach in Asian Perspective." *Exchange* 45 (4) (2016), 321-343.

Veer, Peter van der. *Imperial Encounters: Religion and Modernity in India and Britain* (Princeton, N.J.: Princeton University Press, 2001).

Wang, Angela Wai Ching. "Negotiating a Postcolonial Identity. Theology of the 'Poor Woman' in Asia." *Journal of Feminist Studies in Religion* 16 (2) (2000), 5-23.

Warrior, Robert. "Canaanites, Cowboys and Indians." *Union Seminary Quarterly Review* 59 (1/2), 1-8.

Wilfred, Felix., ed. *The Oxford Handbook of Christianity in Asia* (New York: Oxford University Press, 2014).

Williams, Patrick., and Chrisman, Laura., eds. *Colonial Discourse and Post-Colonial Theory: A Reader* (New York: Columbia University Press, 1994).

Young, Robert J. C. *Postcolonialism: An Historical Introduction* (Oxford: Blackwell, 2001).

Endnotes

[1] Edward W. Said, *Orientalism. Western Conceptions of the Orient* (London: Routledge, 1978). See on the contribution of Said, Adel Iskandar and Rustom Hakem, eds., *Edward Said: A Legacy of Emancipation and Representation* (Berkeley, Los Angeles, London: University of California Press, 2010).

[2] I am not entering into the explanation of postcolonial theories here. An understanding of them could be gained from the vast amount of literature available on this issue. The most recent questions are treated in reviews such as *International Journal of Postcolonial Studies, Postcolonial Studies* etc. Here I confine myself to draw

the attention of the reader to some of the limits of postcolonial theory which are important when we read theology through its lens.

[3] Padmini Mongia, ed, *Contemporary Postcolonial Theory. A Reader* (Delhi: Oxford University Press, 2000), introduction, p. 2.

[4] Edward W. Said, *Culture and Imperialism* (New York: Vintage Books, 1994).

[5] Cf. David Bosch, *Transforming Mission: Paradigm Shifts in Theology of Mission* (New York: Orbis Books, 1991)

[6] Warrior extends this argument and, in the process, turns critical also of liberation theology. According to him, even liberation theology is not free from western epistemology associated with imperialism. For, it uses the Biblical exodus event as liberation motive unmindful of the genocide and destruction of the Canaanites. This destruction and conquest gets celebrated as liberation. He tells how this is reflected in the conquest mentality of colonizers to destroy and rule over the indigenous people. He even goes to the point of considering liberation theology as complicit in the ideology of the empire. However, he suggests alternative forms of liberation theology that is not infected by the "Canaanite" ideology. See Robert Warrior, "Canaanites, Cowboys and Indians", in *Union Seminary Quarterly Review*, 59:1/2 (2005), 1-8. Andrea Smith draws out the implications of the views of Warrior, see his "Decolonizing Theology", in *Union Seminary Quarterly Review* 59, no 1-2 (2005), 63-78.

[7] Cf. Concilium Special Issue, "Reform of the Roman Curia", *Concilium* 2015/5 (London: SCM Press, 2015).

[8] "*Novus habitus mentis*" is a phrase which Pope John Paul II used while introducing the new Latin Code of Canon Law. He intended to say that putting into practice the new code requires a new mindset, since it reflects the spirit of Vatican II.

[9] Cf. Tariqu Jazeel, "Postcolonialism: Orientalism and the Geographic Imagination", *National Geography*, 97:1 (2012), 4-11.

[10] Peter C. Phan, ed, *The Asian Synod. Texts and Commentaries* (New York: Orbis Books, 2002), p. 30.

[11] This orientation is represented by Eric Schwimmer, for example. See John Clammer, "Decolonizing the Mind: Schwimmer, Habermas and the Anthropology of Postcolonialism", *Anthropologica*, 50:1 (2008), 57-168.

[12] John Clammer, *ibid*.

[13] Simon Shui-Man Kwan, *Postcolonial Resistance and Asian Theology* (London, New York: Routledge, 2014).

[14] See Ada Maria Isasi-Diazo and, Eduardo Mendeita, eds, *Decolonizing Epistemologies: Latina/o Theology and Philosophy* (New York: Fordham university Press, 2012).

[15] See Morny Joy, "Postcolonial Reflections: Challenges for Religious Studies", *Method & Theory in the Study of Religion,* 13:2 (2001), 177-95, at 178.

[16] Cf. George M. Soares-Prabhu, *Theology of Liberation: An Indian Biblical Perspective.* Collected writings of George M. Soares-Prabhu, edited by Francis X. D'Sa, vol.4 (Pune: Jnana Deepa Vidyapeeth, 2001).

[17] See Yonghan Chung, "A Postcolonial Reading of the Great Commission (Mt 28:16-20) with a Korean Myth", *Theology Today,* 72:3 (2015), 276-288.

[18] Mrinalini Sebastian, "Reading Archives from a Postcolonial Feminist Perspective: 'Native' Bible Women and the Missionary Ideal", *Journal of Feminist Studies in Religion,* 19:1 (Spring, 2003), 5-25. Her study is based on the archival materials of Basel and Wesleyan Mission.

[19] R. Sugirtharajah, pioneered Asian postcolonial Biblical hermeneutics as can be seen in his numerous publications. See for example, *Jesus in Asia* (Cambridge, MA: Harvard University Press, 2018); *Exploring Postcolonial Biblical Criticism: History, Method, Practice* (Oxford: Wiley-Blackwell, 2012). *The Bible and Asia: From the Pre-Christian Era to the Postcolonial Age* (Cambridge, MA.: Harvard University Press, 2013); *Postcolonial Reconfigurations: An Alternative Way of Reading the Bible and Doing Theology* (London: SCM Press, 2003); R. S. Sugirtharajah, *The Bible and the Third World: Precolonial, Colonial, and Postcolonial Encounters* (Cambridge: Cambridge University Press, 2001); *Postcolonial Criticism and Biblical Interpretation* (Oxford: Oxford University Press, 2002). Postcolonial Biblical approach and Feminist theological explorations share many things in common in their analysis and methods etc. See for example, Musa W. Dube, *Postcolonial Feminist Interpretation of the Bible* (St. Louis, Mo.: Chalice, 2000); Laura E. Donaldson and Kwok Pui-lan, eds, *Postcolonialism, Feminism, and Religious Discourse* (New York: Routledge, 2002.

[20] The doyen of the Enlightenment, Immanuel Kant, writing at the height of European colonialism has left an ambiguous legacy regarding race and colonialism – the darker side indeed of the Enlightenment. See on this issue, Katrin Flikschuh – Lea Ypi, eds, *Kant and Colonialism: Historical and Critical Perspectives* (Oxford: Oxford University Press, 2014).

[21] Enrique Dussel, *A History of the Church in Latin America* (Grandrapids: Wm Eerdmans, 1981).

[22] Ranajit Guha and Gayatri Chakravorty Spivak, eds., *Selected Subaltern studies* (New York: Oxford University Press, 1988).

[23] James Mill, *The History of British India* (London: Baldwin, Cradock and Joy, 1817).

[24] Cf. Samuel Hugh Moffett, *A History of Christianity in Asia,* vol. I (New York: Orbis Books, 1998), 24-90.

[25] See the popularized work of Philip Jenkins, *The Next Christendom. The Coming of Global Christianity* (New York: Oxford University Press, 2002).

[26] As an example, we could cite the several documents produced by the Office of Theological Concerns (OTC) of the Federation of Asian Bishops' Conferences 1987-2007. Vimal Tirimanna, ed, *Sprouts of Theology from the Asian Soil* (Bangalore: Claretian Publications, 2007).

[27] See Beny Liew Tat-Siong, ed, *Postcolonial Interventions* (Sheffield: Sheffield Phoenix Press, 2009).

[28] Hans Küng, *Christ sein* (Freiburg: Herder, 2016).

[29] Cf. Felix Wilfred, "Becoming Christian Interreligiously", *Concilium 2011/2* (London: SCM Press, 2011).

CHAPTER 7

Religions and Competing Identities:
Dilemmas and Trajectories of Peace

Conflicts based on ethnic and religious identities have continued to cause the loss of a lot of precious human lives, many of them buried in mass-graves. They have resulted in many injured and maimed people; forced expulsion, genocide, and ethnic cleansing; missing people, refugees, and displaced people; mass rape and sexual assault; destruction of places of worship, and cultural symbols. These conflicts have been real tragedies with crimes against humanity, as the wars in Bosnia-Herzegovina, in Kosovo, in Sri Lanka, and in many African nations illustrate.[1]

The challenge for all religions today is to refrain from violence, draw from their own resources, and contribute to the cause of peace. There is no need to fear religion as long as it can become a builder of peace. But this cannot be done simply by preaching. Religion is not an isolated entity, but immersed within other social systems and forces – political, economic, cultural, and so on.

Religion and Ethnic Identity

In a modern western society, claiming to live by the ideals of the Enlightenment, and promoting individual freedom, and the construction of an autonomous self (the so-called process of "individualization"), religion, at least theoretically, may not figure anywhere. Religion at the most would belong to the realm of one's free choice rather than something inherent in one's self, collective identity, culture, and tradition. For most people, religion is a very important marker of their identity, as it represents some of the ultimate values and ideals they hold on to. [2]

There are many societies in which religion overlaps with ethnic identity. Serb and Orthodox identity overlap, just as Croatian and Catholic, Bosniak and Islamic identities do as well. In Sri Lanka, the ethnic identity of the Sinhalese is a Buddhist religious identity, whereas Tamil identity is Hindu. In Malaysia, to be a Malay is to be a Muslim; to be Indian is to be a Hindu, and to be a Chinese is to be a Confucian. With multiple religious and ethnic identities, the question arises: in whose image is the modern nation-state to be fashioned, which ultimately is an issue of power. Even at the heart of Europe, there is an undercurrent of right-wing thinking that to be European is to be Christian (*pace* secularists!) and "European Muslim" is, for some, a strange and intolerable proposal. It would appear that at least for some time this kind of thinking was bolstered up during the Balkan war.[3]

Although very often people in everyday life interact across religious borders, there are times when ethnic identities come into conflict for political, economic, and cultural reasons.[4] At this juncture, the religious factor adds strong emotional intensity to the conflict; provides symbols, narratives; and exacerbates the relationship between ethnic communities in the same nation. The political ambitions of the elites, for example, are an important factor in religio-ethnic conflicts. The instrumentalization of religious extremism helps them trump up mass-support.

When religious identity becomes the singular, overwhelming, and comprehensive identity, it is prone to cause conflicts and violence. We also should admit that in the same societies where religion plays the role of identity-marker, we have individuals who distance themselves from the negative aspects of religion, exercise respect, understanding, and compassion towards the religious other, and reach out to the humanity in every person, rather than getting bogged down in socially constructed identities. These individuals play a critical role vis-à-vis their own communities.

Configuration of Identities

Identity, broadly speaking, is the crystallization of the unique elements and characteristics that distinguish one from the other. Since human beings are both individuals and collectivities, there is, obviously, a self-identity as well as a group identity of "we". The important thing to note is that a person has multiple identities or layers of identities.[5] When people, because of various reasons (threat, perception of injustice, past memories) assert one single identity, conflicts arise, get sharpened, and can end in protracted violence. The shaping of identity is both internal and external. Through the socialization process, people construct their self-identities as belonging to a group, and sharing some important commonalities with them. The construction of the identity of the other is often characterized by clichés and stereotypes, and these form part of the socialization process. They get deeply embedded in the psyche of the individual and collectivity.

As regards religious identity, we should pay attention also to internal differentiation within the same religion. These differences are often so marked that two streams or denominations could be in conflict and cause violence. To cite examples: Conflicts between Sri Vaishnava and Saiva traditions have marked the Hindu religious history. Protestantism and Catholicism were locked in conflict through the centuries up to our times as illustrated by more recent experiences in Ireland. The Sunni and Shiite branches within the same religion of Islam could be identity markers for two different groups, and one could violently clash with the other as borne out by contemporary politics in West Asia, for example.

Shaping of Religious Identities in History

Colonialism has led to a situation in which religions have been essentialized. This is done both by the colonizers for easy categorization and classification, and by native people in order to resist the colonial forces. However, if we look at history, religious identities have never been insulated from one another like watertight compartments. A chemically pure religious identity is a myth. The evolution of the different world religions clearly shows how much each one of them has grown by interacting with other religious identities and through absorption of extraneous elements into its doctrines and practices. Most glaring is the example of Hinduism. Its religious identity is but a confluence of many religious streams sourced from different regions of South Asia and from different historical periods. "Hinduism" is a term of relatively recent origin to signify religiosity of many different peoples with a common religious family resemblance.[6]

Christianity itself bears many traces of Judaism and early Greco-Roman conceptions.[7] There was a flourishing Byzantine Christianity and a very missionary Nestorian Persian Christianity. History also witnessed the "Germanization of early Medieval Christianity"[8] with absorption of many elements of its indigenous religiosity and its social structures. The diversity in Christian identity right from the beginning allows us to speak of *"Christianities"* in plural.[9] This plurality has persisted in spite of concerted attempts on the part of the orthodoxy to suppress and marginalise it in the name of a monolithic unity. The concept of inculturation does not capture the richness of this diversity.

Buddhism on its part continued to evolve different forms and identities in relation to the cultures, civilizations, and the religious worlds it encountered. So, we have not only the doctrinally divergent two early forms of Buddhism –*Theravada and Mahayana* – but also Tibetan, Thai, Chinese, Japanese, and Sri Lankan Buddhism. Islam, due to different historical, social, and political circumstances could not have any one single identity. These few examples I cited, are meant to underline the point that the present-day globalisation is not the first time when religious identities meet, interact, absorb, and reinvent themselves through the encounter with other religious identities.

The encounters of religious identities did not happen in a vacuum. It all happened in different social, political, and cultural contexts. The boundaries between religions were fluid and porous, and precisely for this reason, the mutual exchanges among people from different religions were relatively easy. This explains also the fact of religious tolerance and respect for difference, as can be observed in general in the history of Asia. We can make a similar study of religious identities in the global world of today by observing and analysing how people in diaspora or in migrant situation try to live out their religious identity by adopting elements from the surrounding religious world of the country of their migration. One can study, for example, how the Hindu or Buddhist migrant community in Europe or the United States takes on many new elements from the surrounding in reshaping and living their traditional religious identity in the western context of Christian Churches.[10]

Dimensions of Religious Identity

We generally tend to see the identity in the doctrinal tenets or in the belief system. What make a religion different from another one are the different religious tenets. Mostly religious identity is viewed only from this point. Rarely does one refer to other dimensions of religion – worship, morality, law, and way of life. Hinduism is different from Islam because the mode of worship is different with different rituals and accompanying signs and symbols. The difference in identity is to be seen also in the way laws and regulations are formulated. In some religious traditions like Islam and Hinduism laws and injunctions bind the entire gamut of life in all its aspects, whereas for religious traditions that have gone through the historical experience of secularization, these laws relate to only the religious aspects, and do not intend to cover social and political spheres of life. Then, there are identity-markers in daily life, especially in Asia, on the basis of food.[11] Besides the broad category of vegetarian and non-vegetarian, there are a number of aspects in food and diet which speak of different identities, like for example *halal* food for Muslims, *kosher* for the Jews, strict vegetarianism among the Jains, and avoiding of meat by Christians during Lenten season.

Heterogeneity in Religious identity

One of the critical issues in religious identity is the fact that it is not always homogenous. Within the same religious group there is plurality of perceptions, views, modes of action, and behavior. While the identity of any particular group is legitimate, problem arises when the group or community wants to impose on all the members a particular conception of its identity and role. In such cases, religious identity comes into conflict with the rights of the individuals, even though he or she may own the group, but not in terms of what is dictated by the group or its leaders. *The problem here is a dialectics between objective and normative religious*

structures, on the one hand, and the structures of consciousness, on the other.
A reflexive process on the part of the individual leads to who he or she
is, and this could be said as *religious self-identification.* An individual
believer may find a discrepancy between what is prescribed and his or her
own perception of things, leading to dissent. The internal dissent within
religious groups in itself is something creative with a lot of potential
for the group to move beyond an essentialist self-definition. To cite one
example, within the larger Islamic religious identity, one needs to take
into account the fact that Islamic identity may be perceived differently
by the Sunni and Shia groups. The Ahamadiyyas may not be viewed as
forming part of the Islamic identity at all. Then again, we have internal
divisions in terms of the orientation. In the case of Islam, the Sufi tradition
would present a very different understanding of Islam than the Wahabi
Islamic movement, which is concerned about propagating a stringent
version of Islam. When religious identities are stereotyped from without,
these important differences and inner religious heterogeneity get ignored.

Social Construction of Religious Identities

The identity politics of today has given rise to a theorizing on the social
construction of all kinds of identities. This is true also in the case of
religion. Besides the objective elements making up an identity, there
is also an element of construal, namely the way various elements are
deployed and pieced together to create a particular brand of identity. In
the case of nationalism, Eric Hobsbawm, from a historical perspective has
shown how identity gets constructed, and from a theoretical perspective,
Benedict Anderson has argued on the basis of his empirical studies, how
nation is a matter of creation; it is an *"imagined community"*.[12] One may
differ on the degree of constructivism in building identities like nation
or religion, but one cannot deny its working in the identity-creation. The
social construction of religious identities, like in other cases too, happens
through interactions and exchanges with other religious identities. If
for political, economic, historical or cultural reasons, another religious
group is viewed negatively or even as a threat to one's own identity, this
affects the construction of the identity of the religious group to which

one belongs. Hence, there is a social, interactive and relational character to the religious identity-building.

Identity – Perspectives of East and West

As for the issue of identity, in the West itself there is a difference between eastern and western parts of Europe. I find a lot of similarity, for example, between Bosnia-Herzegovina, a country of many faiths, and situation in many countries of Asia. The relationship between different identities – ethnic, cultural, and religious - is very much shaped by the particular history and context. As long as an empire was there and administration was done from a center, local identities did not play any significant role. Each identity tried to understand itself in relation to the major unit of the empire. In the case of Europe, we have the Austro-Hungarian Empire under which there was a great multiplicity of national and ethnic identities. Under the Ottoman Empire the *dhimmi* system served as a safeguard against inter-ethnic and religious conflicts.[13] In the case of India, there was the Mughal Empire followed by the British Empire. During the imperial period, for the reason I cited, there were, by and large, no significant religious or ethnic conflicts.[14] Once the empire collapsed, and there was local autonomy, then the competition began among the various identities in a struggle for power and to garner the best resources available. The leftist claim that ethnic and religious identity would vanish with the affirmation of class-identity and struggles of workers and peasants has been disproved.

Future Trajectories of Peace. Fluid and Porous Identities Vis-à-vis Stagnating Identities

Identities are not to be viewed as ready-made boxes. Rigid and neatly defined identities inevitably lead to their defense. Instead, history attests that identity-building was a process rather than a ready-made product. There have been different types of interactions and levels of interchange among peoples of different religious affiliations. These cannot be set aside. Empirical studies show how, for example, there has been much interchange and communication even at the realm of worship and symbols, as illustrated by popular religiosity.[15] People across religious borders appropriate ideals, values, and symbols of their neighbours. In short, a dynamic and flexible understanding of identity can help prevent religious conflicts.

Stagnating identities, on the other hand, are dangerous as they can be the breeding ground for violence. Ossified identity seeks to secure for itself a space for fear of the other, and it would go even to the extent of ethnic cleansing to make sure that it has an exclusive space. It is awful if religions are found fomenting this kind of identities.

New Role for Religions

Once we are freed from the view of stagnating identity, we will be able to see that in real life, people have multiple identities.[16] Ethnic, religious and linguistic identities are part of many layers of identity with which people live their everyday life. Their multiple identities are shifting, and they often intersect and criss-cross, leaving little room for an insulated identity. Since religions have the tendency to be all-encompassing, they tend to view religious identity as the singular and overarching identity. Hence religions have fostered mostly exclusive identities. The new role religions need to play is to help people free themselves from a singular religious identity and forge relationships with neighbours, not simply as religious believers but as concerned human beings and citizens sharing the same context, history, and conditions of everyday life. Instead of trapping people into a monolithic religious identity, efforts need to be taken to help them feel at home and interact with a plurality of shifting and intersecting identities.

Another important initiative on the part of religious traditions is peace-mediation. In times of conflict and tension, and in post-conflict situations, religious groups and leaders could contribute a lot to the creation of peace. We have a many such initiatives in India. To cite a few examples, when the district of Kanyakumari in Tamilnadu was in the grip of a violent communal conflict between Hindus and Christians, the Saivite leader Kuntathur Adigalar of Kuntathur Mutt and the Church-leaders initiated the "*Thiruarul Peravai*" whose purpose was to bring about peace and harmony among the religious groups. There are innumerable micro initiatives at the grassroots level which contribute to bring down tension and conflict. At the international level, the initiatives of Aytollah al-Sistani in Iraq, and the South African Council of Churches have demonstrated the potential of religions and religious leaders to the cause of peace. We could highlight here also the efforts of the Churches and development of theologies oriented towards peace in the tense situation in East Asia involving the two Koreas, Japan, and China.[17]

Civil Society Initiatives in Multi-Ethnic and Multi-Religious Societies

I think there should be development of civil society initiatives in which various identities and groups participate and share many things in common. In India it has been observed that some cities are prone to Hindu-Muslim riots, whereas other cities are more peaceful, in spite of provocation. Why this difference? There could be many explanations. However, wherever there have been different forms of inter-communitarian associational life and civil society initiatives taking place, voluntary agencies at work, and inter-ethnic marriages are contracted, less conflicts and fewer outbreaks of violence have been observed. For, these everyday practices nurture inter-ethnic and inter-religious understanding and foster mutuality, help build durable structures of peace, and above all, create trust among competing identities. I believe more intense interactions in civil society could help restrain the forces of conflict and violence.

Increasingly, India has been characterized by outbursts of violence and riots among Hindus and Muslims, on the basis of culture, ethnicity, and religion. So, we are able to understand how disastrous conflicts could burst out in the Bosnian-Herzegovinian situation. To sustain peace, harmony and concord among competing identities in a post conflict situation, with lingering trauma, is challenging. There looms always the danger of repeating the past at micro and macro levels. Peace is a very fragile reality, and it requires perpetual vigilance. There is a need for re-education of all the identities involved. It is necessary to take a multi-pronged approach to sustaining peace. As I noted earlier, religions could come out more strongly and critically in the service of peace. This is done not only by drawing resources from the religious traditions, but by helping to activate civil society initiatives across identities and cultivating a sense of common good.

Suppression of Civil Society

But here we face a serious political issue, since the civil society itself is in crisis. Authoritarian and centralized states feel threatened by civil society initiatives. For, in many areas of life, civil society initiatives represent a critical voice challenging the omissions and commissions of the state. With firm roots on the ground, the non-governmental organizations represent a formidable force for peace and harmony among the people. They have the potential to build up peace from bottom up. Unfortunately, even democratic governments tend today to harass and eliminate the NGOs. This is precisely what is happening in India. For some flimsy reason or other, the non-governmental organizations are targeted, and they are forced to close down. A country like India caught up in the communal cauldron require initiatives and movements that go beyond all barriers to bring together people of different cultures and religious persuasions, and to lay the foundations for peace.

Economic Justice and Equal Opportunities

In situations where religious identities are locked in conflict, to come out of the tangle, one will need to heal the situation by addressing the issue of economic justice and equal opportunities. For, in many societies, competition for scarce resources puts different groups against one another. Identity becomes a weapon for claims.

Conflict derives from unequal economic development among particular groups and ethnicities, causing strong feelings of injustice and deprivation. As many analyses show, if the economy weakens, submerged ethnic passions and tensions flare up. Things get worse when there is inequality among the identities in sharing economic benefits. Hence, development needs to take place for all, regardless of ethnic or religious identity. Moreover, the structural causes for inequality also need to be analysed and addressed. In short, the conditions for long lasting peace among multi-ethnic, multi-religious, and linguistic groups are created when appropriate ways and means for equitable development are put in place. Lack of employment and opportunities, low-wages, and corruption are common issues which need to be addressed across ethnic and religious divides.

Recognition of Difference and Interfaith Education

Identity, in the present day, has become a major global issue, politically loaded, with ramifications in all areas of life. There is a temptation to find easy solutions by steamrolling the different identities in favour of a misconceived model of unity and peace. The command to "love one's neighbour as oneself" might have been relatively easy when the neighbor was someone belonging to one's own tribe or ethnic, religious, national, cultural or linguistic group. Today we are in a situation in which our neighbour is someone who has a different mode of thinking, religious belief, and way of life, different history and aspirations for the future. The acid test of our conviction in human dignity and rights is to be shown today concretely in multi-ethnic and multi-religious societies by the respect we give to the difference the neighbour represents.

Recognition of difference needs to be an important component in formal, non-formal and informal modes of education. Here I would like to specify I do not mean advocacy of religious instruction in state-run or state-aided educational institutions. At the Constituent Assembly of India, the question of religious education was debated. Ambedkar and K.T. Shah and others opposed any such initiative adducing different grounds why public money should not be used for religious instruction.[18] What is meant here is something different. Religions could help societies in conflict by contributing to a new educational praxis for recognition of difference and respect for difference. It is something more basic and fundamental than inter-religious understanding. What is at stake is not simply the sacredness of religions and their beliefs as the respect for others in their difference, which is not only a matter of religion, but pertains to many other areas of life. Religion could be a catalyst for the promotion of an education for recognition of difference. This, as rightly Rajeev Bhargava argues, does not contradict the secular character of the state. According to him, "multi- or inter-religious education can, and in some circumstances, must be an integral part of the larger project of secular education".[19]

Since ignorance is the root of prejudices, and stereotypes about other people and their religious universe, today it has become imperative to impart interfaith education. Greater knowledge will go a long way to help in understanding not only the belief system, but also rituals, practices, symbols, and world-view, and value connected with the faith of one's neighbours. Obviously, interfaith education cannot be simply a matter of imparting informations. At one time, probably interfaith education served for the spiritual growth of the individuals. Today, in the context of increasing communalism, we are faced with the urgency of promoting interfaith education for societal harmony and peace.

Knowledge about the faith of others needs to be accompanied by immersion experiences and visits to their religious sites, conversation with them on their faith, since this is what for many people give meaning to their lives, and provide perspectives to see the world. The interaction with and reaching out religiously to the other, would help understand one's own religious identity and belonging better and in proper perspective. It would also be advisable that, as part of interfaith education, one participates in the rituals of one's neighbours at their homes or in their places of worship. Interfaith education becomes additionally effective if it is connected with grassroots activism. People at the grassroots involved in taking up serious human issues as starvation, malnutrition, health-care, questions of women and children, migration, environment etc. will be able to help overcome the feeling of singular identity religions and religious agents tend to create in the minds of the believers. People across different boundaries involved in jointly responding to pressing issues of the people and community will help see their religious identity from a larger perspective.

In India, in times of religious conflicts and tension, much mischief is being done by circulation of rumors.[20] The frenzied masses of people act on the basis of rumors which have, in reality, no foundation, but are capable of causing horrendous violence and destruction. Often, the rumors are deliberately planted by those who instigate communal riots, so that maximum harm is done to the enemy. I think here interfaith education has an important role to play. It can help people to look at rumors critically and see the devastation they can cause.

Though interfaith education should happen in formal, non-formal, and informal ways, it would be important that those directly involved with religion and management of religious affairs, and especially religious leaders are ready to hold interfaith education for their religious communities. This could be very challenging. But coming from the religious agents themselves, it will have great impact on the believers and their relationship to peoples of other faiths. In short, cultivation of interfaith education can help building up harmonious communities and create an atmosphere of understanding, peace, and harmony.

Healing of Memories and Rewriting History with the Other as the Grammar

In post-conflict situation like in Sri Lanka, South Africa, Bosnia-Herzegovina, should we focus on the past, or rather bury it in order to be able to move ahead? Forgetting the past is a pragmatic approach that can be attractive. On the other hand, experience tells that unredeemed memory of hurt is something at work even before conflicts break out. It needs to be addressed.[21] In post-conflict situations, traumatic memories and feelings continue to haunt, and as a festering wound, they afflict life in society. Truth and history need to be confronted for proper healing.

The healing of memories could be a positive role religions could play in conflict and in post-conflict situations. By helping to remove the sting of revenge and hatred, religions could contribute to social harmony and cohesion. Of course, justice needs to be done and truth should come out in the open as a prerequisite for peace and harmony in any wounded society. However, any amount of restorative justice cannot re-establish the situation before violence and destruction were unleashed. That is gone once and for all. Hence, there will always remain a deficit which can be addressed only through a process of reconciliation which remains, to speak in Christian terms, a matter of grace. We see then the great scope religions have in the field of reconciliation in conflict and in post-conflict situations. Conflicts and violence among the identities often stem from fear, insecurity and a sense of threat. Hence, the creation of trust in the other is something religion and religious agents could foster for the construction of peace.

History narrated and written through the lens of ethnic and religious identity invariably turns out to be partisan, especially in the conflict and post-conflict situations. Such a history clouds the facts and strays away from the truth. Curiously, the current interests, concerns, and aspirations of various identities condition the narratives of the past. The suffering and injustice one's group has undergone gets highlighted while the suffering of the other is conveniently forgotten or made light of. Hence, history also needs to be redeemed by being rewritten in the light of truth and reconciliation in the post-conflict situation. It is indeed a very challenging task.

Conclusion

Some years ago, while visiting the concentration camp in Dachau, one thing struck me in particular. I saw in front of the gas-chamber, the statue of an emaciated prisoner representing the thousands of innocent people who underwent senseless suffering and death at this spot. It read: *Den Toten zur Ehre den Lebenden zur Mahnung* - Honour to the dead, and a warning to the living. Religion has been, unfortunately, an accomplice in ethnic and religious wars, if not always by its sin of commission, but certainly by its omission – the failure to do enough to prevent conflicts; the failure to contribute to the process of peace and harmony. Religions have failed to come out of their ambiguities. Christianity could not prevent two World Wars fought practically among the Christian nations with repercussions in the rest of the world. The little border town of Verdun in France which I visited fifty years ago as a student, witnessed a fierce battle and senseless killing. Within about ten months, over 360, 000 German soldiers were killed and equal number on the French side. The war cemetery in Verdun expanding over a large area with white crosses affixed to remember those who perished, stands out as a reminder of the failure of religions to prevent war and violence.

Thousands died in the ethnic and religious wars in Bosnia-Herzegovina, in recent times, and similar wars in other parts of the world. Neither the Catholic Church nor the Orthodox Church was able to prevent the massacre; in a way they were accomplices since they could not prevent the invocation of religious and ethnic identities by the perpetrators of violence and massacre. The war in Bosnia is a lesson to the whole of humanity of what should never be repeated.[22] It is a mine full of lessons.

There should never be another Srebrenica where eight thousand Muslims were killed in a day. It is a perpetual reminder, and indeed a warning to the religions and theologies, that they cannot sit idly when the house is burning, but need to act on a priority basis to quench the fire and take measures to build bridges of peace and harmony, in cooperation with all women and men of good will.

Bibliography

Aloysius, G., *Religion as Emancipatory Identity: A Buddhist Movement among the Tamils under Colonialism* (New Delhi: New Age International, 1998).

Ashiwa, Yoshiko, and Wank, David L., eds. *Making Religion, Making the State: The Politics of Religion in Modern China* (Stanford, Calif.: Stanford General, 2009).

Ayabe, Tsuneo., ed. *Nation-state, Identity, and Religion in Southeast Asia* (Singapore: Singapore Society of Asian Studies, 1998).

Bauhn, Per. *Normative Identity. Values and Identities: Crossing Philosophical Borders* (London: Rowman & Littlefield International, 2017).

Baybars-Hawks, Banu., ed. *Framing Violence: Conflicting Images, Identities, and Discourses* (Cambridge: Cambridge Scholars Publishing, 2016).

Bloch, Esther, Keppens, Marianne, and Hegde, Rajaram. *Rethinking Religion in India: The Colonial Construction of Hinduism* (London: Routledge, 2010).

Cigar, Norman L. *Genocide in Bosnia: The Policy of Ethnic Cleansing* (Texas: A&M University Press, 1995)

Clammer, J. R. *Diaspora and Belief: Globalisation, Religion, and Identity in Postcolonial Asia* (Delhi: Shipra Publications, 2009).

Davie, Grace., Woodhead, Linda., and Heelas, Paul. *Predicting Religion: Christian, Secular, and Alternative Futures* (London: Routledge, 2017).

Duijzings, Gerlachus. *Religion and the Politics of Identity in Kosovo* (London: C. Hurst,1999).

Ferguson, R. Brian., ed. *The State, Identity and Violence: Political Disintegration in the Post-Cold War World* (London, New York: Routledge, 2003).

Forest, Benjamin., Johnson, Juliet., and Stepaniants, M. T. *Religion and Identity in Modern Russia: The Revival of Orthodoxy and Islam* (Aldershot; Burlington, Vt.: Ashgate Pub., 2005).

Henig, David. "Crossing the Bosphorus: Connected Histories of "Other" Muslims in the Post-Imperial Borderlands of Southeast Europe." *Comparative Studies in Society and History* 58 (2016), 908-34.

Jakelic, Slavica. *Collectivistic Religions: Religion, Choice, and Identity in Late Modernity* (London: Routledge, 2016).

Jenkins, J. Craig., and Gottlieb, Esther., eds. *Identity Conflicts: Can Violence Be Regulated?* (New Brunswick, N.J.: Transaction Publishers, 2017).

Klippenstein, Kristian. "Language Appropriation and Identity Construction in New Religious Movements: Peoples Temple as Test Case." *Journal of the American Academy of Religion* 85 (2) (2017), 348-380.

Lee, Robert Deemer. *Religion and Politics in the Middle East: Identity, Ideology, Institutions, and Attitudes* (Boulder, CO: Westview Press, 2010).

Lindemann, Thomas., and Ringmar, Erik., ed. *The International Politics of Recognition* (London: Routledge, 2015).

Liow, Joseph Chinyong. *Religion and Nationalism in Southeast Asia* (Cambridge: Cambridge University Press, 2016).

Mitchell, Claire. *Religion, Identity and Politics in Northern Ireland: Boundaries of Belonging and Belief* (London: Routledge, 2017).

Murphy, Andrew R. *The Blackwell Companion to Religion and Violence* (Oxford: Wiley-Blackwell, 2011).

Oddie, G. A. "Indian Christians and National Identity, 1870-1947" *The Journal of Religious History* 25 (3) (2001), 346-66.

Power, Katherine Anne, *Talking Religion: Discursive Construals of Religious Identity in Rural Canada* (Lancaster: Doctoral Thesis, University of Lancaster , 2010).

Reid, Jennifer. *Religion, Postcolonialism, and Globalization: A Sourcebook* (Bloomsbury: Bloomsbury Publication, 2015).

Saha, Santosh C., ed. *Perspectives on Contemporary Ethnic Conflict: Primal Violence or the Politics of Conviction?* (Lanham, Md., Oxford: Lexington Books, 2006).

Schlee, Günther. *How Enemies Are Made: Towards a Theory of Ethnic and Religious Conflicts* (New York: Berghahn Books, 2010).

Sen, Amartya. *Identity and Violence: The Illusion of Destiny* (London: Penguin Books, 2007).

Shani, Giorgio. *Religion, Identity and Human Security* (London: Routledge, 2014).

Stausberg, Michael. "Advocacy in the Study of Religions." *Religion* 44 (2014), 220-32.

Storm, Ingrid, *Secular Christianity as National Identity: Religion, Nationality and Attitudes to Immigration in Western Europe* (Manchester: Doctoral thesis, University of Manchester, 2011).

Yeomans, Rory., ed. *The Utopia of Terror: Life and Death in Wartime Croatia* (London: Boydell & Brewer University of Rochester Press 2015).

Endnotes

[1] On the contemporary situation of identity and conflicts, see R. Brian Ferguson, ed, *The State, Identity, and Violence: Political Disintegration in the Post-Cold War World* (London; New York: Routledge, 2003); Banu Baybars-Hawks, ed, *Framing*

Violence: Conflicting Images, Identities, and Discourses (Cambridge: Cambridge Scholars Publishing, 2016); Esther Gottlieb, *Identity Conflicts: Can Violence Be Regulated?* (London: Routledge, 2007); Günther Schlee, *How Enemies Are Made: Towards a Theory of Ethnic and Religious Conflicts* (New York: Berghahn Books, 2010); Santosh C. Saha, ed, *The Politics of Ethnicity and National Identity* (New York : Peter Lang, 2007); Santosh C. Saha, ed, *Perspectives on Contemporary Ethnic Conflict: Primal Violence or the Politics of Conviction?* (Lanham, Md: Lexington Books, 2006); Andrew R. Murphy, ed, *The Blackwell Companion to Religion and Violence* (Oxford: Wiley-Blackwell, 2011).

[2] See Slavica Jakelic, *Collectivistic Religions: Religion, Choice, and Identity in Late Modernity* (London: Routledge, 2016). Claire Mitchell, *Religion, Identity and Politics in Northern Ireland: Boundaries of Belonging and Belief* (London: Routledge, 2017); Giorgio Shani, *Religion, Identity and Human Security* (London, Routledge 2014); G. Aloysius, *Religion as Emancipatory Identity: A Buddhist Movement among the Tamils under Colonialism* (New Delhi: New Age International, 1998).

[3] Kurt Almqvist, eds, *Secular state and Islam in Europe; perspectives from the Engelsberg Seminar, 2006* (Stockholm: Axel and Margaret Ax:son Johnson Foundation, 2007), pp. 155-166; Tariq Ramadan, *To Be a European Muslim: A Study of Islamic Sources in the European Context* (Leicester: Islamic Foundation, 1999); ID., *Western Muslims and the Future of Islam* (New York; Oxford: Oxford University Press, 2004); see also Norman L. Cigar, *Genocide in Bosnia: The Policy of Ethnic Cleansing.* (Great Britain: Texas A&M UP, 1995); Rory Yeomans, ed, *The Utopia of Terror: Life and Death in Wartime Croatia* (Rochester: Boydell and Brewer, 2015); David Henig, "Crossing the Bosphorus: Connected Histories of "Other" Muslims in the Post-Imperial Borderlands of Southeast Europe", *Comparative Studies in Society and History* 58 (2016), 908-34.

[4] Masudul Alam Choudhury and Faezy Adenan, "Political Economy of Conflict and Conflict Resolution Between Islam, the Arab World, and the West", *World Futures,* 73 (2017), 376-95.

[5] Peter Gottschalk, *Beyond Hindu and Muslim: Multiple Identity in Narratives from Village India* (Oxford: Oxford University Press, 2000).

[6] Cf. Günther D Sontheimer, and Hermann Kulke, eds, *Hinduism Reconsidered* (New Delhi: Manohar Publications, 1989); Vasudha Dalmia and Heinrich Von Stietencron, eds, *Representing Hinduism: The Construction of Religious Traditions and National Identity* - Symposium Papers (Thousand Oaks, New Delhi: Sage Publications, 1995).

[7] Cf. Jaroslav Pelikan, *Christianity and Classical Culture: The Metamorphosis of Natural Theology in the Christian Encounter with Hellenism* (New Haven & London: Yale University Press, 1993); see also Philip A. Harland, *Dynamics of Identity in*

the World of the Early Christians: Associations, Judeans, and Cultural Minorities (New York: T & T Clark, 2009).

[8] Cf. James C. Russell, *The Germanization of Early Medieval Christianity: A Socio-historical Approach to Religious Transformation* (New York: Oxford University Press, 1994)

[9] See Daniel Pilario, Felix Wilfred, Po Ho, eds, "Asian Christianities", *Concilium 2018/1*; see also Felix Wilfred, *Oxford Handbook of Christianity in Asia* (New York: Oxford University Press, 2014).

[10] Vineeta Sinha, *Religion and Commodification: "Merchandizing" Diasporic Hinduism* (London: Routledge, 2011); Sarita Maurya, *Practice of Hinduism among the Indian Diaspora in South Africa* (New Delhi: GenNext Publication 2017); S. Kulke H.Vertovec, "Hinduism in Diaspora: The Transformation of Tradition in Trinidad", *South Asian Studies* (1997), 265-93; Joanne Punzo Waghorne, *Diaspora of the Gods: Modern Hindu Temples in an Urban Middle-class World* (Oxford: Oxford University Press, 2004); A. Dhand, "Hinduism to Hindus in the Western Diaspora", *Method & Theory in the Study of Religion,* 17:3 (2005), 274-86; H. Foster, "Religious Maintenance and Adaptation: An Example from the South Australian Hindu Diaspora", *Religion Compass,* 2:3 (2008), 316-30.

[11] See Felix Wilfred, ed, "Civilizations and Dietary Practices", *Jeevadhara,* January, 2018.

[12] Benedict Richard O'Gorman Anderson, *Imagined Communities: Reflections on the Origin and Spread of Nationalism* (London:, New York: Verso, 2016).

[13] Christine Isom-Verhaaren and Kent F. Schull, eds, *Living in the Ottoman Realm: Empire and Identity, 13th to 20th Centuries* (Bloomington: Indiana University Press, 2016).

[14] Michael Walzer considers multinational empires as one of the five "regimes of tolerance". But this "tolerance" is to be understood differently as it has different premises. "Imperial rule is historically the most successful way of incorporating difference and facilitating (requiring is more accurate) peaceful coexistence. ...But settled imperial rule is often tolerant – tolerant precisely because it is everywhere autocratic (not bound by the interests or prejudices of any of the conquered groups, equally distant from all of them)". See Michael Walzer, *On Toleration* (New Haven, London: Yale University Press, 1997).

[15] Eric Maroney, *Religious Syncretism* (London: SCM Press, 2006).

[16] P. Lewis, "Muslims in Europe: Managing Multiple Identities and Learning Shared Citizenship", *Political Theology,* 6:3 (2005), 343-65.

[17] Cf. Jude Lal Fernando, "Prophetic Imagination and Empire in Asia: In Search for Peace Theologies in Korea and Japan", in *The International Journal of Asian*

Christianity, 1:1 (2018), 94-116.

[18] Rajeev Bhargava, "Religious Education in a Secular State", *India International Centre Quarterly,* 40:3/4 (Winter 2013 - Spring 2014), 117-130.

[19] Rajeev Bhargav, *art. cit.* 128.

[20] Paul R. Brass has analysed the role of rumours in communal riots. See his work: *Theft of an Idol: Text and Context in the Representation of Collective Violence* (Princeton: Princeton University Press, 1997); J. R. Clammer, *Diaspora and Belief: Globalisation, Religion, and Identity in Postcolonial Asia* (Delhi: Shipra Publications, 2009).

[21] Peter Siani-Davies and Stefanos Katsikas, eds, "National Reconciliation After Civil War: The Case of Greece", *Journal of Peace Research,* 46:4 (2009), 559-75. Institute for Justice and Reconciliation, "Truth Commissions and Transitional Justice: A Select Bibliography on the South African Truth and Reconciliation Commission Debate", *Journal of Law and Religion,* 16:1 (2001), 69-186; James L. Gibson, "The Contributions of Truth to Reconciliation: Lessons from South Africa", *The Journal of Conflict Resolution,* 50:3 (2006), 409-32.

[22] Marija Djolai, *When the Rooftops Became Red Again: Post-war Community Dynamics in Bosnia and Herzegovina* (Doctoral thesis – University of Sussex., 2016); *Justice at Risk: War Crimes Trials in Croatia, Bosnia and Herzegovina, and Serbia and Montenegro* (New York: Human Rights Watch, 2004). J. O Loughlin, "Inter-ethnic Friendships in Post-war Bosnia-Herzegovina", *Ethnicities,* 10:1 (2010), 26-54.

CHAPTER 8

New Impetus for Integral Ecology:
Theological Significance of *Laudato Si*

There is an impression that Pope Francis is pastorally-oriented, but his theology is weak.[1] This kind of view making the rounds requires a more detailed examination of his interventions, discourses, and statements. In any case, his encyclical letter *Laudato Si* should be seen as a fitting response to those who find him lacking in robust theology.[2] This contrast of the *pastoral* and the *theological* betrays a dualism that characterized already certain assessments of Vatican II. The Pastoral Constitution on the Church in the Modern World *Gaudium et Spes*, for example, has been viewed pastorally strong and theologically deficient. It is the same kind of people who would speak of Vatican II as doctrinally weak, whereas Vatican I, is strong on that score.

Lurking behind these judgments is a particular understanding of theology as elucidation of doctrinal truths. It would be unfair to judge the theology of Pope Francis from the perspective of a doctrinal theological tradition that is divorced from the experiences of Christian communities or pastoral realities. We could observe this in the contemporary high-flown and pretentious western theology. This theology has become increasingly narcissistic, and is not able to come to terms with the situation of the faithful who in the last few decades are leaving the Church in droves. There is little correspondence between the theology pursued and the pastoral condition of a worn-out western Christianity. It is also insulated, as it does not seem to enter into dialogue and exchange with global theologies emerging in different parts of the world. *Laudato Si* is a challenge to doctrinal theology (which claims to be *the* theology), its orientation and method.

A Jewel on the Crown

This encyclical marks an important theological turning point in the tradition of Christian social teaching.[3] The social teaching of the Church, as suggested by the word "social", are pronouncements regarding inter-human and inter-community relationships in justice and in the spirit of solidarity. The relationship of the Church with the human realm in its sundry dimensions was characterized as *pastoral*. Here is an encyclical which extends the pastoral relationship of the Church *to the world of nature*, and calls out the world of humans to enter into a harmonious relationship with it, and attend to its rhythm. As inequality and injustice fragment and destroy the fabric of the human community, so do the disruption of the rhythm of nature and the creation of imbalance in its functioning. If *Rerum Novarum* of Pope Leo XIII came at a time of deep crisis in the society through industrial revolution, *Laudato Si* has come out at a time of a double crisis – crisis of human solidarity and a crisis of nature. If *Rerum Novarum* set a "red" agenda to set right the wretched conditions of workers, *Laudato Si* proposes a "green" agenda against the destruction of nature and environment. The new encyclical of Pope Francis shares also something in common with *Pacem in Terris* of John XXIII. They are not simply exhortations to Christian community; they are addressed to the entire humankind on an issue that touches everyone across religious boundaries. As the Orthodox Metropolitan and theologian John Zizioulas expressed, "this Encyclical comes at a critical moment in human history and will undoubtedly have a worldwide effect on people's consciousness"[4] If the previous popes, starting from John XXIII, addressed their social message to *humanity and people of goodwill*; here is an encyclical which focuses on *planet earth* which makes up the life-environment of humanity and other creatures.[5]

A Theological Methodology from Below

The encyclical makes an incisive analysis of the contemporary ecological crisis, its roots, and goes into factors and forces involved. It contains also some important proposals for the future at international, national, and local levels. Both in analysis and proposals, there is an attempt to view the ecological issue as intertwined with the social, political, economic, and cultural questions. This is in marked contrast to ecclesial triumphalism that arrogates to teach without learning. Here, the pope is humble to receive concrete empirical data from science and technology.

Times were when science was subjected to *a priori* formulated doctrines, and this brought Christianity in confrontation with it, as the case of Galileo bears out. In this encyclical we find a clear admission of the autonomy of science, and above all, the contribution it could make to overcome the ecological crisis. "We must be grateful for the praiseworthy efforts being made by scientists and engineers dedicated to finding solutions to man-made problems" (LS. 34).[6] Pope takes into account the data provided by science. But unlike rationalism and positivism, he relates science more closely to the life of humanity. As Jean-Michel Maladam expressed succinctly, "it opens up a door towards a different way of existing in the world".[7]

Pope Francis has benefitted also from the ecological movements which have been grappling with the environmental issue at the grassroots for the past several decades. The data, analysis, and reflections he presents, closely portrays what those active in various environmental movements have been doing. In this sense, his approach is fed from ground realities. The encyclical attempts to pull together multiple discourses – scientific, cultural, economic, philosophical, ethical, theological, spiritual, mystical, etc., drawing insights from all of these towards the burning contemporary issue of ecology. It is certainly not an easy task, but the pope succeeds to a great measure, though understandable inconsistencies propping up in moving from one plane of discourse to the other remain. This is particularly so when he navigates between natural sciences and theology. Striking is the place he accords to natural sciences, more than his predecessors.[8] By and large, the difficult and complex methodology followed in the encyclical has yielded rich dividends.

From a methodological point of view, remarkable is the fact that the encyclical is studded with quotations from bishops' conferences in different parts of the world – Brazil, Canada, New Zealand, US, Philippines, Japan, Dominican Republic, and so on. He is referring to no less than 15 different bishops' conferences. A pope, who defines himself as "Bishop of Rome", willingly listens to other local Churches across the world, and discovers how they have come to terms with the environmental issues. This is highly significant, theologically. For in the last few decades, there were a lot of attempts to water down the role of bishops' conferences whose teaching role was questioned by the doctrinaire theology.[9] Without entering into this debate, the pope, in effect, shows how important it is for the universal Church and for humanity, what the various conferences have to say. The encyclical thus, far from being a Roman monochrome, has turned out like the coat of Joseph, polychrome - rich in colours (Gen. 37:3), thanks to the diverse resources of the local Churches the pope is drawing on. The theological methodology in *Laudato Si* is what the Federation of Asian Bishops' Conferences (FABC) has been trying to follow.[10]

Re-conceptualization of Christian Anthropology

A programme of ecological reform may not prove to be effective unless more basic things are set right. In the case of ecology, it is a question of right anthropology. In his widely discussed article, *The Historical Roots of our Ecological Crisis*, Lynn White laid squarely at the door of Judeo-Christian tradition the culpability for the present day ecological mess. For him, it is the anthropocentrism of this tradition that is to blame. In his words,

> Especially in its Western form, Christianity is the most anthropocentric religion the world has seen. As early as 2nd century both Tertullian and Saint Irenaeus of Lyons were insisting that when God shaped Adam he was foreshadowing the image of the incarnate Christ, the Second Adam. Man shares, in great measure God's transcendence of nature. Christianity, in absolute contrast to ancient paganism and Asia's religions (except, perhaps, Zoroastrianism) not only established a dualism of man and nature but also insisted that it is God's will that man exploit nature for his proper ends.[11]

Let me not enter into the details of Lynn White's thesis here. Even without his thesis, common sense tells us that with traditionally interpreted Christian anthropocentrism we may not be able to come to terms with the present ecological crisis. There is the need, so to say, for a *"sanatio in radice"* – a healing at the root - of this anthropology. It is this that Pope Francis has tried to do in his *Laudato Si*. He has introduced a welcome corrective to a misguided Christian anthropology that saw human beings as the crown of creation. It chimed with the anthropocentrism of western philosophy, Renaissance culture, and the Enlightenment. From a philosophical point of view, as René Descartes expressed, human beings are "masters and possessors of nature".[12] European Renaissance and Enlightenment were the secular versions of Christian anthropocentrism. They fed on mutually. I have been struck by the fact that in Renaissance art, nature figures little. Great Renaissance masters like Michael Angelo, Leonardo da Vinci, Titian, and Caravaggio tried to study the human anatomy, emotions, and behaviour very closely and created great works, but not the rhythm of nature and how it works. If at all, landscapes were used only as backgrounds to highlight the human figures. The male dominated art of the time paid scant attention to nature in itself. Like women, nature was viewed as a subjugated object (*natura naturata*) and not a creative force (*natura naturans*).

This western Christian, Renaissance and Enlightenment traditions stand in contrast to the larger Asian vision and its understanding of the world of humans as intertwined with nature. The life of the humans in Asian tradition is one with the elements of nature. Therefore, when Pope Francis attempts to correct a deeply embedded western theological and anthropological tradition, and speaks of integral anthropology, Asians can understand him immediately without difficulty. For, what he says, resonates with the Asian experience; reflects the vision of Hindu, Buddhist and Taoist traditions; and the way Asian tribals and indigenous people see the reality as interconnected and bonded together. One of the thoughts running through *Laudato si* is the interconnection of the entire reality.

In the encyclical, there is an effort to move from a hierarchical ordering of creatures, to a more teleological understanding in which both human beings and other creatures journey together. If traditional theology saw human beings in his or her relationship to God and to neighbours (society), this encyclical is an invitation to discover a third dimension, namely our relationship to nature, to the earth. We appreciate the novelty of this approach, if we set it against the western understanding of "chain of beings" (*scala naturae*), of Aristotelian vintage. We could further differentiate it from the Neo-Platonist frame of hierarchy of beings that moulded the Christian thought of the Middle Ages, including that of Thomas Aquinas. According to this philosophy, the less perfect is contained eminently in the more perfect; the less perfect is in service of the more perfect. To put it more concretely in terms of our present-day experience, the local superior of a religious house is eminently contained in the provincial; and the provincial is eminently included in the general! So also, the vegetable life is contained in the animal life, and the animal life in the human. Hence, all of nature in a less perfect state is in service of human beings, the crown of creation. This understanding of nature through the hierarchical lens fails to capture the value of each reality in its uniqueness; nor is it able to appreciate the richness of plurality and diversity.

Pope Francis seems to challenge this kind of philosophy and theology, and draws our attention to the truth that the value of anything in nature is not to be judged in hierarchical fashion of high and low (*secundum sub et supra*), but rather from a mystical perspective of unity of all in God. In his words, "The ultimate purpose of other creatures is not to be found in us. Rather, all creatures are moving forward with us and through us towards a common point of arrival, which is God." (LS 83). These words of Pope Francis evoke the symbol of pilgrimage, so dear to Asians. The thought of Francis cannot but strike the Asian readers who are accustomed to see and deal with nature not from a hierarchical perspective but from a mystical perspective of unity of all reality. The sense of bondedness and cosmic solidarity with nature brings forth the spirit of non-violence (*ahiṃsā*) and compassion (*karuṇā*).

Religion in the Public Sphere – A Fundamental Theological Question

The encyclical is manifestly addressed to all people of good will. And yet, we find in chapter two, the pope speaking from the point of view of Christian faith on the "Gospel of Creation". Does that mean inconsistency in his method? I think, though the pope does not explicitly enter into the theoretical question of the role of religion vis-à-vis common good, he is in fact operating from a particular standpoint on the relationship of religion today with public issues and concerns. It is the standpoint that holds that religion and faith have the responsibility towards common good. For the good of the community, religions can and should intervene in the public sphere.[13] There is another argument, which is, again, not stated by the pope explicitly, but which we can read between the lines: The borders of a religion do not end with its adherents; it is not their monopoly. Since religions talk about things that concern all, they will be of interest also to others, to whose perceptions of and engagement with common good they can contribute.

The objection to the assumption that underlies the papal document comes from three different quarters. First of all, states, especially the centralized ones, would find any such intervention on the issue of environment as a political act. The state and politicians claim it to be their competence to speak on public issues such as justice, environment, economic order, etc. They want the religions to keep off from these issues. The claim of the state is problematic. Its stance rests on the presupposition that the good of the society overlaps with the goals of the state. This is simply an unacceptable position. As an integral part of the society, religion can legitimately be concerned about what touches upon its (society's) wellbeing. Recent history illustrates how faith-motivated timely interventions have contributed to the transformation of the political order, and helped societies in their transition to a democratic order. In Asia we could cite the example of Korea, The Philippines, Indonesia, etc. We could further cite the example of the role played by religion in dismantling centralized and oppressive social states in Eastern Europe, the abolition of apartheid regime in South Africa, the transition to democracy of many Latin American countries from 1980's.

A second objection to public role of religion stems from the market economy. In fact, the apostolic exhortation *Evangelii Gaudium*, which was very critical of today's murderous system of economy, came under severe attack by votaries of market economy. Market objects to any state intervention that seeks to restrain it in the interest of social equity and inclusion. Its objection to religious intervention is even more severe. Convinced as they are that market has its own inner logic and dynamics, neo-liberal economists found the pope's intervention as unwarranted. They seem to say that pope should not try to enter into a realm that is not his domain and of his competence. Samuel Gregg from the Acton Research Institute, for example, finds the encyclical of the pope as "well-intentioned" but "economically-flawed".[14] The same kind of objection is raised when the pope comes down heavily on the neo-liberal economy and market for their disastrous consequence on the environment. The contention that religion should have no voice in economy as it has no competence in this field is simply a camouflage for capitalism and market. Don't an impoverished migrant, an exploited woman, a marginalized Dalit, have the right to question an order of economy that denies them the basic means for livelihood? Should not the tribal people challenge a system that destroys their natural habitat and imperils their survival? One cannot brush them aside saying that they have no competence to speak of economy, and should leave it to the experts to decide which economy is best for the society. What we need is a regulated economy in which the entire society, especially its weaker ones, are participants and that the benefits of economy gets shared equitably.

The third objection derives from those who argue on the basis of a narrowly understood secularism or what the French call the "*laicité*". This is a typical western argument deriving from the long European history of religious wars. We realize how flawed is the attempt to extend to Asia the brand of secularism brewed in the West. Our experience in Asia tells us that the secular is not the enemy of religion, as made out in Europe, but a friend and companion in the common struggle for the wellbeing of the society. Few in Asia would find that by speaking about ecology and environment the pope is violating secularism. His words as a concerned Christian believer addressing humanity on the ecological crisis would find welcome among Asian secular groups, actors in civil society, and ecological movements.

The challenge facing nature and humanity beckons us to draw from religious and cultural resources of humankind. Like in the case of human rights, drawing conviction from one's faith can only reinforce the cause. Therefore, Pope Francis, though addresses all people of good will, as a Christian believer and leader draws from the Gospel and the Scriptures insights and vision which support the ecological cause. So, we see the pope referring to the story of creation,[15] to the teachings, attitude and practice of Jesus – all meant to support the care for the earth and its cultivation. His approach is infused with the theology of creation. The traditional theology which rested on anthropocentrism was at home with a theology of redemption of the human race. Pope Francis brings in a breath of fresh air by underlining the need to redeem the earth and nature. Therefore, he makes an integral reading of the Biblical data and highlights the theology of creation. The salvation of human beings cannot be dissociated from the redemption of nature and from the forces of evil and death that seek to disfigure and destroy them. So, in *Laudato Si* we have not only a re-conceptualization of traditional Christian anthropology, but also *a revision of the traditional soteriology* by expanding its scope to include nature and the earth. Such a reinterpretation of Christian faith adds new impetus for involvement with the issue of ecology, and it helps to act in solidarity with many other forces contributing to the same cause.

From the Strategic to the Ethical and Theological

It is remarkable that Pope Francis has shifted the ecological issue from the strategic to the ethical. Strategic thinking goes in the line of finding the technocratic ways and means so as to prevent the degradation of the environment. There is, for example, talk about carbon reduction, carbon trading, carbon credit etc., which are meant to put some restraint on the senseless destruction of nature, and to reduce the warming of the earth. These measures have certain value. But Pope Francis does not rely too much on these measures, but rather goes to the heart of the problem. For him, ecological issue is to be viewed as an ethical issue. This means that human beings have moral responsibility towards the creation of God, and they, indeed, behave unethically if they destroy nature. For Pope Francis, there is a co-relation between the state of ethics and environment. For, as he observes, "environmental deterioration and human ethical degradation are closely linked" (LS 56). The strategic thinking would blame the population growth for the environmental crisis and seek to downsize it. The pope is critical of this view, and points out, instead, to the culture of consumerism and waste, and the absence of sharing and restraint on growth. Here lays the real threat to the environment which needs to be approached from an ethical perspective.

The traditional social teachings had two major foci of ethical reasoning, namely *human dignity and common good*. What pope Francis does is to add to these a third element, that is, *the dignity and sacredness of nature* as God's creation. By adding this new dimension, the understanding of common good itself gets amplified: Common good is no more, as in tradition, the good of human beings, but the well-being and flourishing of nature as well. Therefore, the behaviour of people vis-á-vis nature should touch their moral fibre and conscience.

This ethical approach of Pope Francis rests, as we saw above, on his conviction that nature has *an intrinsic value*. In traditional theology and in philosophical ethics, it is the human beings who have an intrinsic value, and nature has only an *instrumental value* and the value attributed to it by them. Pope raises ecological issue to a real ethical question by acknowledging an intrinsic value to nature.[16] "It is not enough…to think of different species merely as potential "resources" to be exploited, while overlooking the fact that they have value in themselves" (LS 33). This is a major theological contribution of Pope Francis, which, seen from the traditional perspective, could be contentious. On the other hand, seen from Asia, it is a position that brings the pope closer to the Asian way of thinking and acting vis-á-vis nature. What he says is something deeply embedded in Asian culture and religious traditions. The place of nature and the creatures is further corroborated in that he underlines that they are locus of God's revelation as well, and that they proclaim the glory of God. This again is something so much part of the Asian heritage, namely to see the universe permeated by the traces and the power of the divine.

Like human beings, nature too reflects and reveals the mystery of God. And what happens to our co-creatures on earth by environmental destruction? "Because of us thousands of species will no longer give glory to God by their very existence, nor convey their message to us. We have no such right" (LS 33). We can identify a deep connection between the Asian approach that treats all creatures with respect and feel affected when they suffer, and some of the mystical saints in Christian tradition, especially early mystical saints who lived a life of harmony with nature, animals, vegetation etc., feeling in themselves the pain when nature suffered. They lived in the awareness of a harmony and with a sense of interdependence with the entire created realities. Pope Francis goes to the point of identifying Trinitarian structure each creature bears.

> The Franciscan saint [Bonaventure] teaches us that each creature bears in itself a specifically Trinitarian structure, so real that it could be readily contemplated if only the human gaze were not so partial, dark and fragile. In this way, he points out to us the challenge of trying to read reality in a Trinitarian key (LS 239)

This theological and mystical approach to all creatures is why, according to Pope Francis, the world is not simply an arena of problems calling for solutions, but "a joyful mystery to be contemplated with gladness and praise" as well (LS 12).

Moral Support to Environmental Movements

Pope Francis has proposed an ecological theology that is effective in as much as it gives great moral support to the environmental movements all over the world. For the past five decades or so, these movements have grown by leaps and bounds, and have made immense contribution to the protection of nature. The activists in these movements had to struggle against the state and its development agenda, harmful to nature, and against politicians, business interests, keen on exploiting nature to increase their wealth. The encyclical is a fillip to the ecological movements.

In a certain sense, most of what the pope has said regarding the ecological crisis and on the anti-nature model of development has been already said by these movements. But what makes the difference is not so much what the encyclical has said, as the fact that *the pope* has said it. As a moral authority in our contemporary world, the views of a pope in what concerns the global common good, carries a lot of weight and draws world-wide attention. As for Christians, the encyclical is an invitation to see with new eyes the entire creation and to involve themselves to nurture nature with a sense of responsibility. The encyclical is also a great moral support to the unitary vision emerging in the last few decades from vanguard science that seeks to integrate the biological, the cognitive, the social, and the ecological. Pope Francis seems to integrate this new unitary scientific vision into his theology which is challenging. He reveals himself not only a person concerned with praxis and pastoral reality, but also a deep and creative thinker.

Knitting Together

Yet another significant aspect of *Laudato Si* is its effort to bring together ecology and the issue of justice and social equity. Ecological balance should go hand in hand with just and harmonious relationships in human societies. "We are faced not with two separate crises, one environmental and the other social, but rather with one complex crisis which is both social and environmental" (LS 139). The pope speaks also of cultural ecology - the preservation of the cultural heritage. Technological interventions need to be respectful of the culture of the people. What stands out in *Laudato Si* is the unique manner in which the pope links and develops the environmental ecology with human ecology[17] and cultural ecology. This is what the pope calls *integral ecology.*

What is even more significant is that no world leader has ever brought out so persuasively and cogently the environmental, economic, moral and political arguments together in this way. This synthetic view provides a good platform for action and involvement at different levels. Pope Francis speaks of an "inseparable bond ... between concern for nature, justice for the poor, commitment to society, and interior peace" (LS 10). The whole encyclical is an attempt to bind together what were seen and addressed in a disjunct manner in the past.

Moving Beyond the Technological Paradigm

The dominant model of development, outcome of the European Enlightenment, uses technology to exploit nature to produce wealth, prosperity and progress. The boundless growth this model advocates is unsustainable, since the carrying capacity of nature is limited. There should be restraint on growth if humanity and nature were to survive. This caution was sounded already in 1972 by the Club of Rome, but unfortunately has gone unheeded. Things have reached today such serious proportions, the pope warns, that check on growth has become a must for protecting nature and for practicing justice.

> …We need to think of containing [economic] growth by setting some reasonable limits and even retracting our steps before it is too late…The time has come to accept decreased growth in some parts of the world, in order to provide resources for other places to experience healthy growth (LS 193)

Going further, the pope questions the view that economy and technology can solve the environmental problem.[18] Technological paradigm stumbles before the truth that the resources of nature are limited. It stumbles also before the truth that whatever growth is achieved cannot serve only a selected few but should serve all, and therefore needs to be shared equitably. If one does not respect the regenerative capacity of nature and continues to exploit it, the consequences are serious like global warming, floods, soil-erosion, etc. If one fails to share equitably, human community is seriously impaired through this imbalance, and we end up with serious social conflicts and contradictions. Throughout the encyclical, Pope Francis tries to relate closely the ecology of the environment and human ecology.

The technological paradigm of development tells most severely on the life of the poor and the marginalized. A remarkable contribution of *Laudato Si* is the way it relates the protection of nature and the defence of the poor. Both are intertwined. The more we involve in protecting nature, the more we protect the poor, and the reverse is equally true. Destruction of the environment is undermining the survival of the poor – the tribals, fisher people, and impoverished farmers. Symbolically expressed, "the cry of the earth and the cry of the poor" (LS 49) go together.[19] Hence, setting right the earth and healing it is not possible without addressing and healing human relationships in society and in the world at large. Hence his statement:

> We are faced not with two separate crises; one environmental and the other social; but rather with one complex crisis which is both social and

environmental. Strategies for a solution demand an integrated approach to combating poverty, restoring dignity to the excluded; and at the same time protecting nature. (LS no. 139).

Hitting the Nail on the Head

Catholic social teaching has consistently challenged the claims of absolute ownership of the resources of nature. The universal destiny of earthly goods has been supported by Christian Scriptures. Patristic tradition questions the right to private property without restriction. A clear formulation of this key principle is found in *Gaudium et Spes*. "God destined the earth and all it contains for all men and all peoples so that all created things would be shared fairly by all mankind under the guidance of justice tempered by charity."[20] Now, this principle has been invoked in the tradition of Catholic social teaching for the promotion of a society in justice, equity and solidarity. The originality of Pope Francis is that he brings into play this principle not only for the cause of social justice and equity, but also for the promotion of ecological balance.

Unrestrained ownership of private property is a central issue in ecology and the pope hits the nail on the head. Today riches are owned by a few who through the market economy want only to strip nature and destroy it, imperilling the life of other human beings in the process. If there is restriction on the ownership of private property, it would ensure that nature is not over-exploited. Pope Francis sees in the unrestricted private ownership of property one of the roots of ecological crisis. "Natural environment is a collective good" (LS 95) says the pope. As a public good, earth, water and air belong to all. But, unfortunately, land and water are increasingly controlled by a few individuals and corporations, and the air is polluted and poisoned by the same. In order to save nature and common human habitat, the pope has recourse to the non-absolute right of private property. "The Christian tradition has never recognized the right to private property as absolute or inviolable and stressed the social purpose of all forms of private property" (LS 93). The pope's application of this principle to the realm of ecology is very timely.

The Praxial Nature of the Encyclical

"The Philosophers have only *interpreted* the world in various ways. The point, however, is *to change*", so said Marx in his time,[21] and it remains a permanent challenge. It is said of the social teachings of the Church, that they are "the best kept secret". To assume that, spreading knowledge about these documents will solve the problem, is unrealistic and too tall a claim. More is required than knowledge about the social teachings of the Church. Pope Francis is conscious of the importance of *praxis and transformation*. He, therefore, seeks to translate and apply these principles in practice. In fact, a whole chapter (chapter 5) is devoted to practical lines of approach and policies, and proposals of action at various levels – international, national, familial and personal. He has also pertinent suggestions for new practices. New practices call for conversion, new lifestyle, education, and a new spirituality all of which form the next chapter (chapter 6). In all these we can see how the theology of pope Francis touches ground realities and turns out to be vibrant.

Conclusion: The Achilles' Heel

There are at least three issues on which Asian readers would expect more from the encyclical of Pope Francis. The pope is very pointed in all his interventions on the question of poverty, injustice, exploitation, migrants, refugees, etc. And this comes out clearly also in *Laudato Si*. This is a great support to the struggle Asia and the developing world is going through. But Asia is also a world of ancient religions. Here flourish also indigenous religions of tribal peoples. All of them have a great affinity with nature which their religious experience, symbols, rituals, and narratives reflect. Their world-view is not anthropocentric like in the western tradition, and of which the pope is critical. Moreover, these Asian religious traditions have a *mystical approach to nature and environment*. They contain also rich resources for protection of nature. Sacred grove is a typical example. And yet, we find very little in the encyclical that would connect with the Asian religious traditions. One has the feeling a great opportunity for deeper dialogue with other Asian religions on ecology and environment is lost. The reference to St Francis of Assisi and his *Canticle of Creatures*, which lend also the title to the encyclical, could have served as a bridge to relate with Asian religious experience of nature and concern for the environment. These religions practice and celebrate every day the interconnectedness of all reality and acknowledge what the pope calls "an intrinsic value independent of their usefulness" (LS 140). Since the issue of ecology goes across all religious borders and offers a space for common engagement, a deeper treatment of inter-religious aspect of this question would have made the encyclical even more appealing. He does mention the need for such a dialogue when he states, "the majority of people living on our planet profess to be believers. This should spur religions to dialogue among themselves for the sake of protecting nature, defending the poor, and building networks of respect and fraternity" (LS 201). However, he could have gone more deeply into it, highlighting for example the traditions and sources in other religions for ecology to make this dialogue into a concrete reality. Ecological issues present opportunities for the development of public theology today if only we draw inspiration from the scriptures and resources of other religious traditions. They are abundant indeed.

A second shortcoming is the miss to bring out the implications of the encyclical for the Church and its pastoral ministry. Though the document is addressed to all, since the pope draws from Christian resources (chapter 2), logically, some indications for the application of them in the life of the Church would be expected. This would have given the encyclical greater witness value. If everything is interconnected and interdependent as the pope does not cease to tell us, how does it square with the practice of Church governance following a hierarchical model of relationships? The ecological paradigm of relationships suggested in the encyclical does not seem to square with the ecclesiological hierarchical paradigm that is practiced. How does one reconcile both these?

There are also other implications for the life of the Church, especially in what concerns worship. It is time to critically re-examine the Christian liturgy from the perspective of the ecological paradigm.[22] And this is very important for Asia, since its tradition of worship is very close to the elements of nature (*pañchamahābhūta*) – earth, water, fire, air and ether, the five basic elements of cosmic creation. Hindu worship begins by purifying the five elements within the body and outside.[23] The elements of nature are so very important in indigenous traditions and religious practices.[24] All this contrasts with the strong logo-centric (word-centred) worship in the Church which does not bespeak to the Asian genius. Drawing out implications for Christian worship would have been a concrete way to put into practice the lofty vision presented to us on ecology in *Laudato Si*. After all Christian Eucharistic worship implies the materiality of creation symbolized in the form of bread and wine. Through the offering of these sanctified gifts of creation, we celebrate our communion with God.

A third observation concerns the absence of a gender approach to the issue of ecology. Historically environmental and feminists movements have developed together. This is not without reason.[25] For exploitation of nature and environmental crisis affect women as empirical evidence will show in Asia where millions of poor women and their families depend on nature for their livelihood and survival. As the Indian *chipko* movement shows, women have been in the forefront in protecting trees and the riches of nature.[26] Moreover, the same patriarchal forces that are aggressively ravaging nature through technological rationality are also at the root of the oppression of women. A gender perspective both in the analysis of the ecological question and in developing principles and strategies for the future would have made the encyclical more complete.

These limitations, reading from Asia, do not undermine the high quality and substance of this document. All in all, it remains a great document, and indeed a jewel on the crown of the social teachings of the Church, and a great contribution to humankind grappling with the environmental crisis.

When *Laudato Si* was published, I was travelling. I bought a copy of *International New York Times* to find what comments it had on the encyclical. There was indeed a long write-up on the document. More than this write-up what impressed me and captured my attention was a letter to the editor at a corner of this newspaper. It is a comment from an atheist from Mexico, and I would like to cite that as the concluding words:

> As an atheist, I am moved by the brilliant statement from Pope Francis. This is the bravest, most insightful and honest statement I have heard from any international figure, and I only hope that his voice and conscience

will be heard loud and clearly by the self-serving corporate capitalists and greedy others who are willing to sacrifice any and all future good on behalf of short-term gain.[27]

Bibliography

Arogyaswamy, Bernard. "Energy Sustainability and Pope Francis' Encyclical on Care for Our Common Home: National Policies and Corporations as Change Agents." *Consilience* 18 (2017), 1-28.

Byrne, Brendan. "A Pauline Complement to Laudato Si." *Theological Studies* 77 (2016), 308-327.

Deane-Drummond, Celia., Bergmann, Sigurd., and Szerszynski, Bronislaw., eds. *Technofutures, Nature and the Sacred: Transdisciplinary Perspectives* (Farnham: Ashgate, 2015).

Dormor, Duncan, Harris, Alana. Eds. *Pope Francis. Evangelii Gaudium, and the Renewal of the Church* (New York, Mahwah, NJ: Paulist Press, 2017).

Doyle, Eric. "Ecology and the Canticle of Brother Sun." *New Blackfriars* 55 (652) (1974), 392-402.

Edwards, Denis. "Sublime Communion": The Theology of the Natural World in Laudato Si." *Theological Studies* 77 (2016), 377-391.

Faggioli, Massimo. *Pope Francis: Tradition in Tradition* (New York, Mahwah, NJ: Paulist Press, 2013).

Jiao, Zhang Xue. "How St Francis Influenced Pope Francis' Laudato Si." *Cross Currents* 66 (March 2016), 42-56.

Maldame, Jean-Michel. "L'encyclique de pape François sur l'écologie. Une clarification et une invitation à agir." *Bulletin de Litterature Ecclésiastique* 117 (2) (Apr-Jun 2016), 43-67.

Miller, Richard W. "Deep Responsibility for the Deep Future." *Theological Studies* 77 (2016), 436-465.

Montgomery, W. David. "The Flawed Economics of Laudato Si'." *The New Atlantis* 47 (2015), 31–44.

Northcott, Michael. "Planetary Moral Economy and Creaturely Redemption in Laudato Si." *Journal of Theological Studies* 77 (4) (2016), 886-904.

Prellwitz, John H. "Laudato Si, Communication Ethics, and the Common Good: Toward a Dialogic Meeting amid Environmental Crisis." *Journal of Moral Theology* 6 (1) (2017), 144-158.

Ryan, Robert. "Pope Francis, Theology of the Body, Ecology, and Encounter." *Journal of Moral Theology* 6 (1) (2017), 56-73.

Schlichten, David von. "Strange as This Weather Has Been. Teaching Laudato Si' and Ecofeminism." *Journal of Moral Theology* 6 (1) (2017), 159-168

Swidler, Leonard J. "A Call to All the Earth." *Journal of Ecumenical Studies* 51 (2016), 437-442.

Turner, Barrett. "*Pacis Progressio:* How Francis' Four New Principles Develop Catholic Social Teaching into Catholic Social Praxis." *Journal of Moral Theology* 6 (1) (2017), 112-129.

Vechour, Dominic. "The Creation World as a Sacrament: Patristic Moral Thinking and Laudato Si." *Christian Orient* 34 (3) (2015), 122-128.

Endnotes

[1] In response to this impression, numerous theologians, gathered at a conference in Vienna in October 2015 have shown the depth and novelty of Pope Francis' theology. The main papers of this conference are edited and published. See Kurt Appel- Jakob Helmut Deibl, eds, *Barmherzigkeit und zärtliche Liebe. Das theologische Programm von Papst Franziskus* (Freiburg: Herder 2016).

[2] *Laudato Si* proves that Pope Francis has his own theological orientation, which is refreshing. To view his theological position as simply a continuation of John Paul II and Benedict XVI (as do George Weigel, biographer of John Paul II, and Vittorio Messori, author of a well-know book of interviews with the then Cardinal Joseph Ratzinger), is a failure to acknowledge his original contributions. These authors are representatives of neo-conservative (neocon) Catholicism. George Weigel argues, "A change of papal 'administration' does not—indeed cannot—mean a change of Catholic 'views.' Doctrine, as the Church understands it, is not a matter of anyone's 'views,' but of settled understandings of the truth of things."As quoted by Mollie Wilson O'Reilly in https://www.commonwealmagazine.org. [accessed on 4 August, 2015]. All this is to downplay the new course pope Francis is setting in relating the Church to those critical questions of contemporary times such as the environmental crisis. There are others who, unwilling to accept his theology and his trenchant critique of neoliberal economy and free market, want to reduce *Laudato Si* into an encyclical of "climate change" or of "global warming"! As for the critique of Pope Francis' orientation by Vittorio Messori see his write-up in *Corriera della Sera,* (24 December, 2014) titled: "*I dubbi sulla sovlta del papa Francesco. Bergoglio é imprevidibile per il cattolico medio. Suscita un interesse vasto, ma quanto sincero?*" On the theologically imbued pastoral approach of Pope Francis, see Walter Kasper, *Pope Francis' Revolution of Tenderness and Love* (New York: Paulist Press, 2015).

[3] On the background of the social orientation of Pope Francis and the social principles that have guided him as Archbishop Bergoglio in Argentina, and then as Pope Francis, see Barrett Turner, "How Francis' Four New Principles

Develop Catholic Social Teaching into Catholic Social Praxis", *Journal of Moral Theology*, 6:1 (2017), 112-129.

[4] John Zizioulas, "A Comment on Pope Francis' Encyclical Laudato Si", *The Greek Orthodox Theology Review*, 60 (2015), 184-191.

[5] Jean-Michel Maldame, "L'encyclique de pape François sur l'écologie. Une clarification et une invitation à agir", *Bulletin de Litterature Ecclesiastique*, 117:2 (Apr – Jun 2016), 43-67.

[6] LS stands for *Laudto Si*.

[7] Jean-Michel Maldame notes, "L'Encyclique ouvre là une porte vers une manière autre d'habiter le monde", *art. cit.* at 66.

[8] Even then, some find that he has not gone into the question of evolution as presented by biological sciences and has confined himself to a theology of creation. See Celia Deane-Drummond, "Laudato Si and the Natural Sciences: An Assessment of Possibilities and Limits", *Theological Studies*, 77:2 (2016), 392- 415.

[9] See Felix Wilfred, "The Theological and Juridical Status of Episcopal Conferences", in Peter Fernando Episcopal Conferences and Collegiality (Madras: CBCI Commission for Clergy and Religious, 1989), 1-26.

The debate on the question continues even after the "Motu Proprio" Apostolic Letter *"Apostolos Suos"* (1998) by John Paul II.

[10] See Vimal Tirimanna, ed, *Sprouts of Theology from the Asian Soil. Collection of TAC and OTC documents 1987-2007* (Bangalore: Claretian Publications, 2007).

[11] Lynn White, "The Historical Roots of Our Ecological Crisis", *Science* (March 10, 1967), 189.

[12] René Descartes, *Discourse on Method and Meditations on First Philosophy*, translated by Elizabeth S. Haldane (Stilwell: Digireads.com Publishing, 2005), p. 28.

[13] Cf. Felix Wilfred, *Theology to Go Public* (Delhi: ISPCK, 2013).

[14] See www//spectator.org/articles/63160/*Laudato Si*>[Accessed on 3 August 2015]. It is quite strange that Cardinal Dolan of New York should think that the pope's critique of dominant economy in his speeches and in *Evangelii Gaiudium* (and subsequently in *Laudato Si)* does not apply to "virtuous capitalism" of America! See *National Catholic Reporter*, June 6, 2014.

[15] According to Brendan Byrne, the encyclical could have incorporated more of how St Paul interprets the creation story. See "A Pauline Complement to Laudato Si", *Theological Studies*, 77 (2016), 308-327.

[16] Hence his critique of utilitarianism that chimes in with technological logic, but devoid of wider moral concerns.

[17] The definition of the concept of *human ecology* is still very fluid and vague. Broadly speaking, it refers to the interaction of the humans with the environment as part of a larger organic whole. The humans do not stay in splendid isolation from the rest of nature, but impact on the environment and the environment is an important factor affecting human life and behaviour. *Cultural ecology* is the set of attitudes, values, and behaviour patterns this interaction produces in human beings in a particular geographical and environmental context. As a result, different cultures construct their own values and goals with reference to nature. The pope uses both these concepts (human ecology and cultural ecology) in *Laudato Si*. Ecology "calls for attention to local cultures when studying environmental problems, favouring a dialogue between scientific-technical language and the langue of the people" (LS 143).

[18] "Some circles maintain that current economics and technology will solve all environmental problems, and argue, in popular and non-technical terms, that the problems of global hunger and poverty will be resolved simply by market growth" (LS 109).

[19] See Eli McCarthy, "Breaking Out: The Expansiveness of Restorative Justice in Laudato Si", *Journal of Moral Theology*, 5:2 (2016), 66-80.

[20] *Gaudium et Spes* 69.

[21] Karl Marx, "Eleven Theses on Feuerbach", in Marx and Engels, eds, *On Religion* (Moscow: Progress Publishers, 1845), p. 64.

[22] Indeed, the pope says that the Eucharist "embraces and penetrates all creation" (LS 236). If so, it is proper that the concrete way it is structured and celebrated should reflect this truth. In restructuring worship with the elements of nature, Christian liturgy could learn a lot about worship from world religions and from Asian indigenous religious traditions. It needs to go beyond the very limited programme of "inculturation".

[23] Cf. K.L. Seshagiri Rao "The Five Great Elements (*pañchamahābhūta*). An Ecological Perspective", in Christopher Key Chapple and Mary Evelyn Tucker, eds, *Hinduism and Ecology* (Harvard: Harvard University Press, 2000), pp. 23-38.

[24] John A. Grim, *Indigenous Traditions and Ecology* (Harvard: Harvard University Press, 2001).

[25] For a feminist critique of the encyclical see David von Schlichten, "Strange as This Weather Has Been. Teaching Laudato Si and Ecofeminism", *Journal of Moral Theology*, 6:1 (2017), 159-168.

[26] The same is true also of Africa. Symbol of the engagement of women for ecology was the Kenyan Catholic woman Wangari Maathai, educated by Benedictine nuns. With her Green Belt Movement, she valiantly fought against political and economic forces. She mobilized women activists all over the country and succeeded in planting 30 million trees, and initiated no less than 900, 000 women in nurturing plants and trees. Her dedication and sacrifices for the cause of ecology was acknowledged by the award of Nobel Prize for Peace in 2004.

[27] *International New York Times,* 21 June 2015, Weekend edition.

CHAPTER 9

Consumerism as Play of Signs and the Project of Liberation

Some time ago, at a conference in Europe on the theme of life after death, one of the speakers lamented that close to 30% of Europeans believe in reincarnation. He wanted to lay the blame squarely on the influence of "Oriental religions" – meaning Hinduism and Buddhism. But then I intervened to remind the speaker that there may be other reasons for this belief. In the Indian tradition, release from rebirth is considered as attainment of heaven (*moksha*), and people pray to escape from the cycle of births - *samsāra*. Why do the westerners welcome reincarnation? It could be simply because the enticing goodies and cosy comforts the modern world offers are such that one life is too short to enjoy them all; one would like to be reborn again and again to be a perpetual consumer! That is when one could think of being closer to heaven. I am reminded of a saying, "heaven is for those who cannot find anything good on earth". Consumers find everything so good, that heaven becomes redundant.

Consumerism has spread like wildfire to every part of the globe, even in poor countries. During my visits to Manila in the Philippines, I have been struck by the Sunday masses celebrated at shopping malls with large crowds of people, ready to go on their shopping spree at the same spot immediately after the religious service. The sacred temple is located within the dream-world of most fashionable goods in a country that is battling against endemic poverty and deprivation of millions of people of bare necessities of life. Consumerism has permeated every department of life, and none of them is free of its influence.

The phenomenon of consumerism needs closer analysis. What I intend to do in this chapter is to highlight certain facets of consumerism which have gained little attention in the past. The second part of the chapter is devoted to discuss the kind of response consumerism calls for. The idea is not to introduce a set of moral principles and norms, nor propose glib cures. Resuscitating traditional moral values may sound like ethical babblings and may fall on deaf ears, given the general resistance to imposed morality. Alternatively, we could respond reflecting on the sustainability of the consumerist way of life – ecologically and socially - broaching on the issue of environment, justice, equality etc. I have done this elsewhere.[1] In this chapter, I would rather focus on the premises and dynamics at work in consumerism (Part I) and try to move beyond moralizing to look for alternative humanizing conceptions, worldviews, and practices that could come to terms with consumerism more adequately, (Part II).

Part I
The Premises and the Dynamics of Consumerism

A New Conception of Time

Generally, discussions have centred around two models of time – linear and cyclical. But the phenomenon of consumerism would not fit into either of these conceptions. Underlying consumerism is a view of time in which the past and future meet in the present. The present, hence, is not a flow from the past, much less the result of the past. The past and the present are not in a causal relationship. The present is rather the pregnant moment of possibilities which needs to be lived in full. Ideas of progress, development, moving towards future, do not chime with consumerism. Rather than continuity between the past and the present, there is disruption, discontinuity. The present is a moment of surprise and excitement where the unpredictable happens rather than something that happens as a result of previous deliberation and planning. In classical approach, the present has been viewed as precious opportunity to prepare for the 'hoped-for' future with dreams and promises. In consumerism, the future cannot claim the sacrifice of the present, very different from the traditional mindset of the masses of people in India. People built their future by renouncing to the present, postponing or delaying gratification to a future moment. Consumerism has, thus, effected erosion in this traditional conception of time and the building of future.

Representation as the Reality

To be able to grasp consumerism more fully, we need to reflect on the way reality and representation are interrelated. In general, in epistemological thought, reality precedes representation, and truth itself is seen as the correspondence between representation or cognitive process and reality. In the post structural worldview underlying consumerism, reality and representation are differently inter-related. Representation is the realm of concepts, signs, symbols, etc. These *signifiers* are thought to refer to something besides themselves to some *signified*. Poststructuralism has abolished the distinction between the signifier and the signified. We do not have any more signs or signifiers referring to something outside of them. All what we have are signifiers (empty signs) which are inter-related among themselves in a system of codes and symbols.[2] "Signs owe their capacity for signification not to the world but to their difference from each other in the network of signs that is the signifying system".[3] There is an overlap of reality with representation and the former ceases to exist. This is very crucial to be able to understand and interpret consumerism.[4]

In consumerism, what is important is not simply the use value, but the sign value. There is little difference in a consumer good in terms of its use value. For example, when we say that a car is meant for transportation, this use value is equal for everybody. But the coded sign value of a car makes a lot of difference, according to its type and price. In the consumer society, what we have is the play of signs.[5] Communication takes place through the play of signs. As Baudrillard notes,

> The circulation, purchase, sale, appropriation of differentiated goods and signs/objects today constitute our language, our code, the code by which the entire society *communicates* and converses. Such is the structure of

consumption, its language, by comparison with which individual needs and pleasures are merely speech effects.[6]

Signs as words in language have their meaning in relation to other words, signs. The difference a sign makes in this way could become endless and infinite. This explains why there can be no saturation for consumerism as signs of difference, distinction are endless.[7]

This collapse or overlap of reality and representation means there is no more such Kantian duality as *phenomenon* and *noumenon*. There is one single reality that is the *appearance*. Consumerism is in service of appearance and it seeks to embellish it. To put it concretely, consumerism is about packaging, but strangely that is all what we have; it is not that there is anything inside the wrapper! This resonates with what I noted regarding consumerism as a play of signs; play of wrappers. If a value is measured on the basis of the extent one is ready to sacrifice other values for it, then, appearance could be said as the supreme value, and that is why commodities in their sign value is so very important to people. One's consumer practice becomes symbolic capital, manifesting his/her honour, prestige and influence. Particularly when people practice hyper-visible consumerism or "*conspicuous consumption*"[8] with so much extravaganza as to be observed in the high class Indian weddings, parties of the corporates, etc., they enter into the imaginary feudal world, its pomp and pageantry, which all add to their symbolic capital. For example, a wedding of a Kerala NRI billionaire – Ravi Pillai - held in Kollam cost 25 crores with many unmistakable signs of opulence. Imagine, the tent for wedding was spread out to 4.25 lakh square feet to accommodate 40,000 guests![9]

From Use and Exchange Value to Sign-Value

From a global perspective what marks off the present age from the times of industrialization is the shift *from production to consumption*. At that age, the centre of attention was the productive forces, means of production, and the workers as agents of production. However, at this present age of late capitalism, and with the advent of postmodernism, the attention is focused on consumption and all that has to do with it. In the context of a new approach to commodities, the Marxist distinction of use value and exchange value has undergone a transformation. In the present-day culture of consumerism, what seems to dominate is the *sign value* of commodity, almost eclipsing the other two values.

To illustrate what is symbolic value, let me refer to the use of mitre and crosier by the bishops in the Christian Churches. A bishop does not use a mitre to protect himself from rain and sun; nor does he use the sceptre as a walking stick (unless the bishop continues to grow so old that he needs one!). No, these have symbolic value, and not use value or exchange value. The wearing of mitre and carrying of sceptre symbolize power and authority, and these as distinguishing symbols mark them off from the rest of the clergy and the faithful. To change the image, a car, as we noted, is a means of transportation, which is its use value, but whether a person uses a Nano, Indica, Mercedes, Audi or BMW makes a lot of difference in terms of the symbolic value they have. We could make easily a hierarchy of cars and the coded value they represent in terms of status and social identity and recognition.

The problem with Marxist analysis of commodity is that it leaves out the dimension of sign and symbolic value, and consequently fails to understand commodity as *communication*, especially when commodities are exchanged for their sign-value in society. These signs seem to have a life of their own and the whole society seems to function in terms of these exchanges of signs which also represent a hierarchy of distinctions. To illustrate with an ordinary example, clothes serve to cover nakedness and protect us from the environment cold and hot. In cold regions, people tend to wear thick and tight dresses and in hot climates the dress becomes thin and loose. But, wearing dress does not stop there. To clothes are added a sign or symbolic value. When a person uses branded clothes or latest fashion designs, he or she communicates something very important; it shows the person's social and economic standing, and serves as a mark of distinction, a difference. Fashion is a language.[10] The signs of this language are exhibited in public for social recognition and distinct identity. In short, consumer goods are not a source to fulfil needs, but a means in service of social distinctions.[11]

The Self as Commodity

The self is not a pre-existent reality, but something configured constantly and moulded through our freedom and choices.[12] Looking for a hidden self is as real as searching to find something inside the onion. Exercise of freedom creates various layers of the self. Viewed this way, the consumer activity people engage in and their choices make them what they are. To put it in simple terms, "Tell me what you buy, I will tell you who you are".

Individuation and functional specialization are two important features of modernity. Analysing consumerism from this perspective, we could observe how consumer goods help the process of individuation, namely the creation of a unique profile of the self and self-identity. Consumerism, at the same time, exhibits ambivalence. On the one hand, the object of consumption plays a symbolic role, and helps to construct an identity of the self in differentiation. On the other hand, the "self" also gets lost. The subject with his or her agency also now becomes an object like other objects. The system of signs of which the consumer society is constructed, transforms the subject into a commodity. The commodification of the self as a presentable good, leads to various strategies for self-promotion. The transformation of the self as appealing leads people to all kinds of measures that enhance the body. The modern systems from entertainment to education are based on commodification of the self. Whether one applies for an academic position, or seeks one's fortune with film industry, the system forces a person to turn himself/herself into a commodity for others. Social media helps as an important means for self-commodification.

There is an obsessive makeover culture with expansion of beauty parlours, increasing sales of cosmetics, cosmetic surgeries, fashion shows, weight loss recipes, etc., – all on the increase worldwide and also in India. As the *Economist* reports, "worldwide, the cosmetics market (including cleansers and skin creams as well as make-up) grew by 3.6% to € 181 billion ($ 240 billion) in 2014; it is expected to double over the next 10-15 years".[13] The body is so much part of the self that it needs to be continuously remade and remodelled in the consumerist culture, so that it turns out to be culturally and socially valuable. This culture is promoted by movies, TV programmes, advertisements, fashion magazines, and by projection of celebrities of the entertainment field. Driven by all these factors, there is a general craving to appear young and look good to which consumerism responds with endless goods and services. Much of the self-esteem depends today on these factors of appearance and looks. This is especially in the case of women in the patriarchal society where they are made to be perpetually in beauty contest. As it is, frantic quest to edit the body, so to say, has to do with their success in life.

Commodification of Human Relationships

One of the worst consequences of consumerism is in the field of human relationships. Human relationships are recast in the mould of market operating with its logic of supply and demand. Converting human relationships in the image of the market empties them of their depth and trivializes their beauty. In the consumer society, human bonds, including marriage, are for the time being. Any permanent commitment and loyalty are eschewed. I am reminded of an anecdote about the famous British actress Elizabeth Taylor who, when married for the eighth time, told her new husband, "Darling, this is also for a brief time!" The speed with which commodities are acquired, then dumped as obsolescent only to be replaced by new ones, become also the new commodity-grammar, that determine human bonds.

Consumerism – Reinforcement of Casteism

At the global level, consumerism has functioned as a leveller in one sense. For, the goods and services which were once the privilege of the well-to-do and those on the upper echelons of the society are accessible to large masses of people today. In a society of scarcity, wearing silk was a mark of distinction and sign of belonging to nobility. Today, the consumer goods and services are available across the spectrum of various traditional social classes. Yes, consumerism has contributed to eliminate to a large extent class distinctions. Could we say this of caste distinctions? Instead of being a leveller, consumerism seems to have become a new vehicle to reinforce the traditional distinctions and differences. In the Indian tradition, the caste structure was maintained by clear demarcation of symbols and rituals. No one could dare to arrogate the symbols or symbolic roles of the higher castes. Duly elected Dalit panchayat presidents cannot sit peacefully in his or her chair, for it is seen as a provocation by the upper castes and as usurpation of their symbol of local power.[14] To prevent this, the upper castes use many tactics of control and play proxy politics.

As we saw, consumerism is a matter of status, acceptance, and exhibition of power. When it is practiced in a traditional society which is organized around caste-structure, it acquires further significance and new contours. If caste is like the proverbial cat that has nine lives, consumerism in Indian society is a dazzling reincarnation of caste and it is a glorification of hierarchy and social standing. Due to new forces, some aspects of caste may get weakened and even get threatened; but consumerism serves to reinforce it. The consumer power overlaps with caste-position. Thanks to the social and cultural capital, the upper castes also are the ones at the higher end of the consumer society. Those at the bottom of the casteist society, poor and struggling for their basic survival needs, are simply out of the consumer hierarchy; they do not count, and are the outcastes of the consumer society. In this connection, we may recall here that in recent times there was a raging controversy on dietary consumption - eating cow-meat - and unfortunately not a few, incidents of violence based on this issue, as for example, the lynching of a Muslim in Dadri.[15]

There is more to it than what meets the eye. The issue of meat consumption is ultimately about ritual purity and pollution. Those who consume meat are the polluted ones and the vegetarians are the pure, and the unpolluted. There is also a hierarchy here – those who eat other meats are less polluted whereas those who eat cow meet are the ritually impure and most polluted. There is a myth created by the upper castes that the majority of Indians are vegetarians. It is a farce. According to a reliable survey, only 31% of Indians are vegetarians, and has to do mostly with upper castes. When it comes to Southern states, surprisingly, the percentage is much lower – as low as 2% in Kerala; 4% in (old) Andhra Pradesh, 8% in Tamilnadu; 8% in Orissa 8% and 3% in Bengal.[16] What does this mean? The majority of Indians are consumers of meat, and in not few instances, meat-eating is a necessity for survival. Without meat, millions of poor will suffer famine.

What is attempted today is to impose the dietary habits of the high castes on the rest of the society, showing again the underlying caste-chemistry in the issue of food-consumption. Under the influence of globalisation, consumerism in the area of food is getting increasingly diversified with wide variety of choices, especially in the cities. And yet, the caste-based purity pollution continues. Meat-eating is looked down upon, and vegetarian purism is extolled. The *śāstras* have laid down a whole system of dietary and culinary practices and laws governing food consumption. I had a colleague in the University of Madras who was so strict with dietary regulations and purity of food, that for fear of being polluted, he would cook for himself whenever he was forced to travel. No wonder his trips were very short!

Part II: Responding to Consumerism

There have been many critical voices – both in the East and in the West – on consumerism and consumer way of life. Most common critiques spring from an opposition of the material to the spiritual and the otherworldly, and this is to be observed frequently in the response of religions. This orientation was represented in the Christian tradition by the Puritans and Quakers of the past, and by many fundamentalist religious groups of present times. But in most cases, critique derives from ethical considerations which view and judge consumerism in terms of *good* and *evil*, and tries to give ethical prescriptions against consumerism.

Further, in the 1960's there was a scathing critique of mass society and industrialization, and generally against the establishment.[17] It took the form of a counter-culture movement, which meant resisting and protesting by unconventional means, as could be seen in the "hippie" and "beatle" subculture of that era. It found expression in arts, in music, film, attitude to sex, etc. George Romero was a trenchant critique of consumerism as it is bound up with racism (practiced against Afro-Americans) and marginalization of the weaker ones in the society. He was able to weave the critique of consumerism and racism in his classical films such as Night of the Living Dead (1968) and Dawn of the Dead (1978), Land of the Dead (2005). Other criticisms are voiced from the perspective of economy, common good, justice, social equity, and the environment.[18]

Ecological Movements and a New Vision

One of the most significant and fast spreading critique of consumerism stems from the ecological movements. It was Protagoras, the Greek sophist, who said that human being is the measure (*metron*) of all things. The anthropocentrism which developed in the West through the period of Renaissance, Enlightenment and industrialization to late capitalism of today is firmly rooted in the centrality of the humans who continue to exploit nature and its resources. The ecological crisis, as for example, the dangers posed by the warming of the earth has brought about the realisation that there are "limits to growth".[19] It is a clear message that the present form of consumer life is a course that will eventually bring about destruction of humanity and nature. Environmental movements are the ones today strongly critical of consumerism and its impact. They call for restraint on profligate and luxuriant way of life. The ecological summit in Paris is all about containment and restraint so as to ensure a happy life for all human beings, and ensure a sustainable future for planet earth.[20]

I think if the critique on consumerism were to be based only on the fear of survival, it may not turn out to be effective. There is much less chance of succeeding unless the critique is founded on a different vision of reality, and inspired by new convictions leading to alternative practices. If there is the recognition that it is also part of our self and being, then there is the possibility of restraint on the use of nature and the emergence of a a view of it as a value in itself.[21] The ecological movement needs to be also strengthened by a way of life that is characterized by self-restraint or control, and indeed a construction of the self in new terms. We shall consider some of these aspects in the following pages.

Cultural Resources

What we need today is to explore the cultural resources that could help challenge the increasing forms of consumerist way of life. This proposal is premised on the fact that there is an inextricable bond between human development and culture. Culture is not simply a means for development. A better and happy life for individuals and community is not only a matter of economic growth, but also a matter of culture.[22] In consumerism, there is a standardization of happiness linked to instant gratification.

We need to recognize the fact that there is a plurality of conceptions on what is happiness. It is often bound up with culture, geography, and environment. Among many people, happiness is in community, in sharing with others, and being in solidarity. This we find, for example, in many tribal societies.[23] Their culture based on such values tend to foster nature and its flourishing as it is important for their life and sustenance as a community. Challenging consumerism means to foreground many indigenous cultural forms and ways of life that are supportive of human solidarity and sustainability of the environment. With the planetary crisis today affecting deeply humankind and nature, a plurality of ways of life springing from cultures promises hope to get out of this murky situation. The traditional Indian culture in harmony with nature is epitomized in the frugal way of life pursued by Gandhi.

> Gandhi's entire life functioned much like an ecosystem. This is one life in which every minute act, emotion, or thought was not without its place: the brevity of Gandhi's enormous writings, his small meals of nuts and fruits, his morning ablutions and everyday bodily practices, his periodic observances of silence, his morning walks, his cultivation of the small as much as of the big, his abhorrence of waste, his resort to fasting – all these point to the manner in which the symphony was orchestrated.[24]

Moral policing as being done by the fundamentalist forces in the name of culture is not really the proper response to consumerism. Self-restraint way of life that is respectful of nature as reflected in the life of Gandhi would be the kind of response required in the face of increasing consumerism in the country.

The Illusory Self and Perpetual Unhappiness

It is in the very logic of consumerism and in the interest of its own survival that people are kept unhappy. Strange though it may sound, this is how consumerism functions. Satisfied consumption is an oxymoron. Perpetual dissatisfaction with what is, and aspiration towards what could be is that which moves the consumer. To put it differently, consumerism thrives on perpetual unhappiness, and on the discontentment of the consumer whom it goads with promises of new commodities. The absence of consumer aspiration will spell stagnation of economy. The fulfilment of needs and desires do not end with certain commodities and services. There is the thirst to look for something more satisfying, something that is in keeping with the new trends, which will ensure that one is not left behind. Further, the anxiety to keep up with the Joneses, and the sense of insecurity of being excluded, or left behind function as the motor that propels new desires and acquisition of new commodities endlessly with no saturation point.

To be able to understand this phenomenon, we need to be aware of a paradigm shift consumerism represents. In earlier times, the decisions and choices were based on the consideration whether something was *allowed* or *not allowed*. The freedom consumerism has brought about, resists such binary which seems to constrain the freedom of the consumer with an external normativity. Consumerism has replaced this traditional binary, with a new one, namely what is *possible* and what is *impossible*. There is the drive and ambition to be successful and explore all that is possible without restraint, and when one is faced with something impossible, frustration sets in. How do we respond to this?

The Self in Its Humanizing Potentials

The floods that ravaged the city of Chennai in December 2015, and more recently Kerala exhibited two sides of the human – its capacity for the loftiest and the noblest, and also its inclination to evil, deceit and perversity. People risked their lives to save others from inundated homes and from roof tops, and they carried succour to those desperately needed it. On the other hand, there were people who looted houses and pilfered relief materials and sold them for a gain. Given these two polar pulls in the human, it is important to create an environment where the positive and outreaching properties of the human flourish and bear fruit. But the point is that the present market-driven consumerism is creating an atmosphere that makes people centripetal, egoistic, and concerned about the fulfilment of their needs and desires.

The needs of others and the rhythm of nature call for another model of economy and development which will bring out the humanizing potential in the hearts and minds of people, and also will blend harmoniously with nature and planet earth. Let me elaborate the point further. Morality and ethics are not a matter of principles and norms. There is something like a pre-reflexive morality which is spontaneous and not premeditated and planned. The times of crisis are when we see this morality in operation. I find the best illustration of the pre-reflexive morality in the analogy of the Chinese sage Mencius to which I alluded in an earlier chapter in a different context.[25] As we noted, he speaks of a child which is on the verge of falling into the well. Someone snatches the child and saves it. And this person did not think neither of the gratitude of the parents nor of the praise of the community for his action. There is some prompting from within that the child should not die which impels the person to reach out and save it.

Consumerism allows little room for such spontaneous practices. For, in our consumer world, every commodity has a price; so does, every service. The consideration of reward and gain for oneself inhibits people from involving themselves for the wellbeing of others, and of the community. It is enough to reflect how some important areas of life like health care and education were pre-eminently fields of service. These fields evoked the feeling of service and solidarity, and money was never a major consideration. Think how the whole scenario has changed under consumerism. Healthcare and education have been transformed into commodities or consumer goods. As a result, there are star hospitals and premier educational institutions available to wealthy consumers. The state itself has been infected by the consumer environment, and does not consider that it is obliged to provide public health service and general education. Conveniently it leaves these important service sectors to private providers who turn them into fields of plunder and exploitation.

Consumerism as *Artha* and *Kāma*?

Does critique of consumerism mean negation of and alienation from the material base of life? That does not seem to be the case in the Indian classical tradition, which does speak of the materiality of the world and affirms it. In *artha* we have the pursuit of wealth and in *kāma* the sensual pleasure. These are precisely what are at work in consumerism. Now, neither *artha* nor *kāma* are objects of condemnation; rather they are integral parts of life in fullness. *Kāma* was the core of the philosophy of tantrism. *Kāma* also found place in the art of sacred temples as in the world renowned erotic sculptures of Khajuraho temple in Madhyapradesh.[26] Hence, neither *artha* nor *kāma* are to be spurned or suppressed through a normative or negative ethics of rejection and avoidance. Rather, the Indic tradition has insisted relentlessly that the pursuit of pleasure needs to be self-regulated and directed to higher ends. Otherwise, a person will become like a rudderless ship. People need to be guided by *dharma* which again is not a set of rules and norms. Dharma is a matter of practices which form, shape, and mould the self; it is a path on which we need to walk.[27] Without dharma guiding *artha* and *kāma*, they could easily become destructive forces.

Whereas karmic action with its desire for fruits and consequences produce bondage, *niṣkāma karma* (actions without desire for their fruits and consequences) lead to *moksha* – supreme bliss and happiness without end. Consumerism is a process of unfulfilled happiness; it is an endless cycle. Like Sisyphus of the Greek myth, one imagines to climb to the top of the hill with all the bursting energy of one's desires, but the moment it appears the peak of happiness is reached, in no time one is brought down to the abyss of unhappiness. *Niṣkāma karma* brings two results: it pushes us towards the realm of bliss and happiness; it makes the path towards the other a genuine engagement without expectations. *Niṣkāma karma* is often viewed as Indian experience of the Kantian categorical imperative. But in reality, with *niṣkāma karma,* the accent is not on *duty* (as in the case of categorical imperative) but on the *non-attachment* to the fruits of action.

The Dialectics of Expansion and Contraction

As we noted, the right ordering of cosmos, human societies, and the self is paradigmatically represented by the concept of *dharma*. It is not a static order, but more a dynamic process in which at the cosmic level, there is the expansion (modern big bang theory) and contraction, and at the level of the human, there is the dialectic between engagement (*pravṛittidharma*) and withdrawal (*nivṛittidharma*). If consumerism represents the expansion and engagement with senses into the world of *artha* and *kāma*, these are really what they are through a dialectic of negation and withdrawal or renunciation. Engagement and renunciation are two spheres of dharma to be practiced at every stage of life. The contraction or withdrawal is not imposed, but integral part of the fashioning of the self. Mastery of the self is an important component of dharma. A happy life, as experience demonstrates, is not through practices of consumerism, which, as we noted, leaves people unfulfilled and in perpetual unhappiness. This is not to say that one should not seek to fulfil one's needs and desires. The point is that a good life is lived when the self is moulded and transformed through dharma and guided by it both in engagement and in renunciation. At this level, dharma is truly the path to *moksha* - which is both liberation from bondage and ultimate happiness.

Bondage – Freedom and Consumerism

Senses are indispensable parts of human self, and the pleasures of senses are legitimate and lawful. Any morality or ethics that advocates suppression of senses will look at consumerism from an outdated moralist perspective. What is really advocated in Christian, Hindu and Buddhist spiritual traditions is a check on the excesses in the fulfilment of the desires of the senses. Central to Buddhism, for example, is the middle path (*madhyama-pratipadā*) – so central that it has become an alternative name for Buddhism.[28] Middle path is that which avoids extremes both sides and confers greatest richness to human existence and flourishing; it frees life from suffering, because of the balance and equilibrium it represents.[29] Balance and harmony are something important for sustaining all life, including the human and the environmental. The Christian advocacy of temperance is not a negation of senses. It only makes sure that the pleasures of senses do not end up harming the self, the other, the community, and nature. The absence of middle path and temperance in consumerism can make it a bondage. This enslavement and bondage are to be shunned.[30]

Practices of Self-fashioning

We noted how consumer practices go to configure the ego, the self, and its identity. It is a continuous process. But as history and experience show, there are practices of a different kind which shape the ego but in another way. In India and in many civilizations of the world, there have been practices which were advocated for self-mastery, control, restraint, etc. Examples of ascetic tradition disciplining the body and mind in India are well known to us. The Indian practices for mindfulness and single-mindedness (*ekāgratā*) are springboards for enlightenment. Among the ancient Greeks, we could refer to the stoics, and to Plato himself who illustrated the fashioning of the self with the allegory of the chariot – a classic in the western tradition. He imparted the necessity of the mastery of the self amidst divergent pulls, represented by two types of horses harnessed to a chariot.[31]

Buddhism would see in the craving (*trishṇā*) for consumer goods and clinging to them a fallacy of an illusory self, a bondage from which a person needs to be liberated. The way for right kind of self-fashioning is to follow the Eightfold Path to Enlightenment.[32] The mastery of the self is to be distinguished from world-denying ascetic practices which are to be found in all world religions. The former does not oppose materiality but helps to navigate through it without being drowned. The practice of temperance in Christian tradition would resonate with practices for self-control and mastery.

Self-restraint is not a virtue of the ascetics; it is something essential for the growth of the individual, and communities, and humanity at large. In fact, as we noted earlier, for Sigmund Freud, deterrence and sublimation underlie the birth of civilizations. Freud said that without social cohesion and without limits to the freedom of individuals, there can be no civilization.[33] It is built on the principle of restraint. Now, this restraint can be heteronomous when it comes from out, or autonomous, when it is self-generated. The desire, thirst, for consumption driven by market forces need to be counterbalanced by the principles of deterrence and moderation for the sake of common good. This regulation has also a therapeutic effect on the self.

Consumerism, the Realm of Gift and Non-Instrumental Reason

Consumerism is a centripetal movement. What is sought is the self, its needs, fulfilment of its desires, identity, social standing, etc. This centripetal movement requires to be balanced by a *centrifugal movement*. The category of "gift" can enlighten us on this point.[34] Gift is a movement towards the other, including the nature. Gift is where an exchange takes place. In some practices of wedding, as it happens in several parts of Tamilnadu, what is given as gift – money or articles - is recorded carefully and even announced publicly. The recording is important because the family which received the gift needs to reciprocate in the same measure at a future wedding function in the family of the donor. But this is no real gift; it is rather a commerce – *do ut des* (I give you, so that you may give back).

Gifts could be given for various reasons – out of fear, for ostentation or to affirm one's social status like the donation of kings in the past, or to gain a favour as in the case of bribes. Real gift (*danā*) is when no reciprocity and no calculations are involved. Pure gift takes place when it is a sign of sharing of oneself and a sign of love, esteem, and recognition of the other. Any real gift is an end in itself and not in view of something else. Indian tradition presents King Śibi, Karṇa, Vikramāditya and Hariśchandra as icons of generosity who gave to the extent of great personal sacrifice without expecting anything in return. That reminds us of the words of Jesus, "do not let your left hand know what your right hand is doing" (Mt 6:3).

The practice of non-reciprocal gift can transform men and women from the realm of obsessive and neurotic consumerism for satisfaction, comfort, and status, and lead them to the realm of ends. It is a humanizing act. Giving is not a means but an end in itself like the offering of the widow in the temple, whom Jesus praises. "Truly I tell you, this poor widow has put in more than all of them; for they all contributed out of their abundance, but she out of her poverty put in all the living she had" (Lk 21:3-4).

Consumerism is simply on another trajectory. It functions with the logic of instrumental reason, namely the human subject is driven by the goal its actions and choices bring about. It is the same pattern at work in human relationships. The other becomes a commodity with a price, the object of one's desires for the ends the subject determines for itself. It is very evident in the case of women. Patriarchal mindset and attitude see women as a commodity, as an object for use, and not a person with dignity and rights who cannot be instrumentalized for one's ends. But there are realms which defy this logic of instrumentality with which consumerism is vested. Experience of gift-giving, friendship, art, etc., opens up a new horizon of non-instrumentality. Their ultimate purpose is enjoyment. These represent a realm where realities are ends in themselves. Relating oneself to these realms of ends transforms the self and liberates it. Here is at work a centrifugal movement.

Recognition and cultivation of this non-instrumental approach to life could be a great source of power in bringing about a necessary balance and equilibrium. I see ethics as the art of combining harmoniously and judiciously the instrumental and the non-instrumental in life. The non-instrumental reality is first and foremost represented by human persons who are an end in themselves and never to be viewed or treated as means. The non-instrumental realities represented by gift, friendship, art, etc., could bring about certain fashioning of the self. In the experience of friendship, gift and art, there is a non-reciprocity. If they were to be reciprocated, they could easily fall into instrumental rationality, and utilitarian calculus. The movement from consumer to donor, from a self-seeking individual to a caring person is radically a humanizing process which makes ethical injunctions and normativity redundant.

Political Consumerism

Political consumerism could be an important movement towards liberation and the struggle for justice and equity. It presupposes that the consumers are active subjects and not simply helpless victims who are manipulated by the market and its functioning. Political consumerism underlines the active role consumers could play in determining politics, provided they are inspired by deep humanism and thirst for justice, equality and concern for environment. If consumerism is an expression of late capitalism, then response to it cannot be only at the level of individual persons. The very structure and system of needs are to be addressed. The process of production and distribution could be challenged by the consumers for its gross violation of human dignity and rights at the level of supply, production, and marketing. Boycotting those products and goods that are results of exploitation and violation of human rights (for example child labour, unjust wages, etc.,) or harmful to environment, will hit the heart of the market which is bent on profiting at all costs, and enlarging of consumer base.[35] Here consumerism becomes political and the consumers take responsibility for social justice.[36]

Conclusion

The concept of "sign" helped us to analyse the phenomenon of consumerism more sharply. Unfortunately, this sign aspect has been generally neglected or marginalised. What is at stake is sign or symbolic value with which every commodity is inscribed.

What I have tried to argue is that traditional ethics based on good and evil, virtue and vice, duty and rights, ends and means – all these may not come to terms with the world of expanding consumerism. Nor is it a matter of replacing one ethics with a different one. Rather, we need to rely on the substantial critique to consumerism which the ecological movements have brought in. They call for an alternative economy and way of life, and reflect a different vision of the self, the humans and nature. These three realities are interwoven. Ethics is implied here as the path we take to bring harmony and balance into these realities, rather than a system of principles. It is to this kind of ethics, theology needs to relate itself today drawing inspiration from the Gospels.

The continuous stream of consumption leaves in the consciousness of individuals and the community layers of sediments which form new cultural bedrock of values, attitudes, modes of behaviour, etc. The sediments of a new globalised subculture - consumer way of life - needs to come in encounter with alternative visions, values and practices which will be transforming the self and the environment. Moving ahead towards these goals could be assisted by the plurality of cultural resources of peoples, which have been neglected and set aside in the march of a standardized pattern of life, needs, and desires.

The perpetual unhappiness consumerism creates could be encountered by constructing a new identity of the self and by a way of life that is restrained, balanced, and in harmony with nature and the environment.

These resources are amply provided both in the eastern and western traditions. Many practices are associated with control and mastery of the self – a self that is not bent on itself (*homo curvatus in se*) but is in a movement of outreach towards others and the wellbeing of nature. Such centrifugal movement could be sustained further by non-instrumental engagement such as offering of non-reciprocal gift, fostering of genuine friendship, and cultivation of art. They represent in today's world a true spiritual and mystical approach – indeed a "mysticism of open eyes" – which is not the preserve of religions but is accessible to anyone who is seriously engaged for the transformation of the self, the world, and committed to the sustainability of planet earth.

Bibliography

Bailey, Matthew. "Memory, Place and the Mall: George Romero on Consumerism." *Studies in Popular Culture* 35 (2) (2013), 95-110.

Barnhill, David Landis. "Good Work: An Engaged Buddhist Response to the Dilemmas of Consumerism." *Buddhist-Christian Studies* 24 (2004), 55-63.

Bauman, Zygmunt. *Consuming Life* (Cambridge: Polity Press, 2007).

Bauman, Zygmunt. *Does Ethics Have a Chance in a World of Consumers?* (Cambridge MA: Harvard University Press, 2008).

Beck, Ulrich. *Risk Society: Towards a New Modernity* (London; Thousand Oaks, Delhi: Sage Publications, 1992).

Bedford, Tracey Murray. *Ethical Consumerism: Everyday Negotiations in the Construction of an Ethical Self* (London: University College, Doctoral Thesis 1999).

Bhogal, Anoop. *Goddesses of Consumerism. An Interpretivist Study of Young Consumers in Contemporary India* (Leicester: Doctoral Thesis, University of Leicester, 2011).

Davis, Mark. *Freedom and Consumerism: A Critique of Zygmunt Bauman's Sociology* (London and New York: Routledge, 2017).

Himes, K. R. "Consumerism and Christian Ethics." *Theological Studies* 68 (1) (2007),132-53.

Kaza, Stephanie. "Overcoming the Grip of Consumerism." *Buddhist-Christian Studies* 20 (2000), 23-42.

Khalikova, Venera R. "The Ayurveda of Baba Ramdev: Biomoral Consumerism, National Duty and the Biopolitics of 'Homegrown' Medicine in India." *South Asia: Journal of South Asian Studies* 40 (2017),105-22.

Landsman, Mark. *Dictatorship and Demand: The Politics of Consumerism in East Germany* Harvard Historical Studies 147 (Cambridge, Mass.; London: Harvard University Press, 2005).

Micheletti, M., Føllesdal, Andreas, and Stolle, Dietlind., eds. *Politics, Products, and Markets: Exploring Political Consumerism Past and Present* (N.J.; London: New Brunswick, 2003).

Micheletti, Michele, and Stolle, Dietlind. "Sustainable Citizenship and the New Politics of Consumption." *The Annals of the American Academy of Political and Social Science* 644 (2012), 88-120.

Miles, Steven. *Consumerism: As a Way of Life* (London, Thousand Oaks, Calif.: Sage Publications, 2006).

Naomi Klein, *No Logo* (London: Flamingo, 2000).

Neilson, Lisa A., and Pamela Paxton. "Social Capital and Political Consumerism: A Multilevel Analysis." *Social Problems* 57(1) (2010), 5-24.

Reimer, David J. "Biblical Perspectives on Consumerism." *The Scottish Bulletin of Evangelical Theology* 35 (2017), 4-18.

Schor, Juliet. "Combating Consumerism and Capitalism: A Decade of "No Logo"." *Women's Studies Quarterly* 38 (3/4) (2010), 299-301.

Sooryamoorthy, R. "Understanding Consumerism in Kerala." *Social Action* 57 (1) (2007),1-13.

Stolle, Dietlind, Marc Hooghe, and Michele Micheletti. "Politics in the Supermarket: Political Consumerism as a Form of Political Participation." *International Political Science Review / Revue Internationale de Science Politique* 26 (3) (2005), 245-69.

Thomas, Lyn., ed. *Consumption and Public Life* (Basingstoke: Palgrave Macmillan, 2011).

Verma, Pavan K. *The Great Indian Middle Class* (Delhi: Penguin Books, 2007).

Verma, Y. S, and Sharma, Chandrakant. *Consumerism in India* (Delhi: Anamika Prakashan, 1994).

Endnotes

[1] Cf. Felix Wilfred, *The Sling of Utopia. Struggles for a Different Society* (Delhi: ISPCK, 2005). See chapter 11: "Consumerism in a Society of Negations. The Anatomy of a Phenomenon and Its Ethical Implication", pp. 279-306.

[2] Cf. John Sturrock, *Structuralism* (London: Fontana Press, 1993), especially, pp. 136-176; see also Steven Connor, ed, *Postmodernism* (Cambridge: Cambridge University Press, 2004); Jacques Derrida, *Of Grammatology*, tr., Gayatri Chakravorty Spivak (Baltimore: Johns Hopkins University Press; 1997); Jacques Derrida, *Speech and Phenomena and Other Essays on Husserl's Theory of Signs*, tr., David B. Allison (Evanston, IL: Northwestern University Press, 1973).

[3] Peter Childs, *Modernism: The New Critical Idiom* (London: Routledge, 2000); (special Indian edition 2013), p. 71.

[4] If we analyse the phenomenon of consumerism through modern linguistics and semiotics, we will be able to understand its working. While the traditional linguistics concentrates on the genealogy of words and grammar (diachronic approach), modern linguistics has tried to follow a synchronic approach which ties together language with the world and society. The world is not simply represented by language, rather language becomes that through which we have access to the world. It is truer to say that language constructs our world, than language represents the world. To put it differently, given the fact that we are in a play of symbols, in consumerism we do not look for use-value, as we are not to look for meaning in language, but simply its form or its value as signifier in an infinite network of self-differentiating signs.

[5] This aspect is so important that I have highlighted this in the title itself of this chapter.

[6] Jean Baudrillard, *The Consumer Society: Myths and Structures* (London: Sage, 1998), pp. 79-80; see also ID. *Simulations* tr., Paul Foss, Paul Patton, and Philip Beitchman (New York: Semiotext, 1983); see also Guy Debord, *The Society of the Spectacle,* tr., Donald Nicholson-Smith (New York: Zone Books, 2002).

[7] For a highly readable narrative and analysis of consumerism, see Oliver James, *Affluenza* (London: Vermilion, 2007).

[8] The expression was used for the first time by Thorstein Veblen in 19th century. See Thorstein Veblen, *The Theory of the Leisure Class: An Economic Study in the Evolution of Institutions* (New York: Macmillan, 1899); New edition (1994).

[9] See *Outlook* (December 14, 2015), 70-71.

[10] Cf. Roland Barthes, *The Language of Fashion* (London & New York: Bloomsbury, 2005); see also Susan Sontag, ed, *A Roland Barthes Reader* (London: Vintage, 1993); Graham Allen, *Roland Barthes* (London & New York: Routledge, 2003).

[11] This dynamics in consumerism explains also the creation of waste. It is but a logical sequence to consumerism. Things are not made to last as in former times, but only to be discarded and replaced by something new and different. This is the result of "hurried life". Because of the sign value of objects, things are to be discarded, independent of their use-value, so that with new consumer goods, the sign-value and symbolic capital are heightened further to a new level. This is indeed a "planned obsolescence" manipulated by the market and the media. See Zygmunt Bauman, *Consuming Life* (Cambridge: Polity Press, 2007); ID., *Does Ethics Have a Chance in a World of Consumers?* (Cambridge MA: Harvard University Press, 2008). For an anthropological view of consumption, see Grant David McCracken, *Culture and Consumption: New Approaches to the*

Symbolic Character of Consumer Goods and Activities (Bloomington: Indiana University Press 1990)

[12] Cf. Hubert L. Dreyfus and Paul Rabinow, *Michel Foucault: Beyond Structuralism and Hermeneutics*, 2nd ed. (Chicago: Chicago University Press, 1983), especially the interview with M. Foucault, 252 ff (Foucault's interpretative analytic of Ethics).

[13] *The Economist* (December 5-11, 2015), 61.

[14] See a report on this situation in *The Hindu* (February 25, 2010). See also S.N. Chaudhary, *Dalit and Tribal Leadership in Panchayats* (New Delhi: Concept Publishing Co., 2004).

[15] See *Frontline* (Hindutva's Holy Terror), October 30, 2015.

[16] See *The Hindu-CNN-IBN* survey, the results of which was published in *The Hindu* (August 14, 2006). India is the largest exporter of beef in the world.

[17] The theoretical perspectives for this counterculture movement were provided by thinkers of the Frankfurt School of critical theory represented by Max Horkheimer, Theodore Adorno, Herbert Marcuse, and others who advocated a critical appropriation of modernity, especially after the horrendous experiences of World War II. See Herbert Marcuse, *One Dimensional Man: Studies in the Ideology of Advanced Industrial Society* (Boston: Beacon Press, 1964); see also Bernstein, ed, *The Culture Industry: Selected Essays on Mass Culture* (London: Routledge, 1991), 85-92.

[18] Here we may not go in detail into the critiques of consumerism from all these aspects.

[19] Already in early 1970's a study by the Club of Rome under the title of "Limits to Growth" forewarned about the consequences of unbridled development course at the cost of nature and environment.

[20] Cf. *The Economist*, December 5–11, 2015, 73 ff. For a special report on climate change, see *The Economist* November 28–December 4, 2015.

[21] This comes out very clearly in the encyclical *Laudato Si* of Pope Francis. See chapter 8 in this volume.

[22] See John Clammer, *Cultures of Transition and Sustainability: Culture after Capitalism* (New York: Palgrave Macmillan, 2016).

[23] See John A. Grim, ed, *Indigenous Traditions and Ecology* (Cambridge MA: Harvard University Press, 2001).

[24] Vinay Lal "Too Deep for Deep Ecology: Gandhi and the Ecological Vision of Life", in Christopher Key Chapple & Mary Evelyn Trucker, eds, *Hinduism and Ecology* (Cambridge MA: Harvard University Press, 2000), p. 206.

[25] Cf. Jeffrey Richey, *Mencius*, http://www.iep.utm.edu/mencius/ [accessed on 12 January, 2016].

[26] Cf. Desai Devangana, *Khajuraho: Monumental Legacy Series* (Delhi: Oxford University Press, 2000); Shobita Punja, *Khajuraho: The First Thousand Years* (Delhi: Penguin Books, 2000).

[27] See Benjamin Walker, *Hindu World: An Encyclopaedic Survey of Hinduism, vol. I "Dharma"* (New Delhi: Munshiram Manoharlal Publishers, 1983); Sushil Mittal and Gene Thursby, eds, *The Hindu World* (New York and London: Routledge, 2005); Jan Gonda, *Die Religionen Indiens I* (Stuttgart Berlin: Verlag W. Kohlhammer, 1978); see also Rajendra Prasad, ed, *A Historical Developmental Study of Classical Indian Philosophy of Morals*, XII: 2 (New Delhi: PHISPC, Centre for Studies in Civilizations, 2009).

[28] According to a Jataka tale, Gautama Buddha, given to extreme ascetic practices for Enlightenment under the pipal tree, did not refuse milk-rice from the maiden Sujata (later to become his first lay disciple), to satisfy his hunger.

[29] Cf. Takeuchi Yoshinori, ed, et al. *Buddhist Spirituality* (Delhi: Motilal Banarsidass Publishers Pvt. Ltd., 1995).

[30] Cf. Richard K. Payne, ed, *How Much is Enough? Buddhism, Consumerism, and the Human Environment* (Somerville MA: Wisdom Publications, 2010).

[31] See Plato, *Phaedrus* (Minneapolis: Filiquarian Publishing, LLC., 2007).

[32] Allan Hunt Badiner, *Mindfulness in the Marketplace: Compassionate Responses to Consumerism* (Berkeley: Parallax Press, 2002); Stephanie Kaza, *Hooked! Buddhist Writings on Greed, Desire, and the Urge to Consume* (Boston: Shambhala Publications 2005).

[33] Cf. Sigmund Freud, *Civilization an Its Discontents* (London: Penguin Books, 2004); (German original in 1930).

[34] Marcel Mauss, *The Gift: The Form and Reason for Exchange in Archaic Societies* (New York: W. W. Norton & Company, 2000).

[35] Lisa A. Neilson, and Pamela Paxton, "Social Capital and Political Consumerism: A Multilevel Analysis", *Social Problems*, 57:1 (2010), 5-24; Dietlind Stolle, Marc Hooghe, and Michele Micheletti, "Politics in the Supermarket: Political Consumerism as a Form of Political Participation", *International Political Science Review / Revue Internationale de Science Politique*, 26:3 (2005), 245-69; Michele Micheletti, and Dietlind Stolle, "Sustainable Citizenship and the New Politics of Consumption", *The Annals of the American Academy of Political and Social Science*, 644 (2012), 88-120; Micheletti, M., Føllesdal, Andreas, & Stolle, Dietlind, eds, *Politics, Products, and Markets: Exploring Political Consumerism*

Past and Present (N.J.; London: New Brunswick, 2003); Dietlind Stolle and Micele Micheletti, *Political Consumerism: Global Responsibility in Action* (New York: Cambridge University Press, 2013).

[36] Michele Micheletti, and Dietlind Stolle, "Mobilizing Consumers to Take Responsibility for Global Social Justice", *The Annals of the American Academy of Political and Social Science,* 611 (2007), 157-75.

PART - III

RENEWAL OF FAITH AND
REFORM OF THE CHURCH COMMUNITY

CHAPTER 10

Adult Faith and Life in Society

How relevant is Christian faith to our contemporary society in India? Simple as the question may sound, it is not easy to answer. It would be relatively easy to respond to the question in a society where Christian faith is an integral part of the culture and history of the people, as in the case of Europe, especially in its model of Christendom. Here in India, we are in a society, in which Christian faith is viewed, by and large, as an 'alien' faith. What is said of Chinese Christians is said of India too. "One more Christian, one less Indian".

Example of Early Christianity

In many respects, the practice of Christian faith in society in this country today brings us back to the situation of the early centuries of Christianity when the believers faced an ambiguous world of hostility and acceptance, and were marked by great complexity and diversity.[1]

In this particular society, they struggled to position their identity, relate to the state and to forge relationships with various segments of the people. It may be good to recall here that St. Augustine's classical work "*The City of God*" was an attempt to respond to accusations against Christianity and Christian faith in the society of his times. It contributed throughout the Christian centuries of the West to shape the attitude of Christians towards society. The fall of Rome in C.E. 410 and the occupation of it by the Visigoths came as a great shock to the citizens of the empire. There was the accusation that the empire was weakened by Christians because of their pacifism and their abandoning of the worship of traditional gods and goddesses. Augustine's work aimed at responding to these general allegations against Christians by the larger society and its representatives.

New Situation

Any attempt to transpose the model of faith in relationship to society as developed in the various theories in the context of medieval European Christendom would be hardly applicable to the unique situation in India, and Asia in general.[2] Even some of the recent attempts to relate Christian faith to society refer to the socio-political developments in the western context such as the Enlightenment, secularization, postmodernity, etc. In short, in India we need to reflect on the question of faith-society relationship, with reference to our own situation and history, and not depending on any received models.[3]

In reflecting on faith in relation to its impact on society, one should be attentive to avoid two possible misconceptions: understanding of faith in the singular, and de-contextualizing of faith from the society. We speak of faith amidst faiths; of our faith in relation to brothers and sisters of other faiths.[4] In the same breath we speak of our faith, we need to speak of the *faith of our neighbours*. For, we cannot meaningful discourse on our faith without the faith of our neighbours, both of which are exercised in the same society. Moreover, every society has its history, tradition and its unique contours which make it imperative for Christian faith to bear witness in context. However, the question of bearing witness needs to be also framed in relation to the broader issue of religion vis-à-vis society and the public realm - a question that has undergone quite a lot of developments in the past few decades.[5]

The Current Discussion on the Role of Faith in the Life of Society

What are the possibilities for religion to affect the life of the society? How much of space is available in the public life of a society for faith to play a role today? What kind of role could it play for the good of the society without its role being perceived as an unwarranted interference in the legitimate autonomy of the secular realities? When the thesis of secularization reigned supreme – a few decades ago – it was thought that the age of religion had come to an end. Today, the secularization thesis is completely revised.[6] The Iranian revolution of 1979 was an eye-opener. The role of religions in socio-political transformation was further confirmed by the praxis of liberation in Latin America.[7] It played an important role in the overthrow of militarism and dictatorship in the Philippines, Korea, and was responsible to some extent in the dismantling of totalitarian socialist regimes in eastern Europe, as illustrated, for example, in the case of Poland. Moreover, as some recent case studies have shown, contrary to the prevailing views, religion and faith have contributed to democratization of several societies.[8] Peter Beyer has studied the question of religion in general in relation to societies under the condition of globalisation. He makes an important distinction between *function* and *performance*: Religions could function in a society with their rituals, believes, doctrines, etc. But it is only when a religion enters into performance mode, it will have a transformative effect on the society.[9]

For some, as long as faith does not impose itself on the society, its conceptions and its doctrines – what John Rawls calls "comprehensive doctrines" – it could play a role in public life. Faith can intervene to the extent it contributes to *public reasoning*, namely it could become a partner in a common conversation with other people in the polity who have different conceptions of good life, value-system, etc.[10] But the immediate question that could be raised is: Are we reducing faith to its bare minimum? Is faith only part of a common denominator? If faith expresses itself through its symbols, myths, rituals with all their of evocative power, could these also play a role in the life of the society and contribute to its growth? Instead of a theoretical response, let me point out how some of the modern thinkers were able to be active in the public life of the society by bringing in their faith and religious vision to benefit the entire society, without however imposing their convictions on others. We have the example of Swami Vivekananda and Gandhi and their contribution through their faith and spirituality to the regeneration of India. In more recent times, at the global level, Dr Martin Luther King, Bishop Desmond

Tutu and Bishop Carlos Belo have shown what a strong impact faith could have on the transformation of their societies.[11] All the three were awarded Nobel Prize, not for what they did to their faith-communities, but for humanity, drawing on their faith as these were persons of deep faith and lovers of humanity. They lived out and witnessed to their faith for the wellbeing of the society.

Faith free of Absolutism

The well-known story of the elephant and five blind men, is a metaphor to indicate how little we understand, and what happens if the little fragments of our understanding are projected as the whole truth. This is very much true also in the realm of faith. No one can exhaust the riches of faith and its dimensions. The little faith we have and our understanding of it should move us to humility rather than arrogance.

The renouncing of absolutism is not to be interpreted as a failure to be strong in faith or surrender to relativism. The language of "strong in faith" is quite intriguing, since it could conjure up the image of an unassailable fortress which requires to be defended at any cost. We are reminded of one of the best loved hymns of Lutheran tradition "A mighty fortress is our God", originating from Luther - *Ein feste Burg ist unser Gott*". Fortress, citadel, tower, etc. are images that could resonate with medieval life.[12] Christian language of faith has inherited this tradition, and we continue to use them without paying attention to the mind-set and attitudes they could create in our times. God is a mystery of communion, and human community needs to reflect this divine mystery of communion through the creation of a society and world that is respectful of all and promoting understanding, peace, and harmony. Any absolutist statements and claims that do not respect the mystery of love and communion, even if it is made to affirm one's faith, become questionable. Faith needs to be expressed in the language of love and respect for others.[13] This does not diminish the depth and quality of faith which needs to be suffused with love.

Further, in the Christian tradition itself, faith has been experienced not so much as established certainties, but as a struggle of an individual or community in the midst of doubts, obscurity, and disturbing questions.

The life of mystics and saints illustrate how faith was lived as if it were a *tunnel experience*, not being sure of one's direction, confused and assailed by doubts. "For now, we see in a mirror dimly, but then face to face. Now I know in part; then I shall understand fully... (I Cor 13:12). It is far from an arrogant doctrinaire affirmation of ready-made statements and absolute claim of truths. For, in reality we understand only partially and very inadequately the object of our faith. As Vatican I expressed in its *Dei Filius*,

> Divine mysteries by their very nature so exceed the created intellect that, even after they have been communicated and received in faith, they remain covered by the veil of faith itself and shrouded as it were in darkness, as long as in this mortal life 'we are away from the Lord; for we walk by faith, not by sight.[14]

The promise of absolute certainties is a trap into which most people easily fall. It is a trouble-free option compared to the difficult journey of faith one has to undertake to follow the path God shows, as it was the case with Abraham, the father of faith.

Primordial faith

We need to base our reflections on what I would call a *primordial faith* from an anthropological perspective. This will provide the backdrop to understand a historically concretized faith like Christian faith, and to gauge its impact on society.

Faith is a way of being, an attitude, and a way of life that is other-centred. It includes as part of the same coin – the Other (with capital 'O" referring to the absolute mystery that is beyond name and form), and the "other" (with small 'o') referring to our neighbours, the community, the society. Through faith we undergo a radical change in as much as we shift the centre of gravity from ourselves to outside of ourselves – to God the ultimate mystery and consequently to our neighbours. It stands in contrast to the self-referential and centripetal way of life, attitudes, and values. Centri-fugal movement happens when we are taken hold off by the other; seized by what is real, good, and beautiful – *satyam, sivam, sundaram – verum, bonum et pulchrum* (truth, goodness and beauty). The mystics have intuitively seen and savoured this. The other-centeredness is the path to the realm of the Spirit; it is the path of fuller life.

Faith nurtures a centrifugal movement which is also a movement of transformation of the self and of communities. Faith implies a conversion; it brings with it a different vision of reality, another set of principles and values to guide one's life. All this is not achieved just in one single act of faith but through the life-journey of a person or of a community. Hence, there is room to speak of *growth in faith*.

Faith is a universal call given out to all human beings by a God who reveals God's self in multifarious ways (Heb 1:1). This faith as a passionate movement towards the mystery, is something that is fundamental. Without it, tenets, propositions, and doctrines are like lifeless bodies. In Christian tradition, one rightly distinguished between *fides qua* and *fides quae*.[15] But then it is the body of doctrines (*fides quae*) which began to occupy primacy of place and it became identity-marker for religions. The movement of faith towards mystery as the primordial experience uniting people of different religious communities has been underestimated and neglected. Besides, faith became a matter of mind, whereas it is no less a matter of human heart and spirit. Hence, we can rightly speak of believing with one's heart – something we find again in Christian scriptures and in tradition.[16]

Christian profession of faith (creed) does not simply speak of belief in the reality of God as a matter of mind, but says: I believe *in* God (*credo in Deum*) which involves the whole person with mind and heart, with sentiments, emotion and passion. This faith deep into God stands out when we distinguish it from two other forms of faith related to God. One can believe that God exists – which even the devil can do! This was referred to in tradition as *credere Deum*. It is simply an intellectual admission of something or someone -God. Then there is a second level of faith which is the result of our trusting and respecting someone. If a friend tells us something we have faith in her statement. So also, we could believe in what God says, as for example, in the epiphany in Jordan, when the divine voice was heard: "This is my beloved son, with whom I am well-pleased" (Mt 3:17). We believe this because it is God who says that. This second level of faith is described as *credere Deo*. The third level of faith is the one where we really stick out our whole being, and try to immerse ourselves into the depth of the divine mystery. This is a losing of oneself totally in the divine mystery and rediscovering oneself anew in God. It was described as *credere in Deum*. It is the faith that can move mountains, and remain unperturbed in the darkest of nights and deepest of valleys.[17]

There is an open-endedness of the primordial faith towards infinity. Absolutist affirmations could become idols that block the way to see the transcendent, to see the wonderful world of God's creation, and to recognize the divine footprints all around us. It could be a hindrance to communion and peace in society. Far from making an impact on the society, it could harm the pursuit of common good in the spirit of solidarity and togetherness

There is also another important dimension to faith – faith needs to be manifested and borne witness to. Saints and martyrs are called in Christian tradition as *confessors,* precisely because they bore witness to their faith in God. Confession of faith again is not a declaration of whether one believes the body of doctrinal tenets. Confessing one's faith, in the Biblical tradition, is first and foremost a matter of praising and glorifying God with one's heart in an attitude of prayer and devotion. Even the profession of creed is a matter of confession in this sense, namely praising God and not simply declaring the tenets of Christian faith.[18] The movement of faith towards God takes the believer also towards the society, the community. Consequently, mission and evangelization do not become propagation of Christian doctrines, but communication of experiences anchored in the faith élan towards God and one's neighbours. If we understand Christian faith and witnessing in the way we have described, then, there will be less room for suspicion about conversion and Christian proslytisation.

Should religions be characterized by their doctrines, they could easily become source of endless conflicts and violence. If manifestation of faith is linked to one's primordial faith as passionate adherence to God, the believers from various religious traditions will find a path of convergence in manifesting their faith through their involvement for the wellbeing of humanity and the advancement of society. There will be ample room for coming together in a common and primordial faith-experience, and engage oneself for the welfare of the world, society, nature, and entire creation.

Faith and the God of Creation

To be able to understand the implications of faith for the life of the world and of the society, as Christians, we need to think of faith not only in relation to the mysteries of redemption, but also in relation to creation. Perhaps, today, it makes more sense to speak of faith in God's creation, especially in the context of religious pluralism and the ecological crisis. We can rightly speak of God, the Redeemer and even of the mission of the Redeemer (*Redemptoris Missio*). But we need to speak at the same time about our faith in God the Creator. Correspondingly, there is not only *Redemptoris Missio*, but also *Creatoris Missio*. God's creation calls us to mission. It is by expanding this mission that our faith will be able to make any significant impact on our society. A faith in the God of creation has more direct impact on the society and the wellbeing of nature and the universe. In this perspective, bodily realities – food and drink, work and rest (all part of God's creation), and the struggle for justice to make all these available in an equitable manner, are enveloped in the world of faith. All these are an integral part of salvation, though not all of salvation.

For the believer, the social engagement and struggles connected with it, become not simply matters of philanthropy, but an integral aspect of his or her faith-existence. This is precisely what made Pandita Ramabai turn to Christianity. She wanted her engagement for the young widows and marginalized to be illumined by a larger vision and perspective. She wanted her social engagement flow from a deeper spiritual vision.[19] I find convergence between the vision of Pandita Ramabai and Pope Francis. He is very clear that what distinguishes involvement of Christians in society is their faith. For Christians, the engagement with the poor and the marginalized, is "primarily a theological category rather than a cultural, sociological, political or philosophical one".[20] He tells us how faith needs to animate all action in favour of the poor and the downtrodden.

> Our commitment does not consist exclusively in activities or programmes of promotion and assistance; what the Holy Spirit mobilizes is not an unruly activism, but above all an attentiveness which considers the other

'in a certain sense as one with ourselves'. This loving attentiveness is the beginning of a true concern for their person which inspires me effectively to seek their good... The poor person, when loved, 'is esteemed as of great value', and this is what makes the authentic option for the poor differ from any other ideology, from any attempt to exploit the poor for one's own personal or political interest.[21]

As we noted earlier, involvement in the society, its social, political, economic, and cultural realms is a duty flowing from authentic Christian faith. *Gaudium et Spes* of Vatican II has spelt this out in greater detail on the basis of a very sound theology of creation in which human beings are seen as image of God, and therefore having dignity and rights; so also, human community and society are seen not simply resulting through some social contract, but as part of God's creation. Christian faith in creation is a formidable source to foster a world of human dignity, equality and respect. Christian anthropology has such a beautiful vision that it could support and encourage involvement for the dignity of human beings, especially the weaker ones. Implication of this faith is relentless struggle against hierarchical order of the society, against casteism which all threaten the dignity of people and jeopardize unity and communion in human society.

The text of the Constantinople Creed says: "I believe in God, Father Almighty, maker of heaven and earth, and of all things visible and invisible".[22] This is the very first article of faith which needs due emphasis in a country like India where the wonderful creation of God which we share with everyone else is object of our faith. In that sense, the very first affirmation of Christian faith unites us with Hindus, Muslims, Sikhs, Parsis, and peoples of primaeval religious traditions as the tribals are. When we blend this truth with the realization that God reveals God's self in multifarious ways (Heb.1:1), and people respond to the revelation through their faith – a faith exercised not only as individuals but also as a body of religious believers – that would bring about a great spiritual affinity between Christian faith and the faith of our neighbours.

Faith in God's Privileging of the Poor

In Jesus' teaching, the same concern of God for the poor and the downtrodden found in the Biblical tradition continues with a new vigour.

There is no dualism in his teaching as though the world were evil and one should escape from it and keep away from the joys of everyday life. On the other hand, he is emphatically against the riches and accumulation of wealth which destroy people and their humanity, and causes inequality, injustice, and conflicts in society. His teachings are full of caveats against the riches. The love of riches in the vision of Jesus and the false sense of security it causes are obstacles to trust in God and in human beings. Later, the Letter to Timothy would bring out admirably the spirit Jesus' teachings on wealth, saying, "But those who desire to be rich fall into temptation, into a snare, into many senseless and hurtful desires that plunge men into ruin and destruction. It is through this craving that some have wandered away from the faith and pierced their heart with many pangs" (I Tim 6:9-10).

And yet today, there is a strong global trend that is characterized as "prosperity Gospel". It views riches as blessings of God: the wealthier one is, the more one enjoys God's blessings. The modern trends of prosperity Gospel seem to have emerged in early nineteenth century with the New Thought movement, and it got popularized by the tele-evangelism movement in the 1980's. Subsequently, it was taken up in many charismatic movements, in many independent Churches and in mega Churches in Africa, Latin America and Asia. One of the early figures in prosperity Gospel was E.W. Kenyon who was active in 1890's. In mid-twentieth century we have prosperity gospel promoters in A.A. Allen and T.L. Osborn. Widespread in the Pentecostal movement, prosperity gospel is propagated today by such preachers as Joel Osteen, Bruce Wilkinson. It is carried on by local preachers mainly in non-denominational and independent churches in Africa, Asia and Latin America. In the Philippines, the prosperity gospel was introduced into the Catholic Church through the *El Shaddai* movement. In Korea, it is associated with the Yoido Full Gospel Church. Prosperity gospel is also popular in the U.S. among the poor and lower middle-class population, especially among the Hispanics and other immigrant communities.

As one receives generously the riches as blessings from God, one is expected also to donate to the church-community substantial tithes.

There is a kind of pact with God: Those who offer donations, God will bless them "seven-fold" in return. Through entrepreneurship one has to produce more in support of which the parable of talents is adduced. This is nothing but an outright sell-out of the Gospel to capitalism.[23] Capitalism has not spared religion and religious agents to draw them to its own agenda. There are so many varieties of prosperity Gospel, and they all seem to subscribe to the neo-liberal philosophy that rising tide lifts all boats. Poverty, inequality and injustice do not enter into the picture. Increasing of one's wealth and being successful in life are viewed as part of one's faith. There are certain ritualization with money when at services, prayers and blessings are said over it.[24]

The global economic trends and the dominant model of development all indicate more than ever before that we need faith to uphold the cause of the poor, women, and the marginalized. Faith is then a counter-culture. In this, it stands against the ways of the world which privilege the rich and the powerful. This faith has tremendous consequences for the Indian society. But there are also many temptations to forget this truth of God's siding with the powerless and oppressed. Any failure to be on the side of the poor is tantamount to loss of faith in God who has opted to be with the poor and the marginalized. If there is one single message that runs through the entire Bible – from Genesis to the Book of Revelation, it is the truth that God is on the side of the poor and the marginalized; God is a "God of Life" and the defender of the poor.[25]

Faith in the Sermon on the Mount

To have faith in Jesus Christ is to believe, against the contemporary global background, in his teachings, the core of which is constituted by his Sermon on the Mount. The dominant values in our society today, unfortunately, create an environment for dehumanization, social dissension and violence. Competition, greed, and haughtiness continuously spew venom in the life of the society. The Sermon on the Mount offers a different vision of human beings and society. Because of its radicality, Sermon on the Mount represents a great challenge to the dominant vision and values. Precisely because of this, Sermon on the Mount, calls for strong faith to be able to follow its path. Only those who are deeply anchored in God and believe in humanity and its wellbeing will also be able to believe in Sermon on the Mount and try to put into practice its vision and values. "You must, therefore be perfect as your heavenly Father is perfect" (Mt 5:48). What is meant here is not a moral perfection, rather it is an invitation to be whole, and with undivided heart and mind do God's will in love and compassion.[26] The various injunctions in the Sermon on the Mount are an unfolding of this great and noble ideal to which every human being is called to strive after.

There was a time when I thought that the Sermon on the Mount is meant for the chosen ones – the clergy and the religious; and then I thought that it is something meant for the Christian community. Today, I have come to the realization that the jewel the Sermon on the Mount represents is meant for all human beings, and for every society. Without faith in the Sermon on the Mount, there is no future for human life and for humankind. It is in a way the grammar of life – individual and collective.

We have in the Sermon on the Mount things just opposite of what is common place, of what is held as truth and as normal. A world which spawns more and more inequality without concern for the poor and the least ones, cannot sustain itself. Inequality has a costly human and societal price.[27] Hierarchization and inequality affect everyone in the society, and dehumanizes all – the dominator and the marginalised. The spirit of revenge and violence unleash a spiral of violence from which no one is spared and all are affected. Jesus' Sermon on the Mount, his life, and mystery of his death, and resurrection – all these lead us to life in fullness. They do not create a separate code of conduct. The mystery of his life, death, and resurrection is the best embodiment and interpretation of the Sermon on the Mount.

As it touches issues and questions every human being is confronted with, Sermon on the Mount has a universal scope. Gandhi saw this wide reach of the Sermon, when he said, "For many of them [theologists - *sic*] Sermon on the Mount does not apply to mundane things, and that it was only meant for the twelve disciples. Well, I do not believe this. I think the Sermon on the Mount has no meaning if it is not of vital use in everyday life to everyone".[28] There has been a misconception in viewing the way of life Jesus prescribes in the Sermon on the Mount as simply ethics. One failed to see that his injunctions were expressions of faith. It is a kind of practice that flows from faith in God and in human beings; it is the *Dharma* of Jesus.[29] Dharma is much more than ethics.

Sermon on the Mount can be characterized as the response to the call of the Kingdom of God and the way of life it implies. In fact, in the Gospel of Mathew, the Sermon on the Mount follows the narration on Jesus'proclamation of the Kingdom of God and his invitation to repentance. The Kingdom of God, contrary to the worldly domination, has its own ethical and spiritual path. Anyone who comes under the spell of the Kingdom of God will turn to repentance, and attune his or her life and attitudes to the ideals of the Sermon on the Mount. It is not an ethics of commands, but a signpost for a way of life shod through deep faith in God and compassion for human beings, in response to God's own unconditional self-giving in love.

The faith in Jesus' Sermon on the Mount could make a lot of difference in our societies, replete with violence and vengeance. "Love your enemies and pray for those who persecute you so that you may be the sons of your Father who is in heaven; for he makes his sun rise on the evil and the good, and sends his rain on the just and on the unjust" (Mt 5:44f). Following this path cannot but bring about a revolutionary transformation in societies and in the lives of individuals and communities.

In the Indian tradition we could observe two streams of thought and praxis: One goes in the direction of vindicating one's honour by taking revenge – something we note in the great epics of Ramayana and Mahabharata,[30] and which continues to be at work today in the political culture and in the social interaction among the various caste-groups. Historically, this orientation was challenged by a second stream, namely by the advent of Buddhism that preached wisdom and compassion. The India of today is heir to both these traditions, and we could find both these traditions at work. In the desert of communal conflicts and violence, one will find oasis of wisdom and compassion. A great challenge that India faces today is to overcome the sting of violence and revenge through wisdom, mercy and compassion. Christians and people of good will who believe in the Sermon on the Mount and practice it will contribute to strengthen the tradition of wisdom and compassion in our societies.

Faith of Jesus and Jesus of Faith

For Christians, faith of Jesus is an important point of reference. His primordial faith came to expression in his centrifugal movement which is so wonderfully illustrated by his way of life, teaching, his passion, and death. Jesus himself in his deepest being represents the centrifugal movement of God, and hence he is the *kenosis* – self-emptying of God. "Though he was in the form of God, did not count equality with God a thing to be grasped, but emptied himself taking the form of a servant, being born in the likeness of men. And being found in human form he humbled himself and became obedient unto death, even death on a cross..." (Phil 2: 6-8).

To be able to speak meaningfully of the impact of faith in society, we need to speak not only of faith in Jesus, but also *faith of Jesus* – faith of Jesus in God and his communion with the divine mystery, and the living out of this faith amidst the people through his option for the last and the least. Romans 3:21-22 speaks of the faith of Jesus Christ. And it is this faith of Jesus, according to the Romans, which brought about our justification, our righteousness –in other words our salvation. The train of thought about the faith of Jesus Christ is continued in the following chapter in which Paul speaks about the faith of Abraham which was reckoned as righteousness (Rom 4: 1-3).

> But now the righteousness of God has been manifested apart from law, although the law and the prophets bear witness to it, the righteousness of God which is by faith of Jesus Christ (*dia pisteōs Iēsou Christou*) for all who believe (Rom. 3: 21-22; See also Gal. 2:16).[31]

The letter to the Hebrews which brings out the humanity of Jesus refers to him as "pioneer (*archēgos*) and perfecter of our faith". "And let us run with perseverance the race that is set before us, looking to Jesus the pioneer and perfecter of our faith, who for the joy that was set before him endured the cross, despising the shame, and is seated at the right hand of the throne of God" (Heb 12:1-2). He went through the human conditions of suffering in deep faith in the Father. Though many Catholic theologians have been rather hesitant to speak about the "faith of Jesus", quite surprisingly Hans Urs von Balthasar devotes several pages of reflection on the faith of Jesus in the light of the Biblical understanding of faith, and sees in Jesus the model of faith for all believers.[32]

This living faith in God characterized Jesus' entire life and his dealings with human beings and the society.[33] It took the unique form of a filial relationship. Jesus, as the Gospel tells us, addressed God numerous times, and in an unprecedented way as "Abba". There is a continuum in the faith of Jesus in God and in human beings. The following of Jesus in faith will help us overcome the temptation of opposing the divine and the human. Jesus not only had great faith in God which explains his great impact on the society of his times; he also admired those who had great faith. He admires the faith of a centurion who was not one of those belonging to Israel. "When Jesus heard this, he marvelled at him and turned and said to the multitude that followed him, 'I tell you, not even in Israel have I found such faith'" (Lk 7:8). The faith in God is not anything exclusive; it is open to all. Jesus presents his own faith in God and union with him as model for the disciples.

There is a lot of misunderstanding today in relating faith to Jesus. Many scholars see the pre-existent, resurrected and exalted Christ as the object of our faith. This is not disputed. But what should preoccupy us is that Christ of faith is often contrasted with historical Jesus, whose importance in terms of faith tends to be undermined. For, what has been narrated in the Gospel of Jesus of history, is in fact the expression of the faith-experience of his immediate disciples. Jesus of the Gospels is mediated through the faith-experience of the disciples. Hence, Jesus of history is also Jesus of faith.[34] Moreover, the line of reflection we have made referring to God's option for the poor in the life and ministry of Jesus, and in his teachings, especially in the Sermon on the Mount, makes Jesus model of our faith, like in the case of his early disciples. It calls for a lot of faith to follow Jesus' option for the poor and the marginalized and to emulate his counter-cultural model embodied in his Sermon on the Mount. The faith of Jesus and our faith in Jesus of history could be a great force of societal transformation.

Conclusion

Our society, especially its poor, cry for dignity, rights, freedom, justice and equality. The developments in our times, unfortunately, are aggravating the situation, rather than bringing it to an end. It is the time when faith needs to bear abundant fruits of justice. This calls for involvement of all believers in the fields of politics, economy, culture etc., motivated by their faith, its vision and values. A new set of values need to inspire the various realms of human life to bring about a real transformation in the condition of the people, especially the marginalized ones. Faith needs to come to the open, to the market place; it cannot simply be imprisoned in a small world. Tagore tells us why we need to leave the temple to be able to practice our faith in the presence of God and make effective its transformative power.

Leave this chanting and singing and telling of beads!
Whom dost thou worship in this lonely dark corner of a temple with doors all shut?
Open thine eyes and see thy God is not before thee!
He is there where the tiller is tilling the hard ground
And where the pathmaker is breaking stones
He is with them in sun and in shower
And his garment is covered with dust
Put off thy holy mantle and even like him
Come down on the dusty soil![35]

History tells us that some of the great Christian saints and sages tried to translate their faith in the life of the society, as for example, those in mendicant orders of medieval times. The practice of the Gospel of poverty assumed the form of religious orders that will live out the challenges of the Sermon on the Mount. Indeed, a new approach of faith to society was started when the mendicants left the model of enclosed monasteries as the place of practicing faith; instead came in the open to interact with the people and became beggars (mendicants) through voluntary poverty to share the life of the poorest of the poor.[36] This immersion in society and identification with the marginalised ones were for them a sequel to their faith in Jesus who became poor to be one with the suffering humanity. At a time of growth in commerce and urbanization, increasing disparity and marginalisation of the poor, St Dominic and especially St Francis of Assisi put into practice with their companions a different vision of the world and of human beings. What they did represented a social revolution and counter-culture.

In our pluralist and multireligious situation in India, for faith in God and in human beings to have a dent on the society, three important conditions need to be fulfilled: First, Christian believers relate their faith with the faith of the neighbours of other faiths: the believers share in the same faith-movement towards God and humanity which we called the primordial faith. Second, the multifaceted realities of the society beckon the believers to the God of creation. The transformation of the society and world will find an anchor in the faith in a God who has created all humans equal and with same dignity – something foundational for right and just relationships in human societies, and in the common care for nature and its protection. Third, true faith in God will shun the kind of absolutism which excludes and divides. For, faith as a movement towards the divine mystery refracted in the mystery of human beings, could never fathom the object towards which it tends, given the radical inadequacy of believers. As for Christians, their involvement of faith in society will be further enhanced by following the faith of Jesus in God and his compassion for human beings, and by their faith in a God who, as the Christian Scriptures show, has been always on the side of the poor and the marginalised.

Further, in India, Christian faith can make an impact on society by strengthening the deeper humanistic values enshrined in the Indian Constitution, and by helping to create a society increasingly just, free and equal.[37] Another important contribution it could make is to *strengthen the secular fabric of the society.* Christian faith and secularism in India can go together – unlike the way they are opposed in the West, especially in the

French understanding of *laicité*. As Sanjay Subramaniam has noted, when the French oppose the veils by Muslim women, they unconsciously think of the veils of nuns and oppose it as a symbol of the Church-establishment.[38] Secularism is the enemy of faith in the West. Pope Benedict wanted to redeem Christianity from secularism, as Pope John Paul II wanted to redeem Christianity from atheism. *In India, secularism, is a friend of faith.* For, in India, secularism is a matter of *"mediating between different communities"*.[39] In short, by living our Christian faith in service of secularism, we make an impact on the society, help overcome communalism, and enable a life of tolerance and harmony.

Bibliography

Abraham, K.C. *Transforming Vision. Theological – Methodological paradigm Shifts* (Tiruvalla: Christava Sahitya Samithi, 2006).

Amalorpavadass, D.S., ed., *The Indian Church in the Struggle for a New Society* (Bangalore: NBCLC 1981).

Badone, Ellen., ed. *Religious Orthodoxy and Popular Faith in European Society* (Princeton: Princeton University Press, 1990).

Biggar, Nigel., and Hogan, Linda., eds. *Religious Voices in Public Places* (Oxford: Oxford University Press, 2009).

Casanova, José. *Public Religion in the Modern World* (Chicago: University of Chicago Press, 1994).

Chandran, Joshua Russell, and Amirtham, Samuel. *A Vision for Man: Essays in Faith, Theology and Society* (Madras: Christian Literature Society, 1978).

Convey, Martin A. *Keeping the Faith in a Changing Society: Religious Practice and Relief in Ireland in the Light of Vatican II* (Dublin: Columba Press, 1994).

Davie, Grace. *Europe: The Exceptional Case: Parameters of Faith in the Modern World* (Maryknoll: Orbis Books, 2002).

De Lubac, Henri. *La Foi Chrétienne.* 2nd ed. (Paris: Aubier-Montaigne, 1970).

Dinham, Adam. *Faith, Public Policy and Civil Society: Problems, Policies, Controversies* (Basingstoke; New York: Palgrave Macmillan, 2009).

Gandhi, M. K. *Christian Missions: Their Place in India* (Ahmedabad: Navajivan Press, 1941).

George M. Soares-Prabhu, "The Dharma of Jesus: An Interpretation of the Sermon on the Mount." In Francis X. D'SA., ed. *Theology of Liberation: An Indian Biblical Perspective* (Pune: JDV, 2001).

Green, Bernard. *Christianity in Ancient Rome: The First Three Centuries* (New York: T&T Clark International, 2010).

Gutiérrez, Gustavo. *The God of Life* (Maryknoll: Orbis Books, 1991).

Hogan, Linda. *Keeping Faith with Human Rights* (Washington: Georgetown University Press, 2015).

Hollenbach, David. *The Common Good and Christian Ethics* (Cambridge: Cambridge University Press, 2002).

Hollenbach, David. *The Global Face of Public Faith: Politics, Human Rights and Ethics* (Washington D. C.: Georgetown University Press, 2003).

Junker-Kenny, Maureen, and Tomka, Miklós. *Faith in a Society of Instant Gratification, Concilium1999/4* (London: SCM Press, 1999).

Mollat, Michel. *Poor in the Middle Ages: An Essay in Social History,* 1st ed. (New Haven and London: Yale University Press, 1986).

Niles, Preman. *The Lotus and the Sun. Asian Theological Engagement with Plurality and Power* (Barton: Barton Books, 2013).

Pathil, Kuncheria., ed. *Church on Pilgrimage. Trajectories of Intercultural Encounter* (Bangalore: Dharmaram Publications, 2016).

Peter Beyer. *Religion and Globalization* (New Delhi: Sage Publication, 1994).

Rayan, Samuel, *God's Hope Becoming Visible.Indian Christian Reflections on Some Relevant Issues of our Times* (Collected Writings of Samuel Rayan S.J. vol. III) edited by Kurien Kunnumpuram (Delhi: ISPCK, 2013).

Wilfred, Felix. "Asian Christianity and Public Life: The Interplay." In Felix Wilfred., ed. *The Oxford Handbook of Christianity in Asia* (New York: Oxford University Press, 2014), 558-574.

Wilfred, Felix. *From the Dusty Soil* (Madras: Department of Christian Studies, University of Madras, 1995).

Wilfred, Felix., ed. *Leave the Temple. Indian Paths to Human Liberation* (New York: Oribis Books, 1992).

Wilfred, Felix., ed. *Transforming Religion: Prospects for a New Society* (New Delhi: ISPCK, 2010).

Wilken, Robert L. *The Christians as the Romans Saw Them* (New Haven: Yale University Press, 1984).

Endnotes

[1] Cf. Bernard Green, *Christianity in Ancient Rome: The First Three Centuries* (New York: T&T Clark International, 2010); Robert L. Wilken, *The Christians as the Romans Saw Them* (New Haven: Yale University Press, 1984).

[2] In this connection, the social teachings of the Church, in spite of their riches and their élan to make faith active in society, do not sufficiently take into account the fact that in our parts of the world the interaction of faith and society follow a different chemistry.

[3] I have attempted to do this with regard to Asia. See Felix Wilfred, "Christian Social Engagement in Asia", in Felix Wilfred, ed, *The Oxford Handbook of Christianity in Asia* (New York: Oxford University Press, 2014), pp. 327-342; ID., "Asian Christianity and Public Life: The Interplay", *ibid*, pp. 558-574; see also Felix Wilfred, ed, *Transforming Religion: Prospects for a New Society* (New Delhi: ISPCK, 2010).

[4] Cf. S. Wesley Ariarajah, *Not Without My Neighbour: Issues in Interfaith Relations* (Geneva: WCC, 1999); ID., *The Bible and People of Other Faiths* (Geneva: WCC, 1985).

[5] Cf. Felix Wilfred, ed, *Transforming Religion, op.cit.*

[6] Peter L. Berger, ed, *The Desecularization of the World: Resurgent Religion and World Politics* (Grand Rapids: Wm. B. Eerdmans Publishing Company, 1999); Grace Davie, *Europe – The Exceptional Case: Parameters of Faith in the Modern World* (Maryknoll: Orbis Books, 2002); Charles Taylor, *A Secular Age* (Cambridge MA: The Belknap Press of Harvard University Press, 2007).

[7] José Casanova, *Public Religion in the Modern World* (Chicago: University of Chicago Press, 1994).

[8] Cf. John W. De Gruchy, *Christianity and Democracy: A Theology for a Just World Order* (Cambridge: Cambridge University Press, 1995).

[9] Cf. Peter Beyer, *Religion and Globalization* (New Delhi: Sage Publication, 1994).

[10] John Rawls, *Political Liberalism* (New York: Columbia University Press, 1993); John Rawls, "The idea of public reason revisited", *The Law of Peoples* (Cambridge, MA: Harvard University Press, 2001), pp.129-180; see also Melissa Yates, "Rawls and Habermas on Religion in the Public Sphere", in David M. Rasmussen and James Swindal, eds, *Habermas,* II (London: Sage Publications, 2010), pp. 283-292; see also Don Browning – Francis Schüssler Fiorenza, eds, *Habermas. Modernity and Public Theology* (New York: Crossroad, 1992); Maureen Junker-Kenny, *Habermas and Theology* (New York: T & T Clark international, 2011).

[11] Cf. Felix Wilfred, *Theology to Go Public* (Delhi: ISPCK, 2013).

[12] This kind of thinking animates contemporary Protestant Orthodoxy and Evangelical Catholicism. See George Weigel, *Evangelical Catholicism: Deep Reform in the 21st Century Church* (New York: Basic Books, 2014). Reprint edition.

[13] Cf. Werner Jeanrond, "Orthodoxy and Theology: The Ambiguity and Potential of Claims to Orthodoxy", Christian Orthodoxy *Concilium* 2014/2, edited by Felix Wilfred and Daniel Pilario (London: SCM Press, 2014).

[14] *Dei Filius*, chapter 4, DS 3016.

[15] Cf. Avery Dulles, *The Assurance of Things Hoped For* (New York: Oxford University Press, 1994).

[16] Cf. Henri de Lubac, La *Foi Chrétienne,* 2nd edition (Paris: Aubier-Montaigne, 1970).

[17] It is St Augustine who first made a triple distinction: *credere Deum, credere Deo* and *credere in Deum.* The last of this constitutes authentic personal faith. This will be developed further in the Middle Ages by Albert the Great, St Thomas Aquinas and others.

[18] Cf. Henri de Lubac, *op. cit.*

[19] Cf. Uma Chakravarti, *Rewriting History: The Life and Times of Pandita Ramabai* (New Delhi: Kali for Women, 1998).

[20] *Evangelii Gaudium* no. 198.

[21] *Evangelii Gaudium* no.199. Besides the theological motive, the involvement in the society especially with the poor was seen in the Christian tradition from a Christological perspective: the poor were viewed as *"the vicars of Christ".* Hence, service to them was seen as service to Christ. Cf. Michel Mollat, *Poor in the Middle Ages: An Essay in Social History,* 1st ed. (New Haven and London: Yale University Press, 1986).

[22] For Greek and Latin text of this creed, see DS 150. See also J. N. D. Kelly, *Early Christian Creeds,* 3rd ed. (London: Bloomsbury Academic, 2006).

[23] Pope Francis has severest words of critique of capitalism which he views as a murderous system. No wonder that such plain speaking by the pope has provoked negative criticism from libertarian Catholics, especially in the U.S (Samuel Gregg, Marian Tupy, Robert Sirico and others) who try to reconcile the social teachings of the Church with the free market and its philosophy. For those who see Gospel through the lens of capitalism, the solution to the problems the world is facing is to make capitalism function properly. If something is wrong, it is because capitalism is not put into practice in the right way! I am reminded about Margaret Thatcher's interview of 6 January, 1980, in which she referred to the parable of the Good Samaritan. "No one would remember the Good Samaritan", she said, "if he had only good intentions; he had money as well". The subtext of her statement is clear: Accumulation of wealth in the hands of a few, far from being a problem, is an opportunity for works of philanthropy.

[24] For details on this, see Andreas Heuser, ed., *Pastures of Plenty: Tracing Religio-Scapes of Prosperity Gosper in Africa and Beyond* (Frankfurt a.M.: Peter Lang, 2015).

[25] Cf. Gustavo Gutiérrez, *The God of Life* (Maryknoll: Orbis Books, 1991).

26 Cf. Warren Carter, *Matthew and the Margins: A Sociopolitical and Religious Reading* (New Delhi: TPI, 2007), p.157.

27 Cf. Richard Wilkinson and Kate Pickett, *The Spirit Level: Why Greater Equality Makes Societies Stronger* (New York: Bloomsbury Press, 2009); Joseph E. Stiglitz, *The Price of Inequality* (New York: Penguin Books, W. W. Norton & Company Inc., 2012); Naomi Klein, *The Shock Doctrine* (New York: Penguin Books, 2007); Tim Jackson, *Prosperity Without Growth: Economics for a Finite Planet* (London, New York: Earthscan, 2009).

28 M. K. Gandhi, *Christian Missions: Their Place in India* (Ahmedabad: Navajivan Press, 1941), p. 278.

29 Cf. Collected writings of George M. Soares-Prabhu, "The Dharma of Jesus: An interpretation of the Sermon on the Mount", in Francis X. D'SA, ed, *Theology of Liberation: An Indian Biblical Perspective* (Pune: JDV, 2001), pp.153-172.

30 Cf. Rajmohan Gandhi, *Revenge and Reconciliation* (New Delhi: Penguin Books, 1999).

31 In many translations as well as in commentaries such as Jerome Biblical Commentary, the Greek phrase "*dia pisteōs Iēsou Christou*" is translated as "through faith in Jesus Christ" interpreting the genitive as objective Genitive. It means then the righteousness comes about through our faith in Jesus Christ. This translation and interpretation are clearly coloured by traditional doctrinal concerns. If we are to follow the principle of *lectio difficilior*, then it needs to be translated and interpreted as "through the faith of Jesus Christ" in subjective genitive, and not "through the faith in Jesus Christ". In other words, it is the steadfast faith of Jesus in God and his loyalty and filial attachment to God that is spoken about here by Paul as that which brings about justification.

32 Cf. Hans Urs von Balthasar, *Sponsa Verbi* (Einsiedeln: Johannes Verlag, 1961), pp. 45-79.

33 Analysing grammatically the instances where "faith of Jesus Christ" appears, B. Hays concludes: "Thus the balance of the grammatical evidence favours the view that *pistis Iēsou Christou* means faith of Jesus Christ, however that might be interpreted. The case on grammatical grounds for the translation "faith in Jesus Christ" is really very weak. The latter rendering has nonetheless been widespread on the assumption that it makes more sense theologically" H. Bays, *The Faith of Jesus Christ. The Narrative Substitutes of Galatians 3:1 – 4:11*, (Grand Rapids: Wm B. Eerdmans Publishing Co., 2002), 150. For a theological point of view, see L. Malevez, *Pour une théologie de la foi* (Paris: Desclée De Brouwer, 1969), 160ff.

[34] Cf. Collected writings of George M. Soares-Prabhu, "The Jesus of Faith: A Christological Contribution to an Ecumenical Third World Spirituality", in Francis X. D'SA, ed., *Theology of Liberation: An Indian Biblical Perspective* (Pune: JDV, 2001), pp. 267-295.

[35] "Gitanjali XI", in *Rabindranath Tagore Omnibus I* (New Delhi: Rupa& Co., 2003), 6.

[36] Cf. C. H. Lawrence, *The Friars: The Impact of the Mendicant Orders on Medieval Society* (London: Longman Group, 1994).

[37] Cf. John Romus Devasahayam, *Human Dignity in Indian Secularism and in Christianity: Christianity in Dialogue with Indian Secularism* (Bangalore: Claretian Publications, 2007).

[38] *The Hindu*, 30 Nov. 2013.

[39] *Ibid.*

CHAPTER 11

Why Small Christian Communities?

Nothing illustrates more graphically why Small Christian Communities[1] were found attractive in Latin America than the words of an ordinary woman. She simply expressed what she saw on the eve of Christmas. She said, "Christmas Eve, all three Protestant churches were lit up and full of people. We could hear them singing…And the Catholic Church closed and dark! Because we can't get a priest".[2] The need of the hour is a bright Church, witnessing that Jesus is alive in the community of his disciples. Today, the Small Christian Communities led by committed believers keep faith burning and bright. One of the tragedies that befell the Catholic Church is the association of the Church with priests and the hierarchical set up. The renewal of the Church itself was thought to be a reform of the clergy. I believe that the developments that have taken place within the Catholic Church are a pointer. No matter which Church or denomination one belongs to, the challenge of small Christian groups remains the same. The bigger the Church institution, the greater hesitation to focus on the small communities of Christian believers. They are like the active cells that keep the body of the Church alive and vibrant.

Beyond Practical Expediency

There is a danger that small or Basic Christian Communities could be viewed as a pastoral strategy, namely to break down a larger whole of the community into small units for them to be able to function better, and for pastoral agents to reach out to them more effectively. In this case, they could be simply an administrative unit of a parish or pastorate under the direction of a priest or pastor. There is a point in this strategy since large parishes could be unwieldy, non-functional, and impersonal. This approach could give a personal touch to the traditional pastoral care. In some instances, the idea of Small Christian Communities in its origin probably was linked to a situation where there were no priests to serve the people. It led to the activation of the Christian faithful who would jointly read and reflect on the Word of God, and interpret it in relation to their life-situations. In this case, Basic Christian Communities could be looked at as making a virtue out of necessity.

I think it is unwise to be satisfied with our situation of the institutional Church with abundant clerical and religious vocation. The institutional Church is happy with large crowds attending patronal festivities, pilgrim centres, and long drawn-out episcopal ceremonies, jubilees, commemorations, and so on. More than deepening the faith of the people, they serve to strengthen the clerical status and their hold on the people. The clerics, in general, are at home with infantile faith and would go all the way out to increase the number and kind of devotions.[3] There is little effort to inculcate adult faith.[4]

In this context, we need to be aware of two possible future developments. First of all, there is a growing disenchantment of people with the established Church, its power, and mode of governance. This could disengage the people from the present commitment to the official Church, and look for other ways and forms of giving expression to their faith. A clerical Church cannot expect to keep the flock under its mantle for too long. A second possible development is the progressive diminishing of clerical and religious vocation. In the Roman Catholic Church, the growth in the number of vocations has led it to rely on its institutional power. The three ritual Churches (Latin, Syro-Malabar and Syro-Malankara) when they start feeling the drastic fall of clerical and religious vocations in the course of time, will realize the need to work together jointly and give expression to faith in the challenging circumstances of the country. More than all kinds of exhortation for unity and cooperation among the ritual

Churches, what would bring them together is when they begin to feel that the source of their traditional clerical power is drying. It will be an awakening to what is most essential in the practice of faith and Church's commitment to the people.

Clearing the Theological Ground

Be that as it may, it is important to note that Small Christian Communities have a deeper theological founding, and are not to be interpreted in terms of practical expediency. I am referring to the theological status of the local church. Universal versus the local is an important epistemological question which is discussed at times openly; most of the times it is implied in the difference in theological approaches. Whether it is the relationship of the universal Church vis-à-vis local Churches, or universal theological categories versus contextual theologies, a tension can be observed. For the theologian Ratzinger and others, particular or local Church is only a concrete realization in a place of the universal Church which is pre-existent, reminding us of the old Platonic school of de-historicized abstract thought. It has as its consequence a universal theology attached to a universal Church that has "ontological and chronological priority over local Church".[5] Consequently, local Churches and contextual theologies become diluted versions of what is considered the normative and the universal.

In chapter six in the context of our discussion on postcolonialism and Asian theology we discussed about the concept of singularity. Here we shall discuss it in relation to Basic Christian Communities. I think the concept of *"singularity"* could challenge the way the universal and the particular are inter-related.[6] No local Church or Basic Christian Community is a copy of a general repeatable model. Each community has its own unique characteristics. The Basic Communities in Africa is different from the ones in Latin America; the Latin American, again different from the the Asian ones. This socio-cultural situation in which these communities find themselves, make each one of them unique. We will understand a local small community by entering into its narrative and interacting with it. This reminds us of the various communities narrated in the Acts of the Apostles and in the letters of St Paul. Each of the Pauline community was different and Paul interacts with them differently. He does not repeat his pastoral approach from one place to the other, but deals with them in their singularity. This leads us to our next point.

Another important theological basis for Small Christian Communities is provided by the theology of the *people of God* in Vatican II, as well as by its understanding of the Church as a mystery of *communion*. In the post-conciliar discussion, often, the description of the Church as people of God and Church as communion are viewed antithetically. Those who are suspicious that the category of people of God could be a Trajon horse bringing into the Church surreptitiously a sociological category of "people" and encourage a political populism, have been quick to replace it with the categories of mystery and communion. However, Basic Christian Communities represent a happy blending of both the categories – people of God and communion. Without communion, there could be no meaningful discourse about people of God in the Church; on the other hand, without the discourse on real people present in flesh and blood, the category of communion could become an evasive abstraction and a subterfuge. The bonds of loving relationships among the members of the small communities and respect for each one's dignity and charisma will foster communion among them, and spur them on to engage themselves in service to society in the footsteps of Jesus. Basic Christian Communities will reflect the mystery of the divine communion of the Father, the Son and the Holy Spirit in their oneness and mutuality. Institutional structures of the Church may not be able to foster this mystery of the Church as people and as communion, as effectively and in depth as the Small Christian Communities could do. Rightly then we can say of Basic Christian Communities that they "reinvent the Church".[7] It is unfortunate that, while Vatican II allows a lot of space for the life and development of Small Christian Communities, canon law restricts the understanding of the local Church to the diocese. One would expect that canon law would give room to the understanding of the presence of the Church in small communities and think of the order in the Church in the light of this experience.[8]

A Copernican Revolution

Basic Christian Communities represent a Copernican revolution in ecclesiology. A Church that orbited around priests and bishops finally came to be understood as focused on people, on community. This revolution was effected in Vatican II. The very fact that in the Council, people of God were treated as the primary category before talking about hierarchy, is the clearest sign of this revolution which, unfortunately, is not followed through in all its implications. The new theological vision needed to be translated into practice. Since Vatican II, one relied on certain new structures like pastoral council, parish council and similar bodies with the participation of the people of God represented by the laity, clergy, and the religious. However, these structural innovations are far from being adequate.

Some new means were required to live out the vision of the Church as God's people. Small Christian Communities are in a way translation of the grand vision of the Church as a people, and as a communion. Pope Paul VI in his important document on evangelization makes one of the earliest official statements on Basic Christian Communities, acknowledging the role they can play. After analysing the increasing growth of the Basic Christian Communities in its strength and weakness, the document said: "As hearers of the Gospel which is proclaimed to them and privileged beneficiaries of evangelization, they [Basic Christian Communities] will soon become proclaimers of the Gospel themselves".[9] In the post-synodal document on the laity, John Paul II underlined the importance of these communities. It speaks of the "small, basic or so-called 'living' communities, where the faithful can communicate the Word of God and express it in service and love to one another; these communities are true expressions of ecclesial communion and centres of evangelization, in communion with their pastors."[10]

The Conciliar change of vision to people of God and community represents a shift to a new paradigm of participatory Church. To be able to understand what that means, we could recall here the often repeated question, whether the structures like pastoral council, parish council are consultative or deliberative. Bishop Francis Claver of the Philippines, one of the leading figures in the promotion of Basic Ecclesial Communities in his country, noted how such questions fail to recognize the change of paradigm that has taken place.[11] These questions would make sense in a basically hierarchy-centred model in which these structures are thought to be simply some devices to enlist the support of the laity without, however, any basic change in the exercise of authority itself; hence, the preoccupation to ensure the authority of priests and bishops by declaring these bodies no more than consultative. In the new paradigm of truly participatory Church, such questions would not fit in, nor make much sense.

The Becoming of a Local Church

Small Christian Communities can be viewed as the concrete reception of the ecclesiological vision of Vatican II, as we find especially in the documents of *Lumen Gentium* and *Gaudium et Spes*. Against the strong centralized conception of a universal Church, Vatican II spoke of particular Churches, meaning thereby the diocesan and regional Churches. The people and the clergy of the diocese gathered around the bishop celebrating the Eucharist becomes the symbol of the particular Church. What we find in Small Christian Communities is a further step in the concretization of the mystery of the Church. Vatican II rarely used the expression "local Church", while its most frequent and preferred expression was "particular Church". The Small Christian Communities give a new form and shape to the understanding of local Church. A local Church gives greater attention to the socio-cultural environment in which it exists. It is concerned about the people and culture of the society where the Church finds itself.[12] As an expression of local Church, the Small Christian Communities try to immerse themselves into the everyday life of the people around, and live out the implications of faith in concrete circumstances. CELAM – the Bishops' Conference of Latin America expressed the nature and role of these communities from out of their experience in different parts of the continent. In Medellin, the bishops said,

> The Christian base community is the first and fundamental ecclesial nucleus, which on its own level must make itself responsible for the richness and expansion of the faith, as well as the cult which is its expression. This

community becomes then the initial cell of the ecclesiastical structure and the focus of evangelization.[13]

They have reaffirmed the place of Basic Christian Communities in the life and mission of the Church, in their assemblies at Puebla (1978), Santo Domingo (1992) and at Aparecida (2007). Similarly, Association of Member Episcopal Conferences of Eastern Africa (AMECEA) has endorsed the formation of Basic Ecclesial Communities. It may not be historically correct to think of *Comunidades Ecclesiales de Base* (CEBs) of Latin America as the precursor. It would appear that the movement of Small Christian Communities took place in Latin America and Africa simultaneously, and rather independently,[14] whereas the Basic Christian Communities in Asia underwent influences from Africa and Latin America.

Living a Life of Communion

The second great impulse for a new model of the Church represented in the Small Christian Communities derives from the understanding of it as *communion*. It means that the Church is not an ensemble of institutions, structures, and centres of authority, but rather an *inter-subjective reality*. In other words, Church is a matter of relationship which is what basically the word communion denotes. In fact, the relationship among the three persons of the Trinity is the inspiration for the coming into being of the mystery of the Church. Modern life and experience clearly show how systems are impersonal, and each one has an autonomous existence of its own, independent of people. An overly authority-centred and structure-based understanding of Church suffers the same lot. Vatican II took us to a new level by making us realize that the Church is a communion in which people live together in love and fellowship. To be able to understand this, we may recall here, the well-known distinction the German sociologist Ferdinand Tönnies made between *Gesellschaft* and *Gemeinshaft*. Whereas the former focuses on the system, the latter is a reality of communion. The theological aspect of Church as communion - the basis for Small Christian Communities - could be illustrated also by many insights from the theory of communication.

The Small Christian Communities are attempts to live in depth the basic reality of faith which is inherently communitarian in nature. It is not a question of faith of an individual and her God, but a faith that belongs equally to the community. Hence faith to be nurtured requires a living community of persons interacting among themselves. This helps the growth in faith supporting one another. The foundational reality of love has an inherent mutuality. Hope too is something we share as community, since our ultimate destiny is bound together. In short, Small Christian Communities find their foundation in the very nature of faith, love and hope, all of which are communitarian. It is clear then why these Basic Communities are able to provide a conducive environment to live the Christian experiences in depth. This realization led Pope John Paul II to see in these communities, signs of hope for the Church.

> A rapidly growing phenomenon in the young Churches — one sometimes fostered by the bishops and their Conferences as pastoral priority — is that of 'ecclesial basic communities' (also known by other names) which are proving to be good centers for Christian formation and missionary outreach. These are groups of Christians who, at the level of the family or in a similarly restricted setting, come together for prayer, Scripture reading, catechesis, and discussion on human and ecclesial problems with a view to a common commitment. These communities are a sign of vitality within the Church, an instrument of formation and evangelization, and a solid starting point for a new society based on 'civilization of love.[15]

In the Footsteps of Jesus – Good News to the Poor

Small Christian Communities help us follow in the footsteps of Jesus closely and directly. The Nazareth manifesto of Jesus is very clear that the good news is addressed to the poor (Lk 4:18-19). In today's world, there is a calculated attempt to cover up the poor and hide the harsh reality of poverty. With every passing day proving the failure of capitalism as it brings new woes, especially to the poor, one wants to impress that the system is sane, and it has helped to eliminate poverty. This window-dressing attempts to show that there are less poor today,[16] which is contrary to truth. Like in any system, the institutional Church can function on its own, turning the poor into objects of charity and benevolence. The vision of Jesus shows the poor as the main addressee of the Good News of God's Kingdom (Lk 6:20-23). Basic Christian Communities, as we find in most developing countries - in Latin America, Africa and Asia - are communities of the poor. Whereas in these very regions, traditional Christianity was dominated by the powerful, the elites, landlords, those of the upper castes, here is a model of the Church where no such discrimination and distinctions are possible. These Small Christian Communities are communities of equals. They are open spaces where we hear the voices of the poor, their experiences, struggles, their aspirations and hopes.

The Little Flock

A second dimension that reflects the spirit of Jesus is their "smallness". Throughout the Gospel we find Jesus making contrasts. Biblical scholars tell us, for example, about the contrast parables. These contrasts were necessary because the Good News to the poor calls for a different model from the dominant one. The whole tenor of Jesus' teaching highlights for example the small, what is marginal and despised, and what is hidden from the eyes of the world. While the disciples were struck by the magnificent structure of the temple of Jerusalem which was an architectural marvel of the time, Jesus was not impressed by it (Lk 21:5). Rather he points out to the widow in the temple who offers all that she has, and praises her (Lk 21:1-4 and Mk 12:41-44). He speaks about the mustard seed which grows into a big tree (Mt 13:31-32; Mk 4:30-32; Lk 13:18-19), about salt (Mt 5:13; Mk 9:50; Lk 14:34-35), and leaven (Mt 13:33; Lk 13:20-21) hidden but which animates the food and the dough. Further, we find Jesus extolling the wisdom of those who are considered foolish before the world, and speaking of the revelation God has made to babes and children (Mt 11:25-27). Thus, when we qualify Christian communities as "small", in a way, it brings before our eyes the entire Gospel and the way Jesus goes about with his teaching and ministry. These Small Christian Communities are themselves a message about the Kingdom of God, pointing us away from the world of power and pomp. As Small Christian Communities they are agents of Jesus' continuing mission (Acts 2:42-47; 4:32-35).

The great Conciliar theologian Karl Rahner became increasingly aware how the social and familial structures traditionally supporting faith were falling with the process of modernization. He foresaw that the number of Christians will diminish in the course of time and Christian communities will be little flocks, minorities. This is not something to be lamented about but to be taken as a challenge. Christians are called to make their faith more and more deeply personal and become committed to the Gospel mission.[17] This is true today of Christians in every part of the world – in traditional Christian countries as well as in the regions of the South.

The Model of Synagogue

We will understand more closely Small Christian Communities by relating them to the Jewish institution of synagogue. While the temple was in Jerusalem and became symbol of the system and of priestly authority, the synagogues were, so to say, a creation of the laity. It was a community of life of a group of people. It was not bound so much by territory as the bond that united a group of people who met to pray, to read the scriptures, to encounter neighbours, and to sort out various issues of the community. Synagogue functioned as a kind of local "parliament". When the early Christians wanted to follow the footsteps of Jesus, it was not so much the temple as synagogue that provided the model and inspiration. The house Churches (Rom 16:5; 1 Cor 16:19; Col 4:15; Philm 1:2) of early Christianity could be viewed as transformed synagogues.

The evidence in the Acts of the Apostles speaks to us about the meeting together of the disciples in fellowship. It was a life in common and a life in which mutuality and sharing were important. "They devoted themselves to the apostles' teaching and fellowship, to the breaking of bread and the prayers" (Acts 2:42). It would appear that for the first three centuries of Christianity, homes were the meeting place of believers. Lydia for example transformed her home into a meeting place of believers (Acts 16:15, 40). Priscilla and Aquila did not only turn their home into a domestic Church (Rom 16:4-5) but were actively involved in ministry and encouraged Paul and Apollo in their ministries (Acts 18:2-5, 26). More such communities were associated with the house of Gaius (Rom 16:23), Nymphas (Col 4:15), Titus Justus (Acts 18:7).

When the records of early Christianity speak about "houses" where the disciples met, what is meant was not a building in the first place; rather it referred to the *family*. Paul in his letters mentions several of those families who were the points of reference for the community (Rom 16:5; 1Cor

16:19; Col 4:15; Philm 1:2). Domestic Churches or house Churches refer to these experiences of the disciples. These small domestic communities stood for a different set of values than the prevailing ones. Whereas in antiquity bravery, courage, triumph, etc., were extolled, these communities, inspired by a different vision, fostered, for example, values of tolerance, forbearance, forgiveness, benevolence, sincerity, perseverance. We do not find any preoccupation with establishing big structures. Everything is viewed as provisional and transitory, and perceiving God in everything (I Cor. 10:31) was thought very important.

Something that needs to be highlighted is the fact that women played an important role in these house-Churches. Paul allowed them to pray and prophecy in the prayer meetings (1Cor 11:5). In fact, one of the factors that attracted women to Christian discipleship was that they were not discriminated against as was the case in the environment of their times; rather women were called to positions of leadership (Phil 4:2; Phoebe in Rom16:1). This is something we are also witnessing today in Basic Christian Communities. Yet another difference is the spirit of universality. While we find the model of synagogue operative in the early Christian communities, we also note how these were different in other respects. One of the distinguishing marks of these communities was their open-endedness. They reflected the universal spirit of Jesus going beyond ethnic or closed ghetto mentality.

From the Constantine-turn of Christianity to our times, there have been, In spite of heavy institutionalization of the Church, many movements, as for example in the Mediaeval times – movements that gave birth to the Mendicant Orders, which reminded the Church of reforms and solidarity with the poor. Today's Small Christian Communities may not be compared to any such movements in the history of the Church. Rather, they hark us back to the earliest form of Christianity when, in the midst of a lot of uncertainties of their own identity, the disciples gathered together to recall the memory of Jesus, to pray together, to participate in common meals. They pooled together what they had and shared among themselves (Acts 2:42-47; 4:32-35;1Cor 11:17-34). In so doing in the name of Jesus and according to his teachings, the disciples forged a new identity of their own.

The Cultural Matrix

The Basic Christian Communities in Asia, Africa, Latin America, and Oceania have a strong cultural matrix. The ecclesial reality of communion is built up through these communities since the cultures in these continents create a conducive atmosphere for their flourishing. In Asia, the human bonds are highly valued and practiced. Family is something people are attached to and family relationships are fostered through encounter, mutual help, support, hospitality, etc. It is these values and practices which are very supportive of Basic Christian Communities. These become, for many Asians, extended families, as the bonds of love and care unite the members of the Basic Christian Communities. These relationships are deepened and cemented by sharing in the Word of God, worshipping, praying together, and assisting one another. In a society where individualism is at work, it is very difficult to form and sustain Basic Christian Communities. In fact, one would find very rarely such communities in western Europe or in North America. On the other hand, since there is great support of the culture and ethos, they flourish in Asia, Africa, Latin America and Oceania. Speaking of this cultural matrix, Agbonkhianmeghe E. Orobator, an African theologian observes,

> The ecclesiological expression of SCC [Small Christian Communities] corresponds to uniquely African values of interdependence, harmony, cooperation and hospitality that are constitutive elements of the human community. Commonly rendered as "Ubuntu", this anthropological principle grounds the fundamental understanding of person-in-community as wholeness, relationality and solidarity. In light of this understanding, official texts defining SCCs as local churches emphasize the aspect of communal belonging, inter-relationship and a shared vision of and responsibility for the mission of the Church in the local context.[18]

Dialogue, Participation and Growth

We noted how the Base Christian Communities are a fellowship of equals and how their fellowship is nurtured by continuous dialogue. It is by listening to the Word of God and to one another, by mutual sharing, common prayer etc. that the Small Christian Communities are built up. The truth that the people of God are priestly people (cf. 1Pet 2:9) finds concrete realization in the active participation of the people in the liturgical services in these communities, which are not priest-centred, as parishes are. The ordained ministers, like the hierarchy, are in service of the people. The environment of freedom, dialogue, and participation one experiences in these communities opens up avenues for new forms of ministry. In fact, in the early Church, ministries came into being according to the needs, and they differed according to the communities. The warmth, encouragement and support people find in the Small Christian Communities serve them to form themselves and grow in faith as mature human persons. These communities with their flexibility and face-to-face encounter provide an ideal environment for the spiritual-formation of all the members. Every person has his or her unique story. The small communities are the milieu where with ease it can be shared with others to mutual edification and growth in faith and spirituality. This is far from the huge traditional structures where people simply go to attend mass, and where there is little interaction and opportunity to come out with their intimate experiences of faith. Precisely these spiritual experiences and moments of personal transformation will support and encourage the other members of the small community in their spiritual journey. All this helps to bond the group together and make the living of faith a joyful experience.

Small Christian Communities and Public Life

To view these communities as inner-church groupings for better management and administration of the traditional structures of parish and diocese would mean failing to understand their true spirit and nature. The life of faith lived in these communities reach out to the larger society. They are conscious of the mission and leadership Christians are called upon to exercise. Situations are quite different in the various geographical regions. Political engagement of Basic Christian Communities in Latin America has been a very striking feature. History tells us how in the midst of authoritarian regimes and military rules, the Small Christian Communities in that continent functioned as a critical force. These communities were viewed as inimical to the state, and their active members have been sent to prison, tortured, and brutally murdered. This need not be a surprise. For when Medellin and later Puebla advocated the Small Christian Communities, they envisaged also a role of resistance to the structural injustice and poverty plaguing the Latin American continent. These communities succeeded in transforming the rural situation of peasants and marginal groups. They have also great potential for the education and literacy of ordinary people.[19] While critics of religions were sceptical about any role of religion for social transformation, and sociologists were seriously in doubt about the capability of Catholicism for any far-reaching change in the socio-political conditions, the Basic Christian Communities proved them wrong by their radical stand and transformative potential.[20]

In other parts of the world, the situation may not be exactly the same, but these communities have however, faced great challenges to live the Christian faith in the complex socio-political *environments*. In the Philippines, the first Basic Ecclesial Communities were formed in the late 1960's in the conflict-ridden region of Mindanao, and slowly in other parts of the country. The dictatorial regime of Marcos saw in them a likely threat because of the political conscientization and resistance they offered to his rule. These communities were involved, like in Latin America, also in issues of peasants, forestry, land-alienation, and so on. They came to be severely censured and persecuted. From 1991 with the Plenary Council of the Philippines II, Basic Ecclesial Communities became a national programme of the Church and with encouragement by more and more bishops, they began to spread fast. With this, probably, the original prophetic thrust of these Basic Christian Communities also began to decline.

Speaking of Basic Christian Communities in relation to public life, we need to realize their resourcefulness for democratization. In many developing countries, there are military or dictatorial regimes, and even where democracy is the form of governance, it often remains at a formal level. A substantive approach to democracy involves the active participation of the people at the grassroots level. By their spirit of dialogue and cooperation, Small Christian Communities have proved to be veritable schools of democracy. The style of internal organization and practices within these communities provided a model for the democratization of the larger society.

Interreligious Harmony

In multireligious societies like in most countries of Asia, fostering of fellowship needs to reach out to neighbours of other faiths. History and experience show how the big ecclesial structures were perceived by our neighbours as structures of power, and indeed as a threat to their faith. In that sense, the Small Christian Communities have significant witnessing effect for the message of the Gospel. Moreover, these communities in Asia are known for their openness to the religious and spiritual life of peoples of other faiths, and their readiness to collaborate with others. The dialogue here is not simply on doctrinal issues, but a dialogue of everyday life. In short, Basic Christian Communities help us realize in concrete the teachings of Vatican II on other religions in the plan of God's salvation.

Small Human Communities

The Church is a mystery of communion and as the Constitution on the Church "Lumen Gentium" notes in its very first number (LG 1), the Church is a sign of the unity of the entire human family. As such, the Basic Christian Communities could never be simply a communion among Christian faithful alone. It needs to point to the unity of humankind. Whereas in Latin America and many African countries, there is a practical overlap of the Christian community with the larger society, in Asia, this is not the case. Christians live amidst large number of people nurtured by different religious traditions and other conceptions of life. The humanistic aspect of the ecclesia comes out when it has in its very structure this openness to the world, to other people, other religious traditions, and so on. Moreover, in situations of endemic religious conflicts like in South Asia, we need communities that promote common human values shared by peoples of different religious traditions. This has given rise to experiment with the so-called "Basic Human Communities". Given their flexibility, the Basic Christian and Human Communities could contribute to the promotion of peace and harmony in the society. What matters is not the size or number of people in a community but the vision that accompanies them. As the "little flock," the Small Christian and Human Communities will be effective instruments in spreading greater understanding and communion among people. They could sow the seeds for a non-violent and peaceful society. The project of Basic Human Communities goes beyond what is envisaged in inter-religious dialogue. Christians become part of small communities with peoples of other faiths and all of them oriented to transform our society and world into more humane, tolerant, and harmonious one. The very fostering of communion and sharing among members of the Small Human Communities bear witness to a new and different world. Such communities at the bottom could be a great force of support also to various new social movements.[21]

Anxiety about Basic Christian Communities

One of the great achievements of Basic Christian Communities is that they activated the participation of the laypeople, especially women. In these Small Christian Communities, women's voice and leadership come to expression in most unsuspected ways and forms, even though as in the past, there are efforts on the part of male members to control and dominate the small communities. These communities translate into practice the truth that the Church is the people of God, freeing it from clericalism. The active role played by the laity and especially committed women makes the communities very vibrant.

At the same time, precisely for this reason, these communities also became objects of suspicion. This is in spite of the fact that these communities have become part of the policy of many bishops' conferences – regional, national and continental. In a hierarchical Church, understandably, concerns were voiced whether these communities abide by the leadership and direction of the magisterium of bishops, of priests, and whether they respect the ecclesial structures. There was a fear about these communities being manipulated for political ends. The bishops of Latin America, though, as we noted earlier, affirmed the place of Basic Christian Communities, however, were concerned about them setting up a parallel "popular Church" (*Iglesia popular*) in opposition to the official Church. As many of these communities were deeply involved in the work of liberation, fear was expressed that these communities politicize the Church and use Marxism in their theological and pastoral reflections. Since the concept of the Church as the people of God was open to misinterpretation in Basic Christian Communities, one shifted focus to Church as "communion". The matter came up for discussion at the Extraordinary Synod of 1985, and it was argued that "people of God" could reduce the Church to a sociological reality, whereas the notion of communion safeguards its theological character. Often condemnation of liberation theology went along with denunciation of Basic Christian Communities.

There is a debate today that Basic Christian Communities so active in the 1980s in Latin America have lost their momentum; people are turning to Pentecostalism, and hence loss of its original liberational thrust, so it is argued. Often contrast is made between the stagnation of Basic Ecclesial Communities and vibrancy of Pentecostalism. The stagnation of the Basic Communities is often attributed to the control by ecclesiastical authorities. But studies and researches at the grassroots show that the lack of encouragement and even opposition by Church authorities does not explain this phenomenon adequately. Rather, one should look into socio-political factors and conditions outside the Church.[22]

When there was dictatorship, militarism, and authoritarian governments, the Basic Christian Communities of Latin America were a great force of resistance and challenge to the powers, and these communities were very effective at the grassroots level. That kind of situation today is gone, with democratization of many countries of Latin America. But that does not mean that Basic Christian Communities have become simply pietistic prayer groups. Even after transition to democratic rule, we find in many Latin American countries, the situation of poverty, injustice, and exploitation continuing. There is yet "no land of milk and honey".[23] In many parts of the countryside where people still struggle with land alienation and destruction of natural environment, the Basic Christians Communities are still active in resisting exploitation and injustice.[24] The liberational agenda is carried forward in a different form in a new socio-political situation.

In India and in many Asian countries, and in Africa, by and large, Basic Christian Communities lack the radicality we find in these communities in Latin America. Nevertheless, the experiences in Latin America and other parts of the world tell us the great impact the Basic Christian

Communities made, and hence understandably attempts to denunciate and suppress them. In reality, the Basic Christian Communities with their deep ecclesiology and Christology, helped to "reinvent the Church"[25] and to indicate a "new way of being Church".

Conclusion

Basic Christian Communities are like cells that vitalize the organism of the Church. Their phenomenal growth over the years, especially in Latin America, Africa, and Asia points to the need for new forms of community, and for a personalized faith lived in solidarity with others. In their form and spirit, these communities resemble the domestic Churches of earliest Christian disciples. They provide the environment for the believers to grow in faith and hope, and deepen love and communion, following the footsteps of Jesus. Moreover, Basic Christian Communities give concrete expression to the local Church living and practicing faith in a determined cultural and socio-political context; it facilitates the emergence of local leadership of the laity. Small and flexible as the Basic Christian Communities are, they interact effectively with the milieu and bear witness to the Gospel. They also facilitate the integration of faith with daily life, and create the environment for encounter, exchange, and reconciliation with people with whom one lives. In many instances, they play a prophetic role by challenging the existing structures, injustice, exploitation, and violation of human rights. In these communities we experience a new way of being Church. More than any other means, it is perhaps the life and praxis of Basic Christian Communities that have helped to translate into real life the spirit and teachings of Vatican II.

Bibliography

Batangan, Enrique P. and Catholic Institute for International Relations. *Faith and Social Change: Basic Christian Communities in the Philippines. CIIR Justice Papers* (7) (London: Catholic Institute for International Relations, 1985).

Bellah, Robert N. "Small face-to-face Christian communities." *New Oxford Review* 59 (Jun 1992), 17-22.

Boff, Leonard. *The Base Communities Reinvent the Church* (London: Collins, 2001).

Clark, David and Conferences of Major Religious Superiors of England Wales. *Basic Christian Communities: Implications for Church and Society. Pastoral Investigation of Social Trends. Working Paper* 16 (Liverpool: Liverpool Institute of Socio-Religious Studies on Behalf of the Conferences of Major Religious Superiors of England and Wales, 1978).

Cousineau, Madeleine. "Not Blaming the Pope: The Roots of Crisis in Brazilian Base Communities." *Journal of Church and State* 45 (2) (2003), 349-365.

Cowan, Michael A, and Lee, Bernard J. *Conversation, Risk, and Conversion: The Inner and Public Life of Small Christian Communities* (Maryknoll, N.Y.: Orbis, 1997).

De Lima, Gilbert. *Evangelization in India through Basic Communities* (Mumbai: St Pauls, 1996).

Gabriel, Manuel G. *Doing Theology. Basic Ecclesial Communities: A New Way of Being Church in the Philippines* (Manila: Anvil, 2008).

Gajiwala, Astrid Lobo., et al., eds. *Renewed Effort for Inculturation in Indian Church?* (Bangalore: Dharmaram Publication, 2002).

Healey, Joseph G and Hinton, Jeanne., eds. *Small Christian Communities Today: Capturing the New Moment* (Maryknoll, N.Y.: Orbis Books, 2005).

Kerkhofs, Jan. "Basic Communities in Europe." *Pro Mundi Vita* 81 (1980), 30-36.

Maria, David A. *Beyond Boundaries: Hindu-Christian Relationship and Basic Christian Communities* (Delhi: ISPCK 2009).

O'Halloran, James. *Living Cells: Vision and Practicalities of Small Christian Communities and Group* (Dublin: Columba Press, 2010).

Pathil, Kuncheria. "Basic Christian Communities: A New Ecclesial Model." *Jeevadhara* (1985), 326-336.

Pelton, Robert S., ed. *Small Christian Communities: Imagining Future Church.* (Notre Dame, Ind.: University of Notre Dame Press, 1997).

Pinto, Joseph Prasad. *Inculturation through Basic Communities* (Bangalore: Asian Trading, 1985).

Ponnamuthan, Silvester. *The Spirituality of Basic Ecclesial Communities in the Socio-Religious Context of Trivandrum, Kerala, India* (Rome: Pontifical Gregorian University, 1996).

Rahner, Karl. *The Shape of the Church to Come.* Translated from German and Introduction by Edward Quinn (London: S.P.C.K., 1974).

Torres, Sergio and Eagleson, John. *The Challenge of Basic Christian Communities: Papers from the International Ecumenical Congress of Theology, February 20-March 2, 1980, São Paulo, Brazil.* Translated by John Drury (Maryknoll, N.Y.: Orbis Books, 1981).

Vijay, Thomas Scaria, Francis, Colaco, Elvin S., eds. *Breaking Ground.* Papers presented at the International Theological Congress on Small Christian Communities held at Pallotine Animation Centre, Nagpur, India, August 17th-19th, 2011 (Nagpur, India: PAC Publications, 2014).

Endnotes

[1] They are called by different names: Small Christian Communities; Basic Christian Communities; Base Christian Communities; Basic Ecclesial Communities and so on. In this chapter all these expressions are used interchangeably.

[2] Quoted in Leonard Boff, *The Base Communities Reinvent the Church* (London: Collins, 2001), p. 3.

[3] This statement should not be interpreted as if I were against folk religion and advocating a head-level faith. We need to make an important distinction here. There are forms of folk religion in Christianity that emerge from the life and experience of the people; the people themselves are the actors and agents. This is different from an induced popular religion by the institutional Church and the clerical establishment. Here, unfortunately, people are not agents, since these devotional popular practices are fostered by the established Church, wherein commercial aspects are also involved. See Felix Wilfred, "Popular Religion and Asian Contextual Theologising", in Jacques Van Nieuwenhove and Berma Klein Goldewijk, eds, *Popular Religion, Liberation and Contextual Theology* (Kampen: Uitgeversmaatschappij J. H. Kok, 1991), pp. 146-157.

[4] Felix Wilfred, see chapter 10 in this volume.

[5] See Walter Kasper, "On the Church: A Friendly Reply to Cardinal Ratzinger", *The Furrow*, 52:6 (June 2001), 323-332. The author argues why the historical and theological arguments of Ratzinger are untenable.

[6] See Gayatri Chakravorty Spivak, "Scattered Speculations on the Subaltern and the Popular", *Postcolonial Studies. An Anthology* (Oxford: Wiley Blackwell, 2016), pp. 60-70, at p. 60.

[7] Leonard Boff, *The Base Communities Reinvent the Church* (London: Collins, 2001).

[8] Cf. *Concilium 2013/5*, A special issue on Reform of the Roman Curia.

[9] Paul VI, *Evangelii Nuntiandi* 58. Having spread fast in Latin America, Africa, Asia, and other geographic regions, Basic Christian Communities became object of discussion and deliberation at the Synod on Evangelization (1974). The pope cautions against these communities critiquing the established Church and its ways. There is a fear that they could turn out to be simply sociological or political entities. Besides the papal pronouncements, we have numerous regional and continental episcopal bodies coming out with statements encouraging small Christian communities, and these include CBCI and FABC. Going into all those statements may digress us from the main arguments of this chapter. For details on the teachings of the Church, see Silvester Ponnamuthan,

The Spirtuality of Basic Ecclesial Communities in the Socio-Religious Context of Trivandrum/Kerala, India (Rome: Pontifical Gregorian University, 1996).

[10] *Christifideles laici,* no. 26.

[11] Cf. Francis Claver, "Basic Christian Communities in a Wider Context", *East Asian Pastoral Review* (1986), 362-368.

[12] To add a personal note here, when I served as the secretary of the Theological Advisory Commission of the Federation of Asian Bishop's Conferences (FABC) we drew up for the Conference a document called "Theses on the Local Church" in which the accent was set on the socio-cultural context in defining its nature. As the document notes, it "approaches the reality of the local Church as issuing from the encounter between the Gospel and the culture of a people (Theses 5 – 9)". For the text of the document, see Vimal Tirimanna, ed, *Sprouts of Theology from the Asian Soil. Collection of TAC and OTC Documents 1987-2007* (Bangalore: Claretian Publications, 2007), pp.19-68.

[13] As quoted in Klaus Krämer and Klaus Vellguth, eds, *Small Christian Communities. Fresh Stimulus for a Forward-looking Church* (Quezon City: Claretian Publications, 2013), *op.cit.* p.158-159.

[14] See Agbonkhianmeghe Orobator, "Small Christian Communities as a New Way of Becoming Church: Practice, Progress and Prospects", in Klaus Kraemer – Klaus Vellguth, eds, pp.113-125, at 115.

[15] *Redemptoris Missio* 5. Pope Paul VI also spoke about the important place of Basic Christian Communities in the life of the Church and for its evangelizing mission. See *Evangelii Nuntiandi.*

[16] This, for example, was what was done recently by the Planning Commission of India, inspired by liberalism and the spirit of globalisation. But the way the Commission calculated below poverty-line was challenged in the Parliament and also by the civil society.

[17] Cf. Karl Rahner, *The Shape of the Church to Come,* Translation from the German and introduction by Edward Quinn (London: S.P.C.K., 1974).

[18] Orobator, *art.cit* p.114.

[19] Cf. Johannes P. van Vugt, *Democratic Organization for Social Change. Latin American Christian Base Communities and Literacy Campaigns* (New York: Bergin & Garvey,1991).

[20] Cf. Madeleine Cousineau Adriance, *Promised Land. Base Christian Communities and the Struggle for the Amazon* (New York: State University of New York Press, 1995).

[21] Cf. Maria A. David, *Beyond Boundaries: Hindu-Christian Relationship and Basic Christian Communities* (Delhi: ISPCK 2009).

[22] Cf. Madeleine Cousineau, "Not Blaming the Pope: The Roots of Crisis in Brazilian Base Communities", *Journal of Church and State*, 45:2 (2003), 349-365.

[23] Cf. Carol Ann Drogus, "No Land of Milk and Honey: Women CEB Activists in Post Transitional Brazil", *Journal of Interamerican Studies and World Affairs,* 41:4 (1999), 35-51.

[24] Madeleine Cousineau Adriance, *Promised land, op.cit.*

[25] Leonardo Boff, *op.cit.*

CHAPTER 12

Theology Animating Canon Law

C anon law and theology are not polar opposites as is often made out to be, but part of a common journey of the people of God for whose life and growth both of them render distinct services. This indicates the need for close collaboration between them.[1] It hasn't always been so.[2] There were times when canon law and theology followed parallel paths, or when theology itself was pursued so close to canon law as to be qualified as "juridical theology"; and canon law was followed without theological vision guiding it, resulting in its fall into legal positivism. Without any claim of being exhaustive, let me offer a few reflections on some selected issues and questions that emerge in the relationship of theology and canon law.

Presuppositions

When law is viewed as a pre-designed blueprint and expression of the will of the law-giving authority (*ordinatio legislatoris*), the focus is naturally on the compliance to the norms. A vibrant theology will help canon law to adopt a more dynamic conception of itself, as serving the common good and accompanying the people on their journey of faith, hope, and love. Here is both a different presupposition of law and a different theology. That we have moved, as *Gaudium et Spes* notes, from a static conception of reality to a more dynamic one (GS 4-10) applies also to the realm of law in the Church, and it dovetails with the theological conception of the believing community on the move as a pilgrim people. Church on the move towards the fullness of the Kingdom of God has to constantly shift its tent to new locations following new demands and challenges. When canon law is tempted to strike root, theology needs to show the path ahead and invite it to make the necessary changes which ultimately help the people of God in their journey. Theology and canon law can and should work in tandem. Their cooperation is especially to be seen in interpretation of the laws which enshrine values and ideals which both of them share and the promotion of which, albeit in two different but correlated fields, they have as their tasks. Let me cite from one of the great canonists of modern times on why canon law needs to be guided by theology, and not the other way.

> Theology has the capacity out of its own resources to form a judgment over the fittingness of canonical norms for theological institutions. It has the means to determine if the rules are well proportioned for the purpose of upholding the values in question…Canon law has no capacity at all to judge theology because legal *ordinationes* are not meant to be judgments. Besides, it would have no criteria; in its genesis it depends on theological affirmations concerning values.[3]

Their working together will be closer and implementation more effective, when both of them respect the subjecthood of the community and its process of appropriation of laws. This process of appropriation by the people is referred to as *reception* in Christian tradition. This applies as much to doctrines as to laws in the Church. If there is the sense of the community (*sensus fidelium*) in professing faith about which theology speaks, it is to be expected that the laws that bind them need to also vibrate with this sense of the faithful, and find reception among them. That is the best way also to see to the most effective implementation of the laws which will not be seen as an imposition from without (heteronomy) but self-binding laws (autonomy) of the community meant to help produce rich fruits of love, faith, and hope in a common life of communion.

Canon law needs to function under the theological horizon. There is something like hierarchy of truths about which Vatican II spoke (UR 11) and which facilitated the ecumenical initiatives and endeavours in the post-conciliar period. It would be an unrealistic and strange claim if all canons are placed at the same level, or, if each is accorded equal importance.[4] If one were to argue that they all come from the same legislator, that would be simply to claim formal authority for them without reference to the subject matter they deal with, and the degree of their closeness to the central values and ideals the believing community pursues. Some canonical directions on matters of worship may not be placed on par with issues of the equal dignity of all believers and issues of natural justice. This tells us also about the need for canon law to distinguish the grade of authority attached to the different teaching of truths. The fact of having the same legislator does not warrant attribution of equal grade to the laws without distinction.

Canon Law and the Balancing of Faith and Reason

In the history of canon law, there has been two major trends, namely to view it as *ordinatio rationis* (an ordering according to reason),[5] or view it as *ordinatio fidei* (an order according to faith).[6] It is similar to a major problematic encountered in the history of theology, namely the relationship between faith and reason. For anything to qualify itself as law, it should conform to the standards of reason and contribute to common good. This would save canon law from arbitrariness and authoritarian imposition. Applying today the standard of reason - which faith is not expected to contradict – would mean that the laws of the Church be such that they do not go against or undermine human dignity and basic human rights; that there be equality, fairness, and natural justice; and that there be no discrimination on gender basis. All these form part of universal human rights of which humanity has become increasingly conscious. Canon law cannot argue in the name of faith and justify violation of any of these fundamental questions common to human family. This has been strongly bolstered up by Vatican II through a theology of creation in its Pastoral Constitution on the Church in the Modern World. If canon law violates any of these things invoking faith in its support, its (canon law) very legitimacy as a legal instrument upholding justice may be seriously in question. Canon law requires a robust theology that can help it avoid many pitfalls. On the other hand, since the people of God is a community of faith, naturally, the faith-element needs to get reflected in its legal arrangement and ordering. Otherwise, canon law would remain merely at the formal level and will be imprisoned within legal positivism.

Ius Divinum - A Common Theological and Canonical Issue

The nature and binding force of law in canonical tradition have been made to depend on whether a legislation enshrines something deriving directly from divine ordering (*ex ordinatione divina, ius divinum*) or whether something is legislated by the Church for the purpose of common good. The lack of clarity in this matter is seen clearly in comparing the code of 1917 and the code of 1983. Instances where the former referred something as deriving from divine ordering have been deleted when they were reformulated in the code of 1983, and at the same time the new code introduces new canons of "divine law" or "divine institution" (which generally includes in the canonical tradition matters viewed as belonging to "natural law" as well), obviously with the claim of higher grade of authority.

To cite just one example, the code of 1917 speaking of the juridical power of hierarchy in canon 108 states that it consists of papacy and "of subordinate episcopacy" (*episcopatu subordinato*), and this is supposed to derive from divine institution (*ex divina institutione*).[7] In the light of the teaching of Vatican II on episcopacy and on the relationship of papacy and episcopacy, the new code instead sees episcopacy in the light of *collegiality*. This collegial unity following the relationship of Peter and the rest of the apostles is seen in *Lumen Gentium* (no. 22) as coming "from the will of the Lord" (*statuente Domino*), and subsequently codified in CIC can.330. Here is a case of canon law following development in theology, to the extent of abrogating in the code something which was once held to be of divine law. It is also interesting to observe how the use of divine right argument gets redefined in a new perspective in the light of theology. To cite an example, canon 948 of 1917 invokes the authority of Christ (*ex Christi institutione*) to establish the *distinction* between clergy and laity, whereas the code of 1983 follows the spirit of the people of God theology and states that some among the people of God are chosen to serve and shepherd the flock, and this is by divine institution (canon 1008).[8] As we could see, there is a difference in perspective and difference in accent in the use of divine law, underlining once again how important it is for canon law to follow closely theological developments and nuances.

There is a deeper problem, however, in the distinction between the divine law and ecclesiastical law. Canon law may not unilaterally decide upon this matter, but has to seek the help of theology which has to deal with this grey area where clear demarcations between the two are not an easy matter. Ironically, in the theological tradition too there has been no unanimity in this matter in every case. Just imagine that between eleventh and fourteenth centuries, the institution of cardinalate was viewed as coming from divine command (*ius divinum cardinalatus*) and the cardinals were seen by some as "sharing in the fullness of papal power and succeeding the apostolic college" (not the bishops)![9]

Further, if we were to argue on the basis of antiquity of traditions and practices in support of claim for divine right, we need to be attentive to the fact that some of these traditions have been viewed as of divine disposition whereas other traditions and customs are looked at as having been conditioned by the culture and context of the times.[10] In the absence of clarity in this matter, legitimate questions can be raised about crucial issues like the matter of sacraments, and the non-ordination of women — whether they are of divine command or something to do with the culture and traditions of the New Testament times. There is a strong argument for change in this matter, given the fact that in the history of Christianity, what was thought once as of divine right, was subsequently not held so. All these considerations are important also in view of ecumenical relationships in which categorical claims of divine right have been a serious obstacle. Again, theology could be of great assistance to canon law in order for it to become sensitive to issues of ecumenism.[11]

Issues of Discrepancy

There are questions where theology opens up new horizons for canon law, and yet this vision gets narrowed down in legislation, bringing about some serious inconsistency that affects renewal and innovation in the Church. By way of example, I am referring here to the question of power of governance and the question of election of bishops.

According to CIC canon 129, power of governance, called also as power of jurisdiction, is to be exercised by those who are constituted in sacred orders, namely, the episcopate, the priesthood and the diaconate, whereas the laity can only cooperate (*ad normam iuris cooperari possunt*) in the former's exercise of the power of governance. The argument for the legitimate exercise of power of governance derives from the fundamental reality of baptism in which independent of the state (clerical or lay) all believers participate in the priestly, prophetic, and kingly mission of Jesus. Moreover, they are endowed with different charisma and gifts for the life of the community. To this we could add the pastoral argument of the actual exercise of power of governance today in numerous Christian communities and parishes which are directed by lay persons who exercise in practice power of governance. There are numerous example in Christian history of lay exercise of jurisdictional power: emperors convoking councils; laity functioning as legates of the pope and even as Cardinal secretary of the state, not to mention the role of abbots and abbesses in medieval times exercising power of governance over their subjects and administering properties.[12] Nothing then in theology, history nor actual practice- stand against the exercise of the jurisdictional power by the laity. As James Coriden notes,

> The documents of the Second Vatican Council provide ample theological warrant for the possession and use of the power of governance by lay persons. The wide range of conciliar theological themes includes God's call, empowerment by the sacraments of initiation, full membership in God's people and Christ's body, sharing in Christ's threefold priestly, prophetic and kingly functions, active participation in and responsibility for the Church's mission and ministry, and finally the grace, power, and gifts of the Holy Spirit bestowed in abundance.[13]

Canon law has little to invoke in support of its present position of negation of this power to the laity. Here is a case where canon law deviates from theology. A closer attention to the theology of Vatican II would have spared the code from such anomaly of excluding the laity from the power of governance.

One may try to find a theological argument about the fact that, according to the teaching of Vatican II, the bishops, through their consecration receives not only the office of sanctifying and teaching, but as well *the office of governance*. This is a teaching whose importance lies in the fact that the office of governance is not additionally granted by the pope, which could make them appear as officers of the pope.[14] By rooting the power of the bishop in the sacrament, the Council has brought to balance the relationship between episcopacy and primacy. The same, however, should not be extrapolated in the relationship of the laity and clergy, to argue that because they do not have ordination, the laity therefore do not have the power of governance. This is to wrongly apply a teaching, culling it out of context, and to completely misunderstand the spirit and teachings of Vatican II. On the other hand, don't the Christian faithful by virtue of baptismal consecration participate in the kingly (governance) office of Christ, as they do in his priestly and prophetic role?

Selection of bishops is another issue in which tradition and theology are open, but canon law does not correspond to them, nor to the contemporary sensitivities. The entire people of God, clergy and laity, were involved in the election of bishops in early Church, up until twelfth century. Within this general frame, there was a plurality of modalities in choosing the bishop. Historical facts are well-known, and do not need elaboration. And yet, canon law is stuck with a model in which, there is hardly any role to the laity. The process is largely done by the papal legate. It contradicts the principle of subsidiarity and the theology of the local Church as envisaged by Vatican II. Worse is the case when bishops are so to say "air-dropped" for career promotions without any consultation with the local bishops, not to speak of the laity. It is truly an insult to the local Church.

While the Eastern Code is open for a more participatory mode of selection of bishops with its synodal structure, how come the Latin code legislates differently and in a centralized manner? The question becomes anomalous when in the same socio-cultural territory like India, the Oriental Bishops follow participatory model, as per the Eastern Code (cc.181-189),[15] whereas the Christians of Latin Church living in the same territory sharing the same conditions of life, are deprived of such participation. We can only pity the papal nuncios many of whom, in spite of their best intentions, are not in a position to assess the situation of the local Churches, often, on account of their lack of familiarity with the culture, language, life-situation, and history of the people, and yet expected to play crucial role in the selection of bishops.[16] The participation of the people in the selection of bishops, as John Huels and Richard R. Gaillardetz note, may not be dismissed as utopian and impractical. That is to ignore history. To counter such an argument and attitude, these authors have formulated model canons on the matter to show how this could take place concretely.[17]

Contextual Theology and Particular Laws and Customs

Theological pluralism derives from reflections on the life of faith as lived in different cultural, geographic, and historical contexts in which people of God find themselves. In the post-conciliar period, we have witnessed very rich and vibrant theologies emerging from Africa, Latin America, Asia, and Oceania. If theology is to assist the life of faith and make it fruitful relating it dynamically to contemporary experiences in context, then, we cannot have a rigid legal arrangement which is fixated and centralized. Today, canon law cannot model itself after a universally valid and applicable theology. The theological pluralism which was already there in the history of Christianity has now become most effectively realized than ever in the past. Canon law could do its service by meaningfully relating itself precisely to the contemporary realities which contextual theologies try to address. Today, merely invoking formal authority for the enforcement of canonical provisions may not help to maintain freedom and order in the Church community. People would like to see the *ratio legis* (reason for the law) which is important for its acceptance and observance. If, for example, canon law does not pay attention to the theology of marriage as a sacrament and as a covenant, and continues to treat it as a contract of the consenting parties,[18] then the canons could lose their credibility in the community.

Further, failure to respond to new developments in the Church and in the world could fossilize the community as we go ahead with legislations on issues and questions that have become obsolete. For example, penance is something so very much part of Christian faith and life. However, the mode of penitence could undergo changes. It is increasingly becoming evident that auricular confession has been in the process of disappearing for the last few decades, and could get extinct soon. And yet to devote no less than 33 canons to legislate on auricular confession (canons 959-991) with the obligation of the faithful "to confess, in kind and in number all grave sins committed after baptism" (can. 988) could appear belaboring on obsolescence. On the other hand, no one could claim that auricular confession is of divine right. To cite yet another example, the preparation for clerical ministry needs significant changes, so that candidates are trained in such a way as to be able to respond to the challenge of our times, and indeed in different geographical regions. And yet, we have 33 canons (232 -264) dealing with "formation of clerics" that have already become outdated, and which show no sensitivity to changing times and new demands of ministry. Here, theology has the role to help canon law to "read the signs of the times," to abrogate obsolete laws, to formulate new ones, having in mind the changing times and life of the Christian communities.

The code of canon law with its centralizing tendency bears many traces of the Roman and mediaeval laws of western society. Hence, questions can be raised about the suitability of several of those canonical legislations in widely different cultural environments. More basically, there is a difference in the understanding of and attitude towards law itself. Further, translation into practical action of a theology that springs from context, calls for laws and regulations that bespeak to the people, and are convincing to them for the values and ideals they stand for. Unfortunately, there is often a dissonance between theology that wants to be a vital force and a canon law which does not address dynamically the needs of the local community and its specific questions and concerns. This has the consequence of causing ruptures within the community, and thus undermining the witness-potential of the Gospel which both theology and canon law are expected to promote in their journey together. Hence, the importance of developing local customs and particular laws.

However, as it is, there is little scope in the present code for such contextualization of law in the local Churches. In the Latin code, the legitimacy of these customs are made to depend on the approval of them by the legislator, universal and particular, as the case may be (can. 23). The corresponding canon 1506 §1 of the Eastern Code seems to be more open: "The custom of the Christian community, as it responds to the action of the Holy Spirit in the ecclesial body, can obtain the force of law."

History of the Church in early period tells us that the different families of Churches were autonomous (self-governing) – with their own laws and regulations – while maintaining vividly the communion of Churches. Mediaeval times saw innumerable customs and traditions flowing from the life of the local Churches which acquired binding force in the local context. As Andrea D'Auria contends, customs, in fact, enrich the pluriform nature of the ecclesial juridical system, nurture inculturation of ecclesial laws, supply in the wake of *lacuna legis,* and above all else, foster the building of the Christian community under the guidance of the Holy Spirit.[19] With increasing sense of pluralism characterizing the life of the Church in every sphere, it is inevitable that there will also be legitimate space for customs and other particular laws in the Churches. Even more, from a long-range perspective we could envisage the emergence of new *sui iuris* Churches (individual Churches) similar to the patriarchal Churches of the past. In fact, Lumen Gentium 23 speaks in the same breath of the patriarchal Churches of ancient times and of contemporary conferences of bishops (regional, national or continental).

For the emergence of new *sui iuris* Churches eventually with their own canonical structures, the present local Churches need to have already the spaces of freedom and necessary autonomy.[20] This would significantly change the nature and functioning of the existing body of laws in the Church, and their implementation, and thus pave the way for the projected future. In this context, the tendency to water down the theological and juridical status of groupings of bishops into conferences, regional bodies etc. cannot but be viewed as a retrogressive step going against the spirit of Vatican II.[21] There needs to be a lot of freedom for the local Churches to develop their forms and ways of worship which would provide the potential for the development of new rites, since as we know from history, liturgical rite was an important component in the formation and development of *sui iuris* Churches from the early times. In fact, *Sacrosanctum Concilium* (no. 4) not only speaks of the existing rites but seems to open the possibility of new rites in the Church. According to the Code of the Eastern Churches, "a rite is a liturgical, theological, spiritual and disciplinary heritage, differentiated by the culture and the circumstances of the history of peoples, which is expressed by each Church *sui iuris* in its own manner of living the faith" (Canon 28 §1). In all these issues, theology could play a very constructive role in interpreting Vatican II and helping canon law to look towards the future and become more flexible and context-sensitive.

Conclusion

Under the influence of legal positivism, which has a univocal theoretical understanding of law, canon law cannot write off the important role theology needs to play today for a meaningful interpretation of laws governing the community of believers. Canon law is, then, faced with the difficult challenge of reconciling between its own nature as a legal instrument (making it akin to any legal system) and the imperative need to be guided by a theological vision. If it becomes narrative and exhortative, it may be wanting in its legal and normative character for order in the Church community. This is a serious point to ponder for those who would make canon law simply a subset of theology. There are others who would like to see canon law as a subset of law rather than theology. Those who hold this view, face a serious difficulty. They need to account for whether canon law observes human rights and gender equality to be able to pass the test of being a legal instrument to regulate a religious community. How could it be an instrument of justice (which all laws are expected to be) if it is wanting in these crucial matters? Those practicing professional law may not want to include canon law as a branch of the general discipline of law. Another dilemma canon law faces is to reconcile between the demands of justice which it is expected to uphold and the Gospel injunction of mercy which any genuine theology will keep in sight. Canon law cannot afford to lose the delicate balance that is desired.

It is obvious that we may not expect laws of the Church as vehicles for the proclamation of the truths of Christianity. However, there would be no justification for any canonical provision unless it is also the vehicle of a value or ideal to be put into practice. That makes the constant dialogue between theology and canon law an imperative necessity. When the organic unity between the two disciplines – though they may differ in nature and frame of interpretation – is lost, "the Church is bound to suffer: unrealistic speculations or empty legalism can be the harsh symptoms of an internal indisposition".[22]

In other words, self-insulation of canon law could turn it blind to values theology promotes, and a theology that is not oriented to the concrete Christian praxis could end up in a world of abstraction dealing with concepts. The best course for the future is then to continue the dialogue between theology and canon law as they move along with the people of God in their journey to the fullness of the Kingdom of God. This joint journey could help canon law to open up to the signs of the time and overcome some of its inherent limitations.

Bibliography

Austin, Greta. *Shaping Church Law around the Year 1000: The Decretum of Burchard of Worms. Church, Faith, and Culture in the Medieval West* (London: Routledge, 2017).

Corecco, Eugenio. *The Theology of Canon Law: A Methodological Question.* Translated by Francesco Turvasi (Pittsburgh, Pa.: Duquesne University Press, 1992).

Coriden, James A, Pagé, Roch, and Torfs, Rik. *Canon Law between Interpretation and Imagination* (Leuven: Peeters, 2001).

Coriden, James A. "The Canonist's Vocation and a New Church Order." *The Jurist* 51 (1991), 67-80.

Coriden, James A. *An Introduction to Canon Law* (New York: Paulist Press, 2004).

Coughlin, John J. *Law, Person, and Community: Philosophical, Theological, and Comparative Perspectives on Canon Law* (New York: Oxford University Press, 2012).

Edelby, Neophytos., Urresti, Teodoro Jiménez., and Huizing, Petrus., eds. *Postconciliar Thoughts: Renewal and Reform of Canon Law* (New York: Paulist Press, 1967).

Goering, Joseph. "Law and Theology in Fishacre's 'Sentences Commentary'." *New Blackfriars* 80 (941/942) (1999), 360-69.

Green, Thomas J. "The Revised Code of Canon Law: Some Theological Issues." *Theological Studies* 47 (1986), 617-652.

Hansen, Peter. "The Vietnamese State, the Catholic Church and the Law." In *Asian Socialism and Legal Change: The Dynamics of Vietnamese and Chinese Reform*, edited by Gillespie John and Nicholson Pip (Canberra: Australian National University Press, 2005), 310-340.

Hartmann, Wilfried., and Pennington, Kenneth., eds. *The History of Medieval Canon Law in the Classical Period, 1140-1234: From Gratian to the Decretals of Pope Gregory IX* (Washington, D. C.: London: Catholic University of America Press, 2008).

Kasper, Walter. "Canon Law and Ecumenism." *The Jurist* 69 (2009), 171-189.

King, Geoffrey. "The Catholic Church in China: A Canonical Evaluation." *The Jurist* 49 (1989), 69-94.

Koury, Joseph J. "*Ius Divinum* as a Canonical problem: On the Interaction of Divine and Ecclesiastical Laws." *The Jurist* 53 (1993), 104-131.

Loretan, Adrian., and Wilfred, Felix., eds. *Revision of the Codes: An Indian-European Dialogue* (Zürich: LIT Verlag, 2018).

McManus, Frederick R. "The Code of Canons of the Eastern Catholic Churches." *The Jurist* 53 (1993), 22-61.

McManus, Frederick R. "The Possibility of new Rites in the Church." *The Jurist* 50 (1990), 435-458.

Melloni, Alberto., Scatena, Silvia., eds, and Fondazione per Le Scienze Religiose Giovanni XXIII Di Bologna. "Synod and Synodality: Theology, History, Canon Law and Ecumenism in New Contact: International Colloquium Bruges 2003." *Christianity and History* 1 (Münster: LIT Verlag, 2005).

Montgomery, John Warwick. *Christ Our Advocate: Studies in Polemical Theology, Jurisprudence, and Canon Law* (Bonn: Verlag für Kultur Und Wissenschaft, 2002).

Montini-Coleman, James. *Theology and Canon Law: The Theory of Ladislas Örsy* (Washington DC: Catholic University of America, 2006).

Nedungatt, George. "Dimensions of Law in the Church." *Iustitia* 2 (1) (2011), 39-81.

Ombres, Robert. "The Synod of Bishops: Canon Law and Ecclesial Dynamics." *Ecclesiastical Law Journal* 16 (2014), 306-18.

Örsy, Ladislas M. *Theology and Canon Law: New Horizons for Legislation and Interpretation* (Collegeville, Minn.: Liturgical Press, 1992).

Örsy, Ladislas. "Interpretation in view of Action: A Quest for Clarity and Simplicity (Canon 96)". *The Jurist* 52 (1992), 587-597.

Örsy, Ladislas. "Shorter Studies. Corecco's Theology of Canon Law: A Critical Appraisal." *The Jurist* 53 (1993), 186-198.

Patterson, Dennis., ed. *Philosophy of Law and Legal Theory: An Anthology* (Oxford: Blackwell Publishing, 2003).

Rahner, Karl. "Reflections on the Concept of *Ius Divinum*." *Theological Investigations* 5 (London: Darton, Longman & Todd, 1966), 219-243.

Shogimen, Takashi. "The Relationship between Theology and Canon Law: Another Context of Political Thought in the Early Fourteenth Century." *Journal of the History of Ideas* 60 (3) (1999), 417-32.

Stephens, Christopher W. B. *Canon Law and Episcopal Authority: The Canons of Antioch and Serdica* (New York: Oxford University Press, 2015).

Wijlens, Myriam. *Theology and Canon Law: The Theories of Klaus Mörsdorf and Eugenio Corecco* (Lanham, Md.; London: University Press of America, 1992).

Wilfred, Felix. "Episcopal Conferences – Their Theological Status." In Peter Fernando, ed, *Episcopal Conferences and Collegiality* (Delhi: CBCI Commission for Clergy and Religious, 1989), 3-26.

Witte, JR., John and Alexander, Frank S., eds. *Christianity and Canon Law: An Introduction* (Cambridge: Cambridge University Press, 2008).

Endnotes

[1] Cf. Ladislaus Örsy, *Theology and Canon Law: New Horizons for Legislation and Interpretation* (Collegeville, Minnesota: The Liturgical Press, 1992). For a different approach, see E. Corecco, *The Theology of Canon Law* (Pittsburgh, PA: Duquesne University Press, 1992).

[2] From mediaeval times, especially from thirteenth century onwards, a steady antagonism was built between theology and canon law, among other things, on the basis of different positions they held in controversial questions of the time like the issue of Franciscan poverty. The issue often centered on the role canon law sought to play in the ecclesiastical affairs contrary to what theologians of the time held. See, Takashi Shogimen, "The Relationship between Theology and Canon Law: Another Context of Political Thought in the Early Fourteenth Century", *Journal of History of Ideas,* 60:3 (1999), 417-431. For a comprehensive synthesis of relationship between theology and canon law in Mediaeval times, see also, Pier Virginio Aimone, "Il Medioevo", Gruppo Italiano Docenti di Diritto Canonico (a cura di), *Il diritto canonico nel sapere teologico. Prospettive interdisciplinari* (Milano: Edizioni Glossa, 2004), 39-65.

[3] Ladislas Örsy, *Theology and Canon Law. op.cit.* p. 172.

[4] Cf. George Nedungatt, "Dimensions of Law in the Church", *Iustitia,* 2:1 (2011), 39-81, at 78.

[5] Cf. Thomas Aquinas, *Summa Theologiae* I-II, q.90, a.4c.

[6] This latter trend finds its finest expression and evidence in the present code, and the apostolic constitution *Sacrae Disciplinae Leges* (25 Jan 1983) with which Pope John Paul II promulgated it. That the law of the Church must reflect

the image of the Church as much as possible corresponds to the function of law in the Church [Cf. AAS 75 (1983) vii-xiv], notwithstanding the fact that, often, it is difficult to render faith-related doctrines into corresponding canonical arrangements in their entirety. Cf. Jean Beyer, *Il Codice del Vaticano II: Dal concilio al codice* (Bologna: EDB, 1984), p. 7.

[7] CIC 1917 Can. 108 §3. *Ex divina institutione sacra hierarchia ratione ordinis constat Episcopis, presbyteris et ministris; ratione iurisdictionis, pontificatu supremo et episcopatu subordinato; ex Ecclesiae autem institutione alii quoque gradus accessere.*

[8] For further examples see Joseph J. Koury, "*Ius Divinum* as a Canonical Problem on the Interaction of Divine and Ecclesiastical Laws", *The Jurist*, 53(1993), 104-131.

[9] For a brief historical context of the cardinals of the Holy Roman Church, see John P. Beal –James A. Corriden – Thomas J. Green, eds, *New Commentary on the Code of Canon Law* (New York: Paulist Press, 2000), pp. 464-466, at p. 465.

[10] Cf. Karl Rahner, "Reflections on the Concept of *Ius Divinum*," *Theological Investigations,* vol. 5 (London: Darton, Longman & Todd, 1966), pp. 219-243.

[11] Cf. Walter Kasper, "Canon Law and Ecumenism", *The Jurist,* 69 (2009), 171-189.

[12] James A. Coriden, "Lay Persons and the Power of Governance", *The Jurist,* 59 (1999), 335-347; see also Hubert Wolf, *Unterdrückte Traditionen der Kirchengeschichte* (München: Verlag C.H. Beck, 2015), pp. 145-157.

[13] James A. Coriden, *art. cit.* p. 340.

[14] It is true that the *Nota Explicativa Praevia* no.2 of Lumen Gentium specifies that in order for the office of governance to be exercised in concrete, "a canonical or juridical determination" by the pope is required. There are some canonists who bank on this explanatory note to fall back on the pre-Vatican theology of episcopate and to hold that the power of jurisdiction comes as canonical mission from the pope. For example, R. J. Bower says that "the power of orders is conferred by sacramental ordination; (and) the power of jurisdiction, except for papacy, by canonical mission" R. J. Bowers, *Episcopal power of Governance in the Diocesan Church: from the 1917 Code of Canon law to the Present* (Washington D.C: The Catholic University of America,1990), p. 5. This, I think, is simply to take away the novelty of the teaching of Vatican II. An explanatory note is an explanatory note, and nothing more, and it cannot supplant the central teaching of Vatican II found in the main body of Lumen Gentium stating the sacramental foundation of Episcopal power of jurisdiction.

[15] For a synthetic overview, see George Nedungatt, ed, *A Guide to the Eastern Code. A Commentary on the Code of Canons of the Eastern Churches*, Kanonika 10 (Rome: Pontificio Istituto Orientale, 2002), pp. 229-231, and 641-647.

[16] Cf. Felix Wilfred, "Reform of the Roman Curia", *Vidyajyoti Journal of Theological Reflection*, 77:8 (2013), 583-596, at 592-593.

[17] Cf. John M, Huels – Richard R. Gaillalrdetz, "The Selection of Bishops: Recovering of the Traditions", *The Jurist*, 59 (1999), 348-376, at 368 f.

[18] Cf. James A. *Coriden, Canon Law as Ministry. Freedom and Good Order for the Church* (New Jersey: Paulist Press, 2000).

[19] Cf Andrea D'Aura, "Il diritto consuetudinario nella vita della Chiesa", *Euntes docete*, 56:3 (2003), 65-89 at 88-89.

[20] A comparison with the Code of the Eastern Churches will substantiate this. See Frederick R. McManus, "The Code of Canons of the Eastern Catholic Churches", *The Jurist*, 53 (1993), 22-61; ID., "The possibility of New Rites in the Church", *The Jurist*, 50 (1990), 435-458.

[21] Cf. Felix Wilfred, "Episcopal Conferences – Their Theological Status", in Peter Fernando, ed, *Episcopal Conferences and Collegiality* (Delhi: CBCI Commission for Clergy and Religious, 1989), pp. 3-26.

[22] Ladislas Örsy, "Interpretation in View of Action. A quest for Clarity and Simplicity (Canon 92)", *The Jurist*, 52 (1992), 587-597 at 596.

CHAPTER 13

Every Theologian a Community-Researcher

While many areas of Church-life such as worship, governance, art and architecture went through a creative process of indigenization, for a long time, theological research still remained something associated with the West. Even when bright Indian students wanted to do research, they had to travel to the western centres of theological education, and depend upon the scholars in those foreign countries for guidance, and even for choosing themes for research. Often these guides, if at all, had very superficial knowledge of things Indian. The result has been alienation – of the research as well as of the researcher.

At this juncture, creation of theological research institutions and bodies in Protestant, Roman Catholic and other denominations was a bold initiative which has marked a turning point in the Indian theological education. Such one initiative was the founding of South Asian Theological Research Institute (SATHRI), now part of the research wing of Serampore College, with its many doctoral centres all over India. Besides, we have the South Asian Institute of Advanced Christian Studies (SAIACS) and numerous Pontifical Institutes and faculties conferring postgraduate theological and doctoral studies. These institutions need to be strengthened today, not only in terms of infrastructure facilities – which they certainly need – but more importantly in terms of the quality and method of research. This calls for a deeper reflection on the nature and methods of theological research, which we shall attempt in this chapter.

To Search and Research - To be Christian

Research is not simply a technical activity. It is fundamentally a Christian enterprise in the sense that it is a search for truth, for the reality. It is readiness to move from where one is to something new and different. This is an existential aspect of being Christian. Search for truth is to be the character of every believer, and research with its technical instrumentalities, offers the means to fulfil the basic vocation of Christian to be the seeker of truth and to be on a journey towards what lies beyond.[1] A Christian researcher, that is, a theologian, is someone who is in the quest for truth relevant for the church, society, and academia by deploying the necessary technical means for truth-finding. This fundamental aspect of research should not be submerged under the technicalities of the means and methods employed for truth-finding. In a fundamental sense, every theologian as a Christian should be necessarily a researcher.

Revolutionary Character of Research

Without research, there is no progress, no innovations, but only stagnation; without research there is no change, but repetition of the same. Research is crucial in solving problems – whether connected with the human or with the nature. Breakthroughs happen in every department of life through researches. They are very striking in the case of medical research and advancement.

Let me illustrate the point with an example from the field of medicine. Invention of microbes by Louis Pasteur (1822–1895) advanced medical science, and proved to be a great blessing to humanity.[2] The invisible airborne microbes are the cause for many diseases and for putrefaction, fermentation, etc. When Pasteur arrived at this conclusion through hard research, it provoked ridicule from the scientists of his time. It is also his research and experimentation that led to the invention of vaccination against certain diseases like smallpox, rabies, and anthrax that killed millions of people throughout history.[3] Smallpox alone had killed about 500 million people. It was completely eradicated in 1979. You get injected by the same germs to get immunized against the disease they cause; this is the principle of inoculation.[4]

Similar has been the case of Ignaz Semmelweis (1818 -1865), the father of infection control.[5] He was appointed in 1846 as assistant to Prof. John Klein at the Vienna General Hospital. There were two maternity (obstetrical) clinics attached to the hospital – one in which physicians and young medical students handled childbirth and another clinical section was handled by midwives. Curiously the child mortality at birth was high in the cases handled by the physicians and medical students (13 – 18%) whereas the cases of infant mortality were much less in cases handled by midwives. This was quite puzzling and intriguing. Through research and verification of hypothesis, Semmelweis came to the conclusion that the mortality was high in the cases handled by physicians and medical students, because they were doing autopsy of cadavers before attending the pregnant women. His research led to the practice of disinfection, so very important today in medical treatment. Semmelweis recommended washing of hands in chlorinated lime solution. As a result, the mortality rate came down drastically. We can list a number of examples from other fields which have revolutionized our knowledge, and have brought about many beneficial effects to the life of people and of society.

Research is important for informed decisions, formulation of policies, and strategies. It is used in daily life more and more. The modern way of life has introduced a research temper. Even daily life is being governed by mini researches. Once upon a time what our father, mother or teacher told us was the last word. They decided what was best for us and guided us to its realization. But, today, when you want to buy a bike, a car, a cell phone, or household articles, you research; you compare the various products, weigh the various options on the basis of data and information, which leads to an enlightened decision, and you do not depend anymore upon the impression created by the advertisement of a company or the views of your parents, teachers or elders. You study the data on the products, collect information from the net, from those who use the gadgets, and other experts; you compare. Even more, those who sell their products continue to do researches on the demands of consumers, which is known as market-research.[6]

While research environment is all around, and the scientific temper is on the increase, unfortunately, within the Church we lag far behind. Instead of making decisions based on study, research, and findings, those in leadership position, tend to behave arbitrarily following their whims and fancies, likes and dislikes. The lack of a scientific and research-oriented approach leads to unenlightened decisions which continue to do a lot of damage in the Church-community. For lack of research spirit many things happen in the Church in a pre-scientific and even obscurantist manner.[7]

Research orientation is important also in every form of education and human resource development. Text books give you known facts, information, theories, and so on. It is research that takes us beyond what is known, to arrive at conclusions that could challenge received wisdom, and could revolutionize the way we think and do things. The best form of education, then, is not transmission of information, but building the capacity to invent, discover, and create. This makes education a very exciting enterprise. The whole educational process should be characterized by the spirit of research,[8] and it should not be viewed as the final stage of education associated with a so-called "research degree". This is true of all theological education. If our theological and pastoral institutions are imbued with the spirit of research, we could expect a lot of creativity and transformation in all areas of life in the Church.[9]

Three Research Paradigms in Theology

According to its spirit, orientation and foci, we could distinguish conveniently three different research paradigms: 1. The Enlightenment paradigm 2. Liberative paradigm 3. Community-oriented paradigm. Let me briefly comment on each one of them.

The Enlightenment Paradigm of Research

The european Enlightenment was historically the driving force behind western modernity. The development in the field of science and the application of it in the field of technology were all results of acquisition of knowledge. The search for knowledge and collection of data resulted in the so-called *encyclopaedism*. The quest for knowledge in the colonial times and environment led to the gathering of information about peoples and nations, their traditions, customs and manners, their habitat, flora and fauna. This resulted in the so-called *Orientalism* which made the subjugated people and their world object of western research and scrutiny.[10] William Jones, Max Müller, Monier Williams, and others went into the study of India, for example.

The philosophical underpinning in this paradigm of study and research was the conviction that knowledge is power. That explains why today in every sphere of life research has become an indispensable means to acquire power. The more knowledge, there is better control of things and people. A lot of researches in developed countries are done by merchants of death who manufacture and market sophisticated armaments for military use. Research and analysis wing has become an integral part of every military establishment.

The Enlightenment paradigm of research in theology is still dominant in the West. Following this paradigm, theology and theological research are meant to understand and interpret, mostly sacred texts, and it has less to do with praxis. There is little correspondence between the dominant theology in the western theological institutions and the actual reality of Christian communities. Theology continues with its knowledge-production, while people leave the Churches in droves. Some of the researches could be bizarre. The fragmentation of knowledge characteristic of western modernity has also affected theological research.[11] When the Churches in the West are in deep crisis, researches go on in a completely different direction without any reference to actual experiences. There are scholars who, in all their life, have done nothing else than to investigate how Judas died, whether by hanging himself or by falling! And others have, as their research, focus all their life, on how the walls of Jericho fell. I am not saying imaginary things. One of my revered professors knew little about the Scriptures, but he spent all his academic life to study and comment on the apocrypha.

This Enlightenment paradigm of research[12] with its atomization of knowledge may have some methodologically useful points, but it is basically not suited for our country in our theological research. The Enlightenment paradigm of theology with its dominant position given to ideas and their developments tends to view most important questions of life, enveloped in politics, economy, culture, etc., as simply theological corollaries, and they do not affect the process itself of doing theology. Many Western theological departments characterize socio-political issues as "*Practical Theology*".[13] The implication is that pure theology deals with ideas and search for meaning, while practical theology applies them. This dichotomy is very harmful to theological endeavour.

Many times, Indian students are used by western professors to expand and apply their knowledge and research into the South. It is a new and subtle theological imperialism following the Enlightenment model. Let me cite a couple of examples. A student wanted to research on how the Federation of Asian Bishops' Conferences (FABC) has been approaching the question of interreligious dialogue and nurturing a different theology of religions. He could not do that, unless he related this theme to the Dutch theologian Edward Schillebeeckx's theology of religion. Edward Schillebeeckx knew almost nothing of FABC or Asia. The thesis became a hotchpotch one, since the student was constrained to include Schilleebeeckx. In another case, a student wanted to compare my writings with that of the American theologian David Power on the question of Christian sacraments. But he could not do this unless he brought postmodernism into the discussion. This is simply because the supervisor is an expert on postmodernism in theology, and he knew hardly anything of me or of David Power. As I mentioned earlier, SATHRI and other institutions of theological research in India have liberated Indian theology from such constraints as the Indian research scholars today are able to think in relation to our experiences, and design researches that are most helpful to us and to our situation.

Liberative Paradigm of Research

Research in its spirit is a process of liberation. Liberative paradigm of research rests on the premise that knowledge is for transformation. We are on a pilgrimage to the real, the truth. Research is a companion in this journey. "From the unreal lead me to the real, from darkness lead me to light, from death lead me to immortality", so reads the celebrated prayer in *Brihadaranyaka Upanishad.*[14] It is a journey that transforms and liberates us as we move from ignorance and appearance, from impressions and distortions, to the real. This is precisely what liberative research helps us to do. This is beautifully portrayed in Plato's allegory of the cave in his work *The Republic*[15] which is a master-narrative of the european civilization. It portrays the movement from the world of shadows to the world of reality.

The implications of this prayer and this allegory get sharpened when we relate them to actual life-experiences. Let me illustrate this with an example. Most people tend to think that in schools all children are treated equally. This is taken for granted. But if we dig deeper, for which research is very important, we come to understand that things are not as evident as they may appear. Dalit children undergo a lot of discrimination in schools. They are humiliated by the teachers and other children in open and subtle ways. Teachers encourage children of upper castes, whereas they take a prejudiced view of the first generation of Dalit children going to school. These children are put down as wanting in talents, whereas children from high castes are praised for their genius. Dalit children are asked to clean the class rooms, toilets, and the surroundings and the children of high caste are sent to fetch tea and food-items for the teachers. Dalit boys and girls will not be asked to do that for fear of pollution! Someone makes a research on *"Exclusion and discrimination in Schools. Experiences of Dalit Children".*[16] Such an investigation brings to light many such facts about an invisible reality. The facts and experiences dispel false impressions and unmask many make-beliefs. The result of this research could become an important source for a liberative praxis vis-á-vis discriminated children, and a basis for appropriate policy formation that will protect the Dalit children from the discrimination they experience. There are distortions, falsehoods, and shadowy understanding of the actual reality of suffering, of the plight of Dalits, tribals and women. From the shadow knowledge to the realization of truth is a process of search and research. Research has much wider connotation; it has an *existential and ontological base*, and it is not a mere epistemological or technical activity.[17]

In the liberative paradigm of research, praxis and transformation acquire great importance. A new liberative praxis can be supported by researches through a re-reading and interpretation of Christian resources – Bible and tradition. It involves the use of different hermeneutical tools. For example, the Enlightenment paradigm is dominant in Biblical studies. This can be seen in the way historical-critical method is valorized and employed to the point of considering it to be the only approach to truth-finding. This method has serious limitations,[18] but helps us discover what a text says. But beyond what the text says, we need to attend to *what it talks about* – to employ a distinction made by Paul Ricoeur.[19] Theological researches in this paradigm will employ critical hermeneutics and hermeneutics of suspicion. It will move beyond text and meaning to a complex relationship between the text and the context. There will be a dialogue between the reader (individual and community) and the text. Unlike the Enlightenment paradigm, the liberative paradigm of research will be inter-disciplinary in character. It will draw from many disciplines to arrive at transforming truths.

Community Paradigm of Research

The community paradigm is closely allied to the liberative paradigm in research. For, research to be an instrument of social transformation and all-round liberation, has to be community-oriented. Still, the dominant image of researcher seems to be that of a lone investigator insulated within his or her own disciplinary turf. There is urgent need to bring to an end traditional isolationist practices in research, and make it more and more community-centred and interactive. The excessive concentration on individual and his or her success, and promotion of values like excellence, and practices like competition, have led to the loss of community-sense in the process of education and research. And yet, right from the time of Independence, the community dimension was insisted upon in educational practice and policies. This was brought out clearly in the Dr Radhakrishnan Commission Report on Higher Education set up in 1948.

> The most important and urgent reform needed in education is to transform
> it, to endeavour to relate it to the life, needs and aspirations of the people
> and thereby make it the powerful instrument of social, economic and cultural

transformation necessary for the realization of the national goals. For this purpose, education should be developed so as to increase productivity, achieve social and national integration, accelerate the process of modernization and cultivate social, moral and spiritual values.[20]

The community-orientation said of education applies equally to the realm of research. There are many aspects to a community paradigm of research. A simple participant observation does not make any research really community-oriented. For, here the focus is on the agency of the researcher, and the community becomes simply object of observation and study. The community paradigm of research is based on the fact that community is *the subject, agent and source* for truth-finding.[21] This goes beyond participant observation.

More than any other, the field of theology requires the participation of the Church-community. A theology that does not stem from the experience of the community will be a theology simply in the abstract, wrestling with concepts and ideas. This, as we noted earlier, is a tragedy that has befallen much of western theology. There is little correspondence between theological researches and the local Church-community. Research rooted in the community and its situation will indicate also the priority-areas, issues, and questions for innovation. All aspects of the research like formulation of the research problem, working out the research design, and the completion of the project will constantly hark back to the community.

Academic Agency of the Marginalised - Promotion of Research by Dalit and Tribal Scholars and by Women

There is another dimension to community-orientedness. Here we deal with the issue of *inclusion and exclusion*. We think especially of Dalits, tribals and women who are thought as objects of research than *subjects of research*. We can speak of community-oriented research when these subalterns do not suffer exclusion in research, but they themselves become active agents and contributors to theology out of their experiences.[22] Even more, an inclusive theological research will take care that it has reference to the community of the oppressed and marginalised, and that it bring out the issues and questions faced by them.

Ways and means should be devised, structures and institutions created for promoting research actively by this constituency of the marginalized. In the case of reservation, the main argument has been that certain communities have undergone systemic discrimination, and the provisions of reservation are meant to undo the wrongs of the past, and create a level-field. But I think this argument is inadequate. It focuses only on what happens to the marginal groups when they are not included. There is another argument which I would like to apply also to the case of research: By excluding people from active participation, the community suffers. For, we deprive the community of the contribution of its excluded members and their talents.[23] The community is the loser. Applying to research in theology, the researches pursued by the marginal groups and identities bring out perspectives which could correct the community and re-orient it. This would not happen without their participation.[24]

There are many areas in the life of the subalterns that call for research in the direction of transformation. Researches in these areas are done most aptly by the subaltern themselves – Dalits, tribals, women, and other marginalised groups. The subalterns have been, for long the *objects* of research. Today there is an urgent need for them to be *subjects* and agents of research, and especially when it concerns their life-realities. As it is said, even if the best western scholar has brought out excellent study and researches on African traditional religions, a practitioner of these religions has still something to say which the western scholar has not said. So is the case with Dalits, tribals and women. Researches on them which leave out their agency bring out only half-truths. The subalterns need to become pioneers in research on what touches them.

What we said applies as well to theological research. There is a general discourse today of "falling of standards" in theological education and research. This discourse needs to be set in a particular social context. In our casteist and hierarchical society whose values affect also the Church and its functioning, there are those who interpret the falling of standards as a result of the fact that it is now the Dalits and tribals who in increasing numbers are entering into the field of theological education. This is a mischievous interpretation which reveals deep caste prejudices. It is ignorant about contemporary cultural developments that affect everyone regardless of caste affiliation. There is also ignorance of what academic excellence is. Moreover, one fails to recognize that every group has its own unique contribution to the construction of knowledge – including theological knowledge and education. Depriving the community of their contribution to theology would be to impoverish both theology and the community. Often it is the lethargy and lack of educational creativity to bring out the best theological potentials from the students of marginalised groups that masquerade as a fall in academic excellence.

From Doctrines to Study of Practices – New Theological Research Agenda

The community-aspect of research comes to further relief if we shift our attention from doctrines to practices. There is a general assumption that practices embody ideas. So, then, once you have discovered the ideas behind the practice we have advanced in research, so it is claimed. Today, we value the practices in themselves as the mirror of a society, a people and a group. These practices reveal, unlike analysis of concepts, ideas and texts, the "socially negotiated character of meaning" and interpretation. In fact, many disciplines today tend increasingly to distance themselves from texts and concentrate on practices. This should be also an eye-opener for theology which has been overly preoccupied with ideas, concepts, and belief-system.

Embodied institutional practices do not yield meaning by filtering them into ideas. Rather, the practices themselves need to be studied as they are matrix and repository for the generation of meaning. And this is what ethnography does. It does not look out for the concepts behind practices.[25] Think of *rangoli*, which we in Tamil call *kolam*. It is an art-practice of everyday by ordinary people – mostly women. What is important is not the theory behind it, but the very practice of it, even if there is no one explanation of what its meaning is. People continue to perform that ritual, and a cluster of practices and human interactions are involved around this. This is true of religious practices as well of other social practices.

> Briefly, a theory of social practice emphasizes the relational interdependency of agent and world, activity, meaning, cognition, learning and knowing. It emphasizes the inherent, socially negotiated character of meaning and the interested, concerned character of the thought and action of persons-in-activity. This view also claims that learning, thinking, and knowing are relations among people in activity in, with, and arising from, the socially and culturally structured world.[26]

What is said of the social and cultural matrix as constitutive of learning and meaning-making, has also, its implications for research. From a theological research point, it is important to study practices of worship and folk religious customs and traditions, which are not simply instantiation of some theological doctrine, concept or belief. They are to be studied in themselves as practices. Thus, to put in a schematic form, theological researches could go into practices related to the life of the community (*koinonia*), to faith-transmission and education (*kerygma), to* practices in Christian worship and celebration of sacraments (*leiturgia*), the practices relating to pastoral care of the Church-communities and the efforts to reach out to society and the larger world (*diakonia*). The researches into these areas will help rethink, evaluate, and revise existing practices, and lead to new and different ones, more transforming and liberative. Theological research of this kind implies necessarily the deployment of multiple methods and an interdisciplinary approach.

The Empirical in Theological Research

What we said about the community-character of theological research and the study of practices lead us to highlight the importance of empirical study in theological research. Theological researches have generally shunned empirical methodology. But then the community-orientation and study of practices we spoke about, induce us to highlight the empirical in theology. Any empirically based study is likely to be also original when conducted according to best methodological practices. This is what my experience of guiding many theological researches through the years tells me. Empirical study uses primary data, and it is not dependent on secondary sources alone. The empirical approach has a deeper foundation. The ascent to God, to the mystery of human beings, and of the universe can take place most convincingly by moving up on the ladder of symbols supported by senses. The role of senses comes out beautifully in a poem of Rabindranath Tagore.

> My world will light its hundred different lamps
> With thy flame, and place them before the
> Altar of Thy temple
> No, I will never shut the doors of my senses
> The delights of sight and hearing and touch
> Will bear Thy delight.[27]

Theology and Theological Research in the Light of a New Scientific Vision

There are those who think that when you speak of scientific and academic approach to theology, it means that we are not committed to the cause of the poor, the subalterns and their liberation. This is a misconception. A true scientific approach to reality, on the contrary, will strengthen the objective of liberation and free it from clichés. But we need to go further. Theology and theological research are to be imbued by a new vision of the cosmos science is offering us today.[28] Much of present-day theology is based on a conception of the universe that contradicts what science and scientific inventions are telling us. The theological trends which place human beings at the centre of the universe developed a particular brand of anthropology, which is bound to undergo a transformation when human beings are viewed in relation to an expanding universe and in relation to evolution of various living organisms. I think it will do well to every theologian and theological researcher to get a little familiar with astronomy and its astounding facts and figures. Astronomy is a good teacher of humility. Before the immensity and infinity of the universe, we remain flabbergasted and begin to be modest about the truth of our theological statements which look like a small grain of sand on the immense shores of reality. And yet we tend to hold on to them and absolutize them as if they were the only truth. Researches often serve to only confirm such people in their fixated convictions and conclusions, which I would call the model of "ratification research". There is little novelty, but repetition of only old certainties.

Science and scientific discoveries are a great challenge to theology, not in the sense that they are displacing it or rendering it meaningless, but rather they critically question the foundations on which its conception of God, humanity, and universe is based, as well as the way these realities are inter-related. I need not go into the details of these questions at this point. Suffice it to say that theology and theological research need to be aware of the limitations of doctrines and be critical of theological researches that lack sensitivity to the vision of physical and biological sciences of today. Once again, there is the opportunity for theology to shed its tendency to absolutism when it is confronted with a new scientific conception of the universe. Science itself is humble today to realize its own relative character. Every theological research should be inspired by the spirit of deep humility.

Interdisciplinary Nature of Theological Research

Interdisciplinary approach is based on the premise of the unity of knowledge and the limits of each discipline. A single discipline is able to touch only one level of reality, and it leaves out other aspects and dimensions. Especially when the questions and issues are complex, interdisciplinary or multidisciplinary approach is then called for. Interdisciplinary or multidisciplinary approach cuts across the conventional borders separating the sciences, and takes us closer to truth, something which a single discipline alone is not capable of. At this age when we face complex questions, we require the support of many disciplines to answer them. It brings together researchers across different fields and deepens professional relationships. Further, today, when knowledge gets increasingly fragmented, interdisciplinary approach helps to integrate knowledge in its various dimensions. This integration is all the more required in the case of theology which needs to address issues of God, human beings, society, and nature in a holistic manner.

In theology when we speak of interdisciplinary approach, often it is taken to be as something happening within the various branches of the theological field itself. The inputs from Biblical studies, systematic theology, and history of Christianity are interrelated for the purpose of research. This is a limited understanding of interdisciplinary approach, operating within the same field of theology. But today we need to understand inter-disciplinarity in a broader sense, namely doing research in the theological field in cooperation with other fields of study and drawing resources from them, and employing some of the methods they use. This is necessary because without knowledge of, and inputs from disciplines like social sciences, cultural studies, religious studies, history, etc. *theology will remain abstract, de-contextualized, and lacking in impact.* Moreover, inter-disciplinary approach in research will help deepening of theological issues and questions; it will also enable the Church-community to translate concretely the fruits of research into action plans.

The interdisciplinary nature of theology also indicates the importance of team-work. At the general level, in most disciplines, cutting-edge researches are done by teams or groups of scholars. New discoveries in science and innovations in technology are less and less fruit of individual genius, but result of joint venture. It is advisable that every theological institution take up a focus area of theological research and pursue it jointly by the faculty and students. In this way, our theological institutions will also become truly research communities. When the faculty does researches jointly, this will be certainly a highly motivating and inspiring factor for students.

Speaking of interdisciplinarity and team-work, I cannot but refer to the relationship of the guide or supervisor of the research work and the student. The hierarchical mindset so very characteristic of Indian tradition is at work also in the field of research. The guide pretends to be all-knowing master and the student is made to feel as ignorant and incapable. The guide does not see himself or herself as someone accompanying the student in the research journey. In many Indian universities and centres of higher education, the relationship of guide (supervisor) and student is like master and slave. I am told that there are guides who ask their research student even to go to market and purchase vegetable and fish and do household chores! Woe to the student who does not oblige the supervisor, and doomed if he or she dares to critically challenge the views of the guide. Further, there are several instances of abuse and sexual harassment of women research students by the guides. I think we need to bring to an end this revolting state of affairs in research guidance, by encouraging a team of faculty working together to guide and supervise the research work of a student. If the teachers and scholars are open to learning dialogue, and team-work, surely the quality of research is bound to go up. There should be also some mechanisms to protect women research students.

Research Publications

Precisely because research through the advancement of knowledge is meant to serve the community and its wellbeing, its results need to be widely made known and insights brought to concrete applications. Theological researches will deepen the understanding of God's Word, the faith of the community, and its relationships with the larger society and the world. The new insights deriving from researches in various branches of theological studies will nurture innovative pastoral praxis. But, unfortunately, in India, many theological researches remain unknown and hidden. Many valuable doctoral thesis, fruit of several years of hard labour, gather dust in the libraries. This sad state of affairs is due to the fact that they are not published. Publication should be a natural sequel to research.

For any scholar in theology to be able to vibrate with the constantly changing situations of the world and society, it is imperative that he or she continue to reflect, research, and publish. As it is, many of our theological institutions have faculty with high-sounding degrees, but who get rusted academically, and even corrupted due to lure of power and position. A passion for research, and the resolve to contribute to the community will not only make them true intellectual servants of the people but also, free them from the many chains of bondage. "*Omnes doctores non sunt docti* – so goes a Latin saying. It means, all who hold doctoral degrees are not necessarily learned! The theological institutions should create structural means and ways to encourage and support the research of the faculty and students.

On the other hand, despite many handicaps, the theological creativity and output from India is highly significant. And yet, for lack of publication, this contribution remains not known to the rest of the world. Recently I was invited to speak at a conference at the University of Louvain in Belgium. One of the western scholars presented a paper on comparative theology and another one presented a paper on how we need to move towards participation in the religious worship of peoples of other faiths. Apparently, these things were taken as bold ideas and a theological novelty. But then I intervened to say that Indian theology has been practicing comparative theology since many decades. Indian theologians have been reading Bhagavad Gita and John's Gospel and interpreting them inter-textually. I also pointed out that way back in 1988 there was a research seminar in Bangalore at National Biblical, Catechetical, and Liturgical Centre (NBCLC) on the question of sharing of worship with excellent research papers.[29] Even though some of these insights and researches were published, they remain unknown to the larger theological public in the world. I say this not in a national and chauvinistic sense, but because our contributions from India in the field of theological research should benefit global Christianity and humanity. Hence our task of research today in India, seen from a wider perspective, is to publish widely, in India as well as in international publications through books and through innumerable theological journals. It would be great if SATHRI and similar research bodies in the coming years were to concentrate more and more on publication.

Attitudes and Values to Accompany Research

Every scholar needs to be endowed with certain important qualities to be able to pursue serious research. Passion for knowledge is the first and foremost quality. Researches done for the sake of a degree, or simply to be able to get a job cannot be inspiring. The students involved in research should be fired by passion for the subject matter they are investigating. In my experience of research-guidance at the University of Madras, I have come across students whose capacity I am able to spot at the first interview, thanks to the passion they have for the pursuit of a particular question or problem. In other cases, it became obvious to me that the student simply has come for a degree and that is the motivation for research, and indeed a poor motivation. At one time, a student came to me to be enrolled for his Ph.D. I asked him, what is the theme or area in which he would like to research. His reply was, "Sir, give me a theme for research". That was enough for immediate disqualification! There should be an urge to know, to explore. The excitement of exploration should accompany all through the period of research.

Another important quality for research is that of freedom. The search for truth can only be there where freedom is at work. There are pseudo-researches which are not free, but cater to ideological ends, or oriented towards market, promotion of business, etc. Only where there is freedom, there is space for innovation and creativity. Since one of the purposes of research is innovation, it should be accompanied by the spirit of freedom. As for theology, genuine researches could be hampered by the preoccupation of orthodoxy and heterodoxy.

Perseverance is an important quality for any researcher. The topic of research may be very demanding, and clarity may be lacking regarding the direction in which the research is to be steered. There can be many more factors that could easily discourage students. One needs to be guided by a spirit of intellectual adventure and adopt a sportive attitude. This is important, so that the research is not given up in despair. There are many who begin enthusiastically, but then prolong endlessly and some seem to be perpetually research students without being able to complete their thesis. Others end up in frustration. Only the spirit of perseverance could keep up the high morale required for research.

Conclusion

Up until now, due to still continuing colonial influence in theology and theological education, the theological discourse was framed in the West with western conceptual tools and analysis. Anyone who wants to conduct research has to be part of this foreign discourse and fall within its frame. It would seem that the researches done in India and other developing countries acquire significance to the extent they help enhance the theological agenda formulated in the West. We have not fully got out of this. The challenge now is to break loose of this colonial conditioning of our theological research. Theological research institutions in India may need to go beyond, and promote indigenous research projects. More basically, they need to evolve a new framework of theological discourse and research that would be truly Indian in its spirit, nature, method, and scope. A broad vision and programme of this kind could play a good inspirational role for the individual researchers. These institutions will see to it that researches are not simply scattered on umpteen number of topics and issues, but are well-integrated within a larger indigenous theological research agenda.

Towards the above end, let me conclude by raising seven questions. They could help all the stakeholders of our theological research institutions and bodies to reflect on the future of theological research in India.

1. What are the developments in the contemporary world and in India that call for an overhaul of theological education, and theological research?

2. What are the developments in the Churches necessitating new avenues of theological research?

3. Which are some of the areas in the mission and ministry of the Church which call for further study and research?

4. How do the new approaches and insights in the general method of education and scientific methodology impact upon theological research?

5. How do today's transformations in knowledge system (production of knowledge, accumulation, and transmission) going to affect theological research?

6. How could theological research become increasingly inter-disciplinary? What are the methodological issues involved in the inter-disciplinary enterprise?

7. What would be the distinctive features of theological research in India/Asia compared to other parts of the world?

Bibliography

Ballard, Paul H., and Pritchard, John. *Practical Theology in Action* (London: SPCK, 1996).

Bennett, Zoë., et. al. *Invitation to Research in Practical Theology* (New York: Routledge, 2018).

Borgman, Erik., and Wilfred, Felix., eds. "Theology in a World of Specialization." *Concilium 2006/2* (London: SCM Press, 2016).

Boyd, Jason C. *Naked Preacher. Action Research and a Practice of Preaching* (London: SCM Press, 2018).

Butler, Lee H., and Lee, K. Samuel. "Changing the Margins: Mentoring and Research in the 21st Century." *Journal of Pastoral Theology* 27 (2017), 110-20.

Cameron, Helen. et. al. *Talking about God in Practice: Theological Action Research and Practical Theology* (London: SCM Press, 2010).

Clarke, Sathianathan., et al. *Dalit Theology in the Twenty-first Century. Discordant Voices, Discerning Pathways* (Delhi: Oxford, 2010).

Devasahayam, V., ed. *Dalits and Women: Quest for Humanity* (Madras: Dept. of Research and Publications, Gurukul Lutheran Theological College & Research Institute, 1993).

England, John C., et. al., ed. *Asian Christian Theologies: A Research Guide to Authors, Movements, Sources* (Delhi: ISPCK; , Quezon City: Claretian Publishers, Maryknoll, N.Y.: Orbis Books, 2002-2004).

Francis, Leslie J., Robbins, Mandy., and Astley, Jeff., eds. *Empirical Theology in Texts and Tables: Qualitative,Quantitative and Comparative Perspectives* (Leiden: Brill, 2009).

George, P.G., ed. *Theological Research in the Global South* (Serampore: South Asian Theological Research Institute, 2015).

Graham, Elaine. "Is Practical Theology a Form of Action Research?" *International Journal of Practical Theology* 17 (1) (2013), 148-178.

Lorrimar, Victoria. "Are Scientific Research Programmes Applicable to Theology? On Philip Hefner's Use of Lakatos." *Theology and Science* 15 (2017), 188-202.

Nirmal, Arvind P., and Devasahayam V., eds. *A Reader in Dalit theology* (Madras: Gurukul Lutheran Theological College & Research Institute for the Dept. of Dalit Theology, 1990).

Prabhakar, Samson., ed. *Church's Ministry and Theological Education* (Bangalore: BTESSC/SATHRI, 2005).

Prabhakar, Samson., ed. *Inter-cultural Asian Theological Methodologies: An Exploration* (Bangalore: South Asia Theological Research Institute, 2002).

Ricoeur, Paul. *Hermeneutics and the Human Sciences* (Cambridge: Cambridge University Press, 1981).

Said, Edward W. *Orientalism* (New York: Peguine Books, 1977).

Stump, J.B., and Padgett, Alan G., eds. *The Blackwell Companion to Science and Christianity* (Chichester, West Sussex, Malden, MA: Wiley-Blackwell, 2012).

Sugden, Chris. "Identity and Transformation: The Oxford Lectures of Vinay Samuel 1998-2006." *Transformation* 24 (3/4) (2007), 133-50.

Swinton, John., and Mowat, Harriet. *Practical Theology and Qualitative Research* (London: SCM, 2006).

Ven, Johannes A. van der., and Scherer-Rath, Michael., eds. *Normativity and Empirical Research in Theology* (Leiden, Boston: Brill, 2005).

Ven, Johannes A. van der. *Hermeneutics and Empirical Research in Practical Ttheology: The Contribution of Empirical Theology* (Leiden, Boston: Brill, 2004).

Webster, John C.B. "The Contribution of the Historical to Theological Research in India." *Bangalore Theological Forum* 16 (1) (2014), 150-159.

Weyel, Birgit. "Practical Theology as a Hermeneutical Science of Lived Religion." *International Journal of Practical Theology* 18 (1) (2014), 150-159.

Wilfred, Felix. "Crisis in the Christian Narration of God and the Encounter of Religions in a Post-metaphysical World." *Bangalore Theological Forum* 41 (2) (2009), 15-28.

Wilfred, Felix. *Theological Education in India* (Bangalore: Asian Trading Corporation,1985).

Endnotes

[1] In traditional theology, there was little room to speak of research. This is because theology in all its branches was supposed to explain the truths of faith as transmitted by tradition. Any space for research or discovery was excluded. The realm of faith presented by theology called for obedience of faith and not research.

[2] G. Bordenave, "Louis Pasteur (1822-1895)", *Microbes and Infection: A Journal on Infectious Agents and Host Defenses*, 5:6 (2003), 553-60.

[3] Cf. Arthur Allen, *Vaccine: The Controversial Story of Medicine's Greatest Lifesaver* (New York: London: W. W. Norton, 2007); Enrico Salemi D'Amelio and Raffaele Simonetta D'Amelio, "Anti-Infectious Human Vaccination in Historical Perspective", *International Reviews of Immunology*, 35 (2016), 260-90.

[4] At a religious level we had some similar thing connected with the worship of Mariamma or Sītalā, the goddess of smallpox. The very goddess who distributes the smallpox like pearls, is also the one to whom one should pray to get cured from the same illness. See Frédérique Apffel Marglin, and Stephen Apffel Marglin, eds, *Dominating Knowledge* (New York: Oxford University Press, 1990),102-144. But at a scientific level, inoculation was brought about through research. In India we had, so to say, a myth of inoculation, but this was not turned into an empirical reality.

[5] K. Codell Carter and Barbara R. Carter, *Childbed Fever: A Scientific Biography of Ignaz Semmelweis* (London: Routledge 2017); Theodore G. Obenchain, *Genius*

Belabored: Childbed Fever and the Tragic Life of Ignaz Semmelweis (Tuscaloosa: The University of Alabama Press, 2016).

[6] Robert J. Kaden, Gerald L. Linda, and Melvin Prince, eds, *Leading Edge Marketing Research: 21st-Century Tools and Practices* (Thousand Oaks: Sage, 2011).

[7] There is often a subtle and subconscious assumption that matters of faith are not to be on the same plane as other areas of life, and matters of Church are not to be compared to the experiences in society. In other words, it means that faith and Church are to be shielded from any rational and scientific approach. It is such a mode of thinking that permits in the Church arbitrary decisions and authoritarian ways.

[8] Seamus Hegarty, *The Role of Research in Mature Education Systems* (Windsor: NFER, 1997); John Swinton and Harriet Mowat, *Practical Theology and Qualitative Research* (London: SCM, 2006).

[9] Helen Cameron, et al., *Talking about God in Practice: Theological Action Research and Practical Theology* (London: SCM Press, 2010).

[10] Postcolonial studies have critically reviewed Orientalism. The pioneering work was that of Edward W. Said, *Orientalism* (New York: Peguine Books, 1977); See also Felix Wilfred, "Postcolonialism and Subaltern Identity: Implications for Theology", in ID., *Christians for a Better India* (Delhi: ISPCK, 2014), pp. 325-343; Robert Irwin, *Dangerous Knowledge: Orientalism and Its Discontents* 1st ed. (Woodstock, NY: Overlook Press, 2006); Diane Long Hoeveler and Jeffrey Cass, eds, *Interrogating Orientalism: Contextual Approaches and Pedagogical Practices* (Columbus: Ohio State University Press, 2006).

[11] See Erik Borgman and Felix Wilfred, eds, "Theology in a World of Specialization", *Concilium 2006/2*, especially the articles by Sheila Greeve Davaney, "Theology and Religious Studies in an Age of Fragmentation", pp. 35-44; Mary Grey, "From Shaken Foundations to a Different Integrity: Spirituality as Response to Fragmentation", pp. 77-87.

[12] Nicholas Maxwell and Karl Popper, *Science and Enlightenment* (London: UCL Press, 2017).

[13] Cf. Birgir Weyel, "Practical Theology as a Hermeneutical Science of Lived Religion", *International Journal of Practical Theology*, 18:1 (2014),150-159; Elaine Graham, "Is Practical Theology a Form of Action Research?", *International Journal of Practical Theology*, 17:1 (2013), 148-178; Peter Kreeft, *Practical Theology* (San Francisco: Ignatius Press, 2014); Paul H. Ballard and John Pritchard, *Practical Theology in Action* (London: SPCK, 1996).

[14] S. Radhakrishnan, ed, "Brahadaranyaka Upanishad", *The Principal Upanishads*, 1:3/28 (New York: Oxford University Press, 1953), 162-163.

[15] Plato, *The Republic, Book VII*, edited by Benjamin Jowett (New York: The Modern Library, 1941). See also Bowery, A. M. "Drawing Shadows on the Wall: Teaching Plato's Allegory of the Cave", *Teaching Philosophy*, 24:2 (2001), 121-32.

[16] Geetha B. Nambissan, "Exclusion and discrimination in Schools: Experiences of Dalit Children", in Sukhadeo Thorat – Katherine S. Newman, eds, *Economic Discrimination in Modern India* (New York: Oxford University Press, 2013), pp. 253 – 286.

[17] Here we may recall the critique of Heidegger on the western tradition of truth as correspondence of the object and mind (*adaequatio mentis cum re*). He views truth as disclosure, manifestation out of concealment and falsehood. Such an understanding of truth, in my view, could serve to uncover the plight of the victims and marginalised. The unconcealment of the naked reality of suffering and oppression amounts to truth in the primary sense. On Heidegger's approach to truth, see Mark A. Wrathall, *Heidegger and Unconcealment: Truth, Language, and History* (Cambridge: Cambridge University Press, 2011).

[18] See George Soares-Prabhu, "The Historical Critical Method. Reflections on its Relevance for the Study of the Gospels in India Today", in M. Amaladoss, George Gispert-Sauch, and T K John, eds, *Theologizing in India* (Bangalore: Theological Publications in India, 1981), pp. 314-367.

[19] Cf. Paul Ricoeur, *Hermeneutics and the Human Sciences* (Cambridge: Cambridge University Press, 1981), p. 177.

[20] As quoted by Sukhadeo Thorat, "Higher Education in India. Emerging Issues Related to Access, Inclusiveness", *Nehru Memorial Lecture* (Mumbai: University of Mumbai, 2006).

[21] E. Conde-Frazier, "Participatory Action Research: Practical Theology for Social Justice", *Religious Education*, 101:3 (2006), 321-29.

[22] Cf. Sathianathan Clarke, et al., *Dalit Theology in the Twenty-first Century. Discordant Voices, Discerning Pathways* (Delhi: Oxford, 2010).

[23] This is an important argument used in the case of affirmative action in favour of African Americans and other marginalised minorities. See Elaine Kennedy-Dubourdieu, ed, *Race and Inequality: World Perspectives on Affirmative Action* (London; New York: Routledge, 2016); Hugh Davis Graham, *Collission Course. The Strange Convergence of Affirmative Action and Immigration Policy in America* (Oxford: Oxford University Press, 2012); John David Skrentyny, *The Ironies of Affirmative Action, Politis, Culture and Justice in America* (Chicago: University of Chicago Press, 2012).

[24] Cf. Felix Wilfred, "What can 'Upper Caste' Christians Learn from Dalits Christians?" ID., *Christians for a Better India* (Delhi: ISPCK, 2014), pp.105-119.

[25] Partha Chatterjee, "After Subaltern Studies", *Economic and Political Weekly* (September 1, 2012), 44-49.

[26] Cf. J. Lave and E. Wenger, *Situated Learning: Legitimate Peripheral Participation* (Cambridge-New York: Cambridge University Press, 1991), pp. 50-51.

[27] Rabindranath Tagore, *Gitanjali*, LXXIII.

[28] Cf. Ted Peters, *Science, Theology, and Ethics* (New York: Routledge, 2017); Kuruvilla Pandikattu, ed, *Together towards Tomorrow. Interfacing Science and Religion in India* (Pune: Association of Science, Society and Religion, 2006); Christopher Southgate, et. al., *God, Humanity and the Cosmos. A Textbook in Science and Religion* (Harrisburg: Trinity Press International, 1999); Philip Clayton and Arthur Peacocke, *In Whom we live and Move and Have Our Being* (Grand Rapids: William B. Eerdmans Publishing Company, 2004); Philip D. Clayton, *God and Contemporary Science* (Grand Rapids: WM B. Eerdmans Publishing Company, 1997); Charles Birch, et. al., *Faith Science and the Future* (Geneva: WCC, 1978).

[29] See Paul Puthenangady, ed, *Sharing Worship* (Bangalore: NBCLC, 1988).

PART - IV
ECUMENISM AND "WIDER ECUMENISM"

CHAPTER 14

Asian Ecumenism
through Postcolonial Lens

Relationship among the Churches has been an issue touching upon every aspect of the life, worship, mission, belief and history, of the Christian believers. Asia has been in the forefront in steering a new path for the life of the Churches, overcoming the historical divisions of the past. It is a fact of history that the transmission of Christian faith in the past five centuries by the various Christian denominations took place in the context of colonial history. This history has left its marks on the life of the Asian Churches. The future course of relationship among the Christian Churches, however, calls for a re-reading and interpreting of the past through postcolonial eyes. This is precisely what we want to attempt in this chapter.

A Quick Look at the Canon Law

I would like to start by referring to how ecumenism is viewed by the Roman Catholic Canon Law. It is important to take note of this, since canon law is what officially guides the Catholics in the concrete practice of ecumenism. There is but a single canon[1] which deals *ex professo* with ecumenism in the Latin Code, and it reads as follows:

Canon 755: "It is primarily for the supreme Church authority to foster and direct the ecumenical movement among Catholics, whose scope is the restoration of unity among all Christians". And "it is for bishops and episcopal conferences to promote it according to norms of law".

What do we find? Linking ecumenism with the magisterium – with the teaching authority of the Church – the pope and the bishops. How helpful is this position? In spite of all the inspiring things said in *Unitatis Redintegratio*, and in *Orientalium Ecclesiarum* - the Vatican II documents - when it comes to practice of ecumenism, the doctrinal preoccupations have narrowed it down to a matter of the *magisterium*.[2]

Let us look at the word "*restoration*" in the above cited canon. What is implied as goal of ecumenism is a going back (restoring) to the unity that was there before the historical division of the Churches. Implied in this "restoration" is the achievement of organic unity. For, the Roman Catholic Church considers itself to be the true Church of Christ, or sees this Church of Christ "subsisting" in the Catholic Church.[3] Both these claims have been problematic. While the ecumenical discourses and practices have advanced pretty much, and many models have been put forward like conciliar unity, reconciled diversity, receptive ecumenism, etc.,[4] the Roman Catholic Church's official position seems to have got stuck with organic unity. Similarly, while there are attempts to understand and interpret the statement that the true Church of Christ "subsists" in the Catholic Church, we note that the Catholic Fundamentalism, in practice, seems to still profess an equation of the Roman Catholic Church and the Church of Jesus Christ.

As a *method*, the canon follows a top-down approach to ecumenism, and there is nothing on the faithful – the people of God – and their role in ecumenism and its practice. What we have in this canon is, then, *institutional ecumenism*, reflecting the hierarchical structure of the Roman Catholic Church.[5] With this canon, we do not go very far in ecumenism! The Eastern Code, fortunately, has seven canons and has more to say about people of God when speaking of ecumenism. The canon I quoted from the Latin code would explain why Rome is focused on bilateral institutional dialogue with other denominations and agreements on doctrinal points, whereas the developments in the field of ecumenism point to a different direction.[6]

What has been happening in Asia in the field of ecumenism, especially in the light of the experience with "wider ecumenism" – namely inter-religious relationships – and the way postcolonialism looks at unity and plurality could open up new spaces and avenues for innovative ecumenical relationships.

We will deal with the issue in three parts:

Part I: Asian Ecumenical Path

Part II: Insights from Inter-religious Relationship for a New Ecumenical Practice

Part III: Future of Ecumenism from Post-colonial Perspective

All the three parts are tied together by the thread of *postcolonialism*. For, Asian ecumenical path has been one that distinguishes itself from the prevalent understanding of the relationship among Churches during the missionary and colonial period. The postcolonial understanding and interpretation of Asian Christianity leads to talk on the relationship with peoples of other faiths, since it is an issue of unity of humankind which the Churches are called to serve. The future of ecumenism is also envisaged from the postcolonial perspective. Going into these issues of Asian ecumenism is at the same time a matter of realizing its contribution to world ecumenism.

Part I: Asian Ecumenical Path

From Denominations to Indigenous Churches

The same missionary movement that brought denominationalism into Asia, ironically, was also the main source of ecumenism. The spirit of ecumenism was triggered by the need to bear common witness. World Missionary Conference, Edinburgh 1910, was the occasion for the missionaries of different denominations to come together to affirm common Christian witness.[7]

There was a lesser known movement that followed the Edinburgh Conference. It was the move from denominatinalism to autonomous indigenous Churches with their own features. It was an attempt to break the traditional framework of thinking and acting in mission on the basis of past denominational identities. Visionaries like Bishop V.S. Azariah (1874 – 1945), who was a participant at Edinburgh Conference of 1910, already foresaw new forms of Christianities in Asia and in other continents – Christianities not bound by past historical division. It would look that Bishop Azariah and others preferred to invest their energies in the future shape of Christianities in indigenous forms rather than be caught in the agenda of reconciling the historical divisions that occurred in the past. Similarly, a young pastor from China, Cheng Ching-Yi, urged the conference that the Chinese Church exercise its own agency and shape a Chinese expression of Christianity, according to its genius, and with a non-denominational identity.

> Let me quote from the speech of Azariah:

> Through all the ages to come the Indian Church will rise up in gratitude to attest the heroism and self-denying labours of the missionary body. You have given your goods to feed the poor. You have given your bodies to be burned. We also ask for love. Give us FRIENDS.[8]

Through these words, Azariah indicated the importance of mutuality, inclusiveness and dialogue in mission as well as among Churches and denominations – a dialogue based on respect for each other, as indicated by the metaphor "*friends*". He touched a sensitive nerve of the relationship between the missionaries and the native workers which gave him opportunity to reflect on the importance of mutuality, reciprocity and friendship. The relationship of missionaries to the natives was characterized by aloofness, condescendence, and lack of interaction. Implied herein is a postcolonial critique of power relationships in the mission and in the Church. The postcolonial critique of Azariah foreshadowing contemporary postcolonial theories, called for mutuality. Where there is domination, there is no room to talk of friendship or equality. I tend to think that colonial mission was perhaps the greatest religious enterprise in human history, but it was an enterprise lacking in friendship and inter-subjectivity. Azariah was aware how the missionaries, in general, never cared to visit the home of native workers, nor would share meals with them. He apparently said in the same speech in a lighter vein, on how the local people are prevented from deliberations on Church matters. "Too often you promise us thrones in heaven, but will not offer us chairs in your drawing rooms". Unsurprisingly, these words got deleted in the official proceedings of the Edinburgh Conference.[9] There was indeed discussion about cooperation and promotion of unity at the Conference. But it was about mission agencies of different denominations cooperating and avoiding rivalry and duplication in the work of mission.

Thanks to this heritage of V.S. Azariah, Cheng Ching-Yi, and other Asian participants of the Edinburgh Mission Conference, there was a shift of attention from denominations to *indigenous forms of Christianities* in which the agency of the local people became evident.[10] In other words, what has been happening in Asia is similar to the process early Christianity witnessed. Different cultures, histories, and world-views led to the emergence of different ecclesial traditions. The "ecumenical" referred to the communications among the various expressions of Christianity. The possibility of this process is foreshadowed in Vatican II, in *Lumen Gentium* which, while speaking of regional bishops' conferences, points to a possible future development of them into Churches of their own, like the development of Churches in the East and the West in early centuries.

> It has come about through divine providence that, in the course of time, different Churches set up on various places by the apostles and their successors joined together in a multiplicity of organically united groups which, whilst safeguarding the unity of the faith and the unique divine structure of the universal Church, have their own discipline, enjoy their own liturgical usage and inherit a theological and spiritual patrimony... *In like fashion,* the episcopal conferences at the present time are in a position to contribute in many and fruitful ways to the concrete realization of the collegial spirit.[11]

From early twentieth century on, there has been a move in Asia towards non-denominationalism. In China, The National Christian Conference started in 1913 in Shanghai became a common platform of Protestant Churches.[12] The three principles of Contemporary Chinese Christian Patriotic movement – *self-governance, self-support, and self-propagation of the Gospel,* has its roots in the movement of non-denominational Christianity of early twentieth century. Thinkers like T.C. Chao, L.C. Wu and

Y.T. Wu were in the forefront in re-appropriating Christianity in the Chinese way. To belong to one of the western denominational group in colonial times was to reinforce further the "foreign" image of Christianity in China. The Three-Patriotic movement was inter-denominational in one sense, in that it brought the various Protestant denominations together in view of a common mission in China. But in another sense, the development of indigenous Church was trans-denominational, focused on the concrete situation in China. The Korean War reinforced the importance of bridging Christian identity with national identity. This inter-denominational and trans-denominational approach met with opposition, as one could surmise, on the part of the Roman Catholic Church, which threatened to excommunicate any Catholics joining this trans-denominational movement in China.

In India, the formation of the Church of South India in 1947 took place by the merger of Anglican (episcopal), Congregational, Presbyterian and Methodist denominations. It was the first example in the world of an organic ecumenical unity.[13] It was the result of a long process of maturation, starting from the Tranquebar Conference of 1919 which saw the coming together of leaders of several denominations. Following the inspiration of CSI, the Church of North India (CNI) came into existence in 1970.

Ecumenical Forces in Asia

Asian Christians have been aware that denominationalism is not good for the proclamation and witness to the Gospel, and indeed a real scandal in the midst of peoples of other faiths. As C.H. Hwang noted,

> The sad thing is that, before becoming first a confessing Church in the missionary situation, the younger churches were prematurely projected into a "confessional" situation which was not their own; before they became a Community of Christ they were told to become a Presbyterian, Lutheran, Methodist or Anglican church. They were divided without even being able to know why.[14]

In Asia, the meeting among the Churches has been not so much a matter of faith and order (negotiating doctrinal differences), rather the challenges of the world for common mission and witness. This point has been put forward sharply by the Sri Lankan theologian Preman Niles, when he notes, "an important key for grasping theological concerns in the ecumenical movement in Asia is the fact that theological articulations in Asia with some few exceptions, arises at the places where the church meets the world and the world challenges the church."[15] The point could be illustrated by the national struggle for independence of Asian nations from the colonial yoke, followed by the programme of nation-building. The Christian Churches were so scattered and heavily under the control of missionaries, that there was hardly any room for them to come together in the struggle for independence. Opinions were very much divided among the Christians themselves on national issues.[16] However, once independence was attained, the mood changed. The situation of newly independent nations called for all Christians to come together on the basis of a common nationhood, and contribute to the growth and development of the newly liberated countries. The objective of nation-building created the mood for ecumenical cooperation for the benefit and welfare of the people.

Another refreshing ecumenical force in Asia has been the marginalised people, victims, and people at the periphery. From them came new impulses for ecumenism and unity. We name here the Dalit movement, movements of indigenous peoples and tribes, and the stirrings among the discriminated Burukumin of Japan. Groups like the Dalits have suffered discrimination from all the Churches and in different forms. Hence, the ecumenical agenda for them is not reconciliation and unity among the Churches, but a challenge to all of them to overcome caste divisions and create unity of the people of God. For, all of them are divided by caste which is the major source of disunity in the Church. Before this agenda of unity which touches upon their life and dignity, denominational divisions seem to pale into insignificance.

The challenge from the marginalised groups is a challenge of unity – it is a call to the unity of the Church without division on the basis of caste, race, language, etc. Denominational division stemming from past history seems to have had little impact on their Christian faith and life, as the Dalits, for example, cut across different denominations. Whichever denominations they may belong to – an accident of mission history - their goal is unity in the Church and among the Churches. Illustrative of it is the fact that while deciding to convert to Christianity, the choice of the Christian denomination is not based on which one gives them orthodoxy and purity of doctrines, but which one integrates them within the Christian community in the spirit of unity, and respects their human and Christian dignity. "There is neither Jew, nor Greek, there is neither slave nor free, there is neither male nor female; for you are all one in Christ Jesus" (Gal. 3:28). This is the unity the Dalit people seek from the Churches. Dalit and other subaltern groups are contributing to a new and fresh understanding of unity that is yet to come. This is different from institutional ecumenism. The victims, the Dalits, and the marginalised challenge the Churches to reconceptualize ecumenism from the periphery.[17] As Jude Lal Fernando, observes,

> It is the churches' ability to listen to the multiple voices of suppressed others within its own tradition and in other traditions; among the poor, women, different ethnic, tribal and caste groups, among the lives that have been made fragmentary and episodic and the eco-system that is threatened — which is the memory of the eternal Other who is existing in each and every one of us - that could further the process of dialogue. The church discovers itself in the face of the other within the churches, among the churches and in the world at large. The other has been the victim of petty ideological interpretation of doctrine and faith. It is, in fact, the voices of such victims who evoke the moral responsibility of the Church.[18]

Persecution of Christians and their harassment have led to greater experience of Christian unity. For example, the violence and persecution the Christian communities in the state of Gujarat and Odisha suffered have been a force to cement the relationships among various denominations and motive for their coming together. It has also led to jointly rethink the past ways of evangelization. This is an example of ecumenism from below.[19]

The geo-political situations in Asia have also prompted the coming together of the Churches for the cause of peace and reconciliation, as for example through the *Tozanso process*.[20] It refers to the ongoing dialogue and exchange among sub-regional groups that started from 1984 when Churches of North Korea and South Korea met with Churches from Japan and United States. Since then, meeting together on a regular basis, has helped to develop the spirit of solidarity. One of the important concerns in the process is the involvement of the Churches of the region for the reconciliation between North and South Korea. The Tozanso process created opportunities for Church leaders especially of South and North Koreas to make mutual visits and increase mutual understanding among a divided people. This process has also created momentum in the resistance of the Churches to military build-up in Korea.

Institutional and Theological initiatives

At the institutional level, from nineteenth century onwards, the medical, educational, and philanthropic works by the different Churches in Asia gave an opportunity for mutual cooperation among them. Further, movements like Young Men's Christian Association (YMCA), Young Women's Christian Association (YWCA), and World Student Christian Federation (WSCF) played an important role to further ecumenical spirit, and gave new impetus to the institutional initiatives of cooperation among the various Churches. An important institution that has been spearheading ecumenism in Asia is Christian Conference of Asia (CCA) comprising Protestant and Orthodox Churches. At the time of its founding (1953) it was known as "East Asia Christian Conference" (EACC), later in 1973 renamed as CCA. The Christian Conference of Asia and the Federation of Asian Bishops' Conferences (FABC), the Roman Catholic body of Asian bishops, have been in collaboration. Jointly they have taken many major ecumenical initiatives.[21] To give a structural means to carry out common cooperation, both these bodies created a committee of Asian Movement for Christian Unity (AMCU) which has been functioning since 1996. FABC, on its part, has a very actively engaged department dedicated to the issue of inter-religious dialogue and ecumenism – Office of Ecumenical and Interreligious Affairs (OEIA).[22] It is significant that CCA and FABC have come together to think and act in the field of inter-religious relationships – one of the major concerns of Asia. A highly significant consultation of representatives of various Church bodies, thanks to the initiative of CCA and FABC took place in Singapore in 1986 under the caption, "Living and Working Together with Sisters and Brothers of Other Faiths in Asia". One of the crucial points of discussion and agreement was on the relationship of *mission and dialogue* – evangelization and dialogue. The point was under debate in the various Churches. But the Singapore consultation brought greater clarity and nuance to the question of the interrelationship between mission and dialogue. It stated,

> We affirm that dialogue and mission have their own integrity and freedom. They are distinct but not unrelated. Dialogue is not a tool or instrument for mission and evangelization, but it does influence the way the Church perceives and practices mission in a pluralistic world.[23]

What about theologians? D.T. Niles, M.M. Thomas, Stanley Samartha and other Asian thinkers have made substantial contribution to world ecumenism, drawing from Asian experiences. This legacy continues among the present-day Asian theologians. Scholars across denominations meet regularly at Congress of Asian Theologians (CAT). Churches are developing jointly Asian theologies going beyond doctrinal differences among the traditional denominations. They try to re-interpret the Gospel most effectively in the context of Asia, facing the challenges of the times. It is interesting to note that Asian theologians hardly ever meet to discuss doctrinal differences of the various Christian Churches and denominations. It is not a priority for them. The real question is how we could be truly Asian in understanding and interpreting the Christian mission and message.

Finally, it should be pointed out here that Asian ecumenism had wider impact on the political realm. The effort of Churches of the various regions of Asia to come together and engage themselves in mission and witness, has contributed also to create greater regional solidarity among the Asian nations. It is difficult to measure this impact. The ecumenical movement in Asia has created trans-national cooperation and a sense of "Asianness". It preceded political cooperation in the region. We can surely say that bodies like Association of South East Nations (ASEAN) and the South Asian Association of Regional Cooperation (SAARC) are strengthened through Asian ecumenical movement.[24]

Part II: Insights from Inter-religious Relationship for A New Ecumenical Practice

Casting Wide the Ecumenical Net

One of the great contributions of Asia to ecumenical movement is to have widened the concept of "ecumenism," and have included within its horizon the relationship with peoples of other faiths and traditions. It came to be known as "*wider ecumenism*".[25] There were, and are purists who resist any such move, and would restrict the word strictly to relationship among Christian Churches. But the point is that these purists do not understand that the relationship among the Churches which may look disproportionately big, seen through western eyes, are not so when seen from Asia. If the Church is the sign and sacrament of the unity of humankind as declared by Vatican II,[26] then ecumenism cannot but be affected by the issues that touch upon humanity and its unity. One such question is the relationship among different faiths. Greater understanding, harmony, and peace among religions is the goal towards which the Churches are invited to move.[27] By fostering relationship with peoples of other faiths, the Churches are contributing to the unity of humankind; and hence the importance of their coming together for this cause. As the Sri Lankan theologian, Wesley Ariarajah, notes,

> At the global level there is an increasing recognition that the world's problems are not Christian problems requiring Christian answers but human problems that must be addressed together by all human beings. We know that whether it is the issue of justice, peace and human rights, or the destruction of the environment we need to work across boundaries of religions, nations and cultures.[28]

The involvement with peoples of other faiths through wider ecumenism is bound to help the intra-church unity too. During the missionary epoch this was not possible due to a negative theology of other religions. In the past decades, most ecumenical meetings that framed the inter-religious agenda were held in Asia. Ecumenical movement pioneered a different theology of religion than the one that characterized the missionary era. The development of a more positive attitude towards other religions owes a lot to global ecumenical movement. Dialogue with other religious traditions opened the eyes of Asian Churches to see the unity of the Church in a much broader light. This would include the relationship with other religious traditions through inter-religious dialogue and fostering of unity with the whole creation.

However, there is a sense of unease, insecurity, and feeling of threat connected with the use of the term "wider ecumenism." The point is well-formulated by Konrad Raiser in the form of a series of questions:

> Can the churches and those responsible for ecumenical organizations agree on a sufficiently firm common base for the understanding of ecumenism? Does ecumenism in the proper sense relate only to the search for the communion among the Christian churches, or should it be opened up to relations with other religious communities - as is frequently advocated in Asia? Should the ecumenical movement reach beyond the churches to make alliances with other groups in civil society? What is the proper relationship between the commitment to church unity and to social justice? Are common witness and evangelism more important than church unity?[29]

Wider ecumenism need not be a threat to ecumenism among Christian Churches. Experience in Asia has shown that relationship among Churches and dialogue with religions are intertwined and are mutually supportive. As a result, an effective intra-religious dialogue among Christian Churches has strengthened the inter-religious dialogue of the wider ecumenism. Conversely, inter-religious dialogue has called for greater unity and collaboration among Christian Churches and communities. What Andrew Pratt says about the issue in the United States go to confirm the Asian orientation.

> The two ecumenical conversations, interfaith and intrafaith, are connected and may be mutually beneficial. The new religious pluralism in the United States could contribute toward a positive, shared Christian identity that, in turn, might contribute toward healthy and mutually enriching interfaith relationships.[30]

Learning from the Theology and Practice of Inter-religious Dialogue

Asian Theology of religions and the practice of inter-religious dialogue have turned out to be an important source for global ecumenism. Inter-religious dialogue has suggested a non-teleological approach in inter-church relationships. This means that one need not hurry with unity and consensus which would reflect a view from the centre. Rulers and administrators are very concerned about unity that ensures that everything is in order and under control. This imperial model of unity is not what is envisaged for the Churches. Such a mindset and the values attendant on it could be transported also into the practice of ecumenism and in the relationship among religious traditions.

In the theology of religions, for a long-time, fulfilment theory was in vogue, and still it is the dominant theological approach in many Churches, especially in the Roman Catholic Church. Think of a more recent statement in *Dominus Iesus* which says, "Objectively speaking they [other religions] are in a gravely deficient situation in comparison with those who, in the Church, have the fullness of salvation".[31] If other religions have elements of goodness and truth, they are only in an unfulfilled state, and hence one may not rest until the fulfilment is reached towards which one needs to hasten. Such an approach does not really value the richness and uniqueness each religious faith represents and the value of pluralism they all manifest and rainbow-like beauty they exhibit.

A pre-determined idea of fulfilment simply turns them into rungs of a ladder leading to the top of fulfilment. As for the relationship among Churches, this kind of perspective sees ecumenism in terms of solely organic unity. In fact, as we noted earlier, for the Roman Catholic Church the fullness of the Church is to be found in it, while other Churches and communities have some elements of the Church of Christ. This is what I would call a teleological approach to dialogue and ecumenism which seriously undermine them. If in inter-religious relationship we need to focus our attention on the richness the various faiths represent, so it is in the case of inter-church relationships. True ecumenism calls for appreciation of the history and tradition of other Christian Churches for their *value in themselves*. The rush towards organic unity could seriously impair this. *Dialogue is a value in itself*, and not simply a means to a pre-determined end. Hence, dialogue should be continuously fostered independent of pre-determined goals. Setting goals could affect negatively the quality of our dialogue. This applies as much to inter-religious relationships as to ecumenical practices.

Dialogue is what we can do. What comes out of it is not under our control. We need to approach the fruit of dialogue with *a sense of mystery*. Teleological thinking and pragmatic practices may condition our minds to set definite goals for our dialogues. This is to rob dialogue of its true spirit. If we take dialogue as an end in itself, and not a means, then it creates the atmosphere for mutual learning and enrichment.

The attitude and practice of mutual learning creates a welcome opening for each Church-tradition to draw from its own religious sources. However, new impetus for inter-religious dialogue springs also from the world. For example, all the religions are challenged to contribute to justice and peace in the world, and to human dignity and rights. Similarly, ecumenical endeavour could be enlivened today by drawing from *non-religious resources and traditions*. The conversations among Churches need not restrict to their doctrines and worship. The ecumenical net should be cast wider in the sea of humanity to reach the intricate problems it is facing today. "Justice, Peace and Integrity of Creation" sets out an important ecumenical agenda for many years to come; so also, the concerns which forms part of WCC Commission of Churches on International Affairs.

Re-conception of truth is another lesson we learn from inter-religious dialogue. Truth as a set of doctrines to be believed in, offers no real clue or approach to other religious traditions. We need to begin from somewhere else. Inter-religious understanding draws inspiration from what was expressed in Rig Veda: *ekaṁ sat viprāḥ bahudhā vadanti* – truth is one, but sages have spoken of it in a plurality of ways. If we follow the same in ecumenical dialogue, it would mean that, instead of resolving doctrinal differences to arrive at the goal of unity, we will go deeper into the different theological languages and accents in which the truth of the Gospel has been expressed. We contemplate the rich truth of the Gospel as refracted through the prism of different denominations.

Further, the understanding of ecumenism and the relationship among Churches will be different if we employ new insights and perspectives of contemporary hermeneutics.[32] With reference to ecumenism, we could highlight at least two important hermeneutical intuitions. First, every text needs to be placed in the overall context of a broader discourse. For example, Pope Paul VI made it clear in a speech at the beginning of the second session of Vatican II, that the ecumenical relationship with the Christian Churches and communities is an important goal of the Council. If so, it follows that not only *Unitatis Redintegratio*, the document speaking *ex professo* on ecumenism, but all the documents need to be read and interpreted from ecumenical perspective.

Second, every text is open-ended, namely the meaning and significance of a text goes beyond the meaning intended by the author, so that it could be re-interpreted and re-appropriated anew every time and in different situations. This means that whether it is Vatican II or WCC documents or statements of other bodies, they need to be reinterpreted in relationship to the local context.[33]

Moreover, we need to build on what Vatican II said about *"hierarchy of truths."*[34] This helped to facilitate greatly ecumenical understanding in such a way that Catholic Marian dogmas need not be the kind of obstacle it would have been, had not one acknowledged the hierarchy of truths. Similar to hierarchy of truths, we need a *"hierarchy of laws"* which will help for better ecumenical relationships.

Ecumenism and the Issue of Power

There is another set of issues which should also form part of ecumenical engagement. I mean the question of authority and power, and their conception in the Church and in relationship to the world.

Let us begin with the inner-church issue of power. For those who set their goals on the doctrinal reconciliation among the denominations, it is good to remember that *one of the greatest obstacles in ecumenical understanding is the conception of power in the Roman Catholic Church and its juridicism.* Lukas Vischer, a leading ecumenist of his time already indicated where the real problem lies. In his words,

> The question about the proper 'juridical form' of the Church is an eminently ecumenical problem... The 'juridicism' of the Roman Catholic Church is

the object of earnest and radical criticism from the side of the Orthodox as well as from the Churches of the Reformation. They see in the premises as well as in the conclusions of canon law some of the deepest differences which divide them from the Roman Catholic Church.[35]

Let us reflect on the *issue of power in the Churches in relation to its exercise in the larger society*. Some of the Churches have an understanding of power that resonates with mediaeval and feudal models in total contrast to *participatory approach,* based on human dignity and rights, and respectful of modern democratic aspirations. Churches embedded in traditional conception of authority and power are increasingly being challenged by new approach to power in which checks and balances are integral part. An example would be the call to make human dignity and human rights among the fundamental principles of canonical order in the Roman Catholic Church, which would ensure accountability and transparency .[36] But this move, unfortunately, is being resisted. The call from the world for responsibility and transparency in exercise of power and authority poses a challenge to all the Churches in the ecumene. This issue may not be set aside. It needs to be faced by the Christian Churches and communities. The source and channel of power in the Church and the mode of its exercise may not go against the order of creation in which every human being has dignity and inalienable rights. Ecumenical engagements need to grapple with this question.

From a faith and Gospel perspective, to respond to the challenge of power posed by the modern world would be for all the Churches to go back to the understanding of power and authority as service in the early Church. The recovery of this truth will help loosen the rigour of the conception of power and authority which have followed the feudal model in the Church, rather than the Gospel model of service. The model of authority in the Church as service implies in an eminent way participatory exercise of it with due respect to human dignity and rights.

Part III: Future of Ecumenism from Postcolonial Perspective

Postcolonialism helps us to view the future of ecumenism from the perspective of *difference and plurality* rather than think of restoration of a broken unity.[37] There is certainly room to speak of unity but the kind of unity, paradoxical as it may sound, is inextricably bound to difference. There is, of course unity between man and woman when we think of their common humanity. And yet what constitutes deeper union is the *difference* man and woman represent. Precisely the difference among them becomes the basis of their deepest bonds of union. Could we use this analogy for inter-denominational relationships? Are we not in an age when through ecumenical movement we celebrate the *difference?* The ecumenical cause is lost when we interpret difference as *deviance*. The difference the denominations and Christian groups represent is a sign of the richness of Christianity, and not a weakness to be lamented about.

Besides helping us to value difference and pluralism, postcolonialism helps us also to have a *relational self-definition*. The colonizer and the colonized may be interpreted independently of each other. The one is comprised in the definition of the other. Thus, Catholics are implied in any understanding of the Protestants and vice versa. They are relational concepts.

A good ecumenical practice would presuppose a critical approach to the role language and discourses play in constructing the other – the other denomination, the other Christian belief. Further, postcolonialism helps us analyse how "the Catholic" and "the Protestant" are constructed through the use of language and discourses. It would be interesting to study, for example, how traditionally the discourse among the Irish Catholics are constructed about Protestants, and conversely; how the Pentecostals are talked about among the traditional Catholics and how the Pentecostals discourse on Catholics. It would also be interesting to study how Russian Orthodox Church constructs the discourse about the Protestants and Catholics in the context of ethno-nationalism. *Ultimately the underlying issue in ecumenism is something common to contemporary cultural issues.* It is the question of how the "other" is constructed. Postcolonialism could lead to a critical approach to the way the "other" Churches, ecclesial groups, and denominations are constructed.[38]

Not unlike the case of Indian caste, each denomination operates in its discourse of the "other" with an ascriptive identity. The "other" Church, denomination, community is represented as something fixed and unchanging. Postcolonialism helps us to read various *Christian denominations as different discursive practices* with their resources in history and tradition.

Closely connected with discourse analysis in ecumenical practice, is the question of *representation*, which is again a very important thematic in postcolonial theory. Representation is not only an epistemological issue, but a deeply political issue, and a platform for the play of power. Postcolonial theoretical forays have shown that stereotypical representation of the other is a strategy of power and control. This mechanism could also be in the field of mutual representation in the field of religion, and among the Churches too.

Postcolonialism has been critical of abstract universalism and moral globalism that want to transcend the particular and its historical and spatial situatedness. The standard ecumenical agenda has traits of theological universalism which the postcolonial approach could help address, and bring ecumenism at the level of grassroots, of every day practices, of habits and behaviour. Fostering dialogue at the grassroots level would imply a deconstruction of the discourses about various denominations and the kind of language that is used to describe the other in ecumenical circles.

Conclusion

The ecumenical landscape has been changing through developments in the Churches and in the situation of the world. We need to take this into account. We are in a situation which calls for a redefinition of ecumenism itself, thanks to the profound transformations that have taken place in the last couple of decades. What were once the defining characteristics of ecumenism are no more for the new generations. Let me quote the words of Konrad Raiser in his foreword to the second edition of the *Dictionary of the Ecumenical Movement:*

"Now… many of the traditional orientations of ecumenism are challenged or called into question. A new generation has moved into the positions of leadership in the churches for whom the ecumenical struggles and advances of earlier periods are no longer part of their personal memory, but at best a significant feature of recent history." [39]

Times were when *unity* was thought as an important contribution for peace and reconciliation. Times have changed, generation have succeeded. I surmise, the future of ecumenism, and the ecumenism of the future generation lies in *fostering pluralism,* and in appreciating difference, which will define the mutual relationships of the Churches. Promoting jointly pluralism in the society and in the world would be a great contribution of the Churches to peace in the world.

Bibliography

Abraham, K. C. "An Ecological Perspective on Ecumenism." In *Theology Beyond Neutrality. Essays to honour Wesley Ariarajah.* Edited by Fernando and Crusz (Colombo: The Ecumenical Institute for Study and Dialogue, 2011), 193-203.

Ariarajah, S. Wesley. "Wider Ecumenism – Some Theological Perspectives." *Power, Politics and Plurality. An Exploration of the Impact of Interfaith Dialogue on Christian Faith and Practice.* Essays by S. Wesley Ariarajah, edited by Fernando, Marshal (Colombo: The Ecumenical Institute for Study and Dialogue, 2016), 239-256.

Ariarajah, S. Wesley. "Mission and Ecumenism Today: Reflections on the Tenth Assembly of the World Council of Churches, Busan, Republic of Korea." *International Bulletin of Missionary Research* 38 (2) 2014.

Ariarajah, S. Wesley., ed. "Contribution of Asian participation to Edinburgh 1910 Conference." *Power, Politics and Plurality. An Exploration of the Impact of Interfaith Dialogue on Christian Faith and Practice.* Essays by S. Wesley Ariarajah, edited by Fernando, Marshal (Colombo: The Ecumenical Institute for Study and Dialogue, 2016), 257-268.

Ariarajah, S. Wesley., ed. "Sri Lankan Contribution to Ecumenism." *Power, Politics and Plurality. An Exploration of the Impact of Interfaith Dialogue on Christian Faith and Practice.* Essays by S. Wesley Ariarajah, edited by Fernando, Marshal (Colombo: The Ecumenical Institute for Study and Dialogue, 2016), 269-286.

Ariarajah, Wesley. "Wider Ecumenism: Some Theological Perspectives." *Encounters with the Word.* Essays to Honour Aloysius Pieris, edited by Crusz, Fernando and Tilakaratne (Colombo: The Ecumenical Institute for Study and Dialogue, 2004).

Ashcroft, Bill., and Griffiths, Gareth., eds *The Postcolonial Studies Reader* (London: Routledge, 1995).

Ashcroft, Bill., Griffiths, Gareth., and Tiffin, Helen. *Key Concepts in Post-Colonial Studies* (New York and London: Routledge, 2004).

Barker, Francis., Hulme, Peter., and Iversen, Margaret., eds. *Colonial Discourse/ Postcolonial Theory* (New Delhi: Viva Books Private Limited, 2012).

Bhabha, Homi K. *The Location of Culture* (London: Routledge, 1994).

Bilimoria, Purushottama., and Al-Kassim, Dina., eds. *Postcolonial Reason and Its Critique: Deliberations on Gayatri Chakravorty Spivak's Thoughts* (New Delhi: Oxford University Press, 2014).

Brian, Stanley. "Celebrating Century of Ecumenism: Exploring the Achievements of *International* Dialogue." In *Commemoration of the Centenary of the 1910 Edinburgh World Missionary Conference*. Edited by John A. Radano (Grand Rapids, MI, and Cambridge. U.K.: William B. Eerdmans, 2012).

CCA/FABC. *Living and Working Together with Sisters and Brothers of Other Faiths in Asia. An Ecumenical Consultation* (Singapore: July 1987).

Chia, Edmund kee-fook. "Ecumenical Pilgrimage Toward World Christianity." *Theological Studies* 76 (3) (2015), 503-530,

Chow, Alexander. "Protestant Ecumenism and Theology in China Since Edinburgh 1910." *Missiology* 42 (2) (2014), 167-80.

Clifton, Shane. "Ecumenism from the Bottom Up: A Pentecostal Perspective." *Journal of Ecumenical Studies* 47 (4) (2012), 576-592.

Daughrity, Dyron B. "South India: Ecumenism's One Solid Achievement? Reflections on the History of the Ecumenical Movement." *International Review of Mission* 99 (1) (2010), 56-68.

De Achútegui, Pedro S. "Statement and Recommendations of the first Asian Congress of Jesuit Ecumenists Manila." *Philippine Studies* 23 (4) (1975), 18-23.

Dirlik, Arif. "The Postcolonial Aura: Third World Criticism in the Age of Global Capitalism." *Postcolonialism. A Guide for the Perplexed.* Edited by Pramod K. Nayar (New York: Continuum, 2010).

Eilers, Franz-Josef. Ed. *For All the Peoples of Asia. Federation of Asian Bishops' Conference Documents from 2002-2006, 2007-2012*, vols. IV & V (Quezon City: Claretian Publications, 2007 & 2012).

Fey, Harold E. Ed. *1948-1968, the Ecumenical Advance. A History of the Ecumenical Movement* (Geneva: WCC,1986).

Gandhi, Leela. *Postcolonial Theory: A Critical Introduction* (New Delhi: Oxford University Press, 1999).

Gnanadason, Aruna. "The Contributions of the Ecumenical Movement in Asia to World Ecumenism." *The Oxford Handbook of Christianity in Asia*. Edited by Felix Wilfred (New York: Oxford University Press, 2014), 134-144.

Hurley, Michael. *Christian Unity: An Ecumenical Second Spring?* (Dublin: Veritas, 1998).

Jahnei, Claudia. "Vernacular Ecumenism and Transcultural Unity. Rethinking Ecumenical Theology After the Cultural Turn." *The Ecumenical Review* 60 (4) (2008), 404-25.

Joshua Bhakiaraj, Paul. "Forms of Asian Indigenous Christainities." *The Oxford Handbook of Asian Christianity.* Edited by Felix Wilfred (New York: Oxford University Press, 2014),171-181.

Kelly, James R. "Spirals Not Cycles: Towards an Analytic Approach to the Sources and Stages of Ecumenism." *Review of Religious Research* 32 (1) (1990), 5-15

Kichschlager, Peter G. "Human Rights and Canon Law." *Concilium 2016/5* (London: SCM,2016), 65-77.

Kinnamon, Michael and E. Cope, Brian., eds. *The Ecumenical Movement: An Anthology of Key Texts and Voices* (Geneva, WCC, 1997).

Koshy, Ninan. *A History of the Ecumenical Movement in Asia. World Student Christian Federation Asia-Pacific Region, Asia and Pacific Alliance of YMCAs,* vol. I (Hong Kong: Christian Conference of Asia, 2004).

Koshy, Ninan., ed. *A History of the Ecumenical Movement in Asia. World Student Christian Federation Asia-Pacific Region, Asia and Pacific Alliance of YMCAs,* vol. II (Hong Kong: Christian Conference of Asia, 2004).

Kumar Das, Bijay. *Critical Essays on Post-Colonial Literature.* 3rd ed. (New Delhi: Atlantic Publishers, 2012).

Lindbeck, George. "The Unity We Seek. Setting the Agenda for Ecumenism." *Christian Century* (2005), 28-30.

Loomba, Ania. *Colonialism/Postcolonialism* (London and New York: Routledge, 2015).

Lossky, Nicholas., Bonino, Jose Miguez., and Iohn Pobee., eds. *Dictionary of the Ecumenical Movement.* 2nd ed. (Geneva: WCC, 2002).

McLeod, John. *Beginning Postcolonialism* (New Delhi: Viva Books Private Limited, 2012).

McLeod, John., ed. *The Routledge Companion to Postcolonial Studies* (New York and London: Routledge, 2007).

Mongia, Padmini., ed. *Contemporary Postcolonial Theory: A Reader* (New Delhi: Oxford University Press, 1996).

Mullins, Mark R. *Christianity Made in Japan: A Study of Indigenous Movements* (Honolulu: University of Hawaii Press, 1998).

Murray, Paul. ed. *Receptive Ecumenism and the Call to Catholic Learning* (Oxford: Oxford University Press, 2008).

Murray, Paul., ed. "Receptive Ecumenism and Ecclesial Learning: Receiving Gifts for Our Needs." *Louvain Studies* 33 (2008), 30-45.

Nayar, Pramod K., ed. *Postcolonial Studies. An Anthology* (Oxford, Wiley Blackwell, 2016).

Nedungatt, George. "Ecumenism and Canon Law." In *Concilium* 2016/5 *Revision of Canon Law*. Edited by Felix Wilfred. et. al. (London: SCM, 2016), 53-62.

O'Grady, John and Scherle, Peter., eds. *Ecumenics from the Rim: Explorations in Honour of John D'Arcy May* (Berlin: LIT Verlag, 2007).

Parry, Benita. *Postcolonial Studies. A Materialist Critique* (London & New York: Routledge, 2005).

Pratt, Andrew. "'Out of One, Many. Within One, Many': Religious Pluralism and Christian Ecumenism in the United States." *Perspectives in Religious Studies* 42 (1) (2015), 143-57.

Raiser, Konrad. *To Be the Church: Challenges and Hopes for a New Millennium* (Geneva: WCC, 1997).

Rouse, Ruth and Neill, Stephen Charles., eds. *1517-1948, A History of the Ecumenical Movement* vol. 1. 3rd ed. (Geneva: WCC, 1986).

Said, Edward. *Orientalism* (New York: Vintage, 1978).

Sawyer, Mary R. "Black Ecumenical Movements: Proponents of Social Change." *Review of Religious Research* 30 (2) (1988),151-61.

Scholz, Herbert M. "Reviewed Work(s): Towards a 'Dialogue of Life': Ecumenism in the Asian Context," (Cardinal Bea Studies IV) by Pedro S. de Achutegui. *Philippine Studies* 25 (1) (1977), 121-124.

Vischer, Lukas. "Reform of Canon Law – An Ecumenical Problem." *The Jurist* 26 (1966).

Weingartner, Erich. *The Tozanso Process: Ecumenical Efforts for Korean Reconciliation and Reunification* (Maryknoll, NY: Orbis, 1997).

Wilfred, Felix. "Christianity and Religious Cosmopolitanism." *The Past, Present and Future of Theologies of Interreligious Dialogue*. Edited by Merrigan, Terrence., and Friday, John (New York: Oxford University Press, 2017), pp. 216-232.

Wilfred, Felix. "Die Rezeption des II. Vatikanums in Asien." *Vaticanum 21. Die bleibeneden Aufgaben des Zweiten Vatikanishen Konzils im 21*. Christoph Bottlgheimer- Rene Dausner, eds. (Freiburg: Herder, 2016).

Wilfred, Felix., ed. *The Oxford Handbook of Christianity in Asia* (New York: Oxford University Press, 2014).

Young, Robert J. C. *Postcolonialism. A Very Short Introduction* (New York: Oxford University Press: 2003).

Endnotes

[1] The Eastern Code (CCEO), instead, has seven canons on ecumenism (canons 902-908).

[2] See George Nedungatt, "Ecumenism and Canon Law." In *Concilium* 2016/5 *Revision of Canon Law*, Felix Wilfred, et. al. eds, (London: SCM, 2016), 53-62.

[3] Vatican II, *Lumen Gentium* no. 8. On the background of this as well as on the debated term "*subsistit*", see the comments of Aloys Grillmeier, in *Commentary on the Documents of Vatican II*, edited by Herbert Vorgrimler, I (New York: Herder and Herder, 1967), 146ff. Whereas "*subsistit*" became an important point of reference for the post-Vatican opening of the Roman Catholic Church, some of the subsequent documents seem to have set the clock back, and in an effort to maintain orthodoxy, tend to equate the Roman Catholic Church with the Church of Christ. For example, "Letter on Some Aspects of the Church Considered as Communio" issued by the Congregation for the Doctrine of the Faith in 1992; "Responses to Some Questions Regarding Certain Aspects of the Doctrine of the Church" made public by the Congregation for the Doctrine of the Faith on July 10, 2007. Such a trend cannot but promote re-confessionalization and mean "winter of ecumenism".

[4] See Paul Murray, ed, *Receptive Ecumenism and the Call to Catholic Learning* (Oxford: Oxford University Press, 2008); Paul Murray, "Receptive Ecumenism and Ecclesial Learning: Receiving Gifts for Our Needs", *Louvain Studies*, 33 (2008), 30-45.

[5] One may celebrate as a great achievement the accord between the Roman Catholic Church and the Lutheran World Federation on the debated issue of justification. But then, we may be tempted to ask how are the people of God part of this accord, and what does it signify for them. Is it not perhaps a case of "magisterial mutuality"?

[6] See John O'Grady, John and Peter Scherle, eds, *Ecumenics from the Rim: Explorations in Honour of John D'Arcy May* (Berlin: LIT Verlag, 2007), at 498.

[7] Cf. Stanley Brian, "Celebrating Century of Ecumenism: Exploring the Achievements of International Dialogue", in *Commemoration of the Centenary of the 1910 Edinburgh World Missionary Conference*, edited by John A. Radano (Grand Rapids, MI, and Cambridge. U.K.: William B. Eerdmans, 2012).

[8] As quoted in Ninan Koshy, ed, *A History of the Ecumenical Movement in Asia. World Student Christian Federation Asia-Pacific Region, Asia and Pacific Alliance of YMCAs*, II (Hong Kong: Christian Conference of Asia, 2004), p. 24.

[9] Wesley Ariarajah, *Power, Politics and Plurality, op.cit.* 265. I must add that there were individual missionaries who were exceptions. But the point is that the *system*

as such was at best patronizing and at worst arrogant and authoritarian, with little room for reciprocity and inter-subjectivity.

[10] On development of indigenous Christianities in Asia, see Joshua Bhakiaraj, "Forms of Asian Indigenous Christianities", *The Oxford Handbook of Asian Christianity.* Edited by Felix Wilfred, *op.cit.* 171-181.

[11] Vatican II, *Lumen Gentium,* 23. Emphasis mine

[12] Alexander Chow, "Protestant Ecumenism and Theology in China Since Edinburgh 1910", *Missiology,* 42:2 (2014), 167-80.

[13] Dyron B. Daughrity, "South India: Ecumenism's One Solid Achievement? Reflections on the History of the Ecumenical Movement", *International Review of Mission,* 99:1 (2010), 56-68.

[14] See Harold Edward Fey, et al., eds, *A History of the Ecumenical Movement* (Geneva: WCC Publication, 2004), 72f; Michael Kinnamon and Brian E. Cope, eds, *The Ecumenical Movement: An Anthology of Key Texts and Voices* (Geneva: WCC Publication, 1997), pp. 3-4.

[15] Cf. Ninan Koshy, *A History of the Ecumenical Movement in Asia. World Student Christian Federation Asia-Pacific Region, Asia and Pacific Alliance of YMCAs* I (Hong Kong: Christian Conference of Asia, 2004), p. 26.

[16] See Mary John, *Indian Catholic Christians and Nationalism. A Study Based on the Official Catholic Journals of the Period 1857-1947* (Delhi: ISPCK, 2011).

[17] See Shane Clifton, "Ecumenism from the Bottom Up", *Journal of Ecumenical Studies,* 47:4 (2012), 576-92; Mary R. Sawyer, "Black Ecumenical Movements: Proponents of Social Change", *Review of Religious Research,* 30:2 (Dec. 1988), 151-61.

[18] Jude Lal Fernando, in *Swedish Missiological Themes,* 100:1 (2012), 87.

[19] There are numerous other examples of ecumenical streams from the periphery in Asia and across the world. These micro ecumenical narratives need to be highlighted through study and research. See John O'Grady and Peter Scherle, eds, Ecumenics from the Rim (Berlin: LIT Verlag, 2007).

[20] See Erich Weingartner, *The Tozanso Process: Ecumenical Efforts for Korean Reconciliation and Reunification* (Maryknoll, NY: Orbis, 1997).

[21] For detailed historical account, see Ninan Koshy, op.cit. vol. I; see also Ruth Rouse, Stephen Charles Neill, eds, 1517-1948, *A History of the Ecumenical Movement* 1, Third edition (Geneva: WCC, 1986); Aruna Gnanadason, "The Contributions of the Ecumenical Movement in Asia to World Ecumenism", in Felix Wilfred, ed, *The Oxford Handbook of Christianity in Asia op.cit.* pp.134-44.

[22] For statements of recent years of IEIA, see Franz-Josef Eilers, ed, *For All the Peoples of Asia. Federation of Asian Bishops' Conference Documents from 2002-2006, 2007-2012* (Quezon City Claretian Publ. 2007).

[23] CCA/FABC, *Living and Working Together with Sisters and Brothers of other Faiths in Asia*, Final Statement no.5.

[24] Cf. Ninan Koshy, op.cit. vol. II, p. 286.

[25] S. Wesley Ariarajah, "Wider Ecumenism: A Threat or a Promise?" *Ecumenical Review*, 50 (1998), 321.

[26] Vatican II, "The Dogmatic Constitution on the Church", *Lumen Genitum* 1 (November 1964).

[27] Cf. Felix Wilfred, "Christianity and Religious Cosmopolitanism", in *The Past, Present and Future of Theologies of Interreligious Dialogue*, edited by Terrence Merrigan and John Friday (New York: Oxford University Press, 2017), pp. 216-32.

[28] S. Wesley Ariarajah, "The Ecumenical Impact of Inter-Religious Dialogue", *The Ecumenical Review*, 31:2 (2009), 129-297.

[29] Konrad Raiser, *To Be the Church: Challenges and Hopes for a New Millennium* (Geneva: WCC Publication, 1997), p. 15.

[30] Andrew Pratt, "Out of One, Many. Within One, Many": Religious Pluralism and Christian Ecumenism in the United States", *Perspectives in Religious Studies*, 42:1 (2015), 143-57, at 144.

[31] *Dominus Iesus*, 22. Similar view is expressed also from Africa. Method Kilaini writes concluding his article on this subject stating, "the ecumenical effort cannot end with inter-Christian dialogue but must go beyond to inter-religious dialogue. And this will bear more fruit for all - Christians, Muslims, and those following traditional religions - if it is done ecumenically" Method Kilaini, *The Ecumenical Review*, 53:3 (2001), 357-65, at 364-65.

[32] In this connection, I would like to underline the importance of hermeneutics of Vatican II, that is not only diachronic but also synchronic. Such a hermeneutic that relates the various teachings and insights with one another will have great impact in fostering ecumenical relationships.

[33] See Felix Wilfred, "Die Rezeption des II. Vatikanums in Asien", *Die bleibeneden Aufgaben des Zweiten Vatikanishen Konzils im 21*, Christoph Bottlgheimer- Rene Dausner, eds, (Freiburg: Herder, 2016), pp. 426-66.

[34] Vatican II, *Unitatis Redintegratio*, no. 11.

[35] Lukas Vischer, "Reform of Canon Law – An Ecumenical Problem", *The Jurist* 26 (1966), 395-412 at 395, 98.

[36] Cf. Peter Kirchschläger, "Human Rights and Canon Law", *Concilium 2016/5* (London: SCM,2016), 65-77.

[37] Vast literature is available on this growing field of postcolonial studies. The following select number of works will help identify some of the major concepts

in postcolonial theories: Pramod K. Nayar, ed, *Postcolonial Studies: An Anthology* (Hoboken, New Jersey: Wiley Blackwell, 2015); Padmini Mongia, ed, *Contemporary Postcolonial Theory* (Bloomsbury: Bloomsbury Academic, 1997); Leela Gandhi, *Postcolonial Theory: A Critical Introduction* (New Delhi: Oxford University Press, 1999); Edward Said, *Orientalism* (New York: Vintage, 1978); Bill Ashcroft, Gareth Griffiths, and Helen Tiffin, *Key Concepts in Post-Colonial Studies* (New York and London: Routledge, 2004); Homi K. Bhabha, *The Location of Culture* (London: Routledge, 1994); Francis Barker, Peter Hulme, and Margaret Iversen, eds, *Colonial Discourse/Postcolonial Theory* (New Delhi: Viva Books Private Limited, 2012); John McLeod, *The Routledge Companion to Postcolonial Studies* (London, New York: Routledge, 2007); Benita Parry, *Postcolonial Studies. A Materialist Critique* (London & New York: Routledge, 2005); Bijay Kumar Das, *Critical Essays on Post-Colonial Literature. 3rd ed.* (New Delhi: Atlantic Publishers, 2012); Ania Loomba, *Colonialism/Postcolonialism* (London and New York: Routledge, 2015).

[38] Cf. Claudia Jahnei, "Vernacular Ecumenism and Transcultural Unity. Rethinking Ecumenical Theology after the Cultural Turn", *The Ecumenical Review*, 60:4 (2008), 404-25.

[39] Nicholas Lossky, Jose Miguez Bonino, and John Pobee, et al., eds, *Dictionary of the Ecumenical Movement* (Geneva: WCC Publication, 2002), xi.

Indigenous Christianities:
Analysis and Reflections in the Post-denominational Age

By indigenous we mean here forms of Christianity or Churches which are initiated and sustained by the local people, and therefore having its roots in the local soil. Thus, we have a number of Churches initiated by Africans, Koreans, Japanese, Indians, and others. Each one of these indigenous Christianities has specific social, cultural, historical, spiritual, and circumstantial factors for its emergence. This is different from an understanding of "indigenous" connected with such processes as inculturation, syncretism, local theology, borrowing of local worship, and ritual forms. Unfortunately, this latter approach has dominated the study of indigenous Christianities to the neglect of other important questions and aspects that lie behind their origin, and in their interaction with the socio-cultural environment.

From the perspective of freedom and autonomy, indigenous Churches are the ones that are not dependent on instances of authority outside their country or region. Such indigenous Churches define themselves as self-governing, self-propagating, and self-determining. On the other hand, many mainline Churches have been so dependent on outside centres of authority for their direction that they showed themselves to be "phlegmatic Churches" rather than politically active ones. The nature and contours of this type of indigenous Churches are difficult to characterize as they are intertwined with nationalism and state-intervention, as is the case with contemporary Chinese "indigenous" Christianity.

Does the fact of their local origin make the indigenous Christianities[1] politically more active? Historically, could the indigenous Churches claim to have been a force of resistance against political powers and principalities, or were they acquiescing to the dominant political order? Where do the indigenous Churches stand in this respect vis-á-vis mainline Churches? Could the indigenous Churches be viewed as contributors to the process of democratization? In this chapter we shall go into such questions. Our reflections are set in two parts. The first part will explore the background of the emergence of indigenous Christianities, and try to classify them according to different points of reference. This background is indispensable for understanding them in their political role. Against this background and typology, in the second part, we will go into a critical reflection on their political engagement or the absence of it. This will lead to a more complex and nuanced understanding of indigenous Christianities.

Part I
The Background for a Political Understanding of Indigenous Christianities

The Socio-Political Origins

There are two rather simplistic and prejudiced approaches to indigenous Christianities. One is a theological interpretation of them by the mainline Churches as being a marginal, separatist, and sectarian phenomenon. They are seen as a threat to the historical or mainline Churches. The second approach is more sociological which uses the "conspiracy theory". Since many of the independent Churches are Evangelical and Pentecostal in their inspiration, they are viewed as implanted by the American imperial military establishment to counter the movement and theology of liberation. All this fails to get into the complex reality and the diversity independent Churches represent.

Unlike the mainline Churches, indigenous Christianities offer a lot of scope for choice and space for voluntarism. This is in keeping with the spirit of contemporary times. The focus on experience and the direct communication with the Spirit, freed from the mediatory structures of authority in the traditional Christianity, proves to be attractive; so too the integration of the spiritual and the material wellbeing touching upon everyday life. Furthermore, the independent Church movement, as Daniel Bays observes with regard to China, "marked a crucial stage in the maturity of the Chinese Church".[2]

Emic Approach to the Study of Indigenous Christianities

To be able to get closer to an understanding of the indigenous Churches, and especially their political involvement, we need to follow an *emic* approach. It is a fact that many of the studies done by the so-called mainline Churches about indigenous Christianities are highly prejudiced. These indigenous forms are judged against certain parameters that are alien to them. There are others who contrast the mainline Christianity as "great tradition" over against the "little tradition" that indigenous Churches represent.[3] I think this categorization too does not take into account the unique nature of these Churches which foreshadow a new stage in the history of Christianity, not to speak of their highly remarkable growth in the South – Latin America, Africa, Asia, etc.[4] Characterizing them as "little tradition" is tantamount to consider them as marginal.

The indigenous study of Christianities require an *emic* approach that enters into their world of experience. This is an important component in any phenomenological approach to the study of religion, unlike an *etic* approach which treats religious phenomena simply as objects of scientific observation and analysis. *Emic* approach calls for a methodological conversion (different from confessional conversion) to the world of experience and belief of indigenous Christianities, to be able to understand them as they would like to be understood.

Typology of Indigenous Christianities

It may be too ambitious to propose a typology for indigenous Christianities. Even at the risk of some generalization and certain overlap, let me propose a few models within the indigenous Christianities as a heuristic means for their understanding.

Resistance and Identity Based

The opposition by the local people to the ways of missionaries and their association with the ruling colonial powers led to the emergence of indigenous Churches. While several independent Churches came into being as break-away groups from the missionary movement, other Churches sprouted on their own. Protesting against the haughty treatment of the local people by the missionaries and against some of their policies and practices, certain individuals started their own Churches.[5] "*Independent Churches*" is an apt expression, since the local Christians freed themselves from the control of the missionaries. For example, we have the case of the "*Nattu Sabai*" (The Hindu Church of Lord Jesus) in Tamilnadu,[6] and the case of the International Assembly of the True Jesus Church (TJC) founded by Paul Wei in 1917 in Beijing, China.

> Chinese Christians exhibited a strong desire for independence after the outburst of 'The Boxer Rebellion' incidents in 1900. Chinese Christians had long been accused of believing in a foreign religion *(yang jiao)*. They were criticized for being protected by Western missionaries and foreigners ... Chinese Christians, including Cheng and others, were seeking a new identity for themselves. They wanted to demonstrate their independence, fostering a self-reliant Christianity that was freed from foreign funding, from foreign mission direction, and from foreign preaching and theology—that is, the Churches should be self-supporting, self-governing, and self-propagating.[7]

Many independent Churches in South Africa and in West Africa too sprang up as people struggled to free themselves from the authority and leadership of western missionaries. It led to new forms of Christianity, socially vibrating with the African ethos and psychologically satisfying. In other cases, indigenous Churches came to be formed out of conflict and struggle within Christian communities themselves in terms of caste, power-sharing, leadership, etc.[8] Creation of indigenous Churches was also an identity-marker for discriminated against groups on account of their caste or class. The formation of indigenous Churches in India, from the larger socio-political perspective, could be viewed as an expression of the subaltern movement within Christianity. As for China, it is interesting to note that the indigenous Church movement was occasioned not only by disillusionment with missionary movement, but also due to the suppression of Christianity and religion in general during the period of cultural revolution. The socio-political circumstances have led to the formation of many house-Churches of indigenous origin which are, by and large, conservative and evangelical in orientation, and are proselytising.

Messianic and Apocalyptically-Oriented

The indigenous Churches came into existence also because the type of Christianity brought through the missionary movement, could not answer the deeper aspirations of large masses of people marginalised and suffering social, economic and political oppression and disabilities. This was particularly the case in times of crisis – political, social, economic and environmental. When there seemed no humanly possible way out of their plight, they easily turned towards messianic, millenarian, and apocalyptic movements which caught their imagination for a different order of things to come, and inspired exultant hope for survival in the midst of their suffering and marginality.[9] These movements led to a transformation and re-ordering of their lives – individual and collective. Millenarian as most of these Churches are, they expected the sudden appearance of the glorious Lord who will vanquish evil and triumph over the enemy against whom one has to enter into a spiritual warfare now.[10] Apocalyptic streak in these indigenous Christian movements gave its members an insight into things that are hidden to the eyes of the world, but will be revealed at the end of time.[11] Many of the indigenous Christian Churches and movements had charismatic founders.

Spirit-Centered

Most indigenous Churches are strongly Spirit-centered. From a theological point of view, they present a challenge to the Christo-monism of most mainline Churches. The Spirit-based Pentecostal indigenous Churches are to be found everywhere, and each one of them has got its own specific socio-cultural context of emergence. Unfortunately, much of the historiography of indigenous Churches of Pentecostal origin are presented as if they were derived from the American Azusa Street renewal movement at the early beginnings of the twentieth century. This flies in the face of facts.[12] For example, nineteenth century India witnessed Spirit-oriented forms of indigenous Christianity. Pandita Ramabai has been an important figure in the movement. As Allan Anderson notes, one of the earliest Pentecostal movements in Asia was the one associated with the 1905-1907 revival that occurred at a girls' home in Pandita Ramabai's mission in Mukti, India, in which girls baptised by the Spirit had seen visions, fallen into trances, and spoken in tongues. Ramabai understood this revival as the means by which the Holy Spirit was creating an indigenous form of Indian Christianity. Notably, the Mukti revival seems to have preceded and to have been unrelated to the Azusa Street revival.

Indigenous-Religion Based

Many indigenous Churches bear traits of the traditional religions of the people in a particular region. A classical example is the independent Churches in Africa which have integrated several elements from the traditional religions into Biblical Christianity.[13] Christianity is re-shaped through the religious universe they have inherited. We could cite here the example of the Church of the Ancestors of Malawi or the Nigerian Reformed Ogboni Fraternity. These Churches incorporate in themselves the traditional African religious ethos such as healing practices, exorcism, and spontaneity in worship with chanting, drumming, and, of course, dancing. Something similar could be observed in the Korean indigenous Churches in which people have integrated the shamanistic tradition with its belief in the world of spirits – ancestors and divine spirits inhabiting in nature, in trees, rivers, mountains, etc. Far from signifying a break from tradition, Christianity came to be re-expressed in Korean indigenous Churches as extension of the shamanistic tradition, which also explains why these Churches have captured the imagination of large masses of people among the Koreans.[14]

State-Engineered

Religion could play, as history and experience show, a destabilizing role vis-à-vis established political powers. Hence, any authoritarian state will tend to control religion and its public expressions, especially if it goes in the direction of opposition and resistance. The state employs many strategies to counter the power of religion, and one of them is to split the religious group, or support and maintain new splinter religious groups. This dynamic has been at work also in the formation of certain state-sponsored indigenous Churches. The state justifies these Churches on the plea that they are patriotic whereas other Churches imported from the West are anti-national. This type of state-engineered Churches could be seen, for example, in authoritarian and centralized states like China, Vietnam, Myanmar, and so on. Typical is the case of China, where the state sponsors the so-called 'Three Self-Patriotic Movement' (TSPM), namely self-governing, self-supporting, and self-propagating; it also promotes and controls the so-called Patriatic Church through its State Religious Affairs Bureau.[15] In India, though we do not have such type of state-engineered Churches, the idea of a Church that is ideologically oriented to Hindutva can be seen in what is called "*Swadeshi Church*". This has been mooted by the right-wing Hindutva forces.

Part II
The Political Ambivalence

A common feature that can be observed in the history of Christianity in the South is that its theology and praxis were politically divided, with a section of Christians supporting the colonial powers, whereas another section resisting the foreign powers and supporting the indigenous resistance and liberation movements. This is true of the events in Asia as much as in Africa. However, the situation after political independence from colonial powers has been so very diverse, and it is difficult to identify any common pattern. Our purpose here is not to go into the political engagement of the so-called mainline Churches, but that of the independent Churches and communities.

Increasing Political Influence

There is not only a phenomenal increase in the growth of indigenous Churches, but also in their political influence. To cite an example, in Kenya the indigenous Churches of Afro-Pentecostal inspiration, during the entire period of president Daniel arap Moi (1979 – 2002), simply fell in line with the government and supported it.[16] Justification came from the words of St Paul: "Let every person be subject to the governing authorities. For there is no authority except from God, and those that exist have been instituted by God" (Rom 13:1). Indigenous Church leaders were favoured with a lot of gifts by the state, in return for their "prayers"! In the last few years, however, the situation has changed in a new direction. I do not mean, that they started opposing the state; rather the development is more along the line of active involvement in politics, and attempt to wield political power, elbowing out the influence the historical or mainline Churches wielded in public life. It is an irony that these mainline Churches once in the forefront in the struggle against dictatorship and one-political, party system find themselves today marginalised as the political influence of indigenous Christianities has been growing matched only by their numerical growth. The situation seems to be similar in Korea with its mega indigenous Churches of Pentecostal inspiration.

No religion functions in the abstract. Every religion is socially and culturally situated and practiced in a particular political environment. This is true of Christianity as well. But the other-worldly interpretation of Christianity has often led to a-historical approach to its life, beliefs, and practices. Nowhere we see better the historical, social, cultural, and political nature of Christianity (the geo-historical factor) as in the indigenous Churches. The indigenous Churches do not stand on a de-historicized high pedestal. Rather, the history of indigenous Christianity in a particular place becomes one with the history of the people or the group. Reversely, the indigenous Churches serve as a window to the understanding of the life and concerns of a particular people.

In indigenous Christianities we are in a new paradigm. For a long time, Christianity in the South was associated with initiatives from the West and its mission enterprise. Another paradigm came into existence when Christianity was viewed as having no one centre, but being polycentric in nature. The phenomenon of indigenous Churches belongs to a third paradigm in which shaping of Christian life and practices are seen from the perspective of the *agency* of the people themselves and their encounter with and interpretation of Christian life and experience.[17]

From Quietism to Political Activism – A Theological Shift

The political role any Church plays depends very much on the kind of theology it subscribes to, especially its vision of the world and of societal realities. As for political involvement, the general picture of the indigenous Churches inspired by evangelical and Pentecostal spirit, is one of rejection and denial of the world, or at least separation from the "world" (understood in a negative sense) and its affairs, including politics. With their eyes fixed on heavenly matters, these Churches were least interested in the mundane political engagement. The most they were concerned about public matters was when it was a question of their freedom to express and live their Christianity different from the mainline Christian traditions. The situation has changed in all the continents. In Latin America since 1990s certain new developments have taken these Churches to greater political commitment. One of the factors is simply the numerical strength. With its astounding growth, the indigenous Churches have become a political force to reckon with. Secondly, the theological shift towards earthly wellbeing ("prosperity Gospel") in these Christianities called for greater involvement in economic and political fields.

Ad Hoc Political Involvement

The ambivalence we find in indigenous Christianities is also due to the fact that their political involvement is most often *ad hoc*. There is no cogency in their political direction and action. For any such consistency it would require that the indigenous Christianities consciously treat the political realm as a field of sacred duty; should be able to draw from the Bible and other resources; and finally, should be able to motivate and mobilize the Christian believers for political involvement. Since none of this is taking place in a consistent manner, it could be only expected that the responses of the indigenous Christianities to political situations will be characterized by unpredictability and even volatility.

Political Co-optation?

Given their volatility, the indigenous Churches could easily be politically co-opted. A specific case in point is the indigenous Churches in South Africa. They have a distinct origin in the experience of discrimination and racism. In a country and society divided along racist lines, the black people could not feel at home in Churches of white people imported from the West. The indigenous Churches were clearly an identity marker for the black-people. The black people felt at home in the Churches that reflected their tradition and cultural ethos.[18] On the other hand, some of these indigenous Churches allowed themselves to be co-opted by the state and its ideology. Thus, for example, in Zimbabwe, Johane Marange Apostolic Church (JMAC), and African Apostolic Church (AAC) attuned themselves to the authoritarian and nationalist political party and ideology for whose successful election these Churches proved to be indispensable. I referred earlier to state-engineered type of indigenous Churches. It is clear that these Churches get co-opted by the state in return for certain limited freedom to continue their activities, and in some cases to get privileges.

But the question that needs to be raised is whether the indigenous Churches co-opted today will continue so also in future? Could we project a different scenario? To respond, let us take the case of China where Christianity is spreading quite fast, and there is increasingly positive reception of it among the people.[19] Though many of the indigenous Churches are evangelical and Pentecostal in their orientation, the exacerbation of socio-political condition in that country, and suppression of religious freedom and democracy may lead to a situation in which these indigenous Churches may become a significant political force (as it happened decades ago with the Churches in eastern Europe) and rallying point for a different political order.[20] In other words, though these Churches may appear compliant to the state, they could turn out to be a new political force of change and transformation. They may contribute to a democratization process in the long run. This could be surmised from the influence these indigenous Churches and communities wield at micro-level where they, as leaven, are already contributing to the transformation of local situations. Similar developments could happen in Vietnam, Myanmar, and countries in Africa where indigenous Churches seem to take now a conformist position.

The Political Moorings of Prosperity Gospel

Generally, the so-called prosperity gospel is viewed by critics as an example of religion being used for economic gains. The high percentage of tithes to Churches, for example, was supposed to bring abundance of God's blessings and prosperity. What is not sufficiently analysed and studied is the fact that prosperity gospel did not develop in a political vacuum. In some critical instances like that of South Africa under apartheid, while many of the mainline Churches challenged the state theology and its justification of racial segregation and discrimination, and were ready to accept the consequences of this resistance, several of the Evangelical-Pentecostal Churches adopted an a-political posture, and even openly supported the apartheid regime.[21] This pattern of a-political posture or support to the political powers could be identified in many other cases of Evangelical-Pentecostal and indigenous Churches. This mode of behaviour by the indigenous Churches naturally attracted rewards and privileges from the state.[22]

The political patronage created an atmosphere for the propagation of a "Prosperity Gospel" by these Churches. The theology of the prosperity gospel, instead of focusing on life after death, focuses on life before death on this earth, and promotes a life of wellbeing, material prosperity, and abundance as the promise of God for his people. This attitude could be taken as faith-inspired world-affirmation, overcoming a world negation and alienation. So far so good. But then the prosperity gospel considers the lack of prosperity and riches as resulting from lack of faith. In other words, increase in wealth, possession, worldly happiness, blessing, and prosperity is viewed as a sign of increase in faith. Even though, as empirical studies seem to show, there need not necessarily be a link between religion and corruption.[23] However, lacking in critique and ethical concerns, the preaching of prosperity gospel and the theology behind it could easily ignore or cover-up the corruption of the political elites and their amassing of wealth. Moreover, the prosperity Gospel, instead of a faith-based critique, seems to support capitalism, market, and consumerism. Though some of the indigenous Churches are still anchored in prosperity gospel, more recent trends show a different direction. As Anthony Egan remarks with reference to South Africa,

The global Pentecostal movement has backed away strongly from anything that appears to be driven by the 'Prosperity Gospel'. The 2011 Cape Town Commitment is explicitly opposed to it, calls for a firm commitment to ethical stewardship of resources and condemns what it terms 'the toxic idolatry of consumerism'.[24]

Conclusion

The so-called mainline Churches dominated the ecumenical scene and discourse for a long time. In the ecumenical movement, indigenous and independent Churches were viewed as marginal phenomena. They were looked down as "sectarian". The recent decades have witnessed a revolutionary reversal of this. The mainline Churches all over the world – Catholic, Protestant and Orthodox – seem to be declining in the Christian demography whereas the indigenous Christianities of Evangelical and Pentecostal inspiration have gained great momentum in terms of their numerical growth and their impact at the micro and macro levels. In their growth process we could identify different political stands – apathy to politics, conformism to the existing political order, and resistance to the powers that be. It is difficult to discover any consistent pattern. There is a kind of *ad hoc* response. Their political role has been ambiguous, changing according to different conditions and circumstances.

More recent trends in the indigenous Christianities, however, show that they are becoming politically more assertive, especially at the grassroots level with increasing influence in the lives of individuals and small communities. If not explicitly, but implicitly through their local involvement and manner of acting, they exhibit a remarkable potential for the democratization of societies. It is possible that in the course of time, they may even become a critical force to challenge the powers that be. And this could be the case especially in countries with authoritarian and centralized forms of governance. In regions and countries where there is already democratic institutions and rule of law, they could turn out to be a contributor to strengthen the process of democratization. Their contribution in this line could be all the more significant since they seem to provide the necessary skills for a democracy of the ordinary people and of everyday life, rather than a democracy of the elites.

Study of indigenous Christianities, including their political role, helps us develop an anthropology of Christianity, namely how it has been encountered, appropriated, and moulded by the indigenous people in a variety of ways according to their cultural genius, inherited religious traditions, and social and political challenges. Moreover, indigenous forms of Christianity have helped to de-absolutize the Christian tradition, and fashion new ways of living and expressing the Christian experience and message. In fact, this reinvention of Christianity by indigenous traditions, freed from the accusation of being foreign, could make it vibrant in the South and facilitate the play of a more efficacious and convincing political role.[25] Having said that, we need to be aware of the fact that their political involvement past and present indicate unpredictability, volatility, and ambivalence. The same could also characterize the future in spite of their great potential and general appeal.

Bibliography

Ayegboyin, Deji. *African Indigenous Churches: An Historical Perspective* (Lagos: Greater Heights Publications, 1997).

Baago, Kaj. *Pioneers of Indigenous Christianity* (Madras: CLS, 1962).

Barrett, David B., and Padwick, T. John. *Rise up and Walk! Conciliarism and the African Indigenous Churches, 1815-1987* (Nairobi: Oxford University Press, 1989).

Bhakiaraj, Joshua Paul. "Forms of Asian Indigenous Christianities." In Felix Wilfred, ed, *The Oxford Handbook of Christianity in Asia* (New York: Oxford University Press, 2014), 171-181.

Chhungi, Hrangthan., Ekka, M. M., Longchar, A. Wati. "National Council of Churches in India. Commission on Tribals Adivasis, Gossner Theological College, and Senate Centre for Extension Pastoral Theological Research." *Doing Indigenous Theology in Asia: Towards New Frontiers* (Nagpur: Jointly Published by Commission on Tribals and Adivasis, National Council of Churches in India, Gossner Theological College Ranchi and SCEPTRE, Kolkata, 2012).

Cleary, Edward L., and Steigenga, Timothy J., eds. *Resurgent Voices in Latin America: Indigenous Peoples, Political Mobilization, and Religious Change* (New Brunswick, N.J.; London: Rutgers University Press, 2004).

Danielson, Robert. "Independent Indigenous Protestant Mega Churches in El Salvador." *Missiology* 41 (2013), 329-342.

Gampiot, Aurélien Mokoko., and Cécile Coquet-Mokoko. "African Responses: The Birth of African Christianities." *Kimbanguism: An African Understanding of the Bible* (Pennsylvania: Penn State University Press, 2017), 34-61.

Githieya, Francis Kimani. *The Freedom of the Spirit: African Indigenous Churches in Kenya* (New York: Oxford University Press, 1997).

Godwin, Colin. "Indigenous Church Planting in Post Christian Europe: A Case Study of Belgian Pioneers." *Missiology* 39 (3) (2011), 391-408.

Heduland, Roger. "Indian Instituted Churches: Indigenous Christianity in Style." *Mission Studies* 16 (1999), 26-42.

Hedlund, Roger E. "Subaltern Movements and Indian Churches of Indigenous Origins." *Journal of Dharma* 23 (1) (1998), 8-38.

Hsu, Princeton S. *Chinese Indigenous Church Movement* (Kowloon: Baptist Press, 1975).

Jehu-Appiah, J. H. "The African Indigenous Churches and the Quest for An Appropriate Theology for the New Millennium." *International Review of Missions* 89 (354) (2000), 410-20.

Kaplan, Steven., ed. *Indigenous Responses to Western Christianity* (New York: New York University Press, 1995).

Kochupallikunnel, Ipe. *Pentecostal Churches in Kerala and Indigenous Leadership* (Delhi: ISPCK, 2011).

Kraemer, Hendrik. *From Mission Field to Independent Church. Report on a Decisive Decade in the Growth of Indigenous Churches in Indonesia, Etc.* (The Hague: Boekencentrum, 1958).

L. Baker, Donald. "The Transformation of the Catholic Church in Koreas: From Missionary Church to an Indigenous Christianity." *Journal of Korean Religions* 4 (2013), 11-42.

Lian, Xi. *Redeemed by Fire: The Rise of Popular Christianity in Modern China* (New Haven, Conn, London: Yale University Press, 2010).

McLean, Patrica Rose. "Thai Protestant Christianity: A Study of Cultural and Theological Interactions between Western Missionaries and Indigenous Thai Churches." (Edinburgh: Ph. D. dissertation, University of Edinburgh, 2002).

Monshan Wu, Albert. "The Quest for an 'Indigenous Church': German Missionaries, Chinese Christians, and the Indigenization Debates of the 1920s." *The American Historical Review* 122 (1) (2017), 85-114.

Mullins, Mark. *Christianity Made in Japan: A Study of Indigenous Movements.*" (Honolulu: University of Hawai'i Press, 1998).

Norget, Kristin. "The Politics of Liberation: The Popular Church, Indigenous Theology, and Grassroots Mobilization in Oaxaca, Mexico." *Latin American Perspectives* 24 (5) (1997), 96-127.

Oosthuizen, G.C., and Hexham, Irving., eds. *Empirical studies of African Independent. Indigenous Churches* (New York: E. Mellen Press, 1992).

Pobee, John S., and Ositelu, Gabriel. *African Initiatives in Christianity: The Growth, Gifts and Diversities of Indigenous African Churches - a Challenge to the Ecumenical Movement* (Geneva: WCC Publications, 1998).

Shankar, Edward., Devdas, R. V. "Indigenous Church Architecture." *Architecture and Design* 22 (5) (2005), 48-55.

Snaitang, O. L. ed., *Churches of Indigenous Origins in Northeast India* (Delhi: Published for MIIS, Mylapore by ISPCK, 2000).

Vilaça Aparecida., and Wright, Robin M., eds. *Native Christians: Modes and Effects of Christianity Among Indigenous peoples of the Americas* (Farnham: Ashgate 2009).

Wood, Vanessa. "The Part Played by Chinese Women in the Formation of an Indigenous Church in China: Insights from the Archive of Myfanwy Wood, LMS Missionary." *Women's History Review* 17 (4) (2008), 597-610.

Endnotes

[1] In this chapter I use interchangeably the expressions "indigenous Christianities", "indigenous Churches" and "independent Churches".

[2] Daniel H. Bays, ed, "The Growth of Independent Christianity in China, 1900 – 1937," in ID. ed, *Christianity in China: From the Eighteenth Century to the Present* (California: Stanford University Press, 1996), p. 316.

[3] This is the perspective from which Roger E. Hedlund views them. See Roger E. Hedlund, "Indian Instituted Churches: Indigenous Christianity Indian Style," *Mission Studies,* XVI:1/31 (1999), 26-42; ID., *Quest for Identity: India's Churches of Indigenous Origin* (Delhi: ISPCK, 2000) ID., "Indian Expressions of Indigenous Christianity", *Studies in World Christianity,* 10:2 (2004), 185-204.

[4] See Aparecida Vilaça and Robin M. Wright, eds**,** *Native Christians: Modes and Effects of Christianity among Indigenous Peoples of the Americas* (Farnham: Ashgate, 2009); John Pobee and Gabriel Ositelu, *African Initiatives in Christianity: The Growth, Gifts and Diversities of Indigenous African Churches - a Challenge to the Ecumenical Movement* (Geneva: WCC Publications, 1998).

[5] For example, in Japan, Uchimura Kanzo started in 1901 a Non-Church Movement called *Mukyokai.* In the Philippines around 1915 Felix Manalao began the *Igelsia ni Cristo.* For a good overview of indigenous Christianities in Asia, see Paul Joshua Bhakiaraj, "Forms of Asian Indigenous Christianities", Felix Wilfred, ed, *The Oxford Handbook of Christianity in Asia* (New York: Oxford University Press, 2014), pp. 171-181; see also Allan H. Anderson, "Pentecostal Movements in East Asia: Indigenous Oriental Christianity?", *Swedish Missiological Themes,* 87:3 (1999), 319-340.

[6] See M. Thomas Thangaraj, "The History and Teachings of the Hindu Christian Community Called Nattu Sabai in Tirunelveli", *Indian Church History*

Review 5 (1971), 43-67. We have also the case of *Bible Mission* started by Bro. M. Devadoss (1875-1960) in 1938 in an attempt to form an indigenous Church.

[7] Cf. Peter Tze Ming Ng, "Cheng Jingyi: Prophet of His Time", *International Bulletin of Missionary Research*, 36:1(2012), 14-16; see also Lian Xi, *Redeemed by Fire: The Rise of Popular Christianity in Modern China* (New Haven: Yale University Press, 2010).

[8] Today, there are new forms of conflicts within these independent Churches. For a case study of Christ Apostolic Church and Cherubim and Seraphim Church of Nigeria, see Peter Alokan Olusegun Ayodeji, Alabi David Oladunjoye et al., "Critical Analysis of Church Politics and Crises within the Indigenous Christianities in Nigeria", *American Journal of Social and Management Sciences*, 2:4 (2011), 360-370.

[9] This is a point which Waldo Cesar and Richard Shaull make in explaining the phenomenal growth of Pentecostalism in Brazil. See their work: *Pentecostalism and the Future of the Christian Churches: Promises, Limitations, Challenges* (Grand Rapids, MI: W. Em. B. Eerdmans, 2000). As for the development of millennial and apocalyptic type of indigenous Churches in China in twentieth century, see Lian Xi, *op.cit.*

[10] The messianic and apocalyptic language and rhetoric have not remained only within the Churches, but have been employed also for political purposes, as was the case with W. Bush Sr in the context of the Gulf War.

[11] There seems to be today a return in the Churches to Apocalypticism. See *Concilium* 2014/3. The entire issue deals with the *Return of Apocalypticism*. See also George E. Ladd, "Revival of Apocalyptic in the Churches", *Review and Expositor*, 72 (1975), 263-270; Margaret Mollett, "Apocalypticism and Popular Culture in South Africa: An Overview and Update", *Religion and Theology* 19 (2012), 219–236

[12] Cf. Allan Anderson, "Pentecostalism and Charismatic Movements in Asia", in Felix Wilfred, ed, *The Oxford Handbook of Christianity in Asia* (New York: Oxford University Press, 2014), pp.158-170.

[13] Ronald J. Allen, "Creating an Indigenous African Church", *The Christian Century*, March 6 (1991), 265-269.

[14] See Boo Woong Yoo, "Response to Korean Shamanism By The Pentecostal Church", *International Review of Mission*, 75:297 (1986), 70–74; Similar seems to be also the case in Taiwan. See John D. Dadosky, "Shamanism and Christianity: Religious Encounters among Indigenous Peoples of East Asia", Olivier Lardinois and Benoit Vermander, eds, *Variétés Sinologiques* (Taipei: Ricci Institute, 2008).

[15] See Eric O. Hanson, *Catholic Politics in China and Korea* (Maryknoll, New York: Orbis Books, 1980); Philip L. Wickeri, *Seeking the Common Ground* (Maryknoll, New York: Orbis Books, 1998). As a matter of fact, the three-self movement do not originate from the state, but from the local Christian community which used these goals in a bid to assert its agency, and to free itself from the control of western missionaries and mission societies.

[16] For case studies in Africa, see Collis Garikai Machoko, "African Initiated Churches and Party Politics: Zimbabwean Experience", *The International Journal of African Catholicism*, 4:1 (Ontario: Huntington University, 2013), 1-40; Alokan Olusegun Ayodeji Peter, Alabi David Oladunjoye, et. al, "Critical Analyses of Church Politics and Crises within the Indigenous Christianity in Nigeria", *American Journal of Social and Management Sciences*, 2:4 (2011), 360-370; Julius M. Gathogo, "Afro-Pentecostalism and the Kenyan Political Landscape", *Swedish Missiological Themes*, 101:2 (2013), 203-230. See also H. W. Turner, "The Place of Independent Religious Movements in the Modernization of Africa", *Journal of Religion in Africa*, 2:1(1969), 43-63; Linda E. Thomas, "Survival and Resistance in an African Indigenous Church", *Journal of Theology for Southern Africa*, 98 (1997), 13-20.

[17] Cf. Charles E. Farhadian, *Introducing World Christianity* (Chichester: Wiley-Blackwell, 2012). See Felix Wilfred, "From World Mission to Global Christianities", *Concilium 2011/1* (London: SCM Press, 2011), 13-26.

[18] At this point, I cannot but make a reference to the plight of the Dalit people. They do not feel at home in caste-dominated Church-communities and congregations. Should the Dalit people struggle within these communities for dignity, equality and participation, or should they form Dalit Indigenous or Independent Churches where they would feel at home, and at the same time would contribute to reform the entire Church? This is a dilemma the Dalit Christian community is facing today.

[19] Cf. David Aikman, *Jesus in Beijing* (Washington, DC: Regnery Publishing, Inc., 2003).

[20] Cf. David H. Lumsdaine, ed, *Evangelical Christianity and Democracy in Asia* (New York: Oxford University Press, 2009).

[21] Cf. Anthony Egan, "South Africa's Prosperity Gospel Churches", *Concilium 2014/4* (London: SCM Press, 2014), 55-64.

[22] In the case of South Africa, whereas during the anti-apartheid struggles, the mainline Churches by and large supported the African National Congress (ANC) and its political programme, subsequent to abolition of apartheid and democratization, the same Churches turned against ANC and its ruling elite in the new dispensation, and critiqued the rampant corruption that has overtaken

the country. As a result, ANC turned for its support to evangelical-pentecostal and indigenous Churches. In the atmosphere of state-patronage, prosperity gospel started thriving.

[23] This is an important point Anthony Egan makes. See *art.cit.*

[24] Anthony Egan, *art. cit* p. 60.

[25] As is well-known the history of mission was written from the perspective of western mission enterprises. A corrective to this came when the socio-political and cultural aspects were investigated as a necessary background to the understanding of Christianity in the South. Today, I think, we are in a new phase, and this is characterized by a deeper study of the Church movements and indigenous Christianities that came from the peoples themselves. A deeper study of this, especially in relation to its political role in the past and present, will yield a lot of new insights. This remains a task for the scholars of Christian Studies.

CHAPTER **16**

Asia and Interreligious Harmony
Re-Reading of *Nostra Aetate* after Fifty Years

Nostra Aetate was a turning point in the relationship of Christianity to other faiths. Indeed, it is the *Magna Carta* of dialogue for our times. Seen against the general hostile attitude of Christian theologians and missionaries to other religions throughout history, Nostra Aetate was a revolution. It was a landmark in the two thousand years of Christian doctrinal history when an Ecumenical Council accepted positively other religions and their validity. Even more, Nostra Aetate could be considered as signifying the *conversion* of the Church to the religiously other. Over against a long history of a blanket "no" to other religions on the assumption that to be Christian is a state of possessing all truth and wisdom, Nostra Aetate signifies the historic moment when the official Church looked straight into the eyes of the religiously other. It read on the face of the religiously the other, things which it never cared for. What comes out is a humble recognition of the value and richness the faiths of others signify.

> The Catholic Church rejects nothing that is true and holy in these religions. She regards with sincere reverence those ways of conduct and of life, those precepts and teachings which, though differing in many aspects from the ones she holds and sets forth, nonetheless often reflect a ray of that Truth which enlightens all men (NA 2).

We realize the depth and significance of this statement if we compare it with so many other statements and practices through Christian history which rejected outright other religions. A glaring example is the statement of the Council of Florence which stated,

> [The Holy Roman church]... firmly believes, professes and preaches that "no one remaining outside the Catholic Church, not only pagans," but also Jews, heretics or schismatics, can become partakers of eternal life; but they will go to the "eternal fire prepared for the devil and his angels" (Matt 25:41), unless before the end of their life they are received into it.[1]

New Theological Vision

This revolution of Nostra Aetate was strongly supported by *a new theological vision* which the document outlines in a very concise manner. It speaks of the universal salvific will of God, the common origin and destiny of humankind, and the presence of the Spirit in human history. Here, the traditional soteriology and pneumatology undergo a transformation. These are all important elements in the new theological vision which paved the way for a positive relationship with other religions.[2]

Nostra Aetate has taken to a logical conclusion the ecclesiology of *Lumen Gentium* which dissociates itself from the understanding of the Church as *societas perfecta* (perfect society), with closed doors. The Church is characterised as a sign and sacrament of communion with God as well as of the unity of the human family (LG 1). It is a Church that tries to reach out to others (LG 16). What have we to make out of the spiritual legacy of the one human family of which all of us are part? This means we cannot settle down with a realized eschatology, but need to look forward to a futuristic eschatology that has become clear from the orientation of the Council and its different documents. This became evident particularly in considering the Jewish faith in relation to Christian faith, as worked out in Nostra Aetate.

I would like to also highlight here that Nostra Aetate and *Gaudium et Spes* have the same theological axis, and they complement each other. In Nostra Aetate we see a Church blinded by its own exclusive claims of the past open its eyes to see the marvels of God blooming in innumerable spiritual gardens of humanity, whereas in *Gaudium et Spes* we see a Church closed on itself in the past by insulating from the world, reach out to the wonders of temporal realities, thanks to a fresh reinterpretation of the theology of creation. In both cases, the mutual relationship is fostered by continuous dialogue. To be able to understand in depth the dialogue with peoples of other faiths advocated by Nostra Aetate, we need to relate also to the Conciliar document on Divine Revelation (*Dei Verbum*). If Lumen Gentium paved the way for an open ecclesiology pointing to the entire humanity, the document on revelation provided the grammar for dialogue. It sees God's self-revelation itself having taken place through a process of *conversation or dialogue*. In *Dei Verbum* we could hear the echo of the words of *Ecclesiam Suam* of Pope Paul VI which imbued Vatican II with the spirit of dialogue. It states,

> Revelation too, that supernatural link which God has established with man, can likewise be looked upon as a dialogue. In the incarnation and in the Gospel, it is God's Word that speaks to us…the whole history of man's salvation is one long, varied dialogue, which marvellously begins with God and which he prolongs with men in so many different ways.[3]

All this has rooted Nostra Aetate even more firmly in the field of inter-religious dialogue.

Confirmation of Asian Initiatives and Practices

Even before Nostra Aetate, the necessity of dialogue was keenly felt in Asia, especially in India as numerous initiatives pre-dating Vatican II show. Dialogue was already an experiential reality in Asia. The initiatives to explore the riches of other religious traditions, and experience the Christian faith in dialogue with the experience of Hinduism took the form of *ashrams*. Pioneering works in dialogue was done by ashrams, thanks to Brahmabandhab Upadhyay, Jules Monchanin, Swami Abhishiktananda, Bede Griffths and others. At a time when such initiatives were looked upon by many as unorthodox and even heretical, Nostra Aetate came to confirm that such works of dialogue taking place in Asia are in keeping with Christian faith, and even more, such initiatives need encouragement and further expansion. Hence, under the inspiration of Nostra Aetate, further new initiatives were taken. Centres of dialogue were created, and commissions for inter-religious dialogue were established at national, regional, and diocesan levels in different parts of Asia. FABC took the vision of Nostra Aetate one step further when it stated in its very First Plenary Assembly in Taipei as follows:

> In this dialogue we accept them as significant and positive elements in the economy of God's design of salvation. In them we recognize and respect profound spiritual and ethical meanings and values. Over many centuries they have been the treasury of the religious experience of our ancestors, from which our contemporaries do not cease to draw light and strength. They have been (and continue to be) the authentic expression of the noblest longings of their hearts and the home of their contemplation and prayer. They have helped to give shape to the histories and cultures of our nations.[4]

These words bring to mind the millennial Asian practice of living together of peoples of different religious traditions in harmony and mutual respect. Daily life in Asia bears out that people go about respectfully with the religious experience, sacred places, and religious teachings of others. This is something inherent in the Asian way of life and daily existence. Hence, we could look at Nostra Aetate as a confirmation as well of the traditional Asian approach to other religions in the spirit of harmony and understanding.

Dialogue - A New Culture and a New Process

How do we put into practice this new vision about other religions? It is here that the general spirit of all-round dialogue initiated by Vatican II finds its application vis-à-vis other religious traditions. Even before the close of the Council, Pope Paul VI gave a fillip to the Council by highlighting in his *Ecclesiam Suam* (1964), dialogue as the new way of being Church. Dialogue became a key concept that inspired the entire corpus of Vatican II documents. What Nostra Aetate did was to set in motion a new culture and a process of dialogue with peoples of other faiths. It implied a *change of attitude* towards other religions as it viewed them in a completely different light. Dialogue involves also a process of learning.[5]

The spirit and orientation of Nostra Aetate was sustained through the several official documents of the Church, such as the encyclical *Redemptor Hominis* which spoke of the presence of the Spirit outside the confines of the Church (RH. 16) in the various religious traditions; so too *Redemptoris Missio*, where the role of the Spirit outside the bounds of the Church gets even more deeply acknowledged and stated. According to it, the Spirit is present in "individuals…society and history, peoples, cultures and religions" and it goes on to add "the Spirit is at the origin of the noble ideals and undertakings which benefit humanity on its journey through history" (RM 28).[6]

From a theological point of view, if we start from *pneumatology* we will understand the mystery of Jesus Christ more closely. It is the same pneumatology which opens the doors for us to understand the religious experience and traditions of our neighbours of other faiths. Hence, one need not be preoccupied that acknowledging the presence of the Spirit in other religions would water down the mystery of Jesus Christ. Rather when we start from pneumatological considerations we will be able to relate harmoniously our faith in Jesus Christ with the recognition of God's grace and the presence of the Spirit in other religious faiths.

Closer Spiritual Affinity

The landmark event of Pope John Paul II praying with leaders of other religious traditions in Assisi in October 1986 is but a logical consequence of the grand vision of Nostra Aetate.[7] The realization of one common humanity and the experience of sharing in one and the same ultimate mystery in which "we live, move and have our being …" (Acts 17:28), cannot but naturally lead us to invoke together the same mystery in prayer. This was exactly what the event in Assisi was. When Pope John Paul II made his concluding address at the event, one could hear the echo of Nostra Aetate. He said,

> We hope that this pilgrimage to Assisi has taught us anew to be aware of the common origin and common destiny of humanity. Let us see in it an anticipation of what God would like the developing history of mankind to be: a fraternal journey in which we accompany one another towards the transcendent goal, which He sets for us.[8]

The bold initiative of praying with others, made rumbles in certain quarters of the Church, including several ecclesial leaders. The pope defended the legitimacy of a common prayer with others when he spoke to the Roman

Curia in December, 1986. He said, "We can indeed maintain that every authentic prayer is called forth by the Holy Spirit, who is mysteriously present in the heart of every person... every man and woman is capable of... submitting oneself totally to God".[9]

Humanistic Import of Nostra Aetate

The times of Nostra Aetate did not witness the kind and scale of violence, religious fundamentalism and chauvinism we are experiencing today. The developing situations in the world is a crisis of great magnitude. Peace and understanding among religions have become an imperative necessity for the future of humanity. The challenges of the hour globally and in Asia, make dialogue no more an option but a necessity. This shows why relationship of Christianity with other religions should not be treated as a matter of Christian doctrine alone; one has to critically look at whether the professed doctrine contributes to peace and harmony among religions and peoples, or whether it becomes a threat to these ideals all of humanity is called upon to pursue relentlessly. In other words, we have to take into account the humanistic and political implications of Christian doctrines, especially when it touches upon the delicate question of inter-religious relationships, which has become so very crucial for peace in the world. Further, increasing migration of peoples from one geographic region to another, from one cultural and religious setting to another has brought about also intriguing issues of co-existence and tolerance, identity, recognition, and respect.

Even though Nostra Aetate did not envisage such issues and situations, however, if we do a re-reading of it, what we would find is that it is a document not only about a new theology of religion, but also a document about peace and inter-religious understanding on the basis of a larger vision of humanity. As such, Nostra Aetate continues to be an inspiration even as we face new and increasingly complex questions bearing upon religions and religious beliefs. Today we are in a position to draw the implications of Nostra Aetate in terms of its humanistic import.

An Intermezzo – Asia on the Procrustean Bed

When *Dominus Iesus* (2000)[10] appeared, many in Asia were wondering how to reconcile it with Nostra Aetate and many other subsequent documents which corroborated the vision of this Conciliar document. For many Asians, Dominus Iesus was an embarrassment, and it appeared to be the case of one step forward and two steps backwards![11] The language of power, suspicion, intimidation, and threat go back to pre-Vatican II times.[12] Many Asians were asking themselves whether such a regression has indeed taken place. For, the document seemed to speak a different language and set a different tone from Nostra Aetate. It says, "Objectively speaking they [other religions] are in a gravely deficient situation in comparison with those who, in the Church have the fullness of salvation" (no. 22). It was difficult to see for Asians, for that matter anyone who makes a comparative study of texts, how Dominus Iesus could square with Nostra Aetate which is imbued with the spirit of dialogue, and Lumen Genitum which has an inclusive approach. Dialogue takes place when we try to understand peoples of other faiths the way they would like to be understood. We close the doors of dialogue when we are prejudiced, become judgmental, and want to reduce the other within our scheme of things.

Moreover, Asians saw in Dominus Iesus a document written primarily from a doctrinal preoccupation and intended to serve as a caveat. The question of dialogue was approached through neo-scholastic method and spirit. Any essentialist philosophy like neo-scholasticism sees identities as fixated, clearly defined, and demarcated. In actual life, however, identity is not defined by self-isolation but in relationship. One needs to avoid carefully binary like "we" and "they", "inside" and "outside. In the dominant western theological tradition, however, there is an obsession to know clearly who is in and who is out. This is what I would call *theology of "Noah's ark"*. Either you are inside or you are outside the ark. It is difficult to apply this philosophy, and this kind of image in the realm of mystery, which is the case when we deal with the sacred sphere of religious experience. It is a grey zone. Totalitarianism is not only political. It has also a religious version. When we want to create out of Christianity a system of thought, similar to the philosophical system of Kant and Hegel, Christianity is emptied of the sense of mystery, as one seeks to place everything in a particular slot or pigeonhole of an overarching grand system of thought. The religious traditions of our neighbours get truncated when they are forced into our system of thought and belief, reminding us of the Procrustean bed.[13] Moreover, such an approach does not vibrate with the Asian ethos either, which sees the reality organically interrelated; it tries to connect things rather than demarcate and circumscribe one from the other.

Asian theology has been under a cloud of suspicion of not proclaiming the uniqueness of Christ and of having fallen into relativism. To be able to gauge such suspicious attitudes, we need to remember that the pastorally oriented Asian theology is read and interpreted through western systems of thought, categories and preoccupations. Asia is not understood in its context and cultural setting. Generally, when relativism is spoken about, one understands it to mean that "there are many truths which vary according to the subjects who hold different opinions of reality".[14] This is not the way we approach truth in Asia. Instead, Asian spiritual traditions tell us that *truth is not many but one*. This was expressed laconically in Rig Veda, "*ekaṁ sat viprāḥ bahudhā vadanti*" (Truth is one, the sages have called it by many names).[15] The one mystery appears differently in relation to the diverse experience of people which is very important and crucial. Far from a dilution of truth, as being feared, it is an enrichment of truth. If this is applied to the understanding of the mystery of Christ, we arrive not at any indifferent relativism, but an engaging and enriching pluralism.[16] The mystery of Jesus Christ is richly illuminated through a plurality of experiences. The rich pluralism which Asian theology is trying to highlight is being misunderstood through the western understanding of relativism, so much so that the attack on Asian theology often amounts to a shadow-boxing. Is it not a case of mistaken identity? To fathom the depth of Asian theology of religions, especially the mystery of Jesus Christ in its multifaceted nature, one needs to study closely the statements of FABC, in particular, those of the Office of Ecumenical and Interreligious Affairs (OEIA).[17]

Moving ahead with the Spirit of Nostra Aetate in Asia

Thanks to Nostra Aetate and the many dialogical efforts preceding Vatican II, Asia moved ahead to new horizons in developing a theology of religions, and practiced inter-religious dialogue which all became an issue of highest priority, since Christians in this continent live amidst great masses of peoples who are Buddhists, Hindus, Daoists, Confucianists, Muslims, Sikhs, Parsis, and peoples of primaeval religious traditions.

The Roman Synod on Asia saw the theological and pastoral prowess of Asian bishops, under the influence of FABC. That notwithstanding, the end-result of the Asian Synod in Rome in the form of *Ecclesia in Asia* would have left many bishops wondering, whether this was what they really tried to say at the synod. Two months after the Asian Synod, FABC Plenary Assembly gathered in Thailand in January 2000, and its theme has another focus than doctrinal Christology of *Ecclesia in Asia*. The theme is *"Renewal of Church in Asia: The Mission of Love and Service"*. The doctrinal approach of proclamation gives place to an evangelization of love and service in the spirit of the Gospel. Here one hears another language which the Asian bishops could call authentically their own, and not filtered. Their language is not one of other religions waiting to be fulfilled by Christ, rather one of solidarity and partnership. The poor of Asia become the focus of this partnership:

> As we face the needs of the 21st century, we do so with Asian hearts, in solidarity with the poor and the marginalized, in union with all our Christian brothers and sisters and by joining hands with all men and women of Asia of many different faiths.[18]

When the house is on fire, we need to pay attention to save the essentials, and there is no point in disputing who should do the work of saving. Everyone is called today to the mission of saving humanity and nature from the enveloping crisis situation. Our neighbours of other religious traditions become brothers and sisters in a common task of justice, and in the defence of the dignity and rights of human beings – be it the question of the marginalised, women, indigenous people or migrants and refugees. Therefore, simply *missio ad gentes* is not enough; nor missio *inter-gentes*.

We need *missio cum gentibus*. This presupposes a theology of mission and a theology of dialogue from the perspective of the *Kingdom of God*.

That Inter-religious dialogue should not be conditioned by doctrinal preoccupations was clearly brought out by the Japanese Bishops' Conference already in the context of Asian Synod. Reacting to a *lineamenta* overly preoccupied with the proclamation of Jesus as the unique Saviour, the Japanese bishops responded saying,

> Jesus Christ is the Way, the Truth, and the Life, but in Asia, before stressing that Jesus Christ is the Truth, we must search much more deeply into how he is the Way and the Life. If we stress too much that "Jesus Christ is the One and Only Saviour", we can have no dialogue, common living, or solidarity with other religions. The Church, learning from the *kenosis* of Jesus Christ, should be humble and open its heart to other religions to deepen its understanding of the Mystery of Christ.[19]

The approach of Pope Francis, his statements, and many symbolic gestures confirm the position of Japanese bishops and the vision of FABC in general.

New Trajectories of Dialogue in Asia

I would like to present a few thoughts which will help the future of theology of religions and praxis of dialogue in Asia.

To be on the Way

We need to move away from theological disputes to inter-religious collective praxis and transformation. This is what the papacy of Pope Francis beckons us to do. Issues like uniqueness of Christ, the relationship between dialogue and proclamation, which were the centres of attention and hotly debated a few years ago,[20] are receding to the background, as the pope foregrounds the common engagement of all religions to respond to the plight of humanity and of nature. We hardly hear him speaking about those hot theological debates of the past. In his address in Turkey[21], for example, he pointed out areas of common concern which religions need to respond to urgently. The message is the same when he met religious leaders in Sri Lanka and elsewhere. He has articulated it clearly in his *Evangelii Gaudium* (EG).

We can then join one another in taking up the duty of serving justice and peace, which should become a basic principle of all our exchanges. A dialogue which seeks social peace and justice is in itself, beyond all merely practical considerations, an *ethical commitment* which brings about a new social situation. Efforts made in dealing with a specific theme can become a process in which, by mutual listening, both parts can be purified and enriched. These efforts, therefore, can also express love for truth (EG 250).

There are two clear indications in the theology of Pope Francis which will be helpful for our project of inter-religious dialogue in Asia. In the vision of Francis, *to be Christian is to be on the way, to be on a journey with others* – religious, secular – for the transformation of humanity and the flourishing of nature. The orientation of the pope confirms our own vision and practice in Asia. In fact, in 1987 there was a consultation between FABC and the Christian Conference of Asia (CCA) on the question of dialogue with peoples of other religions. It was titled: "*Living and working with Brothers and Sisters of Other Faiths*". FABC General Assembly in 1986 in Tokyo, Japan, meaningfully captioned its final statement as "*Journeying together toward the Third Millennium*". Journey and pilgrimage are very dear imageries in Asia. The motif of journey re-appears again and again in the thought of Pope Francis, his speeches, and documents, including *Evangelii Gaudium*.

Mercy and Compassion

A second theme which is very helpful for our dialogue in Asia is that of *mercy and compassion*. Mercy is the key word to characterize the pontificate of Pope Francis.[22] It is the *mainspring* of the praxis of Francis. This for him, is the hermeneutical key to read the entire Scriptures and the life and teachings of Jesus. It is the jewel of the Sermon on the Mount. "Be merciful as your heavenly Father is merciful" (Lk 6: 36). In the narration of the Last Judgment too (Mt 25:31-46), mercy and compassion are the criteria by which human beings are ultimately judged. If this is the case, then mercy and compassion should also get reflected in our relationship with peoples of other faiths. Instead of claims of superiority or absolute possession of truth which, unfortunately, has contributed to create a gulf between Christians and others in Asia, we need to encounter the other with a lot of love and respect for what they hold and practice as sacred. With this approach, we could join peoples of other faiths to transform the world and society. In fact, Pope Francis during his visit to Turkey, spoke of the need of religions joining together in the struggle against terrorism and fundamentalism. He said, "interreligious and intercultural dialogue can make an important contribution to attaining this lofty and urgent goal, so that there will be an end to all forms of fundamentalism and terrorism which gravely demean the dignity of every man and woman, and exploit religion".[23] Against sceptics on the role of religion in the modern world, pope speaks of the collaboration among religions to contribute to the life of the world. In the words of Cardinal Walter Kasper,

> For Francis it is not only a matter of dialogue about the common as well as different cultural and religious traditions, but also about a common contribution to the well-being of the poor, the weak, and the suffering; it is about common service to justice, reconciliation.[24]

Dialogue and Evangelisation

We do admit that evangelisation and dialogue are inter-related, and they are a mutual enrichment. However, in the past in Asia, we had difficulties to accept the way evangelisation and dialogue were related, especially when dialogue was converted into a means for evangelization. We raised, in Asia, critical questions regarding this position, and it came out very clearly - as we noted in an earlier chapter - in the joint FABC-CCA meeting held in Singapore, way back in 1987. It stated,

> We affirm that dialogue and mission have their own integrity and freedom. They are distinct but not unrelated. Dialogue is not a tool or instrument for mission and evangelization, but it does influence the way the Church perceives and practices mission in a pluralistic world. ...Dialogue offers opportunities for Christian witness.[25]

Today, we can confidently revisit the question of dialogue and proclamation, if we take mercy and compassion as the key point of reference, since they reflect the heart of the Gospel. For, under the inspiration of Pope Francis, there is a fresh approach to mission, evangelisation, and dialogue. Evangelisation is not viewed as an *occasion or opportunity* to justify the doctrinal claims of Christianity. There is a great spiritual depth in Pope

Francis in that he sees proclamation not only related to truth but also to *mercy and love*. The way he thinks of proclaiming the Gospel, and especially the manner he does it, make us realize that we can indeed bring together both these realities harmoniously into Christian life and praxis. If we proclaim God's love and mercy in Jesus Christ, who will be against such an evangelisation in Asia? After all, the message of compassion will vibrate with Asians, seasoned in the Buddhist religious and cultural tradition. The moment Christians raise their pitch and start proclaiming doctrines from a high pedestal making many unique claims above the head of the people, they will put themselves in a position of not being heard, and even could be perceived, instead of being messengers of love, peace, and divine compassion, as a threat to societal harmony.

Ecology and Inter-religious Dialogue

Ecology has become a new and important motive for interreligious dialogue. Integral cosmic vision is characteristic of Hindu, Buddhist, Daoist, Shintoist, and primaeval traditions in Asia.[26] But if we are to dialogue with them, we need to revisit our traditional Anselmian soteriology - *Cur Deus Homo?* The dominant Chritological discourse is associated with a particular and limited conception of salvation. There is need to rethink salvation in new terms, closer to the Gospel. The Gospels tell us that Jesus was concerned about *human suffering* and privations rather than about *sin*. Unfortunately, Christian soteriology came to be constructed around sin, and not on the most important aspects of Jesus' praxis for the wellbeing (*salus*) of human beings and of communities.

We have in *Laudato Si* an attempt to re-conceptualize the traditional understanding of salvation. Salvation – *salus* or wellbeing - is extended to the whole of creation and nature.[27] The new anthropology and soteriology implied in *Laudato Si* brings us closer to Asian religious traditions than ever before. This new and refreshing opening to nature and creation, together with recognition of the universal reach of God's salvation and the presence of the Holy Spirit, offer a new theological basis to dialogue with neighbours of other faiths. By affirming nature as an integral aspect of Christian theological vision, Laudato Si leads us also to rethink present forms of Christian worship excessively centred on the word and preaching, whereas these religious traditions have worship close to the elements of nature – earth, water, fire, air, ether (*mahāpañcabhūta*). We could look at *Laudato Si* as a document that leads *Nostra Aetate* to new horizons.

Feminism, Religious Pluralism, and Interreligious Dialogue

At the time Nostra Aetate came out, one probably never thought that there is an intimate connection between religion and gender. In the past decades, however, feminist movements and studies have given rise to critical approach to the study of religions, their traditions, scriptures, worship, theology, and so on. The result is a plethora of new insights and perspectives to a new understanding of religion as well to the study of religious pluralism. Though Asia is religiously plural as perhaps no other continent is, still little room has been given to study, explore, and draw consequences out of the relationship between feminism and interreligious dialogue.[28] While feminism and feminist studies could contribute to religious pluralism and interreligious dialogue, at the same time, they can also benefit from the practice of interreligious dialogue.

Conclusion

The Challenge of Praxis

Asia, perhaps, is the continent in which this shortest and highly significant Conciliar document Nostra Aetate found most reception. The contribution of FABC to inter-religious dialogue, inspired by Nostra Aetate, is universally recognized. Through the years, FABC has developed a grand vision, and an impressive theology of religions and dialogue. What is missing, however, is *realization* of this theology and its implementation in concrete praxis. The opposition to dialogue and scepticism about it are not only from the outside, but from within too. This is in great part due to lack of an *adult faith*.[29] Infantile faith, nurtured by all kinds of sanctimonious practices and pious devotions, will not find it easy to accept a new theology of dialogue. The conclusion is that we need to cultivate pastorally an adult faith among the believers in Asia for theology of religions and inter-religious dialogue to gain acceptance and bear fruit. The dissonance and asymmetry between infantile faith and inter-religious dialogue need to be overcome with appropriate pedagogical means.

Listening to and Learning from Peoples of Other Faiths

One of the important pastoral means is to include in Christian catechesis a chapter presenting positively other religious traditions and their spiritual experience. For some, this may sound provocative. But I think this should be normal, if we take seriously the grand vision of Nostra Aetate on humanity and its quest for God. If Nostra Aetate is one of the sixteen documents of the Council, forming integral part of its teaching, what prevents us making other religions integral part of Christian catechism? Further, the numerous educational and other institutions run by the Church need to impart the students, knowledge about other religions which will lead to respect and appreciation for them.

Living every day in the midst of the religious world of our neighbours, Christians in Asia will acquire not only the skills to dialogue with them, but also feel at home in their religious places like pagodas, mosques, gurudwaras, temples, etc. This is what I would call *religious cosmopolitanism*.[30] Pope Francis not only visited the Great Synagogue of Rome,[31] but also mosques, and a Buddhist temple in Sri Lanka. Were he to visit India one day, we can surmise, he will visit also a Hindu temple. He has no doctrinal inhibitions when it comes to respecting the sacredness of the religious experience of peoples of other faiths.

Religious cosmopolitanism is the ability to enter into the religious universe of the other, without losing one's identity. It requires a lot of openness. "Men and women do not have to forsake their identity, whether ethnic or religious, in order to live in harmony with their brothers and sisters," Francis said in his address to the religious leaders in Sri Lanka during his visit in January, 2015.[32] Religious cosmopolitanism requires an adult faith, and unconditional openness to the infinite mystery. It calls for a new catechesis and faith-education in Asia. We will go into the issue of religious cosmopolitanism in detail in our next chapter.

Collaborative-Partnership Model

We noted how important this model of partnership is for Asia, faced with many socio-political and ethical challenges. Today, the realisation is growing about the importance of religion in public life and its potentials to create peace and harmony. The issue is not merely that of peace among religions for social harmony. Rather religious resources are increasingly in demand for the creation of peace and justice in the world, and for upholding dignity of human beings and their rights. Besides, at the global level, events like 9/11 have brought to the consciousness of humanity the importance of religion in international affairs. Mere secular pursuits may not be able to create a world of equality, justice, and peace. To save the human, religions pointing to something beyond seem to be very necessary. This is well expressed by Jürgen Habermas when he states, "Among modern societies, only those that are able to introduce into the secular domain the essential elements of their religious traditions which point beyond the merely human realm will also be able to rescue the substance of the human"[33]. Given this overriding importance of religion for harmony, social cohesion, and for saving the human, interreligious dialogue on the model of partnership could substantially contribute to the transformation of the world and societies. Hence, in Asia we are challenged to be *partners* with our neighbours. However, there is more to the joint working of peoples of different faiths than social action or involvement. Religions could bring to our contemporary social and political life a necessary *mystical* dimension of seeing everything interconnected and interdependent. It is not a mysticism of closed eyes; it is a "mysticism of open eyes".[34]

Particularly important would be the working together of religions for peace. "Interreligious dialogue is a necessary condition for peace in the world, and so it is a duty of Christians as well as of other religious communities" (EG 250), reminds us Pope Francis. United Nations and its various bodies, especially UNESCO have proposed inter-religious dialogue as an important means for peace. We need to strengthen the efforts of humanity for peace by promoting inter-religious understanding. The global world rightly awaits a significant contribution from Asia on this question. This challenge takes the Asian Church beyond the walls of the minority Christian communities to the larger agenda of the entire humanity.

Bibliography

Aihiokhai, Simon Mary Asese. "Going beyond Nostra Aetate. The Way Forward for Interreligious Dialogue." In *Journal of Ecumenical Studies* 51 (2016), 386-401.

Andrevon, Therese-Martine. "Des textes et de événements: Bilan de ciqnquante années de réception de Nostra Aetate." In *Recherches des sciences religieux* 103 (2015), 329-349.

Borelli, John. "Unitatis Redintegratio and Nostra Aetate: Reception at the Fifty years Mark in the New Era of Pope Francis." *Ecumenical Trends* 42 (2013), 1-9.

Bristow, Edward. *No Religion Is an Island: The Nostra Aetate Dialogues* (New York: Fordham University Press, 1998).

Cassidy, Edward Idris. *Ecumenism and Interreligious Dialogue: Unitatis Redintegratio, Nostra Aetate* (New York: Paulist Press, 2005).

CCA-FABC. *Living and Working Together with Sisters and Brothers of Other Faiths in Asia*: An Ecumenical Consultation, Singapore, July, 5-10, 1987 (Singapore: CCA-FABC, 1989).

Chia, Edmund. *Towards a Theology of Dialogue* (Nijmegen: Doctoral dissertation, University of Nijmegen 2003).

Clooney, Francis X. "Nostra Aetate and the Catholic Way of Openness to Other Religions." *Nostra Aetate*, edited by Valkenberg Pim and Cirelli Anthony (Washington, D.C.: Catholic University of America Press, 2016), 58-75.

Colberg, Kristin M. "The Omnipresence of Grace: Revisiting the Relationship between Ad Gentes and Nostra Aetate 50 Years Later." *Missiology* 42 (2014), 181-94.

Fredericks, James L. "Nostra Aetate and Pope Francis: Reflections on the Next Fifty Years of Catholic Dialogue with Buddhists." *Nostra Aetate*, edited by Pim Valkenberg and Anthony Cirelli (Washington: The Catholic University of America Press, 2016), 43-57.

Fredericks, James L., and Sayuki Tiemeier, Tracy., eds. *Interreligious Friendship after "Nostra Aetate." Interreligious Studies in Theory and Practice* (New York: Palgrave Macmillan, 2015).

LaRousse, William., ed. "Asian Celebration of the 50th Anniversay of Nostra Aetate." *FABC Paper* 152 (Hong Kong: FABC, 2017).

Madigan, Daniel A. "Nostra Aetate: The questions It Chose to Leave Open." In *Gregorianum* 87 (2006), 781-796.

McLean, George F., Martin, Francis., and Hogan, John P., eds. *Report of Consultations on Nostra Aetate Forty Years Later." 1st ed. Cultural Heritage and Contemporary Change. Series VII, Seminars on Cultures and Values* 23 (Washington, D.C.: Council for Research in Values and Philosophy, 2005).

Muslim Religious Leaders, "Open Letter to His Holiness Pope Benedict XVI." *Islamic Studies* 45 (4) (2006), 604-13.

Niles, Preman. *The Lotus and the Sun: Asian Theological Engagement with Plurality and Power* (Barton ACT: Barton Books, 2013).

Phan, Peter., ed. *The Asian Synod: Texts and Commentaries* (Maryknoll: Orbis Books, 2002).

Renz, Andreas. *Die Katholische Kirche und der Interreligiöse Dialog: 50 Jahre "Nostra Aetate": Vorgeschichte, Kommentar, Rezeption* (Stuttgart: Kohlhammer, 2014).

Roddey, Thomas. *Das Verhältnis Der Kirche Zu Den Nichtchristlichen Religionen: Die Erklärung "Nostra Aetate" des Zweiten Vatikanischen Konzils und Ihre Rezeption Durch Das Kirchliche Lehramt."* Paderborner Theologische Studien. Bd. 45 (Paderborn: Schöningh, 2005).

Root, Michael. "Nostra Aetate and Ecumenism." *Nostra Aetate*, eds. Valkenberg Pim and Cirelli Anthony (Washington, D.C.: Catholic University of America Press, 2016), 27-40.

Scheuer, Jacques. "À 50 ans de Nostra Aetate: Dialogue interreligieux et théologie des religions." In *Revue théologique de Louvain* 46 (2015), 153-177.

Sherwin, Byron L., and Kasimow, Harold., eds. *John Paul II and Interreligious Dialogue* (Maryknoll: Orbis Books, 1999).

Sinkovits, Josef., and Winkler, Ulrich., eds. *Weltkirche Und Weltreligionen: Die Brisanz des Zweiten Vatikanischen Konzils 40 Jahre Nach Nostra Aetate.* Salzburger Theologische Studien. Bd. 28 (Innsbruck: Tyrolia-Verlag, 2007).

Tavard, George H. "Nostra Aetate; Forty years Later." *Ecumenism* 171 (2008), 23-34.

Tirimanna, Vimal., ed. *Sprouts of Theology from Asian Soil: Collection of TAC and OTC Documents [1987-2007]* (Bangalore: Claretian Publication, 2007).

Valkenberg, Pim., and Cirelli, Anthony., eds. *Nostra Aetate: Celebrating Fifty Years of the Catholic Church's Dialogue with Jews and Muslims* (Washington, D.C: Catholic University of America Press, 2016).

Waldenfels, Hans. "Nostra Aetate Vierzig Jahre danach." In *Zeitschrfit fuer Missionswissenschaft und Religionswissenschaft* 89 (2005), 280-296.

Wilfred, Felix. "In Praise of Christian Relativism." *The New Pontification: A Time for Change, Concilium* 2006/1 (London: SCM Press, 2006), 86-94.

Endnotes

[1] Council of Florence, from the Decree for the Jacobites (1442) – For the English translation of the text see, J. Neuner – J. Dupuis, *The Christian Faith in the Doctrinal Documents of the Catholic Church* (Bangalore: Theological Publications in India, 1973), p. 265.

[2] Viewed from Asia, this looks to be the abiding significance of Vatican II. This is different from the view of Rahner, who saw the enduring significance of Vatican II in that the Church got actualized for the first time as universal and Catholic. For critical comments on Rahner's position seen from an Asian perspective, Felix Wilfred, "Vatican II and the Agency of Asian Christians", in Elochukwu E. Uzukwu ed, *Mission and Diversity: Exploring Christian Mission in the Contemporary World* (Zürich: LIT Verlag, 2015), pp. 99-111.

[3] *Ecclesiam Suam*, 70.

[4] Statement of the First Plenary Assembly of FABC, 14 (Taipei, Taiwan: 1974); for the text, see *For All the Peoples of Asia: Federation of Asian Bishops' Conferences, Documents from 1970-1991*, Gaudencio Rosales – C.G. Arevalo, eds (Quezon City: Claretian Publications, 1992), 11ff.

[5] As *Ad Gentes* puts it, "through sincere and patient dialogue they [Christians] themselves might learn of the riches which a generous God has distributed among the nations". (AG no. 11)

[6] When I served as the secretary of the Office of Theological Concerns (OTC), a long document (almost 100 pages) on "The Spirit in Asia" was prepared which brings out more concretely how the Spirit is operative in other religious traditions and in various other expressions in the life and heritage of Asia. For the text of the document see, *For All the Peoples of Asia: Federation of Asian Bishops' Conferences Documents from 1997-2001*, edited by Franz-Josef Eilers (Quezon City: Claretian Publications, 2002), pp. 237-327.

[7] For an overview of the statements and symbolic gestures of Pope John Paul II, see *John Paul II and Interreligious Dialogue*, edited by Byron L. Sherwin – Harold Kasimow (Maryknoll: Orbis Books, 1999).

[8] *L'Osservatore Romano*, weekly English edition (3 November, 1986), 3.

[9] Pope John Paul II, "Address to the Cardinals and the Roman Curia, 22 December 1986," *Assisi: World Day of Prayer for Peace*, 27 October 1986 (Pontifical Council for Justice and Peace: Vatican Polyglot Press, 1987), 146.

[10] *Dominus Iesus: On the Unicity and Salvific Universality of Jesus Christ and the Church* (2000). This declaration was issued by the Congregation of the Doctrine of the Faith. Text of this document as well as other documents

relating to dialogue and evangelization are readily available online at the official websites of Vatican as well as different congregations and offices of Vatican.

[11] To understand how *Dominus Iesus* came across to Asians, see the special issue of *Jeevadhara*, 31:183 (2001). This issue contains the contribution of several Asian theologians - Francis X. D' Sa, Michael Amaladoss, Edmund Chia, Rui de Menezes, José de Mesa, Jacob Parapally, Sebastian Painadath. For reporting, see, "Japanese indifferent to Dominus Iesus", *Union of Catholic Asian News (UCAN)*, 5 (October 2000); "Dominus Iesus Brings Cultural Tension for Vietnam Catholics", *UCAN* (18 September 2000); "Indians of Various Religions Shocked over 'unnecessary' Vatican Document", *UCAN* (19 September 2000); "Theology Institute Initiates Public Discussion on *Dominus Iesus*", *UCAN* (29 December 2000); "Media Say Vatican Document Threatens Dialogue: Communal Peace", *UCAN* (3 October 2000); "Bishops Note Room for 'Theological Inquiry' in Toning Down *Dominus Iesus*", *UCAN* (3 May 2001).

[12] Cf. John O' Malley, et al., *Vatican II: Did Anything Happen?* (New York: Bloomsbury, 2007); see also ID., "Trent and Vatican II: Two Styles of Church", in *From Trent to Vatican II: Historical and Theological Investigations*, edited by Raymond F. Bulman and Frederick J. Parrella (Oxford: Oxford University Press, 2006), pp. 301-320.

[13] Procrustean refers to Procrustes, a Greek mythical figure who attacked people and stretched them on an iron bed, and then cut off their legs so that they could fit into the size of the bed!

[14] The Office of Theological Concerns (OTC) of FABC is of the view that such a position is a misunderstanding. It clarifies how Asia offers space to look at one truth from different perspectives. See OTC document on "Methodology: Asian Christian Theology: Doing Theology in Asia Today", in Vimal Tirimanna, ed, *Sprouts of Theology from Asian Soil: Collection of ATC and OTC Documents [1987-2007]* (Bangalore: Claretian Publication), pp. 255-343, at 258.

[15] *Rig Veda* 1:164.46.

[16] Cf. Felix Wilfred, "In Praise of Christian Relativism", *The New Pontification: A Time for Change, Concilium 2006/1* (London: SCM Press, 2006), 86-94.

[17] An excellent doctoral research work was done by Edmund Chia on the contribution of FABC to interreligious dialogue by analyzing its numerous documents. See Edmund Chia, *Towards a Theology of Dialogue* (Nijmegen: Doctoral dissertation, University of Nijmegen, 2003); see also Preman Niles, *The Lotus and the Sun: Asian Theological Engagement with Plurality and Power* (Baraton ACT: Barton Books, 2013), 150 ff.

[18] Final Statement of VII FABC Plenary Assembly – for the text see, *For All the Peoples of Asia: Federation of Asian Bishops' Conferences, Documents from*

1997-2001, 3, edited by Franz-Josef Eilers (Quezon City: Claretian Publications, 2002), 8.

[19] Peter Phan, ed, *The Asian Synod: Texts and Commentaries* (Maryknoll: Orbis Books, 2002), p. 30.

[20] This question led to the issuing of a few official documents by the Church trying to clarify the relationship between dialogue and evangelization. The Pontifical Council for Interreligious Dialogue (then known as Secretariat for Non-Christians) issued a document called *Reflections and Orientations on Dialogue and Mission* (1984). The Congregation of Evangelization of Peoples and the Pontifical Council for Interreligious Dialogue jointly brought out a document entitled: *Dialogue and Proclamation: Reflections and Orientations on Interreligious Dialogue and the Proclamation of the Gospel of Jesus Christ* (1991).

[21] See https://www.bbc.co.uk/news/av/world-europe-30258527/pope-francis-in-turkey-urges-faiths-to-combat-fanaticism> [accessed 21 July, 2018].

[22] In fact, the Episcopal motto of Jorge Mario Bergoglio read *"Miserando atque eligendo".*

[23] See www.bbc.com/news/world-europe-30250098> [accessed on 21 July, 2018].

[24] Walter Kasper, *Pope Francis' Revolution of Tenderness and Love* (New York: Paulist Press, 2015), pp. 63- 64.

[25] For the text of the statement, see *Living and Working Together with Sisters and Brothers of Other Faiths in Asia: An Ecumenical Consultation, Singapore, July, 5-10, 1987* (Singapore: CCA-FABC, 1989), pp. 104-105. This way of relating evangelisation and dialogue is very different from considering interreligious dialogue as "part of the Church's evangelising mission" (*Dominus Iesus* no. 2), which does not seem to recognise the validity of dialogue in itself. One would defeat the spirit of dialogue if it is made simply an instrument for something else, and not a value in itself.

[26] Western theologians may leaf through the pages of their philosophers – Kant and Hegel, Paschal and Kierkagaard, Haberms and Foucault, Lyotard and Levinas - and they will find in none of them the kind of cosmic and integral vision of reality we note in Hinduism, Buddhism, Confucianism, Daoim, and Shintonism. Hence, the message of Pope Francis in *Laudato Si* cannot be interpreted in the light of these philosophers. Rather here is a call to go to those traditions which have embedded in them a cosmic vision of reality which enlightens us also on the mystery of God, world, and the human, avoiding all kinds of dangerous dualism. In the West itself, there are instances of individuals who have fostered integral vision of reality like St Francis of Assisi, from whose canticle Pope Francis has culled out the title of his encyclical – *Laudato Si.*

However, the tradition St Francis represents is a marginal and neglected one in western history.

[27] Cf. Felix Wilfred, see chapter 8 in this volume.

[28] For a global perspective on this issue, see Jeannine Hill Fletcher, "Shifting Identity: The Contribution of Feminist Thought to Theologies of Religious Pluralism", *Journal of Feminist Studies in Religion,* 19:2 (2003), 5-24.

[29] For more details on this issue see Felix Wilfred, chapter 10 in this volume.

[30] See the chapter 17 on Religious Cosmopolitanism in this volume.

[31] See *L'Osservatore Romano,* Weekly edition in English (22 January, 2016)

[32] http://w2.vatican.va/content/francesco/en/travels/2015/outside/documents/papa-francesco-sri-lanka-filippine-2015.html> [accessed on 21 July, 2018].

[33] As quoted in Michael Reader and Josef Schmidt "Habermas and Religion", *Awareness of What is Missing: Faith and Reason in a Post-secular Age* (Cambridge: Polity Press, 2010), pp. 5-6.

[34] John Baptist Metz, *Mistica degli occhi aperti: Per una spiritualità concreta e responsabile* (Brescia: Queriniana, 2013).

CHAPTER 17

Religious Cosmopolitanism:
Towards an Inclusive and Harmonious World

It is a commonly recognized fact that Asia is the cradle of great religious traditions. Today, these traditions need to engage themselves with contemporary struggles for humanity's unity and future survival. Defining the 'human' cannot be the prerogative of any one civilization; and envisioning the future destiny of humankind and its unity is not the sole privilege of any one religion. Never before has the future of humanity been so critical and elusive as it is today, calling for mobilization of resources from every quarter for its common construction. Never before in history was human co-existence so vigorously debated as it is today – something that has resulted from the innumerable forms of human encounters the present-day life has occasioned.

In the face of the sea of challenges confronting the entire human family, the claims of religions concerning their exclusive identities, *sub specie aeternitatis,* could be as much real and serious as children's playful construction of castles and fortresses on the sands of the seashore.[1] While the divisions are deepening day by day with the escalation of war and mass-murder, starvation and new forms of exclusion, the single most urgent question is about the *destiny of the human family and its salvation.* As such, it is a crucial question for any serious theological enterprise.

It is precisely this vision of the future of the whole of the human family that should take hold of Christianity and its theologies today, and it should be the key hermeneutical approach to define Christianity's relationship with other religious traditions. This is extremely important in the Asian context. For, far too long, questions of Christology, soteriology and ecclesiology have been the nodal points for determining this relationship, thereby turning Christianity into a "*religio incurvata in se*" (a religion bent on itself). Much time and energy have been expended in disentangling the knot Christianity has so masterfully created for itself, thereby leading to the proliferation of theologies of religion – grist for the academic mill. The challenge is to allow the thread of conversation with other religious traditions to stretch to the vast future that is before humankind.

Universal Destiny of Every Religion

All religions belong to the entirety of humankind, and no religion is the sole possession of the immediate community of its believers. From a Christian perspective we could reflect on the foundations of this truth. The narrations of the fall in the account of Genesis (Gen 3:1-24), the depiction of the times of Noah (Gen 6:11-13), the construction of the Tower of Babel (Gen 11:3ff.) – all these refer to the common experience of humankind across nations and races. The question is not what happens to a particular religion, but what it has to contribute to the welfare of the world and the future of humanity.

"The earth is the Lord's and all that is in it" (Ps 24:1); so, do all religions belong to humankind, under divine dispensation. No religion can claim full ownership of its beliefs and practices. Ownership in the Christian tradition, after all, is justified only when it is for the purpose of *autarkia* and *koinonia* (self-governance and communion).[2] Therefore, belonging to a religion does not close the doors; rather, it acquires meaning only so far as it is a means for communion. As for understanding of religions, precisely because they and their Scriptures belong to humankind, they are open to a wide spectrum of interpretations. The classical Indian hermeneutical tradition compared texts to a woman and said that the fact that because a father has generated a daughter need not mean that he is also the best judge of her beauty; the best judge could be her admirer, lover or husband. The modern hermeneutical tradition of autonomy of texts[3] could be profitably applied to the religious traditions whose interpretation need not necessarily be confined to the group of believers, but is open-ended.

First and foremost, all religions belong to humankind as a whole and *in a primary sense*, while a particular religion belongs to the limited community of its believers in a *secondary and derivative sense*. This is similar to what has been said by the Christian tradition on the universal destiny of earthly goods which takes precedence over the right of private property.[4] In the latter case, an appeal has been made to the Biblical injunctions for the year of jubilee, according to which hereditary properties are to be restored to all (Leviticus 25: 8-55). Several Fathers of the Church like Basel, Ambrose, Chrysostom were critical of the rich who amassed wealth at the expense of the poor. In this context they reminded the rich that the goods of creation are the gifts of God to be shared among God's children equitably. Drawing on the Scriptures and the patristic tradition, Catholic social teaching has underlined the social mortgage on private property which cannot be claimed as an absolute right. This tradition is continued in *Gaudium et Spes* which spoke about the universal destination of earthly goods (no. 69) and the same is to be found also in the recent encyclical of Pope Francis, *Laudato Si*.

Two things follow from this approach: (i) Every religion needs to consider itself as being addressed to the whole of humanity, and (ii) Consequently, every human being could draw on the heritage of humanity to the extent that it enhances her quest for life and spirituality.

Second, the mystery about which all religions are concerned is not the possession of any particular religion. It belongs to the entire human family which participates in that mystery. Obviously, no religion can claim to exhaust that mystery, much less to possess it. It would be a sin against humankind to claim for oneself what, in reality, belongs to all. Moreover, to be believers means to be *witnesses*. Belonging to a religious group does not entitle the possession of that particular religion, because believing is, in point of fact, a witnessing to what one has experienced of the mystery. It follows that, that which the witness experiences, surpasses the limited realm of herself and of her community or religious group in which this witnessing takes place.

Third, the various experiences of religions (e.g. creeds, rituals, laws, etc.) are not an end in themselves, but only a means. Even Scripture is only a means, according to Saint Augustine, who distinguishes between *use* and *enjoyment* – the latter identified with the experience of God.[5] Religion is a penultimate reality, and not the ultimate one. It is a means for something greater – and this 'greater' is the mystery that surrounds us all. For, the mystery is that which unites all religions and confers meaning and sustenance to them. The experience and enjoyment of the ultimate mystery to which the whole of human family is called is nourished with a wide variety of spiritual foods offered by the religions, and no one has full control of the spiritual metabolism of the experience and enjoyment the mystery causes.

Religious Resources for Cosmopolitanism

Thanks to its ability to provide fast means of communication, it could be said that globalisation facilitates the emergence of cosmopolitanism. However, to be global does not imply being cosmopolitan, for the deeper kind of relationship and affinity with every part of the world transcends the economic interdependence which is at the heart of the globalisation process. As Samartha rightly points out:

> Fresh criteria for new human relations that go beyond the economic and political structure have yet to emerge. Values that sustain personal life within the community, giving a sense of freedom and participation in large communities, need to be defined. Unless justice and peace are transformed into concrete sharing of power in the community of nations, we may witness merely a rearrangement of old positions.[6]

On the one hand, there are rich resources in the various religious traditions to promote and foster world community and cosmopolitanism, and these relate to the understanding of the human person and human co-existence across boundaries. On the other hand, each religious tradition has its own share of difficulties in accepting and promoting this ideal. As far as Christianity is concerned, there is a major difficulty that originates from its early beginnings and whose legacy still continues: The spiritual community that comes into being through the profession of faith is carefully distinguished – if not separated – from the secular unity represented by political structures as, for example, the Roman Empire. We need to only think of the classical scheme of "*Two Cities*" of Saint Augustine – a thought that has so firmly gripped the Christian imagination that it is still lingering among many Christians in one form or other. We might also think of the image of the "heavenly Jerusalem" representing the unity of the entire humankind. The difficulty is aggravated by the fact that these two cities are viewed as representing two incompatible spheres.[7] In light of this situation, it follows that Christians influenced by such a tradition would conceive of the unity of humanity as a spiritual endeavour centred on faith. The second difficulty lies in the fact that in their efforts for world-community and cosmopolitanism Christians have to grapple with the idea of "chosenness", which is deeply ingrained in its tradition.

To what extent is it then possible for such Christians to accept and promote a cosmopolitanism that cuts across all borders and boundaries, and at the same time is sustained by faith? Fortunately, we have in the Christian tradition, another stream – albeit not so visible – that views Christian life and existence as a cosmopolitan reality. To be a Christian is to be at home everywhere. This is the central thought that we find in one of the earliest Christian documents: *The Epistle to Diognetus*. Responding to the accusation that Christians take refuge in a narrow identity of a "spiritual" community, the anonymous author observes:

> The difference between Christians and the rest of mankind is not a matter of nationality, or language, or customs. Christians do not live apart in separate cities of their own, speak any special dialect, nor practice any eccentric way of life… [They] conform to ordinary local usage in their clothing, diet, and other habits… For them, any foreign country is a motherland, and any motherland is a foreign country.[8]

Cosmopolitanism is not a Greek invention or the heritage of the Enlightenment. Cosmopolitan thought is found among various peoples and nations in different forms and expressions.[9] Those who review history of cosmopolitanism refer to Greek and Roman thinkers like the Stoics and to the Enlightenment heritage, and especially to Immanuel Kant. Such a review leaves the impression that cosmopolitanism is a western creation. This eurocentric history of cosmopolitanism through the lens of the still lingering colonial epistemology needs to be corrected by accounts of cosmopolitanism among peoples and civilizations in different parts of the world. To cite one example, the Indian classical tradition thought of the entire humanity as a single family (*Vasudhaiva Kuṭumbam*). In Tamil culture and civilization, one spoke of "*Yādum ūre, yāvarum kēḷir,*" which means, every village is my village and every person is my kin. Such cosmopolitan visions could also be identified in the cultures and civilizations influenced by Buddhism – reason to rewrite the history of cosmopolitanism. To this heritage, we need to also add the cosmopolitan milieu created by the Islamic civilization in Cordova and Granada, Spain, from the eighth to the fifteenth centuries as well as in Egypt and in the Ottoman Empire. Under Islamic cosmopolitanism there thrived such great thinkers as Ibn Rushd (Averroes) showing the West the way to the forgotten riches of western classical antiquity. The cosmopolitan cultural effervescence favoured the emergence of such inter-cultural thinkers as Maimonides in the thirteenth century.

Hinduism may not have the idea of historical progress (linear conception of time) as moving towards the goal of world community, as is found in the western tradition. However, the vision and way of life that Hinduism inspires is one of a cosmopolitan existence. What is projected in the West as a teleological goal to be worked out through struggles in history, is a presupposition in Hinduism. What may appear as apathy towards the future of the world and the unity of humankind – seen from a teleological scheme – is, in a way, made good by the absence of the idea of election and chosenness in Hinduism. There is basic equality of all human beings in their quest for the divine, which makes them all sharers in one common pilgrimage.

On the other hand, like every other religious tradition, Hinduism too stands in need of re-defining its role vis-à-vis the human community. 'Universal' is something which Hinduism claims to be, when it defines itself as '*sanātana Dharma*'.[10] Modern exponents of Hinduism such as Swami Vivekananda have underlined the universal character of Hinduism. This thought made a worldwide impact after his speech at the World Parliament of Religions in Chicago in 1893.[11] The critical question is how its self-understanding of being universal could actually be realized in present-day circumstances.[12] One important way is *to re-interpret its rich universalistic sources* in relation to the demands of our contemporary times. This would involve a continuous transformation of Hinduism by overcoming any identification of it with particularities such as ethnic identity, caste, and culture. This is a major challenge considering the fact that caste still weighs heavily against its proclaimed universal scope and intentions. For Hinduism, as in the case of other religions, what is required is a new praxis that reflects its transcending of caste, ethnicity, and national ties, and too-narrow identities.

Community of Humankind – The Mission of All Religions

In the post-Westphalian world, nationalism presented itself as a solution to religious conflicts and wars. The idea was to rise above religious identities.[13] Ironically, then, what eventually emerged was nationalism *in the name of religion and religious identities*! Secularism was another effort to contain religions and its dreadful influence. But then it led to the separation of public life and private affair; religion was relegated to the private domain.[14] In spite of these developments, religion continues to retain its place as a source of moral-knowledge and as a system which, though not specialized, could nevertheless respond to questions of momentous significance for humanity – questions that are not raised in other societal systems or remain unanswered.[15] One such pivotal question is the destiny of humanity, its future, its survival, and its unity. This issue needs to be addressed by all religions.

There are heated debates among the religions on such questions as revelation, absoluteness, and universality. There is, however, little discussion, on the *mission* of other religions in regard to what concerns the crucial question of the destiny of humanity. The converging point of the mission of various religions should be *the future shape of the human community and its flourishing*. This recognition of mission of other religions and the awareness of being on a common journey towards a shared future can help to build up the community of humankind as one single family. Respect for other religions necessarily includes respect for the *mission* to which people of particular religious groups feel called, especially when this mission has something to contribute to the unity of the human family and its wellbeing. In this context, the problem with the claim of absoluteness and monopolistic possession of truth is as much a question of the unity and communion of the human community as it is a question of truth and epistemology.

Reverse or Incoming Universality

In order to be able to foster community, Christianity needs to practice what I refer to as reverse universality. From its very inception, Christianity allowed its sacred book to be translated in all languages, and in this way recognised the universality of the human family. In addition, Christianity sent out missionaries to the entire world. These two forms of universality remain incomplete. Christianity needs to allow itself to be interpreted and reshaped by what these peoples, with their cultures and religious traditions, have to say about humanity and human destiny. As long as this reverse universality or incoming universality, in contrast to outgoing universality, does not happen, Christianity is incomplete. The idea of Christianity as mission spanning the whole world is a unilateral universality. In order to be more completely and authentically universal, Christianity requires *multilateral universality* which calls for its message to be interpreted by diverse peoples through their conceptions of the human family and its destiny. The cultivation of doctrinaire dogmatism and the fostering of stratified Christian identity make it difficult to accept incoming universality. Incoming universality is the movement by which Christianity receives the ways of the Spirit from other religions and cultures.

One way in which reverse universality can be kept alive is to ask: What do our doctrines have to say to humanity at large? This is an important criterion which might save the religions from getting entangled in internal discussions, and get lost in texts and exegesis. For example, discerning the significance of polygenism or monogenism[16] for humanity is more important than choosing among these two positions in order to uphold the authority of the Bible. Upholding polygenism and yet believing in the unity of the human family is more important than maintaining monogenism and practicing racism as if human beings do not form one single family, as if some peoples and races are somehow more equal than others. If monogenism could co-exist with the practice of racism, and polygenism could exist alongside the affirmation of the unity of the whole of human family, this serves to show us the urgent need of a self-critique of religious beliefs – including Christian beliefs – regarding what they have to contribute to the creation of human community and its flourishing. The great Thai Buddhist monk Buddhadasa realized this truth when he said:

> If an interpretation of any word in any religion leads to disharmony and does not positively further the welfare of the many, then such an interpretation is to be regarded as wrong; that is against the will of God, or as the working of Satan or Mara.[17]

Religious Cosmopolitanism

The idea that religions belong to humankind as a whole and the notion of reverse universality could be expressed by means of the concept of religious 'comsopolitanism'. The notion of "cosmopolitanism" features in the work of, among others, Martha Nussbaum, Kwame Anthony Appiah and Karl Nielsen. [18] These authors have argued for a cosmopolitanism that transcends the narrow confines of the nation-state, and sees humanity in every person. A moral and humanistic cosmopolitanism was put forward by Rabindranath Tagore even before the outbreak of two world wars. He had prophetic premonition on what impending nationalism could cause to humankind. Seeing the dark clouds of menacing war already at the beginning of twentieth century, Tagore emphasized that we need to unlearn the education that teaches us that a nation is above humanity. He defended the importance of placing our common humanity above nation. These thoughts were expressed by Tagore in his lectures in the United States and Japan, and are published in his booklet *Nationalism*.[19]

The idea of cosmopolitanism has been challenged by those who emphasize the importance of specific identities (geographic, cultural, ethnic, religious, and so forth). A number of authors, including Anthony

D. Smith, argue that cosmopolitanism is an abstraction, something utopian. For them, only particular identities, and not an abstract concept, can motivate loyalty.[20] In response to such criticism, Appiah and others have developed the notion of *rooted cosmopolitanism*, according to which cosmopolitanism must not be seen as opposed to particular identities (community, culture, religion, etc.), but as rooted in one's own identity, while calling for the moral need to transcend one's particular identity.

While cosmopolitanism has been discussed on the political and legal planes, there is little talk about it in connection with religion. One of the reasons for this absence could be the impression that religion goes against the spirit of cosmopolitanism. For many, to be cosmopolitan is to sever the links with religion. Cosmopolitanism is suspicious of religion and the loss of the universalistic perspectives that the association with it could entail.

Religious cosmopolitanism refers to a basic attitude and its attendant mode of practice that considers religions to belong to the common heritage of humanity. It is a mode of existence in which a person has the ability to enter into the religious world of the other. It is a deeply human and spiritual attitude. If political cosmopolitanism is rooted in one's particular nation, but at the same time open to others, the same is true of religious cosmopolitanism. Religious cosmopolitanism challenges religious ontology identified with doctrines, laws, and regulations, in the same way that political cosmopolitanism challenges national ontology.

An empirical enquiry among the religiously pluralist city of Montreal and the region of Quebec has shown how people tend to be religiously cosmopolitan in everyday life. As conclusion to their research, the authors note:

> We have tried to show how religious rootedness is by no means in contradiction to cosmopolitanism; in fact, the opposite would seem to be true in Quebec. We have sought to give an account of the many forms that religious cosmopolitanism takes in Montreal and more widely in Quebec. As we have seen, the recognition of others and the willingness to adapt to their presence that cosmopolitanism implies concerns not only individuals but groups, institutions and urban spaces... In other words, it seems as if the religiosity (or spirituality) – the personal, lived religious "rootedness" –

of our informants, as well as the mobility between religions that so many
have experienced, allows them to be at ease with the religious belonging
and practice of others.[21]

Religious cosmopolitanism tends to bridge religions as a communion
of communities. Syncretism, understood in a negative sense, is the
preoccupation of religious orthodoxy. Any meeting of religions and religious
symbols that does not come under the control of religious authorities is
negatively viewed as syncretic. In a positive sense, syncretism is an effort to
meet with the world of other religious traditions, their signs and symbols,
practices, and rituals. These efforts, often present in people at the margins,
create an attitude of religious cosmopolitanism.

Two Senses of Cosmopolitanism

There could be a bourgeois theory of cosmopolitanism[22] that is at home
with globalisation, transnational projects, western classical antiquity,[23]
and of course, with capitalism. Today, under the capitalistic dispensation,
cosmopolitanism has become the virtue of, so to speak, "frequent
travellers" dealing with peoples across cultural and ethnic boundaries,
involved in the same mode of production, distribution, and aggressive
consumption of goods and services. On the other hand, the civilizational
and humanistic cosmopolitanism is embedded in the particular and is in
solidarity with the local. The particular could be one's nation, ethnicity,
culture, geographic region, or language, and these are not necessarily
in opposition to cosmopolitanism as is often mistakenly assumed.
Cosmopolitan transcendence does not consist in setting aside these
primordial realities of human groups, but in the quest for alternative
modes of life along with other groups, other peoples, and other cultures,
thereby challenging the individualistic cosmopolitanism theory of liberal
stamp with its claim of universal reason. This humanistic and community-
sensitive cosmopolitanism is not a political theory but a praxis that has
civilizational roots, and provides the framework to understand and practice
religious cosmopolitanism.

While we often hear of emperors and rulers whose support of religion
helped it to thrive, we rarely hear of emperors who were inspired by the
spirit of religious cosmopolitanism and co-existence. Among these are the

Indian emperors Ashoka (B.C. 304-232) and Akbar (A.D. 1542-1605).[24] They represent a counter-paradigm to the *cujus regio eius religio* (religion of the ruler – the religion of the region). Though a Buddhist, Ashoka's breadth of vision was such that in one of his edicts he made it known that in harming another religion any one would be harming one's own. It is the same spirit that inspired Akbar, who fostered closer contacts with Christians and Hindus.[25]

Cosmopolitanism in the Indian tradition could be seen in the regular cultural and commercial contacts the western parts of the country had with Greece, Egypt, Syria, Iran, and other cultures. Radhakamal Mukherjee, depicts the cosmopolitan scene of India with other cultures, thus:

> The tolerance of the age permitted a cross-fertilisation of the ancient Brahmanical, Iranian, and Greek cultures, with the Parthians playing an important role as intermediaries; as is clearly indicated by the excavations of the Parthian city of Sirkap in the Taxila area. Indian merchants, pilgrims and scholars not only came from Madhyadesa to Kathiawar, Punjab, Kashmir and Gandhara, but they also visited Syria and Egypt. Both overland and maritime traffic between India and Western Asia was brisk in the Greco-Bactarian and Scythian age and such cities as Taxila, Barbara, Palmyra, Petra and Alexandria became great international centres.[26]

Further, in the Indian subcontinent, the mutual absorption of cultures and cross-fertilization were also fostered by Buddhism in the second century BCE through the first centuries of CE. Thus, India was linked with South East Asia and China in a cosmopolitan relationship.

Today too, cosmopolitanism could be sustained by *solidarity of religions with each other,* since contribution of religions to the future of humanity and its destiny will depend upon the extent they are able to instil, promote, and sustain mutual obligations. Bereft of solidarity, cosmopolitanism will turn out to be a form of contemplative pluralism that marvels at the plurality of cultures, ethnicity, but has little enriching interaction with them. In cosmopolitanism that is imbued with the spirit of solidarity, there is a sense of mutual obligation that is not found in contemplative pluralism or in indiscriminate syncretism and hybridity.

Cosmopolitanism – Rootedness vs Detachment

Cosmopolitanism involves dialectic of identity and transcendence. This could be expressed in the form of two metaphors – *root* and *journey*. To live is to strike roots, and at the same time it is equally true that all of life is a journey. These two metaphors seem to contradict each other. But does not very often the most sublime truths irrupt into our horizons in the form of contradictions? One such contradiction is human existence, which is rooted, situated, circumscribed, and at the same time is also a journey. Both the predictable and the unpredictable meet and merge in the stream of life. This gets reflected also in the field of religion. Belonging to a religious identity and be rooted in it needs to go hand in hand with a journey towards the religious world of the other. To create an enclave to shore up one's identity is to insulate oneself from the stream of the life of others, and this is as much undesirable as the dissolution of the identities in the waters of misconceived cosmopolitanism.

Many people assume it natural to be rooted in one's religion and its tradition. It rarely occurs to believers that one needs to also be, at the same time, detached from one's religion. Religious cosmopolitanism precisely takes place in this dialectic between rootedness and detachment. Viewed from this perspective, religious cosmopolitanism is the attempt at the construction of a collective non-tribal self of a particular religious group. Christianity, like other religions, also has its place of roots and times of journey. To the extent that a religious tradition is able to maintain this tension between rootedness and journey, it will be in a position to commune and share itself with other religious traditions and experiences. Religious cosmopolitanism is a way of life that is open to the riches of the experience of the other as well as its distinctness, while refusing to take the short-cut of hybridity.

Human Solidarity as the Condition for the Creation of Community

If there are no common threads among religions and no strands of convergence, and if religions exist in a scattered way with no communication among themselves, then there is little likelihood of creating true communities. Religious postures claiming discontinuity with other religions disrupt the important goal of creating community to which all religions are called. An interesting instance of the challenges involved here is the first World Day of Prayer for Peace, which was organized at the initiative of Pope John Paul II in Assisi, Italy, on October 27, 1986. This gathering became a matter of hot debate. Some Catholics regarded the Pope's praying with other religious leaders as fostering relativism and syncretism. For them, his action compromised the position of Jesus Christ as the unique saviour of the world. Ironically, Pope Benedict XVI who fought against relativism, and even spoke of "dictatorship of relativism" at the funeral of John Paul II, himself came under critique when he called for a repetition of the Assisi event in 2011!

To ward off the critique of the right-wing Catholics who are scandalized at such prayer meetings, an argument smacking of sophistry was put forward. It claimed that the pope was not "praying together"; rather it was an event "to be together and pray". The argument by the neo-con Catholics is that the pope and others cannot pray to the same God, as they do not have the same understanding of God. In this connection, Michael Amaladoss tells us that, when people of different religious traditions are praying together, they "are experiencing the same God. But they are not having the same experience".[27] One of the standard arguments against praying together is that we do not know which God each one is praying to. This rather curious argument reminds me of some Catholics a few decades ago who objected to praying together Our Father with Protestants. The reason is we do not know what the Protestants mean when they say "Thy Kingdom come"!

If Christians and Christian leaders take offence in praying together with peoples of other faiths (as it happened after Pope John Paul's encounter in Assisi with leaders of other faiths) what kind of community could we expect to foster? This can only discredit Christian efforts for creation of community. The contribution by Christianity to the creation of communities can supplement the political efforts and other initiatives that work for the same goal. The importance of the role of religions in this regard is brought out by Stanley Samartha when he observes:

> The Church is in danger of being considered as the debris left behind by the receding tide of colonialism, if in its fears of syncretism, it tends to

keep itself separate from the neighbours. The problem for India is how, in a multi-religious, multi-lingual, multi-ethnic society, true community life can be fostered so that the nation can move forward. In Pakistan and Sri Lanka, in Malaysia and Indonesia, the problems are the same.[28]

The challenge for the various religious traditions is whether their openness to humanity and its future is such that they can generate witnesses and martyrs who will uphold that harmony of which syncretism is but a poor specimen. On the other hand, claims of absolutism and monopoly of truth divide the human community and diminish the prospects of the unity of the human family to which all religions declare themselves to be committed. Religions play a destructive role when they begin to compare each other in order to demonstrate their superiority over others. Each religious tradition is distinct, and should be understood in its particular context, history and background. As Kosuke Koyama notes, there is no point in the giraffe finding fault with the zebra because it (zebra) lacks a long neck![29]

In every religious tradition we might observe two basic trends in regard to community. The one emphasizes the community of all those who share the same faith, way of life, religious rituals, laws, and traditions. According to Durkheim, the sacred and the religious are identified here with a particular group or community.[30] In some religions, such as Hinduism, this community is loose, thereby creating ample space for diversity. For other religious traditions such as the Semitic religious traditions, the sense of the faith-community is deeply entrenched and strong. In the main, the concern is centred on fostering of the growth of the particular community and its expansion. Mistakenly some of the religious traditions think that the salvation of humankind is identical with the worldwide expansion of itself. We can see this kind of religious ideology at work, for example, in the European missionary movement starting from the sixteenth century. In this perspective, the future of humanity is reached when the entire world becomes Christian, Islamic, Hindu, or any of the other religions that hold this view.

There is another trend in all religious traditions which considers the human community in an open and universalistic spirit. According to this trend, besides one's own faith-community, there is the larger community of the world and of humankind. There is an obligation to foster and promote this universal human community that extends beyond the borders of one's own faith-community. We can characterize this as the cosmopolitan orientation. The spirit of religious cosmopolitanism tells us that it is by fostering the world community that one's own faith-community grows. The relationship is not in inverse proportion; the more the world-community grows, the more one's religious community can also grow. Here, we can recall the words of prophet Jeremiah. "Seek the welfare of the city…for in its welfare you will find your welfare" (Jer 29:7).

Threats to Community: Single Identity and Selective Rationality

In the light of what we have said, it makes sense to state that religions do not belong to a particular community, but belong to the whole of humankind. This claim could serve as a safeguard against the polarization of religion based precisely on a reduction of identity to that of one's particular religion. One of the root causes for violence and terror at the global level is the reduction of the complex and multi-layered identities of people into simplified religious identity, and labelling it. This is not at all helpful for promoting the unity of the human community.

Viewing people solely in terms of their religious affiliation not only distorts the reality of multiple identities of a person, but also ignores the fact that the same religious tradition is lived in a variety of ways depending upon different geographic, social, cultural, and historical configurations. Furthermore, reading history or interpreting history through religious identity could eclipse the interplay of social, economic, and cultural factors that have been at work in the making of history. For example, when Mahmud of Ghazni (CE 979 – 1030) made fourteen incursions into India, he plundered Hindu temples including the marvellous Somnath temple (CE 1024). He did not do this because the places of worship were *Hindu*, but because they were fabulously rich with gold, diamonds, and precious jewels.

Traditionally the claim of superiority for one's religion on the basis of its faith, its privileged revelation, and scriptures was a major source of conflict with other traditions. Today, there is a new threat to inter-religious understanding and world-peace when rationality is claimed solely for one's own religion, while other religions are viewed as irrational or wanting in rationality.[31] Such a mindset makes us wonder, together with Tagore whether "the clear stream of reason has not lost its way into the dreary desert sand of dead habits."[32] It is not infrequent that "dead habits" and tradition pass for rationality, and fuel dangerous confrontation with other religious traditions.[33]

Conclusion

No single religion can determine humankind's destiny. All religions have their role in saving humankind, which is done credibly when they do this jointly. For this to happen, we need to cultivate religious cosmopolitanism by promoting reverse universality. This might not be conveyed and sustained by the project of inter-religious dialogue. I tend to think that inter-religious dialogue, like inculturation, will be soon a dated concept. Inter-religious dialogue presupposes tight compartment-like or essentialized religious identities that are trying to reach out to the other. This could reflect the institutional interest of religions, especially highly organized religions such as Christianity, and may not reflect the real experience of peoples at the grassroots.

I propose that we soon shift from the language of inter-religious dialogue to religious cosmopolitanism. The point of reference in inter-religious dialogue is religious ontologies – doctrinal tenets, symbolic codes, ethical injunctions, ritual practices, etc. In contrast, in religious cosmopolitanism, the point of reference is the *other*, the source for reverse or incoming universality. The difference the other constitutes is not adequately responded to by a mere aesthetic pluralism that endorses diversity, but a cosmopolitanism that is sustained by the spirit of solidarity and praxis.

Religious cosmopolitanism is very often practiced most effectively at the grassroots level and in very localized circumstances where it cuts across opposition between the global and the local. Its scope and moral concerns are not coterminous with one's particular religious affiliation, for they expand to embrace the entire humanity. A person may be exposed to the diversity of the various religious universes, and yet could be chauvinistic and narrow, bent on his or her limited religious community. On the other hand, at the level of local traditions in small places there could be true cosmopolitan religious practice and mode of life.

The spirit of religious cosmopolitanism will help to discredit the historically untenable myth that some religious traditions are rational while others are not – a position which has now posed a new threat to world-peace and understanding among the various religious traditions. Religious cosmopolitanism does not permit any singular overarching understanding of the universal and the rational; rather, it invites us to assume the mutual obligation of engaging the other in the practice of religion in the hope of ensuring the future of humankind.

Bibliography

Adams, David., Tihanov, Glain., eds. *Enlightenment Cosmopolitanism* (New York: Routledge, 2017).

Amaladoss, Michael. *Walking Together: The Practice of Interreligious Dialogue* (Anand: Gujarat Sahitya Prakash, 1992).

Amit, Vered., and Rapport, Nigel. *Community, Cosmopolitanism and the Problem of Human Commonality* (London: Pluto Press, 2012).

Appiah, Kwame Anthony. "Cosmopolitan Patriarch." Joshua Cohen., ed. *For Love of Country: Debating the Limits of Patriotism* (Boston: Beacon Press, 1996).

Appiah, Kwame Anthony. *The Ethics and Identity* (Princeton: Princeton University Press, 2005).

Aravamudan, Srinivas. *Guru English: South Asian Religion in a Cosmopolitan Language* (Princeton, N.J.; Oxford: Princeton University Press, 2006).

Beyer, Peter. *Religion and Globalisation* (London – Thousand Oaks - New Delhi: Sage Publications, 2000).

Cavallar, Georg. *Imperfect Cosmopolis: Studies in the History of International Legal Theory and Cosmopolitan Ideas* (Cardiff: University of Wales Press, 2011).

Delanty, Gerard, and Inglis, David., eds. *Cosmopolitanism. Critical Concepts in the Social Sciences* (London: Routledge, 2011).

Deloanty, Gerald. *Routledge Handbook of Cosmopolitanism Studies* (Oxford: Routledge, 2012).

Fiala, Andrew. *Secular Cosmopolitanism, Hospitality, and Religious Pluralism* (New York: Routledge, 2017).

Forman-Barzilai, Fonna. *Adam Smith and the Circles of Sympathy: Cosmopolitanism and Moral Theory* (Cambridge: Cambridge University Press, 2010).

Hill, Joseph. "A Mystical Cosmopolitanism: Sufi Hip Hop and the Aesthetics of Islam in Dakar." *Culture and Religion* 18 (2017), 388-408.

Hollinger, David A. *Cosmopolitanism and Solidarity: Studies in Ethnoracial, Religious, and Professional Affiliation in the United States* (Madison, Wis.: University of Wisconsin Press, 2006).

Ivanhoe, P. J. "Confucian Cosmopolitanism." *The Journal of Religious Ethics* 42 (1) (2014), 22-44.

Jeanrond, Werner. *Theological Hermeneutics: Development and Significance* (New York: Crossroad, 1991).

Lavan, Myles., Payne, Richard E., and Weisweiler, John., eds. *Cosmopolitanism and Empire: Universal Rulers, Local Elites, and Cultural Integration in the Ancient Near East and Mediterranean* (New York: Oxford University Press, 2016).

Marotta, Vince. *Theories of the Stranger: Debates on Cosmopolitanism, Identity and Cross-cultural Encounters* (New York: Routledge, 2017).

M'Baye, Babacar. *Black Cosmopolitanism and Anticolonialism: Pivotal Moments* (London: Routledge, 2017).

McClean, David E. *Richard Rorty, Liberalism and Cosmopolitanism* (London, New York: Routledge, 2016).

Meintel, Deirdre., and Mossière, Géraldine. "In the Wake of the Quiet Revolution: From Secularization to Religious Cosmopolitanism." *Anthropologica* 55 (1) (2013), 57-71.

Merry, M.de Ruyter, D. "Cosmopolitanism and the Deeply Religious." *Journal of Beliefs and Values* 30 (1) (2009), 49-60.

Mythen, G. "Ulrich Beck, Cosmopolitanism and the Individualization of Religion." *Theory, Culture and Society* 30 (3) (2013), 114-27.

Nielsen, Kai. "Cosmopolitan Nationalism." N. Miscevic, ed. *Nationalism and Ethnic Conflict* (Chicago: Open Court, 2000), 299-319.

Nowicka, Magdalena., and Rovisco, Maria. *Cosmopolitanism in Practice* (London, New York: Routledge, 2016).

Nussbaum, Martha. "Patriotism and Cosmopolitanism." Joshua Cohen., ed. *For Love of Country: Debating the Limits of Patriotism* (Boston: Beacon Press, 1996).

Pierik, Roland H. M., and Wouter, Werner., eds. *Cosmopolitanism in Context: Perspectives from International Law and Political Theory* (Cambridge: Cambridge University Press, 2010).

Samartha, J. Stanley., ed. *Towards World Community: The Colombo Papers* (Geneva: WCC, 1975).

Samartha, Stanley. *Courage to Dialogue: Ecumenical Issues in Inter-religious Relationship* (Geneva: WCC, 1981).

Sellers, M. N. S., ed. *Parochialism, Cosmopolitanism, and the Foundations of International Law* (Cambridge; New York: Cambridge University Press, 2012).

Simpson, Edward., and Kresse, Kai., eds. *Struggling with History: Islam and Cosmopolitanism in the Western Indian Ocean* (New York: Columbia University Press, 2008).

Skrbiš, Zlatko., and Woodward, Ian. *Cosmopolitanism: Uses of the Idea* (London: Sage Publications, 2013).

Turner, B. S. "Cosmopolitan Virtue: On Religion in a Global Age." *European Journal of Social Theory* 4 (2) (2001), 131-52.

Werbner, Pnina. *Anthropology and the New Cosmopolitanism: Rooted, Feminist and Vernacular Perspectives* (Oxford: Berg, 2008).

Endnotes

[1] The perspectives religions adopt for their relationship to the other stem from an essentialistic conception of identity - both of the self and the other, while in fact, the identities are fluid and porous, something that is applicable as much to community and ethnic identities as to religions. Large scale migration in contemporary times, provide concrete evidence to the fluidity of identity. We note how this constant flow of cultures, and religions encountering "new" others reconfigure their (cultures and religions) original identities. The practice of inter-religious dialogue carries with it an essentialistic view of religions, a reason to seek for new frames of reference.

[2] Cf. Charles Avila, *Ownership: Early Christian Teaching* (New York: Orbis Books, 1983).

[3] Cf. Werner Jeanrond, *Theological Hermeneutics: Development and Significance* (New York: Crossroad, 1991).

[4] See Julio de Santa Ana, *Good News to the Poor* (Geneva: WCC, 1977); Donal Dorr, *Option for the Poor: A Hundred Years of Catholic Social Teaching* (New York: Orbis Books, 2002).

[5] Cf. Jeanrond Werner, *op.cit*, 22-23.

[6] J. Stanley Samartha, ed, *Towards World Community: The Colombo Papers* (Geneva: WCC, 1975), p. 5.

[7] The two could form one single ideal of unity only when the political or temporal community was subjected to the spiritual ecumenity represented by the Mediaeval Christendom, so it was claimed.

[8] *The Epistle to Diognetus,* no. 5. For the text of the letter, see *Early Christian Writings: The Apostolic Fathers* (Aylesbury: Penguin Books, 1968), p.176.

[9] Cf. Gerald Deloanty, *Routledge Handbook of Cosmopolitanism Studies* (Oxford: Routledge, 2012); Sudarsan Padmanabhan, "Unity in Diversity. The Indian Cosmopolitan Idea", in Gerald Deloanty, *op.cit.* 463-476; Derry N. MacLean – Sikeena Karmali Ahmed, eds, *Cosmopolitanism in Muslim Contexts: Perspectives from the Past* (Edinburgh: Edinburgh University Press, 2012).

[10] By "*sanātana dharma*", is meant to be universal and inclusive.

[11] For the interventions of Swami Vivekananda on that occasion, see www.viveksamity.org/user/doc/CHICAGO-SPEECH.pdf> [accessed on 23 July, 2018].

[12] Cf. M. Thomas Thangaraj, "Hinduism and Globalization", in Max L. Stackhouse - Diane B. Obenchain, eds, *God and Globalization, vol. 3 Christ and the Dominions of Civilization* (Harrisburg: Trinity Press International, 2002), 213-238.

[13] Cf. Rajeev Bhargava, ed, *Secularism and Its Critics* (New Delhi: Oxford University Press, 1998).

[14] On the chequered western history of secularism and the nuances in its conception and definition, see Charles Taylor, *A Secular Age* (Cambridge, MA: Harvard University Press, 2007). See also Michael Warner – Jonathan van Antwerpen – Craig J. Calhoun, eds, *Varieties of Secularism in a Secular Age* (Cambridge MA: Harvard University Press, 2010); Craig Calhoun – Mark Juergensmeyer – Jonathan van Antwerpen, eds, *Rethinking Secularism* (New York: Oxford University Press, 2011).

[15] Cf. Peter Beyer, *Religion and Globalisation* (London – Thousand Oaks - New Delhi: Sage Publications, 2000).

[16] Monogenism holds that the humankind derives from one parent – Adam and Eve. Polygenism, on the other hand, maintains that humanity evolved from plurality of parents in different parts of the world.

[17] As quoted in Kari Storstein Haug, "Christianity as a Religion of Wisdom and Kamma: A Thai Buddhist Interpretation of Selected Passages from the Gospels", in *Bulletin, The Council of Societies for the Study of Religion*, 35:2 (April 2006), 43.

[18] See Martha Nussbaum, "Patriotism and Cosmopolitanism", in Joshua Cohen, ed, *For Love of Country: Debating the Limits of Patriotism* (Boston: Beacon Press, 1996), pp.131-144. ID., *Cultivating Humanity* (Cambridge MA: Harvard University Press, 1997). Kwame Anthony Appiah, "Cosmopolitan Patriarch", in Joshua Cohen, ed, *For Love of Country, op.cit.* pp. 21-29. Id., *The Ethics and Identity* (Princeton: Princeton University Press, 2005); Kai Nielsen, "Cosmopolitan Nationalism", in N. Miscevic, ed, *Nationalism and Ethnic Conflict* (Chicago: Open Court, 2000), pp. 299-319.

[19] Rabindranath Tagore, *Nationalism* (London: Macmillan, 1917).

[20] Anthony D. Smith, Nations and Nationalism in a Global Era (Cambridge: Polity, 1995).

[21] Deirdre Meintel and Géraldine Mossière, "In the Wake of the Quiet Revolution: From Secularization to Religious Cosmopolitanism", *Anthropologica*, 55:1 (2013), 57-71, at 67.

[22] Today in political theory, one speaks of trans-national world-citizenship, drawing inspiration from Kant's theory of cosmopolitan right, something that has been reconstructed with new impetus and radicality in the work of Jürgen Habermas. Such theoretical exercises may confer legitimacy to the transnational European Union, but the extent to which they are applicable to other parts of the world remains a serious, and indeed unanswered, question. J. Habermas, *The Postcolonial Constellation* (Cambridge, MA: MIT Press, 2001); ID., "Kant's Idea of Perpetual Peace: At Two Hundred Years' at Historical Remove", chapter 7 in *Inclusion of the Other: Studies in Political Theory* (Cambridge, MA: MIT Press, 1998), pp.165-202.

[23] We are here reminded of Diogenes, who, when asked where he came from, replied, "I am a citizen of the world." As quoted in https://www.plato.stanford.edu/entries/cosmopolitanism> [accessed on 11 August, 2015].

[24] A report of the period shows how Emperor Akbar was truly a religious cosmopolitan and had regular dialogue and discussion with different religious groups. It included also Christian missionaries. As a report states, "And later that day the emperor came to Fatehpur. There he used to spend much time in the Hall of Worship in the company of men and sheikhs …when he would sit up there the whole night continually occupied in discussing questions of religion, whether fundamental or collateral…Learned monks also from Europe, who are called *Padre*, and have an infallible head, called *Papa*… brought the Gospel, and advanced proofs for the Trinity. His majesty firmly believed in the truth of the Christian religion, and wishing to spread the doctrines of Jesus ordered Prince Murad to take a few lessons in Christianity under good auspices, and charged Abul Fazl to translate the Gospel" WM Theodore de Bary, et al., eds, *Sources of Indian Tradition* (New Delhi: Motilal Banarsidass, 1988), pp. 39-41.

[25] Cf. Amartya Sen, *Identity and Violence: The Illusion of Destiny* (London: Penguin Books, 2006), p. 64.

[26] Radhakamal Mukherjee, *The Culture and Art of India* (London: George Allen & Unwin Ltd., 1959), p. 131.

[27] See Michael Amaladoss, *Walking Together: The Practice of Interreligious Dialogue* (Anand: Gujarat Sahitya Prakash, 1992), p. 58. See also Gavin Brown, "Praying together in the Dark: Theological Reflections on Shared

Prayer within Inner-religious Dialogue", in *Australian e-journal of Theology*, 20:1 (April 2013), 18-33.

[28] Stanley Samartha, *Courage to Dialogue: Ecumenical Issues in Inter-religious Relationship* (Geneva: WCC, 1981), p. 27.

[29] Cf. Kosuke Koyama, "Observation and Revelation. A Global Dialogue with Buddhism", in Max L. Stackhouse - Diane B. Obenchain, eds, *God and Globalization: Christ and the Dominions of Civilization* (Harrisburg: Trinity Press International, 2002), p. 270.

[30] Emile Durkheim, *Elementary Forms of Religious Life* (London: George Allen & Unwin Ltd., 1915).

[31] Here we can cite the example of Pope Benedict's lecture on faith and reason at Regensburg University on 12 September, 2006. His comments on Islam on this point turned out to be highly provocative and sparked a backlash from the Islamic community. It led to pope's apology to the Muslims.

[32] Rabindranath Tagore, *Gitanjali*, poem 35 (New York: Macmillan & Co, 1913).

[33] What Tagore means by "dead habits" are our way of thinking and acting in a particular manner during a long period of time. We get so used to these habits that we begin to justify them and defend them thinking that they are reasonable. It may be remarked here that in Europe the modern world began when tradition and classical authors (*ipse dixit*) ceased to be criterion of truth, giving place to reason.

Appendix
Sources of the Chapters

1. **Christian Faith and Multiple Rationalities**
    Originally a lecture delivered in French at an International Conference held at L'Institut Catholique de Paris, France, 27-30 May, 2016.

2. **Plurality, Recognition, and Coexistence: Beyond Liberalism and Secularism**

    Delivered as a lecture at an International Conference held at the University of Montreal, Canada, 29 & 30 May, 2013.

3. **Fundamentalism and Kenosis: Multidisciplinary Analysis and Reflections**
    The ideas in this chapter originally presented as the keynote address to the Catholic Biblical Association of India, held in Bangalore, 3 November, 2016.

4. **Religious Freedom in Asia: Diversity, Contentions, and Complexity**
    The main ideas were developed originally as an article for the *International Theological Review Concilium* 2016/4.

5. **Global Inequalities: Through an Asian Window**
    The ideas in this chapter were presented as a keynote address at an International Conference held in Helsinki, Finland on "Mission and Money: Christian Mission in the Context of Global Inequalities", 4-7 April, 2014.

6. **Postcolonial Theories and Asian Theologies**

The initial ideas were developed as a paper for a conference organized at the Institute for Global Church and Mission", Sankt Georgen, Frankfurt a.M, Germany, on the theme "Postcolonial Theory and Theology/Missiology," during 29-31 March, 2017.

7. **Religions and Competing Identities: Dilemmas and Trajectories of Peace**

Originally delivered as a lecture at a conference in Sarejevo, Bosnia-Herzogovina, on the issue of peace in post-conflict societies, 9 & 10 June, 2014.

8. **New Impetus for Integral Ecology: Theological Significance of *Laudato Si***

The reflections forming part of this chapter were first expressed after the release of the encyclical *Laudato si*, at a public lecture in Loyola College, Chennai, 17 July, 2015. Earlier versions of the lecture appeared in English, French, and Spanish.

9. **Consumerism as Play of Signs and the Project of Liberation**

Ideas developed for an article for *Jeevadhara,* and an initial version appeared in the issue of January, 2016.

10. **Adult Faith and Life in Society**

Thoughts presented as a lecture at National Biblical Catechetical and Liturgical Centre (NBCLC) at a research seminar on "The Quality of Adult Faith," 9-13 December, 2013.

11. **Why Small Christian Communities?**

This is an expansion of a shorter version of an article prepared for a special volume on Small Christian Communities, published by Missio, Aachen, Germany, 2013.

12. **Theology Animating Canon Law**

Originally prepared as a paper for an International Conference on Canon Law, organized by the Asian Centre for Cross-Cultural Studies, Chennai, 8 & 9 January, 2016.

13. Every Theologian a Community-Researcher

Main ideas in this chapter were developed as keynote address for a conference to commemorate the 25th anniversary of SATHRI, held at Serampore College, 15-16 August, 2014.

14. Asian Ecumenism through Postcolonial Lens

Prepared as a keynote address for a conference on "Ecumenism in the World Church," organized by the World Centre for Catholicism and Inter-cultural Theology, De Paul University, Chicago, 28-30 April, 2017.

15. Indigenous Christianities: Analysis and Reflections in the Post-Denominational Age

An earlier version prepared as a contribution to a special issue of *Jeevadhara*, Janaury, 2015.

16. Asia and Interreligious Harmony: Re-Reading of *Nostra Aetate* after Fifty Years

Prepared for a conference organized by the Office of Ecumenical and Inter-religious Affairs, FABC, to commemorate the fiftieth anniversary of Vat. II document "*Nostra Aetate*" on interreligious dialogue and understanding, Pattaya, Thailand, 17-19 November, 2015.

17. Religious Cosmopolitanism: Towards an Inclusive and Harmonious World

An earlier version prepared as a paper for a conference organized by the Faculty of Theology and Religious Studies, University of Louvain, Belgium, 14 & 15 November, 2014.

Index